BLOOD CRAVE

BY JENNIFER KNIGHT

RP | TEENS
PHILADELPHIA · LONDON

Books published by Running Press are available at special discounts for bulk purchases in the
United States by corporations, institutions, and other organizations. For more information,
please contact the Special Markets Department at the Perseus Books Group, 2300 Chestnut
Street, Suite 200, Philadelphia, PA 19103, or call (800) 810-4145, ext. 5000, or e-mail
special.markets@perseusbooks.com.

ISBN 978-0-7624-4118-1
Library of Congress Control Number: 2012931677

E-book ISBN 978-0-7624-4699-5

9 8 7 6 5 4 3 2 1
Digit on the right indicates the number of this printing

Edited by Lisa Cheng
Cover image by Steve Belkowitz
Cover and interior design by Ryan Hayes
Typography: Verlag, Knockout, and Mercury

Published by Running Press Teens
An Imprint of Running Press Book Publishers
A Member of the Perseus Books Group
2300 Chestnut Street
Philadelphia, PA 19103–4371

Visit us on the web!
www.runningpress.com

For my mother.
Because you read it first when it was suckiest,
and told me you loved it anyway.
I love you always.

PREFACE

I t starts with heat. A sting. The bite. The fleeting, fragile moment when fangs break skin.

It's cruel, really, that heat is what I feel first. Like a reminder. This is the last warmth I'll ever feel. From the moment the venom seeps into my body until I'm sent willingly, mercifully to my death, I will never feel warm again.

Because immediately after the heat, the coldness begins. It spreads from the puncture wounds in my throat deep into my chest like a rushing river. I can feel it pumping through my veins, spreading throughout my body until I'm burning with cold. Poison incapacitates me completely as the eager, pallid faces of the dead loom above. I am unable to move as fangs slide easily from my throat and my head cracks hard on the stone floor. A delicate bloody wrist appears in my vision, coming closer to my mouth. I want to get away, want to close my mouth. *Fight.* But my body won't respond. All I can hear is my own blood rushing furiously in my ears and somewhere, as though from very far away, the desperate cries of my boyfriend as he struggles to save me.

THE HUNT

ucas, I'm dying."

He approached me on silent feet, head bent to inspect my wound.

"You're such a baby," he said and turned away.

"Seriously," I croaked, clutching my toe. "It's going to fall off."

"Shh," he hissed. "How are we supposed to get the jump on a vampire with you whining constantly?"

I let my throbbing foot drop, carefully avoiding the stray log I'd kicked. "I'm just nervous."

"If you were going to wimp out, you shouldn't have come." He glanced over at me. "Do I need to take you back?"

"No!" I was nervous, but I still wanted to help. After all, how many times does one get to go vampire hunting with a werewolf and live to talk about it?

Well, I hoped I lived to talk about it, anyway.

"Good," he grunted and beckoned me further down the side of the barn. "Because I don't know how much use this will be without you."

I couldn't help but smile at that. The fact that a three-hundred-year-old werewolf needed *my* help was pretty cool. Add in that Lucas had actually let me come on this trip, well, it was just short of a miracle. This wasn't some scenic joyride through vampire territory. No, this mission into a dead vampire's lair was occurring for one purpose and one purpose only: to prove to the pack that there was, in fact, a vampire uprising.

Three weeks ago, Vincent had all but told me it was going to happen in the near future, and maybe it was naïve of me, but I took him at his word. The pack, however, was not so certain. In fact, they dismissed the very idea that the vampires would want to rise up, claiming that they'd never have the guts to challenge the wolf packs.

Even in the face of the continued murders of young girls across Colorado they refused to believe.

Which basically meant Lucas and I had one day to convince them otherwise. Tomorrow evening, he was almost surely going into the silver room as punishment for disobeying Rolf on the last full moon, and our shot at convincing the pack to take action before it was too late would be over.

But I preferred not to think about that. I had to concentrate on the current mission—that way I wouldn't stub my toe on any more logs. Or, you know . . . get eaten.

"Do you smell anything?" I whispered.

"Oh, yeah. This place reeks of the dead," Lucas said. "But it's mostly Vincent's scent."

"So you don't think there are any more around?"

"We'll find out in a few minutes."

I gulped. The sun was slipping below the horizon at a discon-certingly brisk pace, taking our safety along with it. I shuddered, leaning heavily against the wall of the barn.

The barn.

Who ever thought I'd be here again?

The only surefire way to prove the uprising was a reality was to hear it straight from a vampire of the Denver brood. Which, of course, meant that we needed to *catch* a vampire.

Luckily, we already knew of one. Vincent's.

It was a long shot to think there'd be any more vampires sleeping here, since the werewolves raided the place, but it was our only lead. We had to at least try.

"Okay," Lucas said, eyeing the darkening sky. "You remember the plan, right?"

I nodded, throat tight.

"And no matter what happens, you promised to stick to that plan." He rounded on me. "Right?"

Another shaky nod from me.

He began shedding his clothes. "And if something goes wrong, you get to the car as fast as you can and leave. Don't stop till you get to Gould."

"Okay."

He kicked his shoes off and unbuckled his belt. "You have the stake I gave you?"

I held it up in a white-knuckled fist. It was double-ended with a silver tip on one side and a wooden one on the other.

"Good. Don't be afraid to use it."

"But you said I won't have to, right? If everything goes as planned."

"That's the idea." Nude now, he turned away to face the rear entrance of the barn, crouching low. "No more noise now. Try not to let the wind catch you. We don't want your scent to tip them off."

Okay. Be quiet. Avoid wind. Use stake. Got it.

"Be careful," I said, unable to stop myself.

He rose and turned, taking my cheek as he kissed me softly. He pulled away with a devious smile. "You ready to kick some vampire ass?"

I released a reluctant laugh.

His hand closed over mine, squeezing my hold tighter on the stake. Then he turned and began to tremor. My heart went haywire, and I was unable to keep myself from backing up. This was the part of the plan I was most nervous about. My power was still so unpredictable. What if I couldn't forge a connection?

I didn't want him to do this, but if we were going to catch a vampire, we couldn't take any chances. Lucas had to change. And I had to connect to him.

Just please let this work. . . .

In an instant, Lucas exploded and then re-formed into a hulking black wolf. He'd been facing away from me when he changed, but he immediately rounded on me, hackles raised. I had about three seconds to link our minds.

Silver eyes burned into mine, both fierce and terrified at the same time. I inhaled deeply, trying to calm down so I could do this. His deep, gravelly snarl only ratcheted my heart rate up further. I could see his back tensing up, his lips curling more tightly around his gums. Any second now, he would pounce and this would all be over. My hand sweated around the silver stake I was supposed to use against him.

No. I can do this.

I channeled my gift, feeling that familiar zap of electricity ripple though my chest and filter through every limb until I was a live wire. When I focused on Lucas's eyes again, that was it—*bam.* We were one.

His emotions attacked me in a conflicting mess of canine instincts and werewolf protectiveness. He'd told me that werewolves were meant to protect humans from harm, but his wolf instincts told him that humans were potentially dangerous. He wanted to protect me, but was afraid at the same time.

It's okay, I said in my mind, sending him soothing emotions. *I'm here to help you.*

This was part of the plan, too: reminding Lucas's doggie mind of what we were here to do. As a wolf, his instincts took precedent over higher thinking, and although he'd remember vaguely what we were supposed to be doing, he'd need my help to make sure he did everything the way we'd planned.

Gradually, I felt Lucas begin to trust me, felt the fear ebb and his determination to keep me from harm increase. *Good. That's it.*

Lucas's body was almost completely smudged out in the darkness, which meant it was time to get him into the barn to investigate.

Okay, you remember the plan?

I didn't get a clear answer as much as a feeling. He remembered.

Don't kill all of them, if any are in there. We need one to question. And once I'm done asking questions, remember we need to get it into the car, okay? So just do what I say.

Compliance.

I grinned. This was going rather well.

He let out a low growl, and I could feel that he wanted me to stay put.

Okay. Be careful.

He sniffed at me and slunk around the edge of the barn, creeping silently into the fathomless darkness within. It was several minutes before I heard anything, and my stomach was cramping so hard with nerves I felt like I was going to puke. The only thing keeping me together was that I still had Lucas's connection, and could feel that he was alive.

Then someone screamed.

My heart stopped completely, and it took everything I had to keep from running into the barn.

"Get the human!" someone shouted.

An unearthly growling sound erupted and then more screaming. Sounds of a scuffle—banging, grunting, and Lucas's yowling—reached my ears. Pain radiated from his vibe so strongly it hurt me as well. I clutched the stake, flipping it around so that the wooden end faced outward. Any longer, and I was going in. To hell with the plan.

Another high-pitched scream and a thump.

More fighting, and then, without warning, the connection dropped.

I ran into the barn, yelling Lucas's name. It was almost completely dark inside with only the blue light streaming in from the hayloft above. At first I couldn't see anything, then I caught sight of a human lying still on the ground with blood pouring out of her throat. I started to rush to her to help, but a noise to my left made me stop. I whirled around to see—

Oh, thank God.

Lucas was okay. He was just human again.

That wasn't part of the plan, but at least he was alive. And he'd managed to subdue the vampire. It was a man, thin and eerily beautiful as all vampires were, but still sort of creepy-looking when you really looked at him. His pointed, blood-soaked teeth were bared, and he was doing everything is his power to throw Lucas off of him.

"Get off of me, filthy dog!" he yelled, thrashing.

"Yeah, because that's gonna happen," Lucas said. He waved me over, and I handed him the stake. Careful to avoid the silver, he pressed the wooden end directly above the vampire's heart. "Move again and you're history."

The vampire calmed somewhat, but let loose a stream of vile curses.

"Is the human okay?" Lucas asked.

I went over to check. "She's been bitten," I said, voice shaking. "She's paralyzed."

The vampire hissed a laugh and I heard Lucas punch him.

"Leave her and I'll deal with it afterward," Lucas said. "I need you here."

"But she's bleeding."

"*Faith.*"

His tone told me not to argue further, so I returned to the struggling enemies and stood behind Lucas, too afraid to get closer. Lucas was supposed to be a wolf for this part, since he was stronger that way, but I found myself glad he'd changed back into a human. Just the sight of this vampire—of any vampire—was enough to make my brain all slow and fuzzy.

Lucas, however, didn't seem to have the same problem.

"We gotta do this quick. There was another one that got away, and she might bring reinforcements."

"What were they doing in here?" I asked.

"Looked like a feeding frenzy." He nodded to the right and I turned to see—

I choked back a sudden surge of vomit.

"Oh, God," I whispered, looking away quickly.

In the corner of the barn was a pile of dead bodies, some new enough to have been killed tonight while others . . . well, it accounted for the smell of death Lucas had reported earlier, and which I was now privy to.

"The girl," I said, worried about the one who was still alive over there.

"Will die," Lucas said.

"But—"

"It's protocol, Faith. Either I kill her now, or she becomes like this sack of maggots." He slammed the vampire's head into the earth.

At his grunt of pain, I came back to the situation. Now was not the time to lose it.

"We need to find out if he knows anything before we bring him back to the mansion," Lucas said. "So you need to read his emotions when I ask him the questions."

"I know," I said.

"Just reminding you. You look a little freaked."

"I'm fine." I swallowed hard and tried to focus. Looking at the vampire's bloody, beautiful face was not something I was keen on doing, but I had to in order to get the strongest read on his emotions. In fact . . . "I should touch him."

"Screw off, human slime," the vampire growled. Lucas slashed his cheek with the stake.

"You don't speak unless I say," Lucas rumbled. He glanced back at me. "Touch his foot or something."

I bent and pulled his slacks back to touch his calf. At once, a wave of his emotions fell on me like a collapsed building. He was furious and scared, but that didn't take a rocket scientist—or a telepath—to figure out. What I was looking for was signs of deceit.

"I'm ready," I said.

Lucas rounded on the vampire. "Tell me what you know about the uprising."

"What uprising?"

"You know damn well what uprising. Start talking or I'll start taking your eyes out."

Gross. This was definitely a side of Lucas I'd never seen before.

"I don't know what you're talking about." But I could feel differently. He was hiding something—I just couldn't tell what it was.

"He knows something," I said. The vampire hissed viciously at me, cursing me off.

Lucas rammed his head into the dirt again. "Tell the truth. As you can see, we'll know if you lie."

"I don't know anything ab—"

Lucas brought the stake directly over his eyeball, and the vampire cringed. "Lie again. Please. I think I'll enjoy making you eternally blind."

The vampire gulped and then said, "Okay . . . but promise to let me free after."

"Only thing I can promise you is a swift death, leech. Now start talking."

"Why should I—"

Lucas lowered the point of the stake so that it dug into the delicate skin of his closed eyelid.

"Okay!" the vampire screeched. "I know very little, but I know enough. If you just let me go . . ."

"We'll let you go," I said. Lucas turned to me. I shrugged. Why would he tell us anything if he was going to die anyway?

Lucas looked a little stunned by my input, but to my surprise, went along with me. "Sure vampire, we'll let you go, okay? Just tell us what you know."

The vampire deliberated for a long moment, and I felt the mistrust roiling through him as he did so, but finally croaked out with, "I know that the monarch is collecting women. She likes them young and she likes the pretty ones because they make the best hunters. She wants them for the army."

Lucas looked over at me, fire in his eyes.

"He's telling the truth."

"What else?" Lucas demanded. "Who's your monarch? Where is the lair?"

"I can't tell you."

Lucas began to start up with the stake-in-the-eye thing again, but the vampire screamed out, "It's the truth! Ask her! Ask her!"

I felt for it, and found, unfortunately, that he wasn't lying.

"Why can't you tell?" I asked.

"It's forbidden. Vampire magic . . . when we swear our allegiance to the brood, we are bound by a gag. I cannot utter her name nor reveal the existence of our lair without her permission. And I do not have it."

"But it's a chick," Lucas said. "That's something."

"Not enough," I said. "Rolf will need more than this."

Lucas adjusted his hold on the vampire, but made sure to keep the stake poised at his chest. "What can you tell me about the plan to wage war on the wolf packs?"

Something flickered in his vibe—not exactly deceit, but close. I was about to say something, when the vampire began talking.

"The monarch wants to crush Rolf's pack and all others on the planet. We're sick of living in the shadows. We want to kill without consequence, and the only way to accomplish this is if the werewolves are out of the picture."

Lucas looked back at me again and I nodded. It was the truth, all right. It just felt like there was something missing. Whatever it was, it didn't matter at the moment. We had what we needed.

VERDICT

I wasn't sure if there'd ever been a vampire at the werewolf mansion, but if there had, you certainly wouldn't have known it from the ruckus we caused by bringing one into the living room.

Every werewolf within a mile radius—or so it seemed—had smelled the rotting corpse mere seconds after we'd tugged him out of the silver-reinforced trunk. The silver didn't exactly hurt vampires as much as weaken them slightly. It wasn't as bad as it was with werewolves, who'd die if pierced through the heart with silver, but it was enough to keep him from breaking out of the trunk.

Inside the house, the vampire was heavily chained to a chair and surrounded by the pack. Not all of them, but darn near. Rolf stood at the head of the crowd, flanked by Yvette, his human wife, and the other Council members, all of whom were currently deciding Lucas's fate.

Hope this doesn't make things worse. . . .

Lucas and I stood on either side of the vampire, waiting for Rolf to speak. He'd been disconcertingly silent upon seeing what we'd done. Usually when something he didn't like happened, he took to screaming and throwing things. Heavy things. That the eighteenth-century vase behind him was still intact . . . well, it was curious.

After several more moments of tense silence—during which Katie, Julian, and his human fiancée, Melanie, showed up—Rolf finally murmured, "What have you done?"

Hoping this was meant for Lucas, I remained silent, though refused to look away.

"We found the proof we needed," Lucas said, also calm, but firm.

"Regarding?" Rolf asked.

"You know what this is about. Don't feign ignorance."

Rolf's face tightened. "Fine. But I do not see how bringing a bloodsucker into my home is going to change my mind."

"Will you at least listen?" Lucas asked.

He waited a beat, and then, "I will listen."

Lucas kicked the vampire in the leg. The guy had been silent too, probably scared that one false move would turn him into an undead bag of Puppy Chow.

"Tell them what you told us," Lucas commanded.

It seemed to cost a lot of effort, but the vampire obeyed. He was likely hoping we'd hold up to our end of the bargain and set him free if he complied.

Stupid.

When he was done, I turned my attention to Rolf, who had not uttered a word. In the low light from the fire behind him, I could see a vein ticking in his temple—the only clue to the fury raging beneath his calm exterior. And yeah, if I stretched my power, I could feel it. He was *livid*. But, strangely, his voice was subdued when he spoke.

"I thought you claimed to have proof," he rumbled.

I shot a glance at Lucas, who looked about as shocked as I felt.

"What do you mean? This is proof."

"This is nothing but a scared little boy who will say anything to stay alive."

Lucas's mouth thinned. I knew he wanted to tell them all that

I'd read his emotions and confirmed what the vampire said, but that would mean my death along with the vampire's. No way was Rolf going to let me live if he knew what I could do.

"It's the truth," Lucas snarled.

"Prove it."

"What more do you want, Rolf?" Lucas exploded, flapping his arms out to the side. "A vampire from the Denver brood just told you everything he knows about the uprising and you still believe it's a lie? Are you really that damned stubborn?"

"You hold your tongue," Rolf said, voice like a gunshot through the room. "I am over five-hundred-years old, and there has never been a day in my life that I have sunk so low as to trust a vampire. Today will be no different. This creature knows that information—whether false or otherwise—is his only chance to be released. He will say whatever you want to hear to be set free. You should know that, Lucas."

I watched Lucas chew on the inside of his mouth, veins popping out of his neck. Yeah, I too wanted to blurt out that I had confirmed the vampire's story with my power, but I didn't want it bad enough to risk death. Still, if we didn't convince Rolf to take action on the uprising, the gory scene in the barn would be just the beginning.

"So you'll just sit around and do nothing while innocent humans die?" I asked.

Rolf's cold gaze locked on me, and it took everything I had not to shiver underneath it.

"We work every night to hunt the vampires that assault our territory. We always have and always will. But I refuse to waste time preparing for a war that will never come. Do you realize that if I were to accept this war as a reality, I would be obligated to alert every single pack master in Northern America? Word would spread throughout the wolf packs that *I* started this. That *I* initiated the fight. Hundreds of thousands would be mobilized, families evacuated from their homes, curfews, weapons, even riots among the conservative packs! It would be chaos within weeks. And then what if your little theory proves to be false, hmm?"

He peered between the two of us with eyes narrowed. "Do you think everyone will simply shrug and turn back to their lives, as though this happens every day? The werewolves' authority has *never* been challenged by the vampires. The wolf packs will not forget this so easily; they will hold someone accountable for the unnecessary trauma they inflicted on their packs. And who do you think that will be?" He stepped closer to us and pointed his index finger at us as though we'd been naughty puppies who peed on the rug. "If I alert the packs and this proves false, they will be out for blood—*my* blood. So no, Faith. I will not allow the vampires to continue killing on my land. I never have. But as for the uprising? If I hear anyone in this pack even utter the word, I will *personally* declaw you every full moon for the next fifty years. Is this understood?"

Silence echoed for a beat, but I wouldn't be subdued so easily.

"Well, I'm not in the pack," I said, "so does that mean I can talk about it?"

Lucas shook his head slowly—though I thought I saw a hidden grin on his lips—and Rolf straight-up growled at me, which I took as a definitive "no."

"Get out the both of you," Rolf spat. "And take your scum with you."

He swept out of the room, heading for the stairs, and the rest of the pack began to disperse. Julian and Katie found us immediately.

"This was really dumb," Katie said.

"If he wasn't so stubborn, it would have worked," I said sullenly.

"Well, you should have known better," Julian said to Lucas.

"Had to try," he mumbled and then sighed. "Help me take care of him, would you?" He gestured to the vampire, who looked on the verge of passing out. "Oh, and we got frenzy leftovers to clean up, too. Get a crew going, would you, Katie? I think I killed all the live ones before we left so just disposal."

Katie nodded with a jerk and jogged off.

Julian began dragging the vampire—who was now kicking and screaming—toward the back doors. I turned to Lucas.

"What do we do now?" I asked.

"What is there left to do? The verdict's gonna be read tomorrow, and even if by some miracle they don't convict me—which is a pretty slim chance after the stunt we just pulled—Rolf's made it clear that he won't alert the packs no matter what we do. He has to see it for himself."

"But he won't even *try*," I said, halfway stamping my foot in frustration.

"I know it sounds grim, but best we can hope for now is for the vampires to kick it up a notch. Maybe if they kill enough girls, Rolf'll realize he can't turn a blind eye anymore."

I shook my head. What a thing to hope for.

"Lucas, you coming?" Julian asked from the backyard as he struggled with the vampire.

"I gotta go take care of this stuff," he said.

"Okay, I'll be—"

"With Derek," he finished. "I know."

It sucked to hear the defeat in his tone, but I felt that of all nights, I should spend tonight with Derek. He was upstairs in the bedroom next to Lucas's, dead to the world. He'd been asleep since his infection on the night of the last full moon, and had only opened his eyes once, four days later. He'd looked around, I'd cried hysterically, and then he'd passed out again.

Fun times.

Now I spent pretty much all of my time with him, just in case it happened again. And with the full moon tomorrow night, I felt that tonight held the best chance of him waking up prematurely. Or waking up at all, which, admittedly, no one was entirely sure he'd do.

I know Rolf was hoping for it.

He wanted Derek executed, and he wanted to do it now *before* he woke up. I'd fought tooth and nail to keep Derek alive these past weeks, and now, hopefully, I only had hours to wait until he awoke.

"I'll be back late," Lucas said and passed his hand across my cheek before placing a soft kiss on my lips.

"Stay safe."

And he was gone.

• • •

Derek didn't wake up early, although I stayed with him until the last possible moment before Lucas's verdict was to be read. It was dusk, just minutes until the darkness would fall. I stood outside in the snow, holding Lucas's big warm hand and feeling the tremble of his muscles. The extreme nerves he felt were making him want to change. That, coupled with the full moon, minutes away, and being near me was a recipe for disaster. But I didn't care. These precious minutes might be my last with Lucas as I knew him. I wasn't going to hide in the house when I could be in his arms.

The pack was forming a large circle in the backyard. Rolf and the other four Council members stood stoically in the center, while Lucas and I sequestered ourselves just inside the woods next to the mansion. I was so nervous my stomach was cramping, and Lucas's vibe was a mirror of my emotions.

He looked down at me, and I felt my heart skip around in my chest for an entirely different reason. He still did that for me. Just one look and I was mush.

He took my face, his eyes conveying everything he was too scared or too nervous to voice. That he loved me. That he was sure everything would be okay. That after tonight, we'd be going back to CSU and things would return to some semblance of normalcy. That Derek would be better soon.

The darkness of his deep, brown eyes became lighter, almost silvery, betraying his will to change. He bent and pressed his forehead to mine, closing his eyes as if shielding them would stop what we both knew was coming. I heard him inhale a big breath, and I followed suit, breathing with him.

"Okay," he said. "I guess I gotta go now."

I nodded too fast and he took a step back, still holding my hand, unable to let go. Letting go would mean accepting that these would be his last few moments of sanity; that the silver room would make him lose his mind and we'd never be together like this again. Slowly, our palms slid apart, leaving only the fingertips . . . then they broke.

He gave me a brave little smirk and turned, taking that first hellish step away. Suddenly I couldn't stand to see him take one more step.

"Lucas!" I gasped, starting after him.

He spun around and wrapped me up in him. The scent of his skin, his breath against my cheek, his lips on my neck, searing me; his warmth encompassed me and stole the fear from my mind. And all that was left was Lucas. All that mattered were his hands on me, his mouth over mine, crushing against my lips as though this was the last time he'd ever get to hold me.

Suddenly I felt sorry for all the time I'd wasted. The weeks I'd had to kiss him, hold him, and instead had pushed him away to be with Derek. *What if this is it? What if this is the last time I ever kiss him?*

Lucas pulled back, breathing heavily against my lips. His body jerked with tremors; I could feel the change bursting within his vibe like a solar flare. I wondered how he'd managed to keep himself in line at all. He usually never even touched me around the full moon. I guess he figured *what the hell?* He was heading toward his doom anyway. And if he was going to lose himself tonight, I'd rather he took me with him.

"I gotta go," he said hoarsely. "I love you, Faith. No matter what happens next."

I nodded again. "No matter what."

He looked up at the orange sky above us, and for a moment he looked like a wolf—his eyes shining silver and his face so strong and feral, a shadow of the beast he would become tonight. Then he looked down at me, gave me one last devastating look, and left. I watched his body fade into the depths of the trees, becoming one with the darkness.

I stood there for a long moment as the heat of Lucas's embrace seeped out of my body through my fingers and turned me numb. Managing, somehow, to pull myself together, I circled around to the side of the house, where I emerged from the woods near the back patio. I had just started down the slate steps, when someone grabbed my upper arm from behind in a surprisingly strong grip.

I turned and was stunned to see Yvette, her owlish gray eyes urgent.

"Listen to me quickly," she hissed. "If Lucas is convicted, as I suspect he will be, you must stay with him tonight."

I stared at her, confused as hell. "Why?"

"His mind will not survive. You must stay with him. You must help him."

I shook my head. "But how can I . . . ?"

Her gaze pierced mine, willing me to understand something. What, though? I tried to read her vibe, but as always hers was mysteriously absent.

"*Stay with him*," she said again. With that, she released my arm and swept across the lawn to join the rest of the pack.

I remained in place for a moment, attempting to decipher what she'd been trying to tell me. Why would being with Lucas help him stay sane? What could I possibly—

"Faith!"

I turned and saw Katie waving at me from the crowd of werewolves congregated in the center of the yard. I jogged toward her and she smiled worriedly while bouncing on her heels. Her pupils were already elongated, irises like yellow marbles. She was just itching for the moon to rise. As I looked around, I realized that all of the eyes were bright and wild. The energy emanating from the crowd was a tangle of anticipation and ferocity and, suddenly, I felt like maybe I shouldn't be there.

But I didn't have much time to fret over it because at that moment, Rolf began to speak. He stood with the Council in the center of the circle, and Lucas stood before him, straight and tall. His eyes were like starlight as the sunset glanced across his emotionless face.

Rolf's face was equally as grave, as though he didn't enjoy doing this, but he knew it was necessary. I didn't care how necessary he thought this was. I hated that big furry jerk.

Rolf cleared his throat and said, "We have convened on this, the night of the January full moon, to read the verdict regarding the trial of Lucas Whelan. After one week of deliberation, it is this court's decision to convict Lucas Whelan of pack misconduct."

My stomach fell to the ground right along with my mouth. Katie shot me a tense glance as tremors rippled down her back.

But Lucas's face showed no emotion. He stood just as tall as ever, calmly accepting his fate.

"The punishment," Rolf said, "is one night spent in the silver room. The sentence shall be executed tonight." He paused as something flowed across his features. Pity? His energy was regretful, but determined. He said something to Lucas, something I couldn't hear, and then he said, loudly again, "Release him at dawn." Rolf disappeared into the crowd.

Two big human guys attempted to grab Lucas's arms, but he shrugged them off and spun around on his heel. The two men escorted him through the crowd, which parted to let him through.

I watched them take him into the big house, Nora and Julian in tow. I debated a second over whether or not I should follow, but Yvette's words rang in my head: *stay with him.*

So I raced after them, shaking off Katie's hand. The werewolves behind us erupted into conversation, some of them taking off into the woods to await the night. It was getting close. Derek might be waking up soon. And Lucas was going into the silver room.

I didn't know what to do, who to be with. Derek, my best friend, the one I'd been waiting for, for three weeks now, or Lucas—my boyfriend. The boy who had saved my life many times over, the boy I loved without boundaries or any sense of self-control. It was a hard choice to make, but I still had minutes until nighttime, when Derek might awaken.

So, I followed Lucas.

I needed to be there for him, to spend those final moments with my boyfriend, to look into his eyes one last time before they turned loose with madness.

They took Lucas down to the basement and into the ballroom, which was now empty and lightless. There was an invisible door on the back wall, and one of the big guys pushed it in. Nora, Julian, and I followed Lucas through it.

He was silent as we walked down a stark cement hallway toward a room at the end with thick bars on the door, like a prison. The bars glinted in the setting sun, which shone through a small barred window on the back wall of the cell. They were silver bars. Silver-plated walls, ceiling, even the floor.

Suddenly a shrill scream sounded from upstairs, and everyone whirled around at once. Lucas and I made eye contact for a split second, and then he blew past us to fly through the ballroom and up the stairs. Julian, Nora, and the two men followed him, yelling for him to stop. I ran as fast as I could, but by the time I was in the living room, they were already upstairs.

I dashed up the stairs three at a time and ran to Derek's room, hearing a scuffle behind the walls. I rounded the doorway and gasped at the sight before me.

Derek was awake.

And he was pissed.

SANITY

Lucas had Derek pinned down on the bed while he thrashed, blistering the air with curses. There was a girl in the corner—one of the nurses attending to Derek—bleeding from a scratch on her arm. She must have been the screamer. She ran out of the room, still screaming.

Rolf burst through the doorway and shoved me to the side into Julian's arms.

"Get off!" Derek yelled. "What the hell is going on? Where am I?"

"Lucas, release him," Rolf commanded.

Lucas let Derek go with a jerk, but remained close.

Derek straightened and glanced around the room. His eyes were so, so bright, like icicles—cold and sharp. They touched mine and pierced me right down to my soul. I almost gasped. He didn't look anything like himself anymore.

"*Faith?*" he asked incredulously. His voice sounded the same, soft and mellow. "What's going on?"

"There is no time to explain," Rolf cut in. "The moon is about to take us."

Derek frowned, stepping closer and Lucas followed with fists clenched tight. "The *moon*? Where are we? What's—" He took another step and stopped. The pupils of his eyes dilated until even the whites were blackened.

Julian darted in front of me with Nora by his side.

"Derek," Rolf said slowly, inching closer. "Do *not* breathe."

"Why does she smell like . . . like food?" His voice was breathy, ravenous.

"Because you have been turned," Rolf said. "There is not much time left. I fear there will not be time to explain. Remain calm."

Suddenly the room felt like it was shaking. No wait, that wasn't the room. It was Julian's body. Why was I clutching his waist? When had that happened?

"Rolf," Julian said. "I can't . . . hold out much longer. We need to do something."

Lucas shuddered violently and said, "Just bring him outside with us. We can run with him tonight and make sure he's safe."

"There is no us!" Rolf shouted. "You will not run with the pack tonight, Lucas. You will serve your sentence!"

Derek took another step toward me, inhaling deeply. "God, she smells amazing. . . . I could just . . . eat her." His body shook and his head twitched as if he was possessed.

"He's changing!" Nora shouted.

"No," Rolf whispered. "It is impossible."

But it *was* possible.

Derek's body quaked again and then exploded. His roar of pain echoed through the room as a great fissure erupted from the base of his neck to his tailbone. With a sound like ripping fabric, it burst, turning his body inside out. It was slow and grueling compared to the changes I'd seen Lucas endure. It was as though Derek's body was slowly breaking down, each bone, each muscle, each nerve was tearing. Derek's groans scalded the air, and my heart pounded in my chest as his neck elongated, his legs curled underneath him, his ribs—cracking and bending—splayed into the barreled chest of a wolf. He cried out again as his teeth grew to half a foot in length and his body bloomed with flawless ivory fur. Muscles cleaved, sinews dissolved and re-formed, bones cracked like gunshots. And Derek's horrendous screams morphed into the agonized howl of a wolf.

I shrieked and Julian shoved me away as he changed too. I hit the far wall and watched as Derek, now a pure white wolf, lunged for me. Lucas changed in midair and slammed into him. I screamed again as Derek's jaws clamped just inches from my face.

Julian and Lucas wrestled with Derek as Nora ran out of the room. I heard the sounds of her changing on the way downstairs. Then Yvette appeared in the doorway accompanied by two more *huge* human men bearing silver chains.

"Get her!" Yvette shouted, pointing at me. "Get her out of here!"

The men started toward me, but Derek had just managed to get free of Lucas and Julian. He ran past the men, knocking them down, and flew out of the room.

Lucas started to follow, but Rolf, who had yet to change, shouted, "Chain him!"

The big men got to their feet and lashed the chains around Lucas's fur-covered flesh. Lucas howled; the charred stink of burning skin seeped through the room like a poison.

Then Rolf changed, and both he and Julian took off after Derek. I ran to the window and flung it open. I watched a slender white wolf fly across the snow, just a shade darker than the powder. Two dark beasts followed it into the woods, howling shrilly.

"*Derek!*" I shouted. "Run, Derek, and don't stop!"

Lucas's cries of pain made me spin around. Three more men had joined the first four and worked with the others to bring Lucas down. Lucas clawed furiously at them, drawing blood across their arms and backs, but they dodged his fangs with expert speed.

I ran forward—to do what, I didn't know. But I had to help

Lucas. Not only were these men hurting him, but Lucas was the only one who would protect Derek out there. I ran and grabbed at one of the big men's backs, tugging futilely.

Yvette yanked me away and I tried to shove her off, but she was, strangely, much stronger than me. I sagged against her, yelling for the men to let Lucas go. I wished like hell that they were werewolves so I could force them off of him, but they were only human and immune to my power.

They dragged him out of the room as his claws made desperate troughs in the hardwood floors. His lupine face contorted in crazed frustration. Hoping I could soothe him, I tried to forge a connection, but he was too insane and I was unable to catch his eye before they yanked him away. I wanted to do something—to help him somehow—so I went after him, but by the time I ran down the stairs, he and the men were already in the basement. I flew across the tiled floor and made it to the back door just as it was about to slam closed.

I followed the men down the cement hall. Lucas's howls reverberated off of the walls and made my ears ring. His body began to shake and shrink; he clawed at the walls, writhing, trying frantically to keep from being put into the room.

But his efforts were wasted. The seven men wielding silver were too much for him. One of them threw open the door and together, they shoved Lucas inside. He released one last, long keening howl and then morphed into a human. He continued to scream as he shook the chains off. The men strode past me on the way out, bloodied and bruised. One paused and looked back at me.

"We're locking this hallway behind us," he yelled over Lucas.

I spun around. "And?"

"And it's soundproof."

"Does it look like I care?" I turned my back on him.

I heard the door slam and the sound of it locking into place, locking me inside this dark, narrow hallway with a psychotic werewolf.

I ran to the door of the silver room and threw myself to the ground, stretching my arm through the bars. I didn't know what I was supposed to do, but he was in so much pain. I had to do *something*.

"Lucas!" I shouted over his cries. He was bashing himself against the wall, trying to break through it was my guess. But every time his skin touched the silver-plated walls, it sizzled like meat on a burning hot skillet.

"Stop, Lucas! You're hurting yourself. I'm right here! I'm right here for you." I stretched my arm farther in, as though the closer I got to him, the more I could help him, even though that was not the case. I don't think Lucas even knew I was there. The few times I caught sight of his face illuminated in the moonlight, it was manic. Wild, like nothing I'd ever seen before. His body couldn't even heal properly from the burns he caused himself, and there were bloody, bubbling marks on his throat and arms from where the chains had bound him.

I couldn't handle watching him enduring this pain. I stood and paced, furiously trying to figure out how to help him. For once, he was the vulnerable one and I was the one with all the power—but power to do what?

Lucas continued to rage and cry for *hours*. I cried right along with him. And then he must have worn himself out, because sometime around two in the morning, he fell silent.

I looked up, pressing my face against the cool silver bars that burned him so terribly. He was lying curled up in the moonlight as though it was a warm blanket, soothing him. His body was broken, shaking with sobs.

"Lucas?" I said. "It's okay, come here."

Lucas rolled his head toward me. His eyes were darker than I'd ever seen them. They were human eyes, like they must have been before he was infected. Soft—without any hint of the beast struggling to be free within him.

"Faith?"

God, it was amazing to hear him say my name. "Yeah, it's me," I said, mustering a smile through my tears. "Come here. Come here to me."

He drew in a shuddery breath, and I saw a few tears slide across his cheek, making little trails of clean skin against the wounds ripped into his face. "I can't," he rasped.

I sniffled and put my hands back on my side of the bars. "It's okay," I said. "I'm right here. I won't leave you." I felt for his energy; it was so weak. . . . He was losing himself.

That's when it hit me.

I was the one with all the power.

I had to connect with him, control his mind. I hadn't thought of it before because I couldn't connect to unchanged werewolves. I didn't know if it would work now, but I sure as hell had to try. I had the strongest connection with Lucas, so it was worth the shot.

"Lucas, look at me," I said urgently. "I'm going to try and connect with you. Don't look away."

I don't know if it was because he didn't have enough strength to look away, or because he actually listened, but either way, his eyes remained on mine, and I summoned up the electricity inside me. It started just below my heart in that fluttery place where nervousness lives. Like a spasm of light, burning brighter and brighter, expanding throughout my body. I focused fully on Lucas, willing the connection to click into place. I felt resistance, the block in my mind that said it couldn't be done, but I flung it away. I *could* do this.

And then—*snap*.

I was in his head. His emotions were mine, his actions pliable. And, God was he weak. I'd figured this out just in time.

I let my strength flood into him, repeated soothing words, *I'm here, I'm always here, I love you, I'm here.* . . .

But the longer I held our connection, the weaker it became, the more effort it took. I held it steady for what seemed like forever, but it wasn't long enough.

All too soon, it faded and died.

And then Lucas was left alone.

Immediately, he began to groan, raking his hands down his face.

I leaned against the wall, head pounding. I'd never held the connection for so long before, and I was exhausted. But it was nothing compared to what Lucas was enduring. I had to try and do it again; he needed me. So I rested, trying not to watch as Lucas regained his strength and started bashing himself against the walls again. When I felt my strength return, I called out to him.

For a long time, he was too wild to listen, but eventually, he wore himself out and collapsed to the floor. Only then, could I persuade him to make eye contact and give him a few moments of comfort. But then I'd lose it again and the cycle would continue.

・・・

Lucas was close to unconscious when dawn came. I, on the other hand, stood at attention, exhausted as well, but eager to get out of that hell hole. I waited by the door for someone to come let us out. I thought briefly of Derek, wondering if he'd found someplace safe to stay for the day and if he'd been strong enough and smart enough to escape the pack.

Then the door sprung open and three of the gigantic men from last night came to take Lucas back up to his room. I followed, and shooed them away once they'd placed him safely in his bed.

I went about cleaning him off, but I didn't have to apply any first aid to his burns or wounds because they began to heal within minutes.

Once he was cleaned, I put the blankets over him, dimmed the lights, and slipped into bed beside him. I smoothed my hand over his bare chest, loving how the shadows played over the contours and peaks of his flawless body.

I wished I had my camera. I wanted to remember him like this forever. So calm and perfect. I turned my head and kissed his neck. Even in his sleep, I felt the heat surge. I smiled against his skin. Somehow, that made me feel better. I didn't have much energy left to test his emotions, but what I could get was peaceful—or as peaceful as Lucas ever got. There was a tinge of that old craziness at the edges of his vibe, but I couldn't tell if the madness I felt was the werewolf inside him fighting to be released or a madness of a different kind.

True insanity.

THE SENSE

I awoke to kisses—tons of them, on my mouth and down my throat and lower, trailing slowly down my stomach. I smiled, yawning, looking down to see the top of Lucas's head. I grabbed his hair and pulled him up, wanting to see his face.

But the face looking at me was not Lucas. It was Derek. His lips were dripping with crimson liquid, and he had fangs like kitchen knives. I looked down and my body was punctured with bloody fang marks.

I screamed and sat up.

Lucas sat up too, looking around for danger, but as soon as his eyes fell on me, he knocked me back onto my pillows. He hugged me close and tucked his face into my neck, kissing me everywhere.

I panted, totally freaked out . . . and, okay, slightly aroused.

His lips found mine, and I kissed him back.

"Are you okay?" I asked through his lips. "Are you . . . ?" I didn't want to say the word *insane*.

"You . . . are . . . amazing," he said, kissing my nose lightly on each word.

"Me?" I asked, confused.

"You stayed with me," he said, face just inches away. "You kept me sane. I know it was you. I didn't imagine that, did I?"

"No. I was there. I used the connection. I didn't know I could do it when you're human, but it worked. Thank God, it worked."

"Amazing," he said again and rolled over on top of me, kissing me. I felt a blush creep into my cheeks. I wondered if he knew he was naked.

"Lucas," I said. "You, ah . . . you'd better stop."

He shook his head, catching my lips and kissing me harder.

"What's gotten into you?" I asked, laughing slightly.

"I'm tired of being the only one naked around here," he said with a little fake pout that made me want to nibble on his lower lip.

"You're red," he said, smiling devilishly. "So it's okay for me to be naked, but not you? I just don't think that's fair." His hot hand wandered to my shirt and slipped it over my head. I gasped as he began kissing my stomach.

"Lucas!" I said. "Stop it. You're the one who said we couldn't do that."

He came back to my face and brushed his lips over my chin. "Well, maybe I changed my mind. Maybe after last night, I think we should try."

He was actually serious. I sat up. "You know what? I think you *did* lose your mind in there."

Lucas laughed and pushed me back down. "You kept me sane last night using the connection. So use it now. Make sure I don't change. Come on, don't you want to?"

I hesitated. Yes, I wanted to, but . . .

"I don't think now is the best time," I said delicately.

"What's wrong with now? I lived through that hell with my sanity intact—thanks to you." He rubbed his nose against mine. "And Derek is alive, everybody's okay. And this is the safest time. Right after the full moon. With you keeping me in control, it'll be perfect." He smiled roguishly and kissed me so fiercely, I had trouble resisting.

"We don't know if Derek's okay yet," I said.

Lucas stopped and his face slowly settled into a scowl.

Apparently, that was the *wrong* thing to say.

"I'm sorry," I said quickly. I put my arms around his waist. "I didn't mean it . . . like that. I don't know. Just forget I mentioned it." I tried to pull him toward me, but his back stiffened, preventing me from moving him even an inch. "Lucas, come on, aren't you exhausted anyway? I mean, last night was horrible for you. For both of us."

"You don't gotta tell me that," he said. "I know exactly what it was like. What I don't know is why you have to bring Derek up whenever we're alone together."

I felt my mouth open and close as I groped for a good answer. "I'm sorry," I said to avoid a fight. "I promise I won't do it again, okay? I'm sorry."

Lucas rolled off of the bed and pulled on a pair of Levis. He cocked his head at the window and said, "It's nighttime."

"He must not be here then," I said softly. "Rolf would have woken us up."

"Yup."

Finding my shirt lodged in between the pillows, I pulled it over my head and got out of bed. I hated doing this, but . . .

"Will you find him?" I asked.

Lucas's eyebrows lifted just the tiniest bit. "Of course I'll find him," he said. "He's probably hiding in the woods."

"Or dead."

Lucas put his hand on my cheek for an instant and then let it fall. "I'll be back. If you go downstairs, don't tell them where I'm going."

"Thank you."

Lucas looked at me with this odd, pained sort of expression that made me feel horrible for having asked him to search for

Derek, and then turned to leave.

Through the window I watched Lucas run out the back doors. He stripped his jeans, put them in his mouth, and changed in midrun.

As I watched him disappear, I pondered his earlier words. Could I really keep his will to change reigned in? Control his instinct and make him normal? I'd done it last night. It had been grueling, but it had worked.

And I had Yvette to thank for tipping me off. She had seemed to *know* that I would be able to save Lucas. Which could only mean that she knew about my power. And if that was the case, I needed to know how she'd found out and what else she knew. Now.

I straightened and walked downstairs to the kitchen to find a few runts making ice cream sundaes.

"Hey," I said. "Do any of you know where Yvette is?"

They regarded me coldly. A girl with dirty blond hair said, "She's usually in the study with Rolf." She pointed down the hall. "Third door on the right."

"Thanks." I grabbed an apple from the counter and headed down the hallway, hearing the runts' whispers as I went—probably talking crap about me.

I reached the correct door and paused before entering, taking time to lean against the wall and down the apple. I didn't want to do this in front of Rolf, but I needed to know what Yvette knew. Maybe I could get her to talk to me someplace private. Gathering my courage, I stuffed the apple core into my pocket and faced the door again.

But as I poked my head inside, I realized getting Yvette to follow me out wasn't necessary. She was sitting alone beside a wall-to-wall window that opened up to the side yard. The snow-laden trees stood in the distance, their colors muted through the glass panes like a watercolor painting.

Yvette didn't look up from her book when I entered so I closed the door quietly and walked across the room. The study was stacked with books, both old and new, and a mahogany desk stood in the center, cluttered with papers and a laptop computer. I passed it and went to stand beside a gold-upholstered armchair across from Yvette.

She was the only person I'd ever met without a vibe. It had always intrigued me, but now I had a feeling there was a reason I couldn't read it.

"You know why I'm here," I said.

A faint smile tugged on her lips. She placed the book down on her lap and finally looked up at me. Her rounded face was tanned and creased around the eyes and mouth; her wiry black hair was pulled into a loose braid that flowed across her chest. She scrutinized me methodically, taking in every inch of my face.

"I never thought I'd meet another one," she said. Her voice was like the hum of some great machine—low and steady.

"Another . . . what, exactly?" I asked as my pulse began to race. She knew about my power!

But she faltered. "I don't really know *what* you are. But I do know that we are the same. It's a form of telepathy—connecting minds, thoughts. Or in our case, emotions." She leaned in, expression fervent. "What is it like for you? What are your abilities?"

"I can read emotions, like you said. Everyone's, even vampires and werewolves. Actually, theirs are strongest. And I can control any changed werewolf, even on the full moon. But it's difficult."

"And the vampires? Can you control them?"

I shook my head. "How did you know about me?" I asked, sitting down across from her. "How did you know I could save Lucas?"

"I have only met someone like you once before. I knew immediately because I could not sense you."

"Sense me?"

"Sense your emotions."

Oh, my vibe. "I can't . . . sense you either."

"I believe it is because our powers cancel each other out."

"I guess that makes sense. So wait, you said you know someone else like us?"

She looked down at her lap. "Knew. The vampires took him. He is dead now."

I cringed. "I'm sorry."

"They thought he could control them like we control the wolves so they murdered him. But it doesn't work that way. The vampires are undead; their brain functions do not work like ours. We can sense them, but we cannot control them."

"Can you control the werewolves too, then?" I asked.

"Yes," she said. "Though, not when they are human. Well, except for Rolf."

"*Rolf?*" I blurted. He was the last person I'd expect her to be able to control. He'd easily usurped my power over his pack that night at the barn and almost took my connection to Lucas as well.

"Of course," she said, furrowing her delicate brows. "He is my match."

"Your match? What is that?"

"It seems that those with the sense—people like us—have an inexplicable connection to the supernatural world. The magic that runs through the blood of the vampires and werewolves—it binds to us as well, enabling us to sense emotions and temporarily control their actions. For each of us, there is a single supernatural creature whose magic is so similar to ours that they are bound to us by an unbreakable bond. They are matched so perfectly that the werewolf can be controlled even when he or she is human."

Well if that was true, then I supposed Lucas was my match. *Cool.* I wondered what that meant, exactly.

"So can Rolf feel it when you control him?" I asked.

"Yes. He's the only one. But I rarely do it. Only to protect myself from harm. In fact, I have not needed to use my abilities in over a decade."

Huh. Must be nice.

We were silent a moment and, suddenly I heard the shadow of Lucas's voice in my head: *Nobody can ever find out about this. . . . There's no way Rolf will let someone with that kind of power live.*

A flicker of panic flared up as the gravity of what I'd just done hit me. I'd just told the pack master's mate that I could control his entire pack.

Real smart. I was so dog chow.

But then again, he'd let Yvette live.

"Why does Rolf let you control him?" I asked. "He's the pack master; doesn't that threaten everything he's about? I mean you could make him do whatever you wanted—human or not."

"When we first met, Rolf was not the pack master. I stayed with him through many difficult times. He trusts me above anyone else. He would never kill me for what I am because he knows I would never abuse my power over him."

"But what about me? Did you tell him about me?"

Yvette's face closed down—a typical werewolf trick she must have picked up from Rolf. It was impossible to read her.

"Yvette, did you tell him?"

"I have not. I wasn't sure you had the sense, and I didn't want to endanger your life unnecessarily."

"And now that you know, will you tell him?"

She scrutinized me for a long while. "My loyalty is to Rolf," she said and my heart plummeted. "However, you are like me—the only other one I know. We must protect each other." She fixed her gaze on me, serious and intent. "So I will not tell Rolf what you are. So long as you remain a friend of this pack."

"What does that entail, exactly?"

"Remain compliant with Rolf's wishes and I have no reason to tell him what you are."

"I'm not going to let him kill Derek," I said. "You'll have to tell him because I—"

"Shh," Yvette soothed. "Rolf will not kill Derek."

"Wh—what? But he . . ."

"I know Rolf," Yvette said. "He is cautious of change. He doesn't like what a creature such as Derek might do to the dynamics of the pack. If Derek is stronger, he may usurp his leadership. Or if Derek creates more creatures like himself, his very race may be put in jeopardy."

"Yeah, okay, but that still doesn't make it okay to kill someone for something they haven't even done yet."

"Agreed. And that is why I will speak to Rolf. He will listen. I am not the only one who thinks this way—Nora and Tony Nocturn will side with me. Many others, too."

I bit my lip, deliberating. "If Derek is allowed to live, I won't defy Rolf's wishes. So you don't have to tell him about me." I didn't really like the deal, but what choice did I have? I couldn't let Rolf know what I was. He'd kill me, unless . . . unless, I managed to control him—stop him from hurting me.

But Yvette seemed to know where my mind was going.

"I'll block you if you try to control Rolf," she said. "He's my match, and I will feel it if you enter his mind."

Damn it.

"You can do that?" I asked. "Block people?"

"It takes practice, but yes. I learned to do it with Kevin—the last person I met with the sense. There are some humans who can do it as well, subconsciously, of course. And there is the chance that you will meet a vampire who can block you, since they know of our existence."

"Will you teach me to do it? So I can protect Lucas against . . ."

Yvette's face split in a rueful grin. "Against me?"

I flushed and shrugged. "Make it an even playing field?"

She flipped the pages of her book with one hand. "Perhaps one day."

Lame. "Can Rolf block *you* out?"

Her lip curled. "Unfortunately."

I smiled at that. "Hey, you have to let him have his way *sometimes*."

The shadow of a smile played around her mouth. "Yes, I suppose so."

5

THE WAITING GAME

I left with my head spinning in twenty different directions. I was excited that I'd met someone else with the sense, as Yvette had called it. And I was out-of-my-mind eager to tell Lucas about the whole matched thing. I wanted to start experimenting with him ASAP, to test the limits of our connection and my power. What other cool benefits came with our superlink and how could I use them for both my own safety and his? Not to mention for some of the more tantalizing activities.

But I was also still worried about Derek, and if he had even survived the night with the pack after him. As usual, the thought of what he must be going through because of me, brought my high right back down to the floor, and by the time I was back in Lucas's room, I had returned to biting my nails off in anticipation of Lucas's call.

Before I'd even had a chance to sit down, I heard a knock at the door. I turned to see Katie pop her head in.

"Hi," she said. "Can we come in?"

"We?" I asked, pushing myself onto the edge of the bed.

Julian stuck his head in too, and I waved them in. Katie sat down on the desk, and Julian came to lean beside me on the bedpost. I didn't need to sense their vibes to read their emotions; it was written all over their faces. They were scared.

"Where's Lucas?" Katie asked tentatively. "Is he . . . okay?"

"He's fine," I said.

"Was it bad?" Katie asked, awed.

"Kate," Julian said sharply. "Come on, she doesn't want to relive it."

"No, it's okay," I said and leaned back on my elbows. "It was bad . . . really bad. But he's healed now and he went out for a run. I think he needed a release."

Katie and Julian nodded like they could imagine what I was talking about.

"So, last night . . . ," I started, not really knowing how I would continue.

"We didn't see Derek," Julian said.

I felt my lungs empty with a long breath. "Thank God," I whispered. "I thought the pack would kill him."

"I think he has too much vampire in him to make him easily locatable."

"That's sort of good, I guess."

It was good because that meant he was able to lose the pack. It was bad because that meant it was more than likely that he was dead inside. No feelings. No love. No Derek. "Let's talk about something else," I said quickly.

Katie, never one to play shy, jumped right in.

"Guess what!" she gushed.

I cracked a smile. "What?" I asked.

"I'm going to CSU this semester!"

"What?" I asked again.

"As a lab assistant." She smiled at my blank expression. "I'm a chemist, didn't Lucas tell you?"

"No."

"Loser. Well, I am. And I finally got a job!" She clapped her hands together. "It's been ridiculous trying to find someplace to hire me because I look sixteen—and, let's be honest, who wants to hire a sixteen-year-old chemist—but Rolf made a call to the dean of the chemistry department, and they said they'd take me."

"That's great, Katie," I said, genuinely happy for her. And, yeah, a little relieved that she'd be on campus with me. Over the past few weeks, I'd really come to rely on Katie for support and a little levity in what was swiftly becoming the worst time in my life. She was a good friend, and I'd been dreading leaving her for school.

"We'll be together more," Katie went on with a sneaky wink. "I'll be able to help Lucas keep an eye on you. Oh, and Derek now, too. That is if he's not all crazy and—"

"Kate!" Julian snapped, cutting her off.

"Oh, sorry," Katie made an exaggerated grimace.

Julian rubbed his temples. "Ignore her," he said wearily.

Katie's outraged expression made me laugh. "It's fine," I said. Katie threw a triumphant look at Julian, which made me smile again. I sighed. Just being around these two was like a glass of ice water in the desert. "I'm so glad you guys aren't like the rest of the werewolves. They're all such jerks."

Julian lifted an angular brow. "What are you talking about?"

"Oh, please," I scoffed. "Don't pretend like you don't know. I'm sure everyone talks trash about me when I'm not around."

"I don't know about that, but I do know that they are afraid of you."

"Afraid?" I asked incredulously. "Of me?"

Julian nodded and Katie bobbed her head enthusiastically.

"Why?" I asked, totally confused.

"Lucas is one of the oldest members of the pack," Julian said. "Second only to Rolf and our father—our real father. Tony. Lucas would be one of the most influential members of the Council if he'd ever agree to be on it."

"Why doesn't he?" I asked.

"He doesn't much enjoy politics. He's more of a . . . a vigilante, I guess."

"Yeah, I can see that about him," I said.

"Anyway," Julian went on. "You hold a lot of sway with Lucas. He refused to put you in danger to kill Vincent. He even threatened to leave the pack if it came down to it, which was a drastic move."

"Why?" I asked. "What's the big deal about leaving the pack?"

"Because once you leave, you can never return. It's a huge sacrifice. Not one many would make for a human. But he would have. I know Lucas, and when he says something, he means it." Julian's gaze held mine as my heart leaped at his words. "That's why someone like you, who holds that kind of power over a pack member—especially one like Lucas—well, let's just say it's dangerous. Our loyalty is to our own kind, and our pack, specifically. Not to a human." He smiled kindly. "So if you're not feeling the love from some of the pack, that's probably why. They don't like you holding the cards when it comes to him."

"Wow," I said. "I never really thought of it that way, but I guess it makes sense." If they only knew just how much sway I had over Lucas I might not have even been alive.

"Melanie has the same problem," Julian said, "though not as bad since I'm not as old or important as Lucas."

Lucas had told me that Julian's relationship with Melanie had caused a big rift between Julian and his parents since most werewolves were firmly against romantic relationships with humans. They even threatened to appeal for Julian's exile from the pack if he wouldn't end it. But Julian refused to let her go. Nora and Tony finally accepted their relationship—however reluctantly—when Julian proposed to Melanie about a year ago. I found the saga sweet and romantic. Lucas thought it was dumb and believed that all relationships were doomed to end—that no love could last eternity. Not that it mattered to me if he wanted to spend the rest of his immortal life festering in a pit of everlasting loneliness.

Okay, so it mattered. A little.

"But everyone seems to like Melanie," I said, coming back to the conversation. "I've never seen anyone be mean to her."

"That's because my parents are on the Pack Council." He threw me a wry smile. "I may not be ancient like Lucas, but I do have influence of my own."

"But why are they mean to me and not Melanie?" This was so unfair.

"Well, she's been around longer. So even though she's human, the pack trusts her. And,"—Julian's eyes twinkled with mischief—"she didn't bring a potentially blood-thirsty hybrid into the house either."

He chuckled at my dirty look. "It also helps that I'll be infecting her soon," he said between laughs.

"What!" I exploded.

Katie began giggling behind her hand.

Julian's smile faded. "What's wrong?"

"You're in-infecting Melanie?" I managed to sputter.

Julian's expression resembled someone who'd just been told to eat an anthill. "Yes," he said. "Of course. I'm marrying her, aren't I?"

How could Julian want to do that to Melanie? She'd be tormented for years before she could learn to control her triggers.

Even then, she still had to succumb to the change every month. She'd be tortured by it forever. What was Julian thinking?

Katie kicked her legs against the desk, obviously amused by my reaction. "She thinks you're crazy, bro."

"Lucas and you never discussed this?" Julian asked.

"No," I said. "Never. Why would we?"

"Don't you want to be with him forever?"

"I—I don't know. I mean, it just never seemed like an option. We've only been together a few months."

"Don't you love him?" Julian asked. The way he said it wasn't accusatory, or suspicious. It was matter-of-factly. As though this was the most obvious question in the world.

But it had taken me years to be able to answer that question with a *yes*. Now, I was more certain of it than ever. I loved Lucas. More than my own life. But to let him infect me? I wasn't so sure.

"Yes," I mumbled finally. "I love him."

"Then let him infect you," he said simply.

My world jolted at his casual tone. As if what he suggested was nothing more than getting a haircut. "But that'll make me a were-wolf," I said vacantly.

Katie barked a laugh. "Duh! That's the whole point! Being a werewolf rocks!"

I stared at her. Lucas never made it seem that way. With him it was all torture and angst. Sure, he liked his enhanced strength and senses, but as far as his transformations went, he always seemed tormented by it. I'd seen his art—he was a wreck inside. Why would I ever want to live like that—especially if it was an eternal life?

"Melanie *wants* to be a werewolf?" I asked.

"She wants to be with me forever. And this is the only way to do that. We've spoken about it and she's willing to endure a few . . . difficult years in exchange for an endless life together."

"But—Lucas is over three hundred years old and he still seems to hate his transformations," I argued.

"That's because Lucas rarely lives with the pack," Julian said. "He only just returned after living alone in Russia for the last twenty years. Enduring the transformations alone is much more difficult than when you have a pack. It's close to unbearable when you're alone."

"But why?" I asked. "Why does having the pack help?"

"Because changing with a pack creates a bond," Katie chimed in. "Like a support system. When we all change together and run in groups, it makes it easier. We stay away from the humans and hunt in the woods instead. And Rolf is always there, the voice in the back of our heads, helping us stay out of trouble."

"So Melanie will join the pack?" I asked, mulling everything over.

"She will try," Julian said. I sensed nerves in Julian and I wondered at the cause. As I watched him, he shifted his weight and the light caught on something shiny on the inside of his elbow. Two jagged scars, both about three inches in length and no thicker than the width of a pencil. They were identical to the ones on Lucas's arm. His mark. Then the reason for Julian's nervousness clicked: Melanie had to pass the initiation rites to get into the pack. The first of countless dangers she'd have to overcome once she'd changed.

"When are you going to do it?" I asked.

"Late spring. When she turns twenty-one. We will be wed

here, at the mansion and then we will have the ceremony."

"Ceremony?"

"To infect her," Katie cut in. "We do it every six months. Anyone who wants to be infected gets bitten together."

"Why do you have to have a ceremony?" I asked.

"We don't *have* to have one," Katie said. "But it's fun. And it makes it easier for the runts to have company when they're enduring the change."

My mind focused on the word *enduring*. So it hurt to change . . . probably tremendously. Yet another reason *not* to do it. As I sat pondering everything I'd heard, I could only pinpoint one true reason to be infected: Lucas. Forever.

It was a concept I could definitely fall for, but Lucas's words still nagged at me: *No relationship is strong enough to last an eternity.*

As depressing as that thought was, I pressed it away because it didn't matter. I didn't want to become a werewolf anyway—even if it meant being with Lucas forever. I just wasn't cut out for that kind of life.

"It's all right," Katie said.

I looked up. "Huh?"

"That you don't want him to infect you. It's all right."

I frowned at her. "How do you—?"

"Because I can see it on your face. And it's okay. Lucas would never want it anyway."

Well, she was right about that much. Lucas seemed to hate letting me into the supernatural world even in general, so making me a part of it . . . well, I didn't want to be around to see the hissy fit he'd pitch at that idea.

"Lucas should be back by now," Julian commented. "If he was only running."

I winced up at him. I wasn't supposed to tell anyone where Lucas had gone, but I figured these two were the exception to that rule.

"He went to look for Derek," I admitted.

Julian nodded as if he'd expected me to say that. "Well, if anyone can find him, it'll be Lucas. He's the best tracker I've ever known. And in truth—" He cast a sidelong look at Katie and then away, ashamed. "I caught Derek's scent last night."

Both Katie and I gasped.

"Julian!" Katie hissed. "How could you keep that from the pack? Do you know what Rolf would do to you if he found out? Why didn't you tell them?"

"Because they would have killed him," Julian said calmly, but still adamant. "And I'm not sure that's the right thing to do."

I smiled appreciatively at Julian.

"But that doesn't mean I won't support killing him, if it turns out Derek is malicious," he qualified and turned to look firmly at me. "If he's a danger to the humans or the pack, then, I'm sorry Faith, but he's got to go."

I stopped myself from looking away from Julian's fierce expression, thinking to myself that of all the realities I'd been faced with tonight, that was one I could never, ever accept.

Just as I was about to defend Derek—again—a high-pitched shrieking noise cut me off.

My cell phone was ringing. And it was Lucas.

NO BREATHING

I pressed my cell phone to my ear, glancing at Katie and Julian.

"Hello?" I said.

"It's me," Lucas's voice sounded through the receiver. He waited a beat . . . a gut-wrenchingly long beat, and then said, "I found him."

The knot in my stomach tightened. "And?"

"He's alive. I had to, ah . . . hit him, though. He's out of it, but he seems okay."

"You *hit* him?" I gasped.

Lucas ignored me. "Tell Julian to take you to the cabin in the woods where you and Derek stayed and leave you there. I'll be inside."

It took a moment for me to process everything. Derek was alive, he was *alive*! And I was going to get to talk to him, hug him, and tell him how sorry I was about everything.

It was euphoria for an instant before I realized that none of those things were going to be possible. Derek wanted blood now. *My* blood. I wasn't going to get to touch him or even get too close.

"You there?" Lucas asked. "Did you pass out?"

I snapped out of it. "Yes," I said quickly. "I mean, no, of course not. I'll be there as soon as I can."

• • •

Thirty minutes later, Julian, Katie, and I were squashed into Julian's black Jag. The top was down, and my face felt frozen against the arctic wind whooshing through the car as we raced up the winding mountain road. The night sky was muted; blue clouds had smudged out the moon and completely erased every silver star in the sky.

When we're close to the cabin, Julian pulled over onto the side of the road and without even bothering to roll the top up, or even open the door, he pounced out of the car and landed lightly on the snowy ground. Katie, too, just hopped out in one graceful leap. I, on the other hand, had to use the door.

I walked shakily toward the cabin with Katie by my side. Julian entered and stood next to the door, watching something in the cabin, presumably Derek. When I was close enough, Lucas pulled me to his side and nodded for Katie to stand guard over Derek as well.

A fire crackled on the moldy hearth, warming the room and casting flickering shadows across the walls. Everything seemed exactly the same as the last time I saw it—filthy, dank, and swathed in cobwebs. Except that there was one very new addition. Derek sat calmly on the dirty couch. His chalky face was bathed in orange light from the fire, making him look almost human. He might have fooled me, but his eyes gave him away. They were so, so blue—like a winter sky. No human on earth had eyes that blue. They widened when he saw me.

"Remember what I said," Lucas warned. "No breathing."

Derek nodded quickly, his gaze darting from me to Lucas several times. I saw his throat move as he swallowed.

"I brought food," Julian said, indicating a bag slung over his shoulder.

Derek perked up as Julian reached into the bag and pulled out two extremely rare steaks. He tossed them to Derek, who took a ravenous bite.

"I was so hungry," he said with a moan. I watched a little color flow into his ivory cheeks, and I felt a weight lift.

"You like the food?" I asked.

Derek nodded, chewing. He finished the steaks and leaned back, rubbing his stomach just like he always did after a huge meal. I felt my heart lighten at the familiar gesture.

Derek scratched his chin for a second, looked around at everyone and then said, "Okay, I've been pretty lax about this whole deal so far, but I'll admit: my patience is running low." He looked dead at me. "Someone tell me what's going on."

"He still doesn't know?" I asked, staring up at Lucas.

His face scrunched up. "I thought it'd be easier for him to take coming from you."

"Well?" Derek asked. "I'm listening."

It felt so weird saying it like this—so clinically. Maybe if I could be near him, it wouldn't seem so cold.

"Can I sit by you?" I asked, looking at Lucas instead of Derek. "You're all just two feet away in—in case."

Lucas didn't look happy about it, but shrugged and dropped my hand.

I sat down on the couch beside Derek. He still seemed calm, but his gaze was expectant. I could feel every eye in the room on us.

"Derek," I said, trying to sound more confident than I was. "I don't know . . . I don't know where to start, really. This is going to sound crazy. I'll just say that first." I paused to inhale deeply and then said slowly. "You've been infected. On the last full moon, you were bitten by a vampire and fed his blood, right after that you were bitten by a werewolf. You passed out for three weeks and woke up last night."

The word dumbstruck didn't even begin to describe Derek's face. It was dumbstruck times a million. Then, amazingly, he began to chuckle. I winced at the sight of his teeth. They were blindingly white and the incisors were elongated just enough so that they didn't look quite human.

"This is a joke, right?" he asked. "You all are playing a joke."

I shook my head.

"So what?" Derek said. "I'm supposed to believe in vampires and werewolves now? Is that it?" He laughed again. "Come on, Faith. I'm not the smartest guy in the world, but I'm not an idiot either. I know that stuff is fake."

"It's not fake," I said evenly. "You spent last night as a wolf, didn't you? How else do you explain that?"

Derek stopped laughing and his forehead wrinkled up like white satin sheets. "I was expecting you to tell me I'm crazy."

"You're not crazy. You saw Lucas change, right? And you heal quickly, run faster, the sun . . ." Something caught in my throat at that and I started again. "The sun hurts you. All of that is new. It's all because you're a . . . a crossbreed between a werewolf and a vampire. A hybrid."

"That's impossible," Derek said. He looked around the room for confirmation, but found only the steely gazes of three werewolves. "It's impossible, isn't it?" He was begging me, pleading for me to say it was fake, that this was all some evil joke—some horrid nightmare.

But it wasn't. It was so very real.

"I'm so sorry, Derek. I know how scared you must be." I

reached out to grab his hand, and all three werewolves started forward, warning looks on their faces. I stopped and returned my hand to my lap. Yeah, touching was probably not smart.

Derek began to nod his head like he was forcing the information inside his brain. "I guess I should have figured it out, huh?" he muttered. "It's pretty obvious once you hear it out loud. Turning into a wolf, the sun." He faced me. "The way you smell."

I gulped and stood up slowly. He had a funny look in his eye all of a sudden. I crossed the room and melted into Lucas's side.

"So what does this mean?" Derek asked. "I'm a hybrid . . . thing. What does that mean?"

"Means you got a lot of work ahead of you," Lucas said. "We gotta figure out exactly what you are, what you're capable of. If you turn out to be a dangerous psycho-mutant, then we gotta figure out some way to keep you away from the pack."

"The pack?" Derek asked.

"Our pack," Lucas said, gesturing to Katie and Julian. "Our family. The pack master is convinced that you're a monstrosity— that you're gonna be the end of everything. The only thing that'll save you is if you can control yourself. And fast."

"I feel controlled," Derek said. "I feel fine. Great even. Still kinda hungry, but that's easily fixed."

Lucas's hand tightened around my waist, heat flowing. "You don't feel sick at all? Sick to your stomach?"

Derek shook his head. "No. Why?"

Lucas and Julian exchanged glances.

"But Faith smells like food to you?" Lucas asked.

Derek blinked and this strange, pained expression fluttered

over his features. "I want her blood," he said, as if just realizing it. "That's why she smells so freaking amazing. That's so *gross*."

Katie giggled.

I cut her a look. Derek wanting to eat me was so not funny.

She sobered up, but remained smiling. "He seems fine, you guys," she said. "It looks like he can eat regular food, and he hasn't tried to kill Faith. I think we can relax."

"Hush," Julian said. "We've got to be sure. We've got to test him. What if he has venom?"

Katie's eyebrows rose, and she watched Derek with renewed caution.

"Venom?" Derek asked.

"Vampires have venom on their teeth," I said. "You might have it too." I looked up at Lucas. "How do we tell?"

Lucas heaved a sigh and went to Derek. He held his arm out in front of Derek's face.

"Bite me," he said.

Katie snorted in the corner, and Julian elbowed her in the ribs.

Derek withdrew, looking utterly repulsed.

"Look," Lucas said. "I'm not keen on you gnawing on my arm either, but if you have venom, I'll feel it."

"Can't you just smell it?" I asked. I didn't like this idea. What if Derek's maybe-venom hurt Lucas? Or what if this sparked some sort of fight? This was a bad idea.

"I don't smell any venom," Lucas said, "but it might be something different than I'm used to. We have to be sure."

"What if he infects you?" Julian asked. "You might not be immune."

Lucas waved us off. "Just do it," he said, putting his arm closer to Derek's mouth. "And don't get too excited. My blood's not gonna taste good—I think."

Derek made another grossed-out face and then looked pleadingly in my direction.

I threw my hands up. This seemed like the best, quickest way to find out, and I didn't really have a choice.

Derek took hold of Lucas's forearm and brought it to his lips. He grimaced up at Lucas again, but Lucas just motioned lazily for him to get on with it. Then he bit into Lucas's flesh. Lucas's face tightened, blood gushed from Derek's mouth, and then Lucas yanked his arm away. Derek wiped his mouth on his sleeve, making a face like he'd just tasted dirt.

"Well?" Julian asked.

"It's clear," Lucas said as the bite mark closed, leaving a line of blood dripping down his fingers. He wiped it off on his jeans and came back to me.

"That was sick," Derek said. "You taste like ass."

"That's because vampires don't eat werewolves. Our blood's not supposed to mix. You need human blood to take the place of yours."

Derek didn't look convinced. "What do you mean?"

"You're dead. Dead people don't have blood. It dried up when you turned. It's why you crave human blood—it's your life force. If you don't drink it regularly, you'll go crazy and probably commit suicide or walk into the sunlight or something. At least, that's how it is for regular vampires."

Derek's expression was blank—he didn't seem to have heard anything Lucas had said. "Dead?" he whispered. "Did you say I'm *dead*?"

"Vampires are undead," I said as delicately as possible. What little color left in Derek's face drained away. "But you're not all vampire," I said quickly. "You've got some werewolf in you, too."

"No," Derek said. "I'm dead. I know I'm dead. . . ." He began to breathe hard, which made me extremely nervous since he wasn't supposed to be breathing. Then he gagged and ran out of the door. Lucas and Julian started after him, but the sounds of vomiting made them stop.

A moment later, my heart broke open as Derek staggered back into the room, his face so gaunt I really believed he was dead. He collapsed onto the couch again. "Water?" he rasped, looking to Lucas.

"No. Sorry."

Derek grimaced and nodded, swallowing hard. "I think . . . I think I need to be alone for a little while. I need some time to get my head around all of this."

Lucas nodded like he knew the feeling. "We'll be right outside," he warned. "Don't take too long. We only have a few hours till daybreak, and I still gotta find someplace lightless for you to crash." Then he paused, frowning as though just thinking of something. He stole a look at me and said slowly, "Where'd you sleep today?"

"Found a cave," Derek croaked. "Had to fight a bear for it, but it seemed to work. I didn't die anyway. . . . If I *can* die anymore."

"You fought a bear?" I asked incredulously.

Derek shot me an uneasy glance. "Just a small one."

"We'll be right out there," Lucas said again. "And I'll find you again if you run."

"I'm not running," Derek said. "No place to go."

Lucas took up my hand and began to lead me to the door, when

Derek said, "Faith can stay."

My heart skipped about ten beats, and I looked up at Lucas hopefully.

"Ah . . . I don't think that's smart," Julian said.

Lucas glanced from Derek to me several times and then said to Derek, "You even *think* about touching her and I'll kill you so fast, you won't even know it happened."

Derek's eyes burned into Lucas so hot, I had to stop myself from taking a step back. At once, I believed he could rip my throat out in seconds.

"I'd never hurt her," Derek swore.

"Not yet you won't," Lucas sneered and let go of my hand with a sharp flick of the wrist. All three werewolves exited the cabin, leaving me alone with my best friend.

BLOOD PACT

I stood in front of the hearth, watching Derek anxiously. His gaze swept down my body, freezing me like a winter breeze.

"Hey," I whispered.

I didn't know what else to say, what to do.

Derek rose and came to stand before me. I just now realized that he wasn't wearing much—a pair of too-loose blue jeans and a grungy white T-shirt that almost matched the hue of his skin. He should have been frozen in his scanty attire, but he acted as though the cold that bit at my fingertips didn't affect him at all.

As he came toward me, I noticed something different in the way he walked, in the gait of his step. He had always been graceful, but now it was like he'd oiled all of his joints; they moved without any hint of effort. His body was more toned than ever, and it looked as if he'd grown a few inches too.

As frightening as he was, and as different, I had to say: being a hybrid agreed with him. His skin, though unearthly pale, was smooth as untouched snow and his platinum hair fell across his forehead, grazing the very edges of those ice-blue eyes. The lips I'd once kissed when he was human were petal-pink and puckered out just slightly where his fangs hit them.

Even though I'd practically lived by his bedside for the past month, I felt like I hadn't seen him in years. I'd never been so nervous around him. His vibe, which I was finally able to read now that his transformation was complete, revealed that he was equally apprehensive.

Derek stood close to me, just a foot away.

"I can feel the warmth of your body," he said. "Even from right here." He held his hand out in front of my chest, not even coming close to touching me, yet burning me nonetheless.

"Are you cold?" I asked shakily. Another dumb thing to say, but anything to break the silence.

Derek shook his head, his eyes never leaving mine for an instant.

"Can they hear us?" he whispered, nodding to the door where Lucas and the others stood, probably poised to storm in at any moment.

"I don't know," I said honestly. "Can you hear them?"

"Yes. They're talking about someone named Rolf." Derek's pupils dilated just slightly, and his voice came out cracked when he spoke next. "I can hear your blood pounding, too."

I swallowed hard, wishing that I could somehow muffle the sound of my heart throbbing. No need to tempt the poor guy.

"Well," I said, ignoring the comment about my blood, "then, I guess maybe they can hear us too." I paused. "Why? Is there something you don't want them to hear?"

"I don't think the boyfriend would appreciate it," Derek said, "but I don't care." His faced melted into a sad little smile. "I missed you."

My heart was careening off my rib cage by now, and Derek had to hear it, which made my cheeks flush—another temptation. I looked away, trying to hide it. I felt like a flashing neon sign that said, *eat me!*

Something icy touched my chin and pulled it up. It was Derek's fingers. The fact that he was touching me, especially against Lucas's wishes, was about all I could take. Tears began to form and clog my throat. Reluctantly, I met his eyes.

"What do you feel now?" I asked. "Anything?"

Derek put his hands over mine and I shivered. "I feel scared," he murmured. "I feel . . . alone. I feel like I'm dreaming, mostly, but overall I'm just happy you're here. I want to keep you with me, Faith. I don't know if I can take this if I don't have you around, even if it means watching you with . . . with him." He clamped his jaw shut.

Mine clamped shut, too. I had been ready to tell Derek how this was all my fault. To apologize and tell him how bad I felt, how much I wanted to take everything back. But I looked into those crystal eyes, so different from the ones I was used to seeing on his baby-face, yet somehow still shining with that everlasting warmth and love.

I couldn't tell him this was my fault. It would crush the last little bit of hope and humanity out of him. He was standing there telling me I was all he had left and that he'd lose it without me. How could I tell him the truth? That I had done this to him?

It would destroy him.

So instead, I sidetracked to the second most important thing and asked, "You feel all of that? *Really* feel it?"

"Yeah," he said. "You sound like you don't believe me."

"It's just that vampires don't feel things, regular human things. They lose their humanity over time. I was scared you wouldn't be the same—that you wouldn't be my Derek anymore."

Derek reached up and wiped a tear from my cheek. "I'll always be yours," he said. "You have to know nothing will ever change that." He smiled a little. "Not even death, apparently."

I let out a little laugh that was mostly a sob. "I know it now. I can still see *you* in your eyes."

Derek pressed his hand closer against my cheek "You feel like you're on fire," he said. "Or am I just cold?"

"You're cold."

His face closed down. "Because I'm dead. I don't *feel* dead."

"You don't look dead either," I said earnestly. "You look alive. Perfect and alive." I tried to smile, but the truth was that he looked like a corpse. Felt like one too. I removed my hand from his skin, but he kept his on my face.

"At least I can be around you. Touch you, if I want." He rubbed my cheek, spreading the death around my skin. It was so gross. "The boyfriend won't like that."

"He can suck it up."

Derek's eyebrow twitched. "Speaking of sucking," he said, with a hint of humor in his voice. "This whole blood-drinking thing . . . it's not really my style. What'll happen to me if I never drink anybody's blood? Will I go nuts like a vampire?"

I was so relieved to hear those words pass his lips. I might have had a hard time accepting Derek's habits if he'd been spending his nights murdering people to satiate his thirst.

"I have no clue," I said. "Nobody knows anything about you. You'll just have to experiment and find out."

"So how long have you known about all this?" Derek asked, narrowing his gaze. "That night we spent in this cabin . . . you knew didn't you? That's why you were so scared of the dark . . . and Julian. Jesus, he *changed* that night, didn't he?" He looked around as if the dingy cabin hid more secrets he could now decipher with this new knowledge.

"I couldn't tell you," I said. "The pack would have killed me for it."

"I wouldn't have believed you anyway. But—damn. I knew there was something up with that guy." He glowered at the door where Lucas stood, probably listening raptly to every word we said.

"You were right," I said. "And I'm so, so sorry I got you involved."

"I—I can't say it's all right, yet," he said. "Because it's not. But, I have a feeling that with you to help me through it, one day it will be."

"It will," I promised, though I had no idea if the words were true.

Derek was silent for a while, probably mulling things over. I watched the strange angles of his face darken and bloom with the firelight, felt his vibe fluctuate from anger to confusion to grief and back to anger again. He was a mess.

"So, I'm the only hybrid . . . thing out there," he said at last. "Seriously?"

"It seems that way. Lucas told me once that mixing vampire and werewolf blood is like, the worst of the worst in this world. Vampires and werewolves are eternal enemies. They don't work together as far as I know. So no one's really tried mixing their blood into one person before—at least not on record. You're unique, Derek. And everyone's scared of you—of what a hybrid race means."

A smile spread across Derek's lips. "Werewolves are scared of me. That's wild."

"You have no idea," I grumbled dryly.

Then Derek's smile faded. "Are they going to try and kill me?"

I swallowed as my smile died as well. "I really don't know." I grabbed his arms even though they felt dead and gross. "Listen to me, Derek. You *have* to control yourself. All the time. From now on. If you slip up even once and kill someone, and the pack finds out—they'll hunt you. They'll find you. And they won't have any misgivings about killing you."

Derek gave me a look as though I was acting melodramatic. If only he knew how serious this was.

"I'm under control," he said. "I'm not planning on killing anyone."

"*Ever*," I said. "No biting. No changing too close to people. No sucking of any blood. Ever."

Derek nodded, his eyes still hooded with a scowl. "Got it."

There was a knock on the door and Lucas entered.

I withdrew my hands from Derek's arms and took a step back.

Lucas's eyes flipped to me and shifted silver. I think I actually *saw* him bite his tongue.

"Time to go," he said.

I went to him and took his hand. He was like a furnace. I didn't know if that was because I'd just been holding Derek's icicle arms, or because Lucas was ready to change at any second. All I know is that I liked it. Blood rushing, pulse pounding . . . *life*.

"Are we going back to campus now?" I asked. And would Derek be coming, too?

"Nope," Lucas said. "Rolf called. He's summoning us."

"What's that mean?" Derek asked.

Lucas answered for me. "Nothin' good."

Panic fluttered in my chest. "But—we can't just hand him over," I sputtered. "Rolf will kill him." Despite Yvette's assurances to the contrary, I didn't trust Rolf. At all.

"He won't," Lucas said surely, already tugging me out the door. Derek followed closely with a look of immense concern on his face. Katie and Julian were trudging along ahead of us, already at the tree line.

"How do you know that?" I asked. "He's wanted to kill Derek since he came to the house. How can you just trust him all of a sudden?"

"Because I do."

I stopped walking. I needed a better answer than *that*.

Lucas rounded on me.

"You trust me, right?" he asked.

I nodded.

"Then you trust Rolf."

"He put you in the silver room," I hissed. "I can *never* trust him after that."

"Rolf won't hurt Derek. He gave me his word. If he breaks it in front of the whole pack, he might as well resign."

"How do you figure that?" I asked.

"A pack is based on trust, Faith. I trust Rolf, he trusts me—even though he put me in the silver room," he said, reading my outraged expression. "If he breaks his word, it's over for him. Rolf's been leading this pack for over two decades. He'd never give that up just for a kid who *might* be a danger to us."

I wasn't convinced.

"He won't hurt Derek, all right?" Lucas said. "But it's one night only. We have till dawn, so unless you want to wait until tomorrow and take your chances, I suggest we get going."

Defeated, I cast a glance at Derek's petrified face and set off toward the car without another word. I could only pray that Lucas and Yvette were right.

. . .

The five of us walked up the slate steps of the werewolf mansion in total silence. Lucas's vibe was whirling around manically and Derek seemed paler than ever. I couldn't even begin to think how scared he must've been, knowing he was about to enter a house full of werewolves who wanted him dead.

Inside the massive recessed living room, about twenty pack members and all of the Pack Council were convened. They seemed to have been discussing something controversial—probably us—because a lot of the faces were angry. But angry or not, every single face turned to Derek when we entered the room.

For almost ten seconds, the only sound was the crackling of the fire and blood rushing through my ears.

A chair scratched against the wood floor as someone stood up. It was Rolf, looking poised and disconcertingly calm.

I was instantly suspicious.

"Lucas," Rolf said. "Glad to see you are well." He smiled warmly at Lucas, but I understood the subtext of that snide little statement: *I'm glad you didn't go crazy after suffering that sadistic punishment I gave you for no good reason other than to prove my place as pack master.*

Jerk.

I glared him down with my most venomous look, but he wasn't paying attention to me.

"I am also glad that you have found your friend." Rolf went on, turning his black gaze on Derek. "Won't you please introduce us?"

"This is Derek Turner," Lucas said, even though Rolf already knew who Derek was. He probably knew more about him than I did, since he was rumored to have connections with the CIA. "Derek, this is Rolf. The pack master."

Derek's eyes shifted to mine, they were lighter than normal— white with black rims encircling them. His wolf eyes. The nerves were really starting to trigger him. I prayed he'd keep it under control. The last thing we needed was for him to change and start trying to rip the house apart.

"It is an honor to meet you, Derek," Rolf said. "Please, all of you sit down. We have much to discuss."

Something was definitely up. Rolf was acting way too nice, even if he'd promised he wouldn't hurt Derek. I reached out for his vibe and felt it boiling beneath his blasé exterior. He was frustrated. But why? I tried to get a handle on what specifically was irking him, but before I could delve deeper, something sliced its way around his emotions, cutting me off.

My eyes flicked to Yvette, who sat next to Rolf. Her steely gray gaze was locked on mine. She knew I'd been feeling Rolf out. I hastily withdrew my feelers and looked away.

Julian sat on the couch beside Melanie and Katie sat cross-legged on the floor by his feet, eyes bright with anticipation. Derek cast a worried look in my direction, and I grabbed his hand. I heard a few people gasp at this, and I glared at the room, holding tighter. I pulled him to the couch in front of the fire and sat beside him with Lucas on my other side.

"So," Rolf said. "He can touch you, after all. He does not have the blood crave? After the other night, I just assumed . . ."

Lucas answered for me. "He has it. But he can eat regular food, too. If he doesn't breathe, the crave seems manageable. He hasn't eaten anyone, anyway."

"That is good." Rolf's face relaxed somewhat. "That is very good." He observed Derek levelly. "The dawn is soon approaching, and we do not have much time left with you. I assume Lucas and Julian have told you all that you need to know about your condition—at least for now?"

Derek nodded.

"Well, I must admit, that I have questions for *you*, Derek Turner," Rolf said. "And some words of caution." His eyes darkened, and he leaned in, clasping his hairy fingers together. "The Pack Council has decided that your life will be spared as long as you remain under *complete* control. If you find that the need for blood is too much, we have ways in which you can satiate your thirst without resorting to murder. We urge you to come to us before you lose control. We do not want to kill you. Despite what you might think"—he shot me a scathing look—"that is not our way. However, if you become a danger to our territory, we will have no other choice. The safety of the humans and of our pack is our priority. Is that clear?"

"Yes, sir," Derek said.

That sounded strangely fair, coming from Rolf. I wished I had the guts to ask him what his angle was, but I remained silent. Maybe he was just trying to prove to the pack that he would honor his word and not hurt Derek for tonight.

Derek opened his mouth as if he wanted to say something, but pressed it shut again without saying anything.

"What is it?" I asked gently.

"I can go back to CSU now?" he asked softly.

"No," Rolf said, leaning back in his chair. "I apologize, but that is simply impossible. You're in an extremely unstable state right now and being in the vicinity of so many humans will put them at risk. I cannot allow it."

Derek's face fell.

"Then where will he stay?" I asked, speaking up for him.

"Here," Rolf said.

Alarm bells fired off in my head. *Whoa, whoa, whoa.* Derek live here? At the mansion . . . *alone?* There was no way that was happening.

"No," I said at once. "He needs to come back to school with us."

Rolf's eyes could have laser-beamed through my head and into the wall behind me. "That is not for you to decide."

I turned to Lucas, waiting for him to speak up. At first, he looked down at me as though I was being difficult. Then, without even really meaning to, I opened the connection and spoke to him through it: *Help me convince Rolf.*

"She's right," Lucas said suddenly. But it hadn't been Lucas's will that made him stick up for Derek, it had been mine.

Startled by what I'd done, I let the connection drop. I hadn't meant to *make* him do it—just ask him to. But I guess my power didn't work that way. Heck, I hadn't even been sure I could speak to him the way I had. Good information for later, but it didn't excuse what I'd done.

Lucas shook himself slightly, seeming to come out of a trance. His eyes shifted silver, and I felt the change rage within him like an angry bull. Controlling him that way must have increased my threat and made him want to change.

I was a total scumbag.

"I—I mean," Lucas said, sounding sluggish. "I'll be there . . . and Katie. We'll be at CSU to guard Derek."

But Rolf shook his head with a single jerk. "We need you, Lucas. Now that this mess with Vincent Stone is done with, there is no reason for you to remain at the school. Your duties are here, hunting with your brothers and sisters."

Lucas's jaw shifted. "So put me on Derek's guard." His tone was reluctant; he was only saying this for me, but I was grateful. "Me and Katie. We can watch him."

"You and Julian are our most skilled trackers," Rolf said, nodding at Julian. "We need you."

"You got along just fine without me," Lucas grumbled. "And Julian's still here. Besides—" Lucas's eyes narrowed and his voice was clipped with contempt. "The Council seems to think the vampires in this area are manageable. There's no uprising, right?"

Rolf's nostrils flared with annoyance. "We see no evidence of an uprising."

"Then one tracker's more than enough to handle any vampire threats. Julian's here. He'll do it."

I saw Julian nodding adamantly.

"Grant me permission," Lucas urged. "I'll guard Derek and continue at CSU."

For a moment, Rolf seemed cornered, but then he spat, "And what if the crave presents itself in the midst of one of his classes? Then what?"

None of us spoke for a while. He had a good point there. . . .

"I'll take his classes with him," Katie said suddenly. All eyes turned to her, and a rather adorable blush crept into her cheeks.

"What?" Rolf barked.

"I—if it's all right with you, pack master," Katie stammered. "I'll take Derek's classes with him and guard him."

Rolf studied her for a long time with something close to how I might look at roadkill.

Lucas cut her a crooked grin and turned to Rolf with victory in his eyes. "See? With me there too, there's no reason he can't continue his life at CSU. He'll have to take night classes, but that's not a problem."

"Yeah, I work during the day," Katie chipped in. "Now I won't be bored all night."

I beamed at her.

A vein bulged in Rolf's neck. "If I allow this," he said stiffly. "I will want weekly reports, and he is to be brought to Gould at every full moon. I will not have him roaming the town during that time. We do not yet know the full extent of his capabilities."

Lucas nodded curtly.

"And," Rolf continued. "You will need to find him a place to sleep during the day. Some place lightless."

"Fine," Lucas agreed.

Everything was silent for a moment.

"I will allow it," Rolf said. "On a trial basis."

I let out a long breath and glanced up at Derek, who smiled back at me, relieved.

"So we are in agreement?" Rolf asked. "You will keep Derek under control, and we shall not harm him."

"Sounds good to me," Lucas said. He started to get up to leave, but I'd finally found my courage.

"Wait," I said. "How do I know you won't just come around during the day when he's asleep and kill him? You seemed pretty hell-bent on it up until just now. And Lucas said this truce thing is only good for one night. How can I believe you won't hurt him after it's over?"

Rolf regarded me stonily. "The Council members have illuminated the error of my thinking, and I have changed my mind. They believe that destroying a life out of fear is dishonorable and wrong. As wary as I am of Derek's potential for murder, he has not harmed anyone or proved himself malicious in any way. He has committed no crime and cannot be condemned simply for existing."

He seemed truthful, but it was just so difficult to believe. Then Yvette's gaze caught mine again, and a small, almost nonexistent smile was etched into the creases of her face. And then I realized: she'd done as she said and influenced Rolf. Whether she'd used her power, or simply spoken to him on my behalf, I couldn't know. Either way, I was grateful.

"I want some kind of insurance," I said. "Sorry if that insults you or whatever, but you locked Lucas in the silver room and campaigned to kill Derek for three weeks straight. I just don't believe you."

Suddenly, Rolf stood up, and I jumped, pressing myself into the couch as he walked toward us. But he turned on Lucas.

"I will make a Blood Pact with you, son," he said. "Hold out your hand."

Tony, Nora's husband, spoke up at once. "Are you sure that's wise, Rolf?" he asked. His deep, gravelly voice thundered through the room, startling me.

But Rolf ignored him. "Your hand," he said, eyes pinned on Lucas.

Lucas stood without a word and obeyed. Rolf produced a slim silver knife from his pants pocket and pressed it into the center of his palm. Thick, rich blood gushed from the wound, and I glanced worriedly at Derek, but he shook his head.

Oh, right. Werewolf blood smells like ass.

I watched Rolf take the knife and puncture Lucas's hand as well. Lucas didn't even wince. I would have been screaming.

Rolf held on to Lucas's wrist as the dark blood dripped from their hands, pooling on the floor, spattering as it hit. It was sickening.

"I, Rolf Farrow, swear with every drop of blood in my body, that I will not harm the hybrid creature, Derek Turner, unless he proves himself to be a danger to our territory." He clasped his hand with Lucas's. "I swear this in blood, the unbreakable bond." He looked Lucas in the eye for a solid minute and then released his hand. By the time they let go, the wounds had healed. He turned to the room. "The Blood Pact has been made. You all bear witness to it. Hear this and spread it within the pack: No one is to touch this boy, Derek Turner. If he is thought to be a danger, I will call for him and *I* will be the one to dole the punishment. Is that clear?"

Every head in the room nodded except mine and Derek's.

Then Rolf turned back to me. "Satisfied?" he asked.

I felt my chin lift. "Yes. Very."

I couldn't ask for more than that, could I? Sure there was still the chance that Rolf was lying, but with his pack watching and what Lucas had said about trust, I thought the odds were much lower. This would have to suffice.

Rolf returned to his seat. "Find him a place to sleep for the day," he said, waving his hand as if swatting a fly.

Derek and I rose and followed Lucas to the door that led to the basement. I felt every eye on our backs as we crossed the room and filed into the ballroom. The door clicked shut behind us, and I let out a huge breath, sagging against the wall.

"That was nerve-racking," I gasped.

"What happens if Rolf breaks the Blood Pact?" Derek asked Lucas.

"I get to kill him," he said flatly.

Derek and I stared.

"Don't get excited," Lucas grumbled. "Rolf is almost two hundred years older than me. Even if the Council allowed me to fight him, I'd never survive. It was all for show."

I deflated. *So much for that.*

"What about everything you said?" I asked. "About trust binding the pack together? Everyone just saw him make the Blood Pact with you. If he breaks it, won't it make him look bad?"

"Yeah," Lucas grunted. "He won't break the Pact. But he wouldn't have broken his word either. You didn't need to make him do that."

I bit my tongue, unable to believe that Lucas was actually defending Rolf. But I let the issue drop.

"What was all that business about getting permission to stay at CSU?" I asked. "Rolf acted like you were supposed to be here hunting or whatever."

Lucas leaned against the wall and said, "Pack members have to hunt vampires. It's a duty we all swear to when we join. It's like a job. If you don't do it, you get fired—aka, kicked out of the pack. And nobody wants to get kicked out."

Derek was paying close attention to this and asked Lucas, "So you kill vampires?"

"Yup."

"Why?"

"Because they're evil. And they kill people. And if werewolves didn't protect the humans, they'd turn into fodder."

"So why don't you hunt?" I asked Lucas.

"I do. Well—I did before I went to CSU." At my blank look, Lucas continued. "Remember I told you I went to CSU to try and hide from Vincent?"

I nodded.

"Yeah, well, I was kind of on a special . . . scholarship."

"Meaning?"

"We can appeal to the Council for permission to live in the human world. So we can go to college or med school or get into politics—stuff like that. The scholarship only lasts about ten years and then you have to stop and come back to do your duty. It's how pack members get connections for the pack, both legal and illegal."

"But you'd been to school before," I said, recalling that he had several degrees. "Why'd Rolf let you go to CSU if you already have so many degrees?"

"These were special circumstances. Rolf knew about the deal with Vincent and allowed me to go incognito for a while to try and shake him off. He gave me a year. Normally, someone with as much school as me would have to wait until some of the younger ones were out. But, like I said. Special circumstances."

"So you have the rest of the year to be at CSU? And then what?"

Lucas shook his head. "I killed Vincent before the year was up. I should be back with the pack now—that's what Rolf was saying. He's only letting me stay because of Derek. I'll probably be there until he graduates and then have to come back." He stifled a yawn behind his hand and cast a meaningful look up at the ceiling.

Yeah, I was tired, too, but I wanted to make sure Derek was settled before I crashed. "Derek needs a bed," I said. "And clothes and a shower."

"He doesn't have time tonight," Lucas said. "It's getting close."

"Well, we can at least get him something to sleep on."

Lucas huffed as he trudged up the stairs. He returned in less than a minute bearing a sleeping bag and some food. He even brought some water like Derek had asked for earlier.

"See you in the . . ." I stopped. I almost said see you in the morning. Derek just shrugged sadly. "See you tomorrow night," I said finally.

Way to rub salt in the wound.

I went to Lucas, and he slung his arm over my shoulders as we exited. I knew he made the little possessive gesture to stake his claim over me in front of Derek and it ticked me off—nobody wants to feel like a tree that's just been peed on—but I let Lucas do it. If this was how Lucas dealt with helping Derek, then I could deal with it.

For now.

INFLAMED

Lucas and I slept all day. It was becoming a nasty habit I'd have to break once class started up again. But for now, there were still five days left of winter break, and I was content to sleep the days away snuggled next to Lucas. He was great to sleep with, so warm and cuddly. Like my ideal teddy bear.

Or teddy wolf . . . or whatever.

I awoke at dusk with a smile on my lips. I could feel Lucas all the way down to my toes, pressed up against my back, molded to my body perfectly.

"Lucas?" I whispered, wondering if he was awake.

"I'm up," he said softly. "Hi."

I wriggled around to face him and watched his eyes grow lighter. I gave him a look, and a wry smile twisted his lips. "No fair," he said. "I wasn't ready." He closed his eyes, breathing deeply. When he reopened them, they were a perfect dark brown. Beautiful.

I tilted my face upward and brushed my lips against his, inhaling against his skin. The familiar scent of sweetness and pine needles reached my nose, sending warmth coursing through my body. I kissed his neck, feeling the stubble of his five o'clock shadow prick my lips. Lucas sighed, pulling me on top on him and sweeping my hair to the side. I let him kiss my throat, loving the goose bumps he raised on my skin.

Tension built between us as we teased each other with kisses, touching everywhere but lips. Just when I thought I'd die if he didn't kiss me, he took my face and pressed his lips to mine. Fire bloomed in my chest and I deepened the kiss, reveling in the warmth of his mouth.

As we kissed, I let myself feel the happiness he brought me, and it bathed me in a warm beam of sunlight. All I wanted was more of it.

My fingers found the bottom of Lucas's shirt, and he let me pull it over his head. I felt the smoothness of his skin with my lips, tracing down his ribs. He pulled me back up with a lopsided smile on his face. I ate it up with my kisses, heart beating erratically. Lucas's hands grazed the small of my back. I wanted him to go further, to take my shirt off—take everything off. But it was out of the question.

Then I remembered that it might not be impossible anymore. I'd pretty much dismissed Lucas's suggestion that I repress his change with my power while we made out because I'd been worried about Derek. But Derek was fine—for the moment—and well, Lucas and I hadn't kissed like this in weeks. His suggestion was definitely starting to look good at the moment. Especially with everything Yvette had said about "matches" and whatnot. If Lucas and I had this superconnection or whatever, then I had more of a shot at calming his change than anybody else's.

Was I completely sure that I could suppress his triggers well enough and long enough for us to make love? Nope. But damn it, I was going to try.

I pulled back, leaning on my elbows over him. I could feel that he was curious, but it was laced with the hunger of desire. A little crease puckered between his brows and I kissed it.

"I have something to tell you," I said.

"Oh yeah?" His hands still ran up and down my hips, making it difficult to concentrate.

"Mm-hmm," I hummed. "I'm ready to try that whole suppress-your-trigger thing while we make out."

"Are you, now?" He grinned sleepily.

I nodded. "I've recently acquired some new info about my power, and I think it's time I test out the limits. What do you think?"

He furrowed his brow. "What new info?"

I smiled mischievously. "I'll tell you later." I bent in to kiss him, but he dodged and rolled over so I was below him. It happened so quickly, I was left a little disoriented.

"Tell me now," he said, and I could hear that stubborn edge to his voice. The one that told me he wasn't about to drop this without an explanation.

But I was probably the only person in the world who could make Lucas's obstinacy melt away like snow at sunrise, and it was a power I liked to play with every once in a while. Especially at times like these when—amazingly—I knew something he didn't. It wasn't very often that I had the upper hand, but when I did, I didn't give it up easily.

"Tell you, or what?" I arched my hips into his and he groaned.

"Or . . ."

"Yeah?" I smiled innocently, a stark contrast to what I was doing with my hips.

"Or . . . something . . . bad . . ."

"You're very scary," I said, pouting my lip out. "But I think you're all bark and no bite."

"I'll bite," he said and hissed inwardly as I ran my fingernails lightly up his spine.

Oh, this was much too easy. He wasn't even putting up a decent fight. I smiled, smelling victory. I licked my bottom lip, giving him my best smoldering gaze. One leg wrapped around his waist, and that was all it took. He grumbled something that sounded like *screw it* and began kissing me. Only this time, I dodged.

"Wasn't there something you wanted me to tell you?" I asked between his lips.

He made a deep throaty sound that was half arousal, half warning.

It was all I could do not to make a fist-pump into the air. I loved winning when it came to us.

"Are you sure?" I asked, doing my best to keep my voice innocent while my body told a totally different story.

"Shut up and kiss me back."

"But then I can't tell you my news."

"To hell with your news." He began pulling my shirt up.

I laughed, pulling it back down. "You're too easy."

"You're too evil."

"I know. But seriously, I want to tell you what Yvette said."

"You brought this on yourself." He pried my hand away from my shirt and brought it all the way past my chest.

"Lucas!" I gasped, pulling it back down again.

He growled at me.

"Bad dog," I said with a nervous laugh. "Don't make me knee you in the crotch."

Defeated—for the moment anyway—he collapsed heavily on top of me, muttering swear words.

"Lucas," I panted. "Can't. Breathe."

He rolled to the side, still fingering the hem of my shirt as though waiting for me to lose focus so he could whip it off.

"Fine, fine," he grumbled. "But make it quick. I have big plans for this trigger-stopper thing you can do."

"Maybe do," I qualified.

"You did it in the silver room," he said.

"That's because . . . well, that's what I wanted to talk to you about." I gave him a brief recap of how I'd discovered that Yvette was like me, and that she and Rolf were like, link-mates or something. And that we were, too, or so it seemed.

"Apparently each person with the sense has a werewolf match," I said. "And with that werewolf, the connection is so strong that they can control them even when their human. That's how I was able to save you in the silver room. Because you're my match." I beamed at him.

Lucas's face betrayed his amazement, and for a long while, he was silent. "Wow," he muttered at last. "I—ah, I don't know how to feel about that, exactly."

That hadn't been the reaction I'd wanted. "What do you mean?"

"Well, I was already a little iffy about you controlling me when I'm changed. I was only okay with it because it protected you and it could keep me from doing some bad stuff. But controlling me when I'm human? That seems like a little much."

"But I'd never use it to make you do something you didn't want." I didn't mention that I'd accidentally done it last night. Thankfully, he hadn't even noticed. It had been a mistake. One I would never let happen again if I could manage to stop it.

"I don't know, Faith."

He looked so upset about this—so the opposite of what I'd wanted. Why wasn't he seeing the positive side here? And then I remembered: "You can block it," I said at once. "Yvette said it takes practice, but you can keep me out. So if you ever get ridiculously stubborn about something and don't want me to try and sway you—not that I ever would—you can stop me." Well, I wouldn't use my power to sway him. I'd use my other charms, which, I was happy to say, were in excellent working condition. Go me.

Lucas chewed on his bottom lip. "Well, I guess that's okay. We'll practice with it sometime." He tucked a stray lock of my hair behind my ear. "It's not like you can stop it. I'll just have to trust you." He gave me an adorable half smile. "If you can trust me not to change around you, I can trust you not to abuse your power over me."

"Deal."

"Odd," he said, still smoothing the lock of my hair in his fingers. "There's never been a human in existence that had any power over me. And you—the one person with the power to make me do anything you wanted," he shrugged. "Hell, you don't even need it. I'd already do anything for you."

It was kind of strange to think that a three-hundred-year-old werewolf was Jell-O in my hands, but if we were going to be together, then I really wouldn't have it any other way. After all, I was Jell-O in his. Might as well make it even.

I was about to dive in for another exquisite kiss, when he said, "Hey, you know what this means?" A devious smile crept over his lips. "If we're matched or whatever, then I'll bet you really can suppress my trigger. We might be able to . . ."

Now he was getting it. "Yeah, I thought of that, too." I settled closer against him. "Actually, that's the whole reason I brought it up."

He began kissing me, harder now, and my body felt like it was on fire. "Try it," he said against my lips. I could feel his energy growing more and more uncontrollable along with the passion of his kisses. He began to shake.

I wanted to try and repress his trigger, but I couldn't think about anything except how amazing his hands felt as they crept lower along my sides and the fact that if this went well, we might actually be able to make love for the first time ever. Like now. And, yeah, I was nervous. "It's . . . kind of hard . . . to concentrate. . . ."

He laughed lightly, pulling back. "Yeah, I guess. And there's one small problem, too."

Panting slightly, I gave him a questioning look.

"You smell," he said.

"Bad?" I asked, mortified.

"Sort of. Like vampire, but different. I guess it's Derek."

I pressed my nose against his chest and sniffed his skin. He smelled like an aphrodisiac, but I wasn't about to admit it.

"You don't smell so hot yourself," I said.

Lucas buried his face in my hair. "Do you want to shower with me?" His voice was husky in my ear. "We can test this theory out in there."

My heart thrilled at the thought, but I was still nervous that I wouldn't be able to do it, matched or not.

"Maybe," I managed to say.

"I think you do."

Lucas hopped off the bed and scooped me up in his arms. I squealed as he hauled me to the bathroom across the hall and set me down. Eyes burning into mine, he locked the door behind us.

• • •

It worked. Oh, did it work. Lucas and I didn't make love, but I managed to keep him from changing during a *very* long shower. It had been difficult at times because I was so easily distracted. To my credit, trying to concentrate while Lucas was pressed up against me, totally naked and dripping wet was more than a little unfair. And God, Lucas looked amazing wet. The way his hair plastered itself to his forehead made me crazy, his lips dripping with water, the rivers running down his chest, over his hips . . .

Plus, I had never been naked in front of a guy before, and I'd certainly never been naked *with* a guy so I was more than a little nervous. But the obstacles were part of the fun, and by the time the hot water ran out, I'd almost gotten his trigger completely subdued.

Once we'd toweled off, it was well past nightfall, and it was time to check on Derek—a much less pleasurable event. Not that I didn't want to see Derek. I did. But dragging ourselves out of that shower was torture.

Lucas and I walked hand in hand across the living room. The house was now empty of most of the werewolves that had been here last night. I could hear murmurings in the kitchen as we passed, but I saw no one. We stood in front of the door to the basement, staring at it.

Lucas pecked me on the cheek one last time as if to signify that it was the last time he'd do it for a while (a thought that deflated the happy bubble bouncing in my chest) and pulled the door open. Derek was sitting on his sleeping bag, his chin resting on his hands. He perked up when we entered and stood up in a superfast movement that rivaled Lucas's speed.

"Hey, guys," he said. "Jeez, I was bored. I was too scared to go up there—you know—since everyone pretty much hates me."

"Nobody hates you," I said, but quickly changed the subject. "We're going back to CSU tonight. It's time to get back to—well, some semblance of normalcy, anyway. You got all your stuff?"

Derek made a face at me. "The only stuff I have is me. These aren't even my clothes."

"Oh!" I suddenly remembered that Derek was still in need of a shower and clothes, not to mention a big honking meal so that he wouldn't feel inclined to eat me on the way home. Shame overtook me when I thought of him sitting down there in the dark, filthy and starved, while I luxuriated in the shower with Lucas.

Lucas sent Derek to the guest shower and instructed him to get his stuff from the bedroom he'd stayed in while he transformed. Once Derek was off, Lucas led me to the now abandoned kitchen to cook him some thick, bloody steaks.

Twenty minutes later, Derek came downstairs in a pair of Lucas's jeans and a black AC/DC concert tee. I smiled at him and handed him the plate of steaks like it was an Olympic gold medal.

Lucas had his own towering plate of steaks, while I contented myself with some cereal. All three of us sat at the breakfast nook in the kitchen and dug in.

"My mom's gonna freak," Derek said as he chewed. "I saw

myself in the mirror just now. I look like a corpse."

I squeezed his arm briefly. There was nothing to say about that. He did look dead.

"And what the hell are *these*?" Derek asked, baring his teeth. He pointed at his elongated canines.

"Fangs," Lucas said flatly. "I got 'em too, you wanna see?"

"No!" Derek and I said at the same time.

Lucas leaned back in his chair, seemingly proud of himself for scaring us.

I turned to Derek. "You can just tell your mom you haven't got much sun since you moved here."

"That's a heck of a way to put it." He sighed. "Man, I'm gonna miss the sun. I remember you and me at the beach, baking all afternoon." He smiled for a moment and then turned to his plate. "Guess that's not gonna happen anymore, huh?"

"We can still go to the beach," I said. "We'll go at night. The sun causes cancer anyway."

For a long time, the only sounds in the kitchen were of silverware clinking and Derek clearing his throat awkwardly the way he did when he was feeling anxious.

"So, speaking of the beach," I said, trying to maintain the conversation. "We still have six days left before class starts. Why don't we go to San Diego to visit? I know my mom misses me, and your parents will want to see you—even if you look a little . . . peaky."

"How're we going to get all the way over there when I can't be in the sun?" Derek asked. "And don't you think it'll look pretty suspicious to my parents if I only visit them at night looking like

I just crawled out of the grave?"

"Since when do your parents notice anything?" I reasoned.

Derek lifted his eyebrows and nodded, taking a massive bite of his steak. His parents were divorced and totally into their own lives.

"Come on," I cajoled him. "Don't you want to feel the sand again? Smell the salt of the ocean? See our old friends?"

Derek was still silent as he chewed on a bite of steak. I was about to start mentioning our favorite hot dog stand near Del Mar beach, when Lucas said, "Yeah, well, I'm not sure I'd go, either."

"What?" I asked, crestfallen.

He shrugged. "A vacation sounds great right about now, that's for sure, but, I don't know . . . with the uprising . . ."

"What uprising?" Derek asked loudly.

"Shh!" I hissed.

Lucas and I exchanged glances. Last thing we needed was for Rolf to hear we were still discussing this. I motioned for Derek to come closer and quickly whispered everything he needed to know.

When I'd finished, he sat back looking a little paler than usual.

"So yeah," Lucas said. "With all of that still unresolved. It feels a little frivolous to be jet setting to Cali."

Under normal circumstances, I would have agreed, but these were not normal circumstances. Over the course of the last four months, I'd not only discovered a secret world of supernatural creatures, I'd also been kidnapped by a vampire, almost turned against my will, attacked by a rapid pack of werewolves, and been forced to turn my best friend into a mutant. I needed to get out of Colorado and I needed it now.

"Look," I said firmly. "Rolf has straight-up refused to believe that there's an uprising, even in the face of overwhelming evidence. We've risked our lives to try and make him believe and all he does is resist us. What more are you going to do without the help of the other packs, Lucas? We don't know where the lair is, we don't know how to find it without more clues, and we don't know where the vampires will strike next. I'm just as upset as you are about the murders. I want to stop them. But there is *nothing* we can do." I leaned in and held his gaze, making sure that he grasped the magnitude of what I was about to say. "And honestly, babe, if I don't get out of this place and around some normal people soon? I. Will. Lose it."

To my surprise, a small, almost impressed, smile turned his lips up at the corners and he said, "You convinced me."

I did? Score.

I rounded on Derek, fixing him with the same menacing stare.

"Okay," he said, relenting.

I relaxed. "Thank you."

"But I don't think I'll be visiting the parents," Derek said. "They'll definitely notice I'm different. I wonder what they'll say when they find out I'm off the football team." His expression darkened. "Do you think they'll kick me out of school? I don't have the money to afford it without my scholarship."

I opened my mouth to spew some comforting bull, when Lucas spoke up.

"I'll take care of it," he said.

"What?" I asked. "Take care of what?"

Lucas's eyes met mine and they were kind, but laced with something sour, maybe sadness. "I'll pay for his classes for the next four years," he said. "He won't get kicked out."

My heart just about melted onto the tile as I gazed at Lucas. I entwined my fingers with his under the table and squeezed his hand. "Thank you," I whispered.

"Yeah," Derek said. "Thanks, man. I don't know what to say. I wish I could pay you back, I just—"

"Don't worry about it," Lucas cut him off. "I got more money than I know what to do with. But you *are* off the football team. Rolf's gonna call the school and explain that you got sick. Leukemia. You can use that as your cover if you ever get stuck. We'll forge all the documentation you'll need to back it up. I'll give everything to you when we get to campus."

Derek's mouth had parted slightly. "You guys are good at this, huh?"

Lucas shrugged. "We do it a lot for the runts."

"Well, thanks. Really."

I squeezed Lucas's hand again, loving like crazy that he was doing this for me, even though I could sense how much it was killing him.

• • •

h, the heat, how I missed you.

I was baking in the sun and loving every glorious second of it. I lay on my big hibiscus-print beach towel and shaded my eyes as I watched Lucas play Frisbee with some of my friends from high school. The beach was exactly what I needed. It was hot, full of life, full of regular people doing regular things. Nobody was changing into wolves, trying to suck anybody's blood, or running for their lives. The sand, the warm breeze, Lucas smiling, my old friends chatting next to me.

I was in heaven.

The only thing missing was Derek. He was sleeping—dead to the world until the night woke him. I had him stashed in an abandoned fallout shelter not too far from our old high school. It was underground, which was perfect. Lucas and Derek had spent the first night fixing it so that it was lightless. Lucas even went to some expensive home security store and bought a high-tech-lock thingy that only he and I had the keys to. It locked from the inside too, so Derek could get out if need be, and also lock himself in when I left him. It was safe. Derek was safe.

But, boy I wished he could see this sun with me.

It had been such a perfect vacation thus far. I hadn't realized how much I'd been missing my mom until I saw her face, bright with awe, as we greeted each other. She was totally stunned when I showed up at her door at eleven o'clock at night, with a pale Derek on one side, and a tall devastatingly sexy—okay, and somewhat scary—boy on my other side. She was wild with happiness once she got over the shock, but I could tell she was thrown by Derek's new look. We told her that he was getting over the flu, since we couldn't use the leukemia spiel. She'd obviously call Derek's parents to send her condolences, and they didn't know about this yet.

Surprisingly, my mom really liked Lucas. My mom's a lawyer, and she's one of those overly opinionated people that's sometimes hard to get along with, but she and Lucas seemed to have the same views on pretty much everything. They spent hours griping over politics and global warming and other stuff that put me to sleep.

I was glad that my mom liked Lucas so much. She was kind of my moral compass when it came to life and if she approved, I approved.

The deal was officially sealed.

Lucas jogged toward me from the surf, the sun glancing off his damp, caramel skin in the most enticing way. The girls lying next to me, Nicole and Alexis, suddenly stopped talking. I looked over and had to smother a laugh. They were staring at Lucas with their mouths hanging open. Yeah, he was cute when he was happy.

Lucas crashed in the sand next to me, spinning the Frisbee on his finger.

"Wanna play?" he asked.

I smiled. "Careful, I think your tail is wagging."

Lucas flicked the Frisbee at my stomach, and I grimaced, acting injured.

"Play for just five minutes," Lucas wheedled.

"Fine, but don't laugh at me when I trip over myself."

His smile widened. "Never." He tugged me up and ran down the beach, holding his arms over his head for me to throw.

I threw it and he returned the thing with lightning speed. I fell over in the water trying to catch it and Lucas laughed at me. He laughed at me big time. Not that I cared much. I was just enjoying having fun with him instead of trying to evade death. I think he liked it too.

• • •

New Year's Eve was the following day, and Lucas and I decided to do something special together since we'd had little time to ourselves lately.

It wasn't the warmest, but I took Lucas surfing anyway. He admitted to trying it once, a couple decades ago, but gave up quickly because salt water didn't gel with him. Apparently, it tasted too much like blood for his liking.

"You're not supposed to drink it," I said. "Don't be a grump. Just roll with it."

He turned out being better at it than I had ever been. Which was expected. And annoying. He actually ended up helping *me* improve, something he teased me about to no end. After we were spent, we ate lunch on the pier and fed the pelicans our scraps as we talked about school and what classes we wanted to take this semester.

Later Lucas took me to a club where they throw glowing paint on the crowd, and we spent the night dancing. I expected Lucas to refuse to dance with me—he didn't seem the dancing type. More the brood-in-a-corner type—but he'd astounded me by refusing to actually *stop*. At twenty seconds to midnight, I was panting and exhausted, but Lucas had never looked more alive. Or happy. As the music blared and the countdown began, he pulled me close, pressing his hips against mine.

I heard his rough voice in my ear, sending my heart flying.

"Three . . . two . . . one . . ."

And then his lips consumed me. I threw my arms around his neck, peeking only to see the crowd around us going insane and people knocking into each other as they scrambled to find someone to kiss. I closed my eyes tight again, thanking everything I knew that I'd never have to find someone to kiss again. Lucas would always be right here.

N ot long after that, we drove back home, ears buzzing—mine anyway—and hearts still throbbing erratically.

"That was fun," Lucas said.

Actually it sounded more like *zz zzz zzzz*, but I got the gist. I nodded at him, and suddenly he got this funny look on his face. A spark in his vibe told me he'd just decided something, but I couldn't tell what. I was also a little tipsy, which affected my power.

"What is it?" I asked.

I heard the hissing sound of his laugh. "Loud much?"

"I can't hear," I admitted, knowing I must still be yelling.

"In that case . . ." He started moving his mouth as though speaking, but I couldn't hear a word.

I swatted his arm playfully and he laughed.

"I wanna show you something," he said, checking to see if I'd heard.

"What is it?" I asked.

"Something I painted. It's ah . . . kind of big."

"Cool. Where is it?"

"On the back wall of your mom's building."

I stared as he pulled into the overhang of my mom's apartment and got out. He came around and opened the door for me in an uncharacteristically gentlemanly gesture. "You coming?" he asked, offering a hand.

I took it warily. "Suck up," I accused.

"As long as you don't rat me out to your mom."

I wouldn't have done that anyway, but I liked the special treatment. "Keep it up or I just might."

The tip of his mouth curved upward as we walked around the alley between the two apartment complexes and around to the back of my mom's building. It was a narrow space with a chain-linked fence on one side and some Dumpsters in the distance. Five back doors punctuated the brick wall at intervals, the third one being my mom's place. We walked down the alley, but I stopped when the bright white moonlight hit the wall and illuminated Lucas's piece.

It was a building, like a skyscraper. Silver and blue paint melded to create the metal structure and what seemed like hundreds of windows. Inside each pane was a picture; it looked like a film strip had been laid down to depict someone's life. There were people, animals, houses, cars, eyes, and . . . was that me? I moved in closer. Yes, I was in some of them. Lucas was in others. I recognized Julian in wolf form and some other werewolves I couldn't tag. It was really, really cool.

But I couldn't truly appreciate the beauty of his work. Mostly because the building which housed these precious scenes was on fire. Yellow, orange, and blue flames licked the building, the colors moving and undulating so flawlessly I could swear the fire was real.

I felt Lucas come to stand beside me as he looked up and up at the painting. It actually went about halfway up the wall, which made me wonder how he reached so high.

"When did you do this?" I whispered. I was equal parts amazed and horrified by the piece.

"Over a couple of nights. While you hung out with Derek."

"I thought you watched the news with my mom."

"She goes to bed at nine. And you're out till two or three, usually, so there's a lot of downtime. It's a good distraction when I can't stop thinking about you."

I could almost hear the words *with him* tacked onto the end of that sentence, but he kept it in.

I turned to look at his profile.

"So . . . I make you think of a burning building?"

He half smiled. "At first I didn't get it either," he said, still contemplating the wall. "When I paint, whatever I'm feeling just comes pouring out of me, and I don't necessarily understand it until afterward. But now it all makes sense. The building is my life." He crouched down and touched the brick at the bottom of the wall, where the building was blackened and smoldering as though the fire had died a long, long time ago. The window panes depicted scenes of a little girl playing on a grassy hill with dark hair and almond eyes like Lucas's, an older man and woman standing with arms around each other in a small wooden cabin, a handsome boy holding a bow and arrow, who looked suspiciously like a younger version of Vincent. "When I first started painting," Lucas said softly, "I drew these scenes at the bottom here. Those two are my parents and my sister—what I remember of them anyway."

He choked on the word sister and my heart stopped. Lucas *never* spoke about his sister. And this was the first I'd ever heard him speak about his parents. Or his life in Scotland. I watched him anxiously as his eyes darkened, his vibe becoming so saturated with grief it was like a wall of smog. Suffocating. Even in my semi-inebriated state, it overwhelmed me, and for a moment, I could actually see what Lucas must have: Vincent latched onto his sister's neck as she screamed his name. I felt the helplessness he felt three hundred years ago as she was killed in front of his eyes. In his mind, the pain was as fresh now as it was then.

A blast of hatred hit me and then a stark contrast of remorse. Lucas touched the pane with the young boy wielding the bow and arrow. Vincent. The way Lucas probably remembered him. Human. Flushed with warmth and life.

In the past. I could almost hear his voice as his vibe intensified. *Let it go. . . .*

He moved up a level, and the scenes grew more sinister—giant beasts with glowing eyes and a moon looming behind them, bloody battles and, at the very end of the row, a hand coming down on Lucas's shoulder that looked as though it offered a comforting squeeze. "And then there's some of my infection," he said, explaining the panes, "finding my pack, running from Vincent." He scraped his palm over the one where a werewolf fought a slender, pale figure, their bodies so distorted it was almost impossible to look at it without grimacing. "For so long that was my life," he murmured. "I was dead inside. Repressing everything, never letting anyone in; like I kept a glass pane between me and the world. One I could never break."

He stood and moved his hand up the wall, and I began seeing my face inside the windows. "Then I met you. Suddenly, life became worth enduring the pain of my curse. Because it meant living with you. That's when I started painting the flames. When I was done, I thought—damn, there's something wrong with me. Why'd I just set my girlfriend on fire?" He cast a sidelong grin at me. "And then I figured it out." He stepped closer, taking up my hand. "For so long, I was cold. Lifeless as any vampire. But now I'm alive with loving you." He looked back at the wall, his gaze sweeping the entire beautiful thing. "You set my life on fire."

His voice cracked at the end, and I felt my heart fill with emotion. The strength of his vibe all but capsized me so that I had to clutch his arm to keep steady.

"This is really amazing," I said softly, meaning both the painting and what he'd said about it. The way my heart was overflowing with love.

Lucas shrugged, back to his old gruff self. I wished he'd remained open just a little longer.

"I was gonna paint over it," he said. "So you or your mom wouldn't see it and think I was a psycho. But then, in the car you had all that dried paint all over your face and it reminded me of this. And I just wanted you to see it first."

"I'm glad," I said, though I was secretly scrubbing paint flecks off my face behind his back.

"You're not afraid I'm a pyromaniac?" He smiled back at me, stopping me from scrubbing my face.

"Believe me, that's the least of my worries." I walked up and touched one of the panes where Lucas and I were embracing. "But you're right. We can't leave it up here. My mom might get in trouble with the building's owners. I hate the idea of getting rid of it, though."

"No biggie."

Then I had an idea.

"Wait a minute," I said and flew in the apartment through the back door to grab my camera from my room. I returned and said, "We'll photograph it. That way we'll still be able to remember it, and you can just stick the photos in a scrapbook."

He walked over and cupped my cheek. "How'd I get such a smart girlfriend? I'm pretty damn lucky."

I shrugged, feeling all proud of myself—which was rare around creatures that were naturally better than me. "We're both lucky."

9

EXPERIMENTATION

The following night, Lucas and I drove to the fallout shelter to let Derek out. Lucas usually let me do this little chore alone, preferring to watch the news with my mom—or graffiti her building, apparently. And since I got to spend the days with Lucas, the least I could do was give my nights to Derek. But tonight was different. Tonight we were going to begin our "experimentations" with Derek.

When we reached the fallout shelter, I jumped out of my mom's rusted Cadillac and fumbled around in the darkness, looking for the correct key. I found it, thrust it into the fancy lock on the door, and punched in the twelve-digit key code when it started beeping at me. Once the door unlocked, I hefted it open and found Derek standing on the first step smiling up at me.

"Hey," he said. "Took you long enough."

I blushed. "Sorry. Traffic."

There was no traffic. Lucas and I had been tangled up in my bed the whole afternoon while I practiced suppressing his trigger. We'd yet to do anything too exciting because of the distraction issue, but it was heavenly nonetheless.

Derek leaped out into the night and stretched a little. He didn't bother to greet Lucas, who hadn't even gotten out of the car.

"How'd you sleep?" I asked Derek.

His eyes glinted. "Like the dead."

I cut him a disgusted look. "Are you ready for tonight?"

"Yeah, I've been thinking about that—are you really sure you want to come? It might not be safe."

"I'm going," I said firmly. "Lucas and I already discussed it." Fought about it, was more the way the conversation had gone, but

Derek didn't need to know that. I'd finally convinced Lucas that I could use my power on either of them if they lost control. Granted, I wasn't completely sure I could use my power on Derek since he was part vampire, but still. It won me the argument.

Derek shrugged and bent to open the car door for me.

"It's your funeral," he said as I passed him into the backseat of the car.

We set off into the night. Lucas drove farther and farther into the desert along a lonely highway that curved through the sea of sand like a ribbon blowing in the wind. No one spoke, though I tried several times to initiate friendly conversation. After my third attempt, and an exasperated glare from Derek, I fell silent and contented myself with watching the empty land roll by my window.

Twenty minutes later, Lucas stopped the car at a seemingly indistinct point in the middle of the desert. I got out and let the crisp, dry wind fly through my hair. *God, I've missed this place.* I looked across the hood of the car at Derek. He, too, seemed to enjoy being home. We exchanged grins and an electric current passed through my body—Derek's vibe. Strong, too. Not enough to pick out an exact thought, but he was nervous and excited at the thought of what we were about to do. It wasn't such a far cry from my own emotions.

Lucas, who had been rustling around in the trunk, came around and handed me an armful of supplies.

"What's all this?" I asked.

Derek leaned against the hood of the car and listened in.

"The stopwatch is so we can time him," Lucas said. "Pen and paper to record everything—for Rolf. And the camera because I have a feeling Rolf's gonna want to see it for himself once he sees the numbers."

"And the flashlight?" I asked as Lucas set up the tripod on the roof of the car.

Lucas gave me a withering glance and said, "So you can see us. Or have you gained the ability to see in the dark?"

Well, he was in a mood tonight. I narrowed my eyes at him and tried to push myself onto the hood of the car. Unfortunately, my hand slipped and I ended up in the dirt, cursing and rubbing my elbows. I heard Lucas snickering, but Derek squatted down and helped me up.

"Klutz," he accused, his tone playful in my ear.

"Mutant," I snapped back vindictively. I started to push myself onto the hood again, but Derek took my waist and placed me on it before I could protest. The skin on my hips burned where his clammy hands had touched it, but it was nothing compared to the scalding look Lucas threw us as he stomped off into the desert.

"Better follow him," I told Derek. I avoided his eyes by turning the flashlight on and arranging my recording tools.

I shined the beam of the flashlight on the faraway forms of Derek and Lucas, standing together among the cacti and brambles. They seemed ghostly under the dull glow of the half moon and the harsh white beam from my flashlight. I couldn't hear what they were saying, but Lucas looked sullen and Derek, nervous.

Then, with a final jerky nod from Derek, Lucas started back to me, arriving more quickly than I could blink. My hair blew into my mouth as he came to a stop next to me.

"What did you tell him?" I asked, watching Derek take off his T-shirt.

"I told him to change," Lucas said nonchalantly.

"What?" I choked. Despite my insisting on coming tonight, the reality of the situation hit me like a truck. A vampire-werewolf hybrid was about to transform mere feet from me. Why hadn't that scared me earlier when I could have opted out and spent the night watching movies with my mom? "Why—are you sure it's safe, I mean . . . what if he—?"

"What? Attacks you?" Lucas peered at me through slatted eyes. "What do you think I'm here for? Decoration?"

"Well, no, I just—"

"Besides, you said you could control him if he loses it, right?"

"I think so—I mean, yes. Of course I can."

He looked about to say something, when Derek called, "You ready over there?"

I looked around and started at the sight of him standing underneath the beam of the flashlight, clad in only his underwear. He was unnaturally pale, but God, was he ripped. I hoped I hadn't gawked too much and shot a hasty glance at Lucas. Thankfully, he was switching on the video camera and didn't notice my blush.

"Go ahead," Lucas called back. Then he said, softer to me, "You sure you're good with the connection thing?"

I nodded, too afraid to speak. As eager as I was to be involved in all of this, I couldn't help but feel just a smidge terrified at the thought of what might happen. Fangs and blood and lots of screaming were a potential future for tonight's events. Hopefully it wouldn't happen and I'd be able to connect to Derek if it came down to it.

Lucas took my hand. "I'm right here," he said, sensing my nerves.

Then, without warning, Derek changed. After several long, agonizing moments on Derek's part, my best friend was gone and in his place was a stunning, dangerous white wolf.

Dangerous, in theory, however, because all he did was sit calmly in the sand, panting and swishing his tail gently. His eyes were white now save the slate gray pupils and ebony rings around the irises; he watched us with unnatural intelligence and serenity. It was a human's gaze, completely different than when Lucas changed. When Lucas changed, he was *wild*.

"I don't think he'll hurt me," I murmured. "He seems tame."

"Let's find out," Lucas said, starting forward. "Come on."

Lucas towed me over to Derek while I mumbled things like, "I'm not sure this is safe, maybe I should wait by the car, Lucas I don't want to . . ." Ignoring my ramblings, Lucas bent down a little to Derek's eye level. I had no need to bend over—Derek was taller than I was, even as a wolf. Standing there in front of him, even with Lucas, was totally petrifying.

"Can you understand me?" Lucas asked Derek.

Derek released a little yip that quite obviously meant yes.

"Then sit," Lucas commanded.

Derek's throat bubbled with a growl, but he sat down with a thump.

I giggled nervously.

"Well, this makes things easier," Lucas said. "If he can understand us, that'll save him the trouble of changing back and forth."

"Good," I said. "It seemed to hurt him. Changing, I mean."

"That's probably because it *did* hurt him."

I looked up at Lucas, concerned. "It hurts you?"

"Not anymore. I'm sure it's still hard for him now." He jerked his head at Derek, who had wandered off to root around a deep hole in the sand. "The more times you change the more your body and mind grow used to it. The first time is unimaginable pain."

My heart ached for him, for his pain—his curse. His body could never be at peace.

I put my hand on his shoulder. "You don't deserve this life," I murmured. "I can try to numb your triggers more often. Not just when we . . . you know, fool around. It'll take some time to work up my strength, but I can try." If there was anything I could do to make this easier on him, I wanted to do it.

He placed a slow kiss on my lips, but Derek barked viciously and I drew back. Lucas scowled and his body quaked slightly.

"Okay, stop it both of you," I said, taking a few steps away from Lucas and gathering my scattered emotions. "I'm sorry I kissed him in front of you," I said to Derek. "It was insensitive."

Lucas looked as if he wanted to tell me off for apologizing, but he clamped his mouth shut. A deadly silence penetrated the night and I felt my pulse quicken. How quickly the mood had changed.

"Let's keep going," I said. "What else do we need to test?"

Lucas ran his hand through his hair. "Well, I think it's pretty clear already, but I guess we gotta be sure." Lucas turned to Derek, who had come to stand right beside me. "Do you still have the blood crave?"

Derek looked up at me balefully, and I knew it was a no.

"He doesn't," I said for him. "Look." I held my hand out to

Derek's muzzle, and he sniffed it vigorously, tickling my palm with his whiskers. I laughed and Derek licked me. "Ew . . ." I rubbed his saliva off on his fur.

Derek didn't look pleased.

"He's like a really smart dog," I said, smiling over at Lucas. "Not like you at all. When you change, you're scary and wild. Derek's still Derek underneath all that fur." I reached out with my power to feel him relaxed and excited to start experimenting, but as I looked into his eyes, trying to ignite the connection, I felt a wall. It was impassable. Derek didn't seem to notice a thing as I centered my gaze on his white eyes.

At last, Derek whined impatiently and I stopped, frowning. *There must be too much vampire in him. Not good.*

"He's right," Lucas said. "We'd better get on with this. I think we should try running first. That's safest." He glanced around and pointed to a peculiarly shaped cactus about a hundred yards in front of us. "Run there," he said to Derek, "And when I say go, run back as fast as you can. Stop before you hit the car, though, all right?"

Derek sniffed as though this last statement was obvious and trotted off to the wonky cactus in the distance.

"To the car," Lucas said, setting off.

We both leaned on the hood, and I held the stopwatch in my hand, poised to click it once Derek passed the rock I thought was shaped like Courtney's head.

"Ready?" Lucas asked me. "This is gonna be fast."

"Ready when you are."

"On three, all right, Derek?" Lucas yelled. "One . . . two . . . *three!*"

Instantly, there was a blur of white, and wind whipped by me so strong it blew my hair straight back. Derek stood before us, windblown and yapping happily. It was a few seconds before I realized I hadn't clicked the stopwatch.

"Holy crap," I murmured.

"You didn't time him," Lucas said irritably.

"That was . . . really fast."

Lucas's lip curled. "I'll have to do it. My reflexes are faster." He held out his hand for the stopwatch.

Derek paced restlessly, tongue lolling out. He seemed all too proud of himself.

"You like to run, huh?" I asked. Derek let out a short howl. "It must be a wolf thing."

"It's a pack thing," Lucas said shortly. "We run in packs. It binds us. Running on our own is nice and all, but it's nothing compared to running with your brothers beside you. He'll never have that."

"What is your *problem* tonight?" I asked, fed up with him.

"Nothing."

"There's something—"

"Do it again," Lucas said to Derek, cutting me off. "I'll time it this time."

Derek reset back to the wonky cactus and Lucas counted down. Once more, Derek blew toward us in a whip of wind. I saw Lucas click the stopwatch and then stare at it, eyebrows raised.

"What?" I asked nervously.

"Nothing, it's just . . ."

"Is he slow or something?"

Lucas ground his teeth. "I wanna see something." He threw the stopwatch on the hood of the trunk. I picked it up and gawked at the time on it: 0.5 seconds. With my mouth hanging open slightly, I turned to watch Lucas walking to Derek.

"What are you doing?" I asked.

"Get in the car," Lucas shouted back roughly.

I heard Derek growl at him, probably as disgruntled as I was at his tone.

"Why?" I called.

"Can't you just do what I ask for once?" he said, stripping his T-shirt.

"Are you going to *change*?" I gasped.

"Get in the car, Faith!"

I threw the stopwatch onto the hood and stomped into the car, slamming the door behind me. I didn't care what horrors Lucas had seen in his past, he was being a dick. I watched through the window as he tossed his jeans to the side. Without warning, his body tore apart, distorting and convulsing for less than a second and then he was a wolf, darker than the ink sky above us. My hands were trembling on the steering wheel. This was so unsafe.

Lucas released a short bark and ran back to the cactus with Derek loping along after him. It was then that I realized what Lucas had in mind: he wanted to race.

I waited with bated breath, staring at the empty beam of the flashlight, for the two wolves to appear.

Then a whip of dust told me they'd started. Derek arrived in half a blink and Lucas a few seconds later. My stomach dropped. Lucas had lost. Majorly. I watched from inside the car as they repeated the race twice more. Then it seemed Lucas couldn't hold his form any longer, and he shifted back into a human.

This was not going to improve his mood.

Cautiously, I cracked the door open and emerged, not knowing if I should say anything to Lucas or not. Snatching up his clothes, he returned to the car silently and thumped down on the hood, which dented beneath his weight.

"Did you record his time?" Lucas grunted.

"Wha—oh, no I forgot." I grabbed the pen and paper and scrawled the time Lucas had taken on the stopwatch. "How come he doesn't change back?" I asked after a short silence.

"I guess it doesn't work that way for him," Lucas grumbled as he tugged on his belt with a pointed jerk. "I don't know how long he can hold it."

"Should we wait and see?"

"No. I wanna know what else he can do."

"Maybe that's enough for tonight. I'm sure he's tired." I was eager to be done with tonight's experiments. It wasn't going at all well, and I didn't know how much longer cordiality would hold out between my men.

"I want to see how strong he is," Lucas rumbled. "And then we can go if you want."

"Okay," I agreed meekly. "How are we going to test his strength?"

Lucas eyed the car with interest, bent down and pulled on the bottom of it, as if testing its weight.

"Don't even think about it," I said. "My mom's already going to kill you for denting it."

Lucas seemed unconcerned. "I'll buy her a new one. This car's a pile anyway."

"Lucas," I pleaded. "I don't think this is smart."

He ignored me and beckoned Derek over. Derek padded across the asphalt and sat before us, luminescent white eyes inquisitive.

"Change," Lucas commanded.

Derek sniffed and galloped out of the beam of the flashlight, for a little privacy, I guessed. When he returned, he was sweating and paler than usual, but his face was alive with excitement.

"Going well, huh?" he asked, taking his time shrugging his shirt over his sweaty skin. "How fast was I?"

I said nothing, but handed the notebook containing his time to him.

Derek sucked his bottom lip in and made a low whistle. "Pretty fast, eh, Lucas?"

Lucas could not have looked more murderous.

"So," I said loudly, catching Derek's attention. "You, ah ... didn't feel like you had to change back at all?"

Derek shook his head, still smiling with that superior glint in his now turquoise eyes. "Should I have?" he questioned Lucas. His voice carried a deviously innocent note in it. "Werewolves can change any time they want," Lucas said stiffly, "But if it's not the full moon, the time we have while we're changed is limited."

Derek looked genuinely interested now.

"Why?" he asked.

"Just the way it is. If there's a human in danger, we can keep the form longer, but without a reason to change, we can't hold form for much longer than five minutes."

"How long can you hold it if there's a vampire around?" Derek asked.

"Till it's dead, usually. But I don't need to be a wolf to kill a vampire." The menacing timbre of his voice made me truly believe that last statement.

"So I don't count, then?"

Lucas regarded him curiously. "Guess not. Either that or you don't pose a threat." His tone had a bite to it at the end that made me sure he'd meant that as an insult.

I gulped as they glowered at each other.

"Well," I mumbled weakly, "should we . . . ?"

"Yes," Lucas said harshly. "We're gonna test your strength now," he told Derek. "With the car."

Derek bent and tested the weight of the car, much as Lucas had.

"What are we doing to it?" he asked.

"Lifting it," Lucas said.

Derek bent obligingly and I shouted, "Wait!"

They both stared at me.

"We have to get the camera off the roof."

Lucas snatched it up and set it down again about ten feet away, making sure that it was aimed directly at my mother's poor car. She was going to kill me for this. Lucas had better get her something nice.

"You go stand by the camera," Lucas barked at me.

"And you can shove the camera up your—"

"Ready?" he called out, ignoring my grumblings.

"As I'll ever be," I said. "*Try* not to total the car. We still need it to get home."

Derek grinned wickedly, his ghostly face shining in the darkness. I held the flashlight's beam steady on them, watching Lucas bend and pick up the car with apparent ease. He held it cradled in his arms for a few seconds and then set it back down again as gently as if it were a child.

I let out a breath I didn't know I was holding.

"Good job, babe!" I called out, trying not to sound too asinine.

Both men gave me death glares. *All right. I give up tonight.*

Now Derek moved toward the car and bent at the knees, pulling up under his arms and all the way over his head. He showed a bit more strain than Lucas had, and he didn't set the car down nearly as gently.

But Lucas was not satisfied. He wanted to *beat* Derek, not just match him, and he wouldn't be happy until he did.

"Throw it," he said.

"What?" Derek asked, glancing at me.

"Throw the car," Lucas repeated.

"What? Lucas—no," I said, stepping forward. "Can't you at least try to save the car?"

He rounded on me. "Shut up for ten seconds, would you?"

I stopped short. I didn't care how hurt his pride was, that was not okay. I was about to yell back, when Derek cut in.

"Don't talk to her that way!" He snarled.

Lucas spun around. "Don't tell me what to do, runt."

Derek stared Lucas down, face more unearthly pale than I'd ever seen it. "Careful, Fido, your fangs are showing."

Lucas's eyes turned to slits. "You wanna see my fangs? Cuz I'll be more than happy to show 'em to you." He started forward and I could tell Derek wasn't about to back down. Their feral energies radiated through the night, so strong I almost saw them. This was not going to end well.

I came up behind Derek, intending to get between the two of them. But I only got as far as Derek's flank. Appearing out of nowhere like that must have triggered a reflex or something, because the next thing I knew, Derek had swatted me back—his open palm hitting me square in the chest—and I skidded across the sand, landing in a pile.

That was it. Final straw.

Lucas charged, pummeling Derek to the ground. They both began fighting, and it wasn't more than three seconds before Derek's unstable emotions made him change.

I got up and started back toward them. "Stop!" I screamed uselessly. As if they would listen. "Derek, stop! Lucas, I mean it!"

Neither of them paid me any attention.

Then Lucas changed too, and the fighting grew more vicious. I heard yelps and teeth gnashing. I didn't want to get too close, but I had to stop them somehow. Lucas was three hundred years stronger than Derek. If I let this go on, Lucas would kill him. But what could I do? I could try to hit them with the car, but that might seriously injure one or both of them. Or make them turn on me.

"Stop, damn it!" I yelled, actually stamping my foot in frustration.

Lucas got Derek's throat in a choke hold. Blood gushed beneath his teeth. I gasped, screaming, "STOP!"

Lucas's metallic eyes met mine, his jaws still clamped to Derek. But that was all I needed. I couldn't let Lucas kill Derek. I forged the connection, summoning the electric power that hid somewhere in my chest. *Stop*, I spoke to Lucas. *Stop it now, before you kill him.*

I felt his resistance. A resounding *no* filled my head, but I brushed it aside. *Yes, Lucas. Let him go.*

Lucas's jaw slackened, and Derek darted away.

Now change, I spoke to Lucas. *This is too dangerous.*

He obeyed, and I released the connection. Lucas crouched on the ground, panting. His eyes tore holes in my heart when he looked up at me. Total betrayal.

He opened his mouth to speak, when Derek came at him out of nowhere. His claws dug deep into Lucas's smooth flesh and I heard him cry out. A sharp *crack* made my pulse sputter.

Lucas let loose a string of hot curses as he clutched his broken arm. He kicked Derek off of him and stood, grimacing.

But Derek wasn't through. He charged Lucas again, his slim white body like a spirit in the darkness. I made contact with his eyes, trying to forge the connection, but there was nothing to latch onto. Derek's mind had a wall built inside it, something I couldn't cross.

"Stop!" I screamed as Derek tore into Lucas again. His pained cries rang in my ears, too horrible to accept. "*Please!*" I shouted. "Derek, don't!"

Lucas changed again and fought back, rolling away from Derek's jaws just in time to avoid a neck wound. Derek came to a stop in front of me, facing Lucas. His lips were churned into a snarl, his body coiled as if he was protecting me from . . . what? Lucas?

The two animals stared each other down, hackles raised and vibes clashing. Then, with a low, furious snarl, Lucas turned and ran through the night, limping on his front leg.

I panted as I watched him go, falling to my knees in relief. Though I was upset that he'd left, it was for the best. His arm would heal quickly, and he needed time to calm down. This whole experimentation thing had pushed Lucas past his limits as far as Derek went. Deep down, I knew he hadn't meant any of the jerky things he'd said to me and that he was just irritated at being beaten by a runt—even if that runt wasn't the same species as him. He'd be back once he'd calmed down, and we would work everything out.

But Derek—what the hell was his problem?

I stood on shaky knees and rounded on him just in time to see him change back into a human. I averted my eyes from his nakedness and heard him go to the trunk of the car where we kept a duffel bag filled with spare clothes for moments like these. He pulled it open and began rifling around for something that fit him.

"What the hell is wrong with you?" I said, watching him step into some jeans.

He cast an indifferent glance at me. "What are you talking about? That guy is a jerk. He needed to be taught a lesson."

I scoffed loudly. "He's over three hundred years old, Derek. He would have killed you."

"Then how come I just kicked his ass?"

I stopped short, debating on whether or not to tell Derek what I had done—that I had, in effect, saved his life by using my power. But Lucas had been adamant that I not tell *anyone* about my power. I'd already gone against that and told Yvette. That was enough. So I said, "He knows how much you mean to me. He does have some self-control when it's not the full moon."

"Yeah, right," he grumbled. "And that's why he was treating you like shit? Because of all his wonderful self-control?"

"He was just angry because you're faster than him. He's not a good loser, I guess."

Derek seemed to like that. A leer appeared on his face. "Nah, he's a loser all right."

"You'd better not do what you just did again, Derek. Next time he might not be so nice." Or maybe I wouldn't.

Derek looked skeptical as he began packing up the camera equipment. "Yeah, yeah . . . whatever. Can we just go now? I'm sick of this."

I'd never seen Derek like this before. He'd been more than ready to start a fight with Lucas, *eager* for it, even. And when Lucas had stopped, he'd kept coming after him, intent on killing him, or so it had seemed. Derek wasn't like that. Sure, he'd defend someone if it came down to it, but he never started fights if they could be avoided. The supernatural magic had changed him, after all. He now had the ruthlessness of a vampire packed in with the impulsiveness of a werewolf. Question was: Could he make the two sides work together, or would they tear him apart?

Derek hopped into the driver's seat and beckoned me over. I obeyed on numb legs and went to the front seat. "Where to?" he asked, with a tentative smile.

But I was still mad at him and I turned away, jaw set.

Derek sighed. "Fine. I'm sorry, all right? But I don't like to hear him treating you like that. You deserve better."

I rounded on him. "Lucas and my relationship is none of your business, Derek. He treats me just fine." Not totally true given tonight's events, but that wasn't the point. I'd deal with Lucas later.

"Whatever," Derek said.

"And you need to apologize to Lucas, too. You practically tore his arm off." I hoped he was okay.

Derek looked as if I'd just told him to lick the car tires.

"Derek," I warned.

"Fine," he grumbled. "Now will you get over this?"

I smiled victoriously. "Yes."

"Excellent." Derek started the car. "Beach?"

"Perfect."

VIRAN

D erek drove us to Del Mar beach and parked a little ways from the public parking lot. It was closed at this time of night, so we had to kind of sneak in and walk through the nettles and tall grass toward the ocean. Derek leaped down over the ledge overhanging the sand and held his arms out for me. I let him help me down, mostly because he wanted to. I could certainly get down by myself.

We kicked off our shoes and began shuffling through the grainy sand to the surf. The night was crisp and clear, no clouds to mar the perfection of the sky. It was almost chilly, but when you're used to withstanding weather in the teens, fifties feels like a sauna. There was nobody around at this late hour, only us and the waves crashing around our ankles. I glanced up at the navy sky and saw the waning half moon looking back at me.

"I've been thinking," Derek said, bending to pick up a shell. "I need a name."

"You have a name," I said. "Derek Wendell Turner."

He gave me a look. He hated his middle name; he thought it was girly. I thought it was adorable.

I kicked sand at his ankles and he said, "Hybrid sounds lame. And I'm sick of the werewolves calling me a mutant. I've been playing around with mixing vampire and lycan together. You know, because lycans are werewolves?"

"Uh-huh," I said, humoring him. This was such a boy thing to do—needing a badass name. "So what'd you come up with?"

"Viran."

"Viran," I repeated. "Wouldn't a cross between vampire and lycan be vican?"

Derek tossed the shell into the ocean and said, "Yeah, but I like viran better. Sounds more threatening."

I smiled. "I like it, too. From now on I'll be sure to call you by your proper name. I'll spread it around."

Derek looked like he was going to ask something, but stopped himself.

"Spit it out," I said. "I hate when you hold stuff back, it makes me nervous."

Derek tossed another shell into the surf and said, "I was just wondering. . . . Can Lucas only change into a wolf? Like, is that his only form?"

"I guess so. He can change into the regular-looking wolf when it's not the full moon. Then he changes into the giant half-man, half-wolf thing on the full moon. Why do you ask?"

"Curiosity."

"I'm curious about something, too."

"Hmm?" He still looked like he was thinking about something else.

"Do you have any triggers?" My worry was that the rash violence I'd witnessed earlier would manifest in view of the humans, and if so, how he would manage to keep that in check at CSU.

Derek shook his head, seeming to come out of whatever he was pondering. "Not really. I don't think my, ah . . . trigger is as sensitive as a regular werewolf's. I really only feel overwhelmed when I get a sudden rush, you know? It makes it difficult when I get angry or sad, because it also . . ." He broke off and cleared his throat. "It also makes me crave blood."

"What?" I whispered, aghast.

"The trigger doesn't just make me want to change—it makes me want blood, too. And I don't *want* to drink blood, but I can't help what I'm feeling. Sometimes the only way to stop the blood crave from taking over is to change. It's confusing and annoying to try and figure out which craving to deal with—blood or beast—but, I don't know, it's manageable for now. I just hope it doesn't get worse."

"Me, too."

Something in my voice must have tipped him off to the upset roiling within me, because his tone lightened significantly when he said, "Anyway, it's not all bad. The strength and speed—man, I never thought I could be so powerful." He stretched his arms out in from of him, twisting his wrists around as if he'd just awoken from a long nap. "If only I could play ball like this." He smiled over at me. "And the wolf thing is sweet, too, once the transformation is done with. Sometimes after you . . . go back, I change and run along the beach or in the desert. It feels good to just run. It's like a release."

I nodded, knowing exactly what he meant. It had been so long since I ran, and I suddenly realized how much I'd been missing it. I made a little vow to myself to get back into track during the coming semester.

I'd realized during this trip to California just how much of myself I'd given up since coming into the underworld. All of my old friends with their happy, carefree faces and stories of frat parties and straight-A's sent a sliver of jealousy through me. I loved Lucas, yes. And I loved Derek—even if it was platonic—but that didn't mean I had to let them consume my life the way they had since Derek's infection.

I listened to the waves for a little while and then asked, "Are you scared?"

Derek frowned down at me.

"Of the full moon, I mean."

"Oh . . . that." He sighed. "Not really scared, just nervous. I can't remember what it was like last time, so I don't know what to expect. I don't want to lose my mind. . . . Be all crazy like Lucas talks about."

"You won't," I said surely. More surely than I felt, for certain.

Derek sighed again. "Hope you're right." He reached his long arm out and slung it around my shoulders, pulling me close. We walked in synch, and I felt his fingers flicker up and down my arm. "You're getting tan again," he said.

I shrugged, hoping he didn't take it as a betrayal of our friendship that I'd been basking in the sun for the past week.

His fingers continued to stroke my arm in an increasingly sensual manner, and our pace had slowed so much we were barely moving anymore. My heart began to hammer. I worried about his intentions and whether I'd have the strength to hurt him again by refusing his advances. Even though I forgave Derek of his past mistakes—and I truly did forgive him now—that didn't mean I was willing to let Lucas go for him. I loved Derek. Always would. But our relationship would never be romantic again with Lucas in my life.

Derek stopped walking and turned to face me, looking down at me with a million different emotions playing across his features. He moved to close the distance between us, and whether he was going for a hug or a kiss, I couldn't tell, but either way, we couldn't go there. It was wrong and unfair to . . . well, to everyone.

So I pulled away, tucking my hair behind my ear as I averted my gaze. I didn't want to see the look on his face.

"I wasn't going to kiss you," he said.

I glanced up at him, surprised and a little shaken. "I know," I lied.

"I am capable of being your friend, Faith. I've been doing it for years."

"Yeah, but now . . ."

"What? What makes now so different that you can't even hug me?"

Now there was Lucas. I had a boyfriend. One who was, okay, a smidge possessive and probably wouldn't appreciate smelling Derek all over me when I went back to him.

But how did I tell Derek all of that? Especially after their macho-wolf battle tonight?

And even taking Lucas's feelings out of the picture, there was still the fact that no matter how much Derek tried to pretend that he held only platonic feelings for me, I knew he was full of garbage. I could feel his emotions, and knew that every touch of my hand on his, every smile, every kind word, translated into hope for him. I had to be more careful than ever to keep our relationship strictly friendly, because Derek—no matter what he said— was still in love with me.

I opened my mouth to try and—somehow—break this to him, when I was saved by my cell phone. The high-pitched ringing sliced through the night, ripping us apart. I grabbed it from my pocket and held it to my ear.

"Hello?" I said. I watched Derek throw his hands on his hips and stalk away.

Way to piss off the newborn viran. Real smart.

"Hey," Lucas's voice came through the receiver.

"Hey," I said. "Where are you? Are you all right?"

"Yes, I'm fine," Lucas said tartly.

"Are you still mad?"

Silence blared on the other side of the phone. I took that as a *yes*.

I lowered my voice and turned away from Derek. Even though he could still hear me—and Lucas through the phone—I hoped he'd take the hint and not listen in.

"I'm really sorry," I whispered. "You know—for what happened during the fight?"

"You promised you'd never do that, Faith."

"I know I did, but you would have killed him."

"Don't be ridiculous. I was making a point. I've dealt with uncontrolled runts before and I don't kill them. They just need a firm hand in the beginning. I never would have seriously hurt him."

I wasn't so sure of that, but he had a good point. Maybe I'd overreacted. "I'm sorry," I said again. "I was just afraid one of you'd turn on me." Partly true.

"Well, what happened to using it on Derek?" Lucas's voice was so low I had to strain to hear it.

I cast a nervous glance at Derek, who was eyeing me interestedly. "I can't," I told Lucas.

He rumbled a low curse. "Then I guess I get why you did what you did. I might have done the same thing in your position. But, still. You need to trust me more than that, Faith."

I was about to argue back that he'd made it difficult for me to trust him by repeatedly telling me what a wild killing machine he was when he changed, but decided against it. I didn't want to fight. Especially not in front of Derek.

"Okay," I said.

"Tell him from me he better stop treating you like shit," Derek snapped at once.

I turned on him. "Shut up!"

"I don't treat you like shit," came Lucas's voice on the phone.

"Well, you were pretty mean to me tonight," I said, turning away from Derek again so he'd get the hint. "I know your pride was hurt or whatever, but still. Treating me like that is not okay no matter what mood you're in."

There was a long stretch of silence, during which I wondered if he'd hung up, but finally I heard him sigh. "You're right."

Whoa.

"But you have to understand, Faith, sometimes I overreact or react wrong. It doesn't mean I don't love you or even that I think it's okay to talk to you the way I did. I just can't control it. Which isn't an excuse. I'm just trying to explain that I'm not some chauvinistic jerk. I'm a werewolf. And I'm sorry."

I nodded to myself, feeling uncomfortable because Derek was listening. "It's okay. Just try to tamp it down from now on all right?"

I rounded on Derek, who straightened suddenly, looking guilty for eavesdropping. "And you said you'd apologize," I reminded him.

Derek's lips thinned. "Sorry."

I mouthed *thank you* at him, and then Lucas spoke up.

"Believe it or not," he said, "I didn't call to fight."

"Why'd you call then?" I looked out at the ocean, trying to let the rhythm of the waves soothe me.

"I have bad news."

My pulse stuttered, and Derek whipped around.

"I went back to your mother's house," Lucas said. "She was watching the news, and I overheard the headlines. There was another murder in Fort Collins."

The bottom dropped out of my stomach.

"It was a girl," he continued. "Same type of thing as before . . ." He paused. "Faith, we gotta go back to Colorado. Rolf's summoning us again."

THE BREAK-UP

We were back in Colorado before dawn the following day. Julian and Katie were at the airport to pick us up. We all packed our things into the trunk of Julian's minute car and hopped in. Okay, Derek and Lucas hopped. I shuffled. I had been unable to sleep on the plane ride and was utterly exhausted.

I sat in the back between Lucas and Derek, leaning into Lucas's side to keep myself warm. The other side of my body was pressed against Derek's ice block of a thigh. It was an odd sensation, one I never really wanted to have again.

"Why's Dad calling us?" Lucas asked as Julian got on the expressway, heading toward Gould.

"The murders have started up again," Julian said.

"I know, but what's that got to do with us? We were in California."

"Your vampire uprising theory is starting to catch on. Dad wants to ask you about it."

"Wait," I said. "Seriously?"

Lucas and I exchanged eager glances.

"Yeah, well, he can't claim it was just Vincent doing the killing anymore," Julian said. "He's still a little iffy about it, but the Council is coming around, especially after the whole vampire-interrogation thing you two did." He winked at me in the rearview mirror.

"Is he alerting the other wolf packs?" Lucas asked.

"Not yet. I don't think he's up for that. I'm betting the plan is going to be to eradicate the Denver brood ASAP and hope the whole thing goes away."

Well, that was a decent solution anyway. It made me feel better to know that an end to the murders would soon approach.

"So this has nothing to do with Derek?" I asked.

"Nope," Julian said. "Don't think it does."

I glanced at Derek and saw his face smooth in relief. I nudged him with my leg, and he smiled, nudging me back harder.

Then I felt Lucas's body sizzle with heat, and I stopped playing with Derek. The car suddenly felt like a grenade. If I made one false move, if I pulled that pin out, I'd set Lucas off and the car would explode with werewolf jaws, leaving me slashed to bits in between them all.

Not a good thing.

I snuggled closer to Lucas and closed my eyes.

"Can Derek and I go back to campus then?" I asked, yawning. "I really don't want to go up there. We always get stuck staying for way longer than we wanted to."

Lucas didn't answer for a moment, and I felt the heat of his body intensify.

"If that's what you want," Lucas said.

"We have to get Derek's room situated anyway," I said. Then a thought occurred to me, one I hadn't really considered until now. All these details were such a pain. "What are we going to tell Pete and his other roommates?"

Lucas's jaw flexed, but his voice was relatively calm. "We got Derek a single in my building. Already moved his stuff in and blocked out the windows."

"Oh . . . ," I said. "You guys *are* good at this."

Lucas shrugged. "Take Faith and Derek to campus," he said to Julian. "She's right. We always end up staying way too long, and we've got class on Monday." He kicked the back of Katie's seat. "Stay with them till I get back. I know you're not technically on duty till Monday, but there's still a vampire killing people out there. I don't want to take any chances."

"Okay," Katie said, shooting a shiny white smile back at me.

The rest of the ride was silent, and I alternated between sleep and watching the streetlamps play along Lucas's angular profile.

Once at CSU, I kissed Lucas good-bye and waved as he and Julian headed up to Gould. It was close to dawn already, so we didn't have time to dawdle. Katie and Derek carried all of our stuff up to the top floor of Lucas's building. Derek shoved the key into his new room and let us girls in before him.

It was pitch dark inside. I couldn't see my hand if I put it in front of my face, but I heard Derek and Katie walking around.

"The human needs light," I said, stumbling over something on the floor.

Katie giggled and I heard Derek's hand scrape against the wall as he hit the light switch. Then the florescent lights flickered on and the room was illuminated. The shape of the room was identical to Lucas's, but that was where the similarities ended. Lucas's room was dim, red and black, and papered with disturbed art that made you feel like you were in a macabre cave of sorts.

Derek's room was filled with sports stuff and posters of cars and a calendar with sexy girls on it. He was such a boy. Whoever had set up Derek's room had done a great job. Everything was in place, down to his blue toothbrush in the bathroom cabinet and his Rams helmet hanging on the bedpost.

"We even got you a new car," Katie said from behind. She tossed a pair of car keys onto his desk. "You know—because the last one got squashed."

I smiled over at Derek, but found that he was standing stock still in the middle of the room with this haunted, zombie-like look on his face.

"What's wrong?" I asked.

Derek dropped the bags and shook his head, closing his eyes. "We gotta take this stuff down."

"Why?" I asked and put my hand on his arm. "This isn't how you want it?"

"I can't look at this stuff," he said, face burning with pain. "This life doesn't exist anymore!" He spread his arms around the room, gesturing to the green and gold Rams paraphernalia and the pictures of the beach and his family. "This isn't me. This life is gone!" His eyes met mine, stabbing me with intensity. They were almost white. "All I have left is you." His voice broke. Then he winced and dragged his hands over his face. "But I don't even have you anymore, do I?" He smiled bitterly. "All I've got is myself and this sick blood crave I have to deal with."

I was so stunned by the suddenness of his outburst that I couldn't speak.

"I can't look at this stuff anymore," Derek said again, quietly this time. "It's not me." He crumpled to the floor, shoving his face in his hands. I knelt beside him and heard Katie leave the room.

As soon as the door closed, Derek threw his arms around me, pulling me against his body. He shook with sobs; his tears were like ice water against my cheek. I felt the corner of his lips brush mine.

I felt so incredibly sorry for him, for what I'd done to him. I wanted to make him feel better—to help him in some way, but that didn't mean I could kiss him. I pulled away from his searching lips and put my hands over his cheeks.

"You always have me," I said firmly. "Whether or not I'm with Lucas, I'll always be here when you need me. Remember that, okay?"

"Sorry," he rasped. "I guess, seeing my old life all laid out in front of me was kind of a shock. It's just luck that I didn't change. I got close."

"We'll take it all down," I said, trying to sound comforting. "Get you some new stuff this weekend."

Katie popped her head back in, seemingly relieved that the crying was done with.

"Sorry," Derek said, looking embarrassed.

Katie just shrugged. "I'll help you take the posters down," she offered.

Derek cracked a grateful smile. "Yeah, thanks."

We set out removing anything that would remind Derek of his past life. When we were done, all that was left was the calendar of sexy girls, some pictures of me and him in high school, and the blank wall. Katie went down to the Dumpster and trashed everything else. When she returned, it was minutes to dawn and Derek was fading fast.

"Me and Katie will go to my room," I said as Derek climbed into his bed, eyes drooping closed.

His face wrinkled into a frown, and he held his arms out for me.

I went and hugged him. "See you tonight," I whispered. "Come to my room when you're up, okay? We'll hang out."

"No," he said. "Stay here."

I cast a look at Katie.

"I can't," I said. "We don't have a place to sleep."

Derek tugged me onto the bed with him and held me in a vice. "Sleep with me. . . ."

Trapped in his arms, I looked up at Katie pleadingly.

"Help?" I asked, still trying to escape.

Katie giggled and watched me squirm.

Derek squeezed me tighter. "I love you," he breathed in my ear. "I'll always love you."

My heart wrenched, and I stopped struggling. I watched his face settle into stillness and his body grew even heavier. He was asleep. Dead.

"Love you back, idiot." I turned to Katie, snickering in the doorway. "Get him off of me."

She came over and lifted Derek's arms as if they were nothing, and I escaped, rubbing my ribs.

"Let's get out of here," I said. "I feel like I'm in a crypt."

Katie giggled. "We kind of are."

• • •

In the morning, I was awakened by the screeching sound of my cell phone. I flung my arm out and accidentally smacked my lamp. It hit the floor and landed on Katie, who let out a funny woof-like sound.

"Sorry," I grumbled, reaching for my phone.

I heard Katie groan and saw her hand put the lamp back where it was supposed to be.

I dragged the phone to my ear and glanced at the time. It was eight o'clock in the morning. I'd only been asleep two hours. Why in God's name would Lucas call me at eight o'clock? There was either something wrong or Lucas was becoming a sadist.

"Hello?" I croaked into the receiver.

I heard sniffling from the other end of the phone and I sat up. Something was definitely wrong.

"Who is this?" I asked.

"It's Heather."

"Heather?" For a moment my brain couldn't grasp the concept. Heather seemed like such an alien word after weeks of were-wolves and full moons and blood. Why did she sound so upset? Why was she even calling me? We hadn't spoken in almost a month. I'd assumed she hated me for being the worst friend in the history of the world. "What's wrong?" I asked.

"Sorry it's so early," she said thickly. "I didn't know who else to call. I don't have many friends."

"I'm your friend," I said. At least, I wanted to be. Heather and my other friends were yet another thing I'd sacrificed to be with Lucas. Something I intended to get back this semester. "Tell me what's wrong."

Heather broke into sobs.

I watched Katie give me the stink eye and pad into the bathroom. I guess she was a light sleeper, too. Ashley was out on the bed next to us. A bomb could've gone off, and she wouldn't have noticed.

I shushed Heather. "Just tell me what happened. Is it the murders? Are you scared?" We'd all received notifications on our doors the other day that there was to be a curfew from now on, meaning nobody could be out past eleven p.m. It was a testament to how seriously the human community was taking this "serial killer," and it had everybody on edge.

"No, it's not that," Heather grumbled. "Pete broke up with me for some *girl*. Paula or something."

After everything those two had been through last semester, I couldn't believe Pete would just dump her that way. Then again, he was a scumbag as far as I was concerned. I still hadn't forgotten his manipulation of Heather for sex. I tried to sound genuine when I spoke, but was secretly glad he was out of the picture.

"Aw . . . I'm so sorry, Heather. That really sucks."

Heather cried harder.

Okay, not the right thing to say.

"Is there anything I can do?" I asked helplessly.

Suddenly Heather stopped crying and said, "Yes. Yes there is. That's why I called you. I want to go out tonight. I want to go out with someone really cute and really smart and funny that'll just *crush* the life out of Pete."

I stared across the room at my desk. "Ah . . . I'm flattered that you thought of me, but I'm not really into girls."

Heather laughed a little. "No, dummy. I meant that guy you used to date. Vincent Stone? Would you mind terribly if I went out with him, just for one night? Just to make Pete jealous?"

I groped for an excuse that didn't involve decapitation via werewolf. "He moved away," I said lamely. "Sorry."

"Oh . . ."

Katie came out of the bathroom and sat on my bed. "Offer her Derek," she whispered.

I put my hand over the receiver and turned to Katie. "You heard Heather all the way in the bathroom?"

"Dog ears." She grinned toothily.

I removed my hand from the receiver. *I want superhearing. . . .*

"What about Derek?" I asked Heather.

It was a good idea after all. Derek could use a night out with a nice girl to distract himself, and Heather needed someone hot to make Pete jealous. Heather was definitely a nice girl, and Derek was *definitely* hot even considering his creepy paleness.

"Oh, no," Heather said. "I couldn't. I know you and Derek . . ."

"Derek and I nothing," I said, glancing nervously at Katie, who was pretending not to listen. "We're just friends."

"Still, Derek is Pete's friend. He might not want to."

"Don't worry about it," I assured her. "Derek would love to go out with you. Really. I'll set it up."

"Okay," Heather said. "But you have to come, too. Come to Zydeco's with us and keep me company in case something goes wrong."

I wrinkled my nose. I hated Zydeco's. And as eager as I was to get Derek involved with someone besides me, I didn't want to actually witness it. "I don't know, Heather. It might be weird."

"No." Heather's voice was firm. "I need you. You have to come. Bring Ashley if you want so it's not so weird, but I want you to come with. Please."

"You really should go," Katie put in. "I know Derek seems in control, but he's still young. *I* should definitely go, anyway."

"Okay," I whispered, hand on the receiver again. "But we're not bringing her." I jerked my head at Ashley. I liked Ashley and everything, but I didn't want her getting involved in werewolf-vampire drama. As it was, I felt a crush of nerves at getting

Heather into it. I consoled myself with the fact that Heather—hopefully—wasn't going to find out about our underworld and that she would take tonight's outing at face value, never knowing what she was really dealing with. The same went for Ashley, theoretically, but I didn't want to take chances. Better to keep the human involvement to a minimum.

"All right, I'll come," I said to Heather. "I'll bring my friend Katie. See you tonight at nightfa—I mean, at eight. That okay?" God, I was getting weird. See you at nightfall. . . . Sheesh.

"Thanks, Faith. I owe you big time."

No, I owed her after the way I'd treated her lately. Which is exactly why I'd agreed to this. And the fact that I missed having her around to talk to. She'd always been a loyal friend to me, and I'd dumped her. Not anymore. I said good-bye to her and hung up, hoping that tonight would help fix things between us.

"So . . . ," Katie said. "You and Derek were together, I take it?"

"In high school," I said. "Why? Does it matter?"

"No," Katie said quickly. She looked away, fidgeting with the nose on my stuffed panda.

"I'm going back to sleep," I yawned. I gave Katie a piercing look. "*Don't* tell Lucas what we're doing."

She threw a look at me, one that said plainly, *we'll talk about this later*, and settled back down on her makeshift bed.

I lay back too, pulling the covers over my head.

Yeah, I knew somewhere inside that what I was doing was reckless and immature, but the larger part of me didn't care. I wanted to get out. To have fun like a normal college kid. And that's exactly what I intended to do tonight—without Lucas's knowledge.

PUNCH-DRUNK

J ust after eight thirty, Heather and Derek, followed closely by Katie and me, walked along the cobblestoned streets of Old Town toward Zydeco's. The usual crowd of people angling to get inside blocked the sidewalk and our group joined the fray.

Getting to this point had been a marathon of manipulation and lies. First, there was convincing Katie not to tell Lucas. Not only did I fail to see the point in it—besides pissing him off and starting a fight—but I also sort of resented the notion that I had to ask permission to go out. Lucas wasn't my dad (thank God), and I didn't have to ask him permission to do anything—least of all hang out with my friends. And as long as Katie was there to guard Derek, there was no reason we couldn't go. That was what she was there for, after all. I spewed all of this to Katie, and she'd backed down, consenting only to call Lucas if something bad happened.

Next there was the issue of coercing Derek to go on a date with Heather.

Derek was not into it.

I had to use every ounce of cunning in my body to cajole him. In the end I owed him one steak dinner, doing his homework for a week, and one marathon movie sleepover night, which was to be relinquished after Zydeco's tonight. A small price to pay to get Derek out on a date with someone besides me.

And then there was Heather. She noticed Derek's change of appearance immediately. Her mouth hit the floor and her eyes went all soft, like she'd just seen Ryan Reynolds or something. She turned to me when Derek wasn't looking and mouthed the words, "Oh my God!"

The line outside of Zydeco's was exceptionally long tonight, not because there were more people, but because of the new security measures in effect to keep weirdoes out. Since the murders had yet to abate, it seemed the whole town was on high alert. Nobody out late, doors locked, shop owners applying new alarm systems to their buildings, not to mention CSU's annoying new curfew. Zydeco's was in on it, too, meaning we all had to empty our pockets before entering, and submit our purses for inspection by two beefy bouncers with tattooed arms.

After we'd been deemed safe—which I thought was hilariously ironic—we were allowed to pass. A sexy lady in Mardi Gras attire threw beads over our heads by as we walked through the door and into the loud, colorful, and slightly cheesy atmosphere that was Zydeco's. Instantly, Heather rose onto her tiptoes and peered around over the tops of people's heads, probably trying to look for Pete. Katie and I followed Heather and Derek to the back where the tables were.

We sat down, submerged in total awkwardness. Heather bit at her nails as she looked around the club. Derek on the other hand was expressionless and completely motionless. Why did I agree to this again? I'd never felt more out of place. Watching Derek on a date with Heather? Talk about uncomfortable. Thankfully, Katie dashed away and showed up again with a platter full of shots.

Forgetting all about my former conviction to abstain from alcohol consumption, I knocked one back. Derek made a grab for one, but I caught his wrist and leaned in to whisper in his ear, "Are you allowed to drink? You know . . . with the blood crave?" Derek's vibe rang with exasperation and then knocked his shot back.

"We'll see," he said.

"That was dumb," I said. I grabbed another glass and downed it.

"Oh, my God!" Heather suddenly gasped and spun around to look at me. "Pete and Paula are right there!" She pointed discreetly at a couple sitting in the back corner.

Sure enough, it was Pete with some other girl who must have been Paula.

Paula looked like a sex goddess. She had siren-red hair and big pouty lips to match. Her body was shaped like an overly exaggerated hourglass, and I swear I saw her thong through her black leather dress.

There was no way this chick was in college. She looked like a Playboy bunny. I found it utterly laughable that she was with Pete, who looked more like Goofy than anything else.

"I have to go over there," Heather said.

"What?" I hissed. "Are you crazy?" Heather's face drained, and she coughed down a shot.

"Come with me, Faith," she said. "I need support."

Heather took hold of Derek's hand and dragged him to Pete and the sexpot's table. I glanced back at Katie helplessly and shuffled along reluctantly.

"Hi," Heather said loudly to Pete.

Pete about jumped out of his freckly skin when he saw Heather—and Derek clasping her hand. "Derek?" he asked, slightly aghast. "Dude, what happened to you?"

"Flu," he said shortly.

"You might wanna get that checked."

"He's fine," Heather said. "*We're* fine." She hugged herself closer to Derek, and I saw her shiver. I bit my lip, hoping she was too upset to notice Derek's frosty, marbled body.

Pete's face fell. "We?"

"Yes," Heather said triumphantly. "We. Me and Derek. We're on a date."

Pete gawked, but his girlfriend spoke up. "What a coincidence," she said. "So are we." She smiled and put her hand on Pete's gangly thigh. She had an oily voice that matched her oily vibe.

I was instantly suspicious. I thought maybe if I got closer I could pick up more about her, so I leaned in and said, "Hi. I don't think we've met. I'm Faith." I extended my hand.

Paula turned to me. "Paula Tourmaline," she said. She touched her fingers to my hand and shook it lightly. I immediately felt a wave of crazy hit me—that same crazy, snarled-up energy I felt from all supernatural beings I'd ever come in contact with.

Then something else registered as Paula slid her hand from mine: she was wearing long, black, silken gloves.

Oh crap.

"Tourmaline?" I asked, trying to sound normal. "Is that French?"

"No," she said shortly. She returned her big brown eyes to Heather. "It was nice to meet you, Hannah."

"Heather," I corrected loudly.

I tugged Derek's sleeve and steered him away from the table, leaving Heather to fend for herself. She gave me a narrow look, but rounded on Pete saying something that looked snide.

Derek let me tow him to the hallway near the bathrooms, but then snatched his arm away.

"You need help going to the bathroom?" he asked. I heard the fury in his tone, but now was not the time for fighting.

"That chick is a vampire!" I all but screamed.

"Shut up," he said, though he must have seen the urgency in my gaze because he straightened and inhaled deeply. His pupils dilated, and he rolled his head back, staggering into the wall. "Jesus," he gasped. "Don't let me breathe again."

"Why'd you even do it at all?" I asked, voice high.

"I was trying to see if I could smell her . . . but *damn*." He opened his eyes, and I saw that his pupils had filled his entire eye, his mouth was parted, and I could see the tips of his elongated incisors.

Suddenly, he looked terrifying.

"Close your eyes!" I squeaked, glancing around anxiously.

Derek did so and reached out to hold my hand. I took it and squeezed as hard as I could.

He groaned and slammed his fist against the wall, making a little depression in the brick.

Great. This was going *so* well.

Some girl with too-big hair gave us a frightened look, and I wrapped myself around Derek, pretending to make out with him. People usually averted their eyes from such a sight.

"It's okay," I said in his ear. I ran my hand over the back of his neck and then had a horrible thought. "Am I making it worse?"

"Yes," Derek said. "But don't stop."

"Masochist," I teased.

Derek laughed shakily. "Guess I didn't realize how bad I wanted it."

"You haven't been breathing this whole time?"

He shook his head. "One of the benefits of being dead."

"Derek, I'm pretty sure Paula is a vampire."

"How do you know?"

I didn't want to tell him that I felt her vibe. Derek knew that I felt people's energies, but he'd never actually believed it. I barely ever talked about it with him. But that was before he'd become a viran. Still, now didn't seem like the time to go into it. Instead, I asserted my next-best reason, which was infinitely less convincing. "She was wearing gloves," I said lamely.

Derek pulled back and opened his eyes, which were back to normal. "Faith, lots of people wear gloves. It's winter."

"But I felt this freaky vibe coming off of her!" I protested.

Derek put his hands on his hips. "Are you still on about that? Seriously?"

"What? So you can believe in vampires and werewolves, but you can't believe that I felt something weird about her?"

"I don't think there'd be a *vampire* in Zydeco's."

"This is where I met Vincent," I said.

"She's not a vampire," he said firmly. "You're being paranoid."

"No, you're being a jerk!" I yelled, halfway into hysterics. "Pete—your *friend*—is in danger!"

Derek's jaw clamped shut and his pupils widened a smidge. "You're crazy," he spat. "I gotta get back to my *date*."

But when he turned, Heather was gone.

"Where'd she—," Derek started, looking around.

"Maybe she went back to the table," I suggested, heading there. But when we returned Katie was sitting alone, looking bored. "Where's Heather?" I asked.

"No clue," she said with a shrug. She slurred her words a little, and I realized five of the shots were gone.

Awesome.

"Go check the bar," I instructed Derek and closed in on Katie. "Are you drunk?"

"Only a little," she said. "Why? Who cares?"

"Because you're supposed to be our guardian tonight!" I said, sounding more than a little hysterical. "What if Derek loses control? And did you know that Paula is a vampire?"

Katie's eyes widened. "Seriously?"

I faltered. "I'm pretty sure."

Katie cursed, seemingly angry with herself now. *Well, good,* I thought vindictively. *She's being totally irresponsible.*

"Should I go check and see?" Katie asked. "I can smell it if she's a vampire, but I have to get closer. All these humans are obscuring the scent."

"I don't know, I think we should—"

Just then, Derek returned without Heather, and I broke off. "I didn't see her," he said curtly.

"This is a disaster," I muttered, running my hand through my hair. "We need to leave."

"I'll check the bathroom for Heather," Katie said and took off, stumbling.

Derek sat at the table and downed another shot.

"Will you stop that, please?" I said as I sat next to him and put my head in my hand.

"What's your problem?" he asked. "You're acting completely insane."

I just stared at him. How could he not see the danger here?

Was I the only one left with any sense? Or maybe I was just the only one who'd been repeatedly attacked by a vampire and a pack of werewolves in the last month. Maybe Derek was right—maybe I was being paranoid.

I sighed, trying to release the tension squeezing me from the inside out. "I guess I'm just on edge. I'm not used to being out like this. With a werewolf and a newborn viran." I smiled ruefully at him.

He didn't return it.

A hand touched my shoulder and I jumped, turning around. It was Katie.

"I found her," she said. "She's in the bathroom."

"Oh good," I said. "Get her and we'll go."

"Ah . . . that might be a problem."

"Why?"

"Because she's in there with a bunch of blood bitches."

"What!" I shrieked.

Derek turned. "What's a blood bitch?"

"Humans who drink vampire blood," Katie said. "They do favors for the vampires in return for small amounts of blood. They're like drug addicts. It's disgusting."

"How do you know they're blood bitches?" I hissed, glancing around to make sure nobody was listening in, which was dumb because the club was ear-splittingly loud.

"I can smell the vampire blood in their systems," Katie explained. "Plus, I'm pretty sure I recognize one of them. I can't place her, but I'm thinking I must have seen her during a raid or something."

"Oh, God," I moaned. "So what do we do?"

"I don't know," Katie said. "Maybe we should call Lucas?"

I pressed my lips together. I really didn't want to do that. He'd be so mad that we'd gone out, and it wasn't like he could help us from two hours away. "No," I said. "I'll handle this. Just—stay with Derek."

She nodded and sat beside him as I headed off toward the bathroom. I didn't know exactly what I planned on doing, but Heather was my friend—sort of—and I couldn't let her go down this path. Maybe she'd listen to me.

I entered into the yellow light of the bathroom. The brick walls gave the room a rusty odor that mingled unpleasantly with the scent of bleach and toilet bowl cleaner. As Katie had said, Heather was there, sitting on the counter and talking with four other girls, all of whom looked over when I entered.

Three of the girls were close to identical. Dull brown hair pooled around their shoulders, skanky clothing covered their anorexic bodies, and a glazed look hung in their eyes. The fourth girl looked very different. She had reddish-brown hair and gorgeous jade-green eyes that pierced into mine, indicating that she wasn't high on drugs or large quantities of vampire blood. She wore a brown leather jacket and red heels, both of which I liked very much. Had this meeting been under different circumstances, I would have asked her where she'd gotten them. But as it was, I fixed the girls with my best I'm-a-badass stare and went up to them.

"Heather, I've been looking everywhere for you," I said pointedly.

She seemed unconcerned and just giggled.

"We're ready to get out of here," I went on. I waited for her to jump off the sink and come toward me. But she just smiled dazedly.

She was high, but whether she was vamped or on drugs was beyond me. Nor did I care. I just wanted out of there, and Heather, too. "Come on," I said, holding out my hand for her to take.

"She doesn't want to go," said the girl with reddish hair.

I rounded on her. "And you would be?"

A grin spread on the girl's strawberry-kissed lips. "Danni," she supplied. "And who says you get to decide when she leaves?"

"I do. I'm her friend."

"Some friend," Heather grumbled.

"What?" I turned back to her, seeing that her freckled face had gone sour.

"You're a crappy friend," she said. "You never call me, and I practically had to drag you out tonight. And then you totally left me with Pete and Paula!"

She was right, but regardless of how sucky I'd been to her, I still cared about her and I didn't want her anywhere near these people. "Look—I'm sorry, but I've been going through some . . . things. Can we please just leave now and we can talk about it in private?"

"No," she said. "I'm happy right here." She folded her arms over her chest.

"Why don't you stay?" Danni said to me. She gestured to the grimy bathroom as if she was asking me to stay in some posh penthouse.

I had to repress the urge to laugh. "No thanks," I said. "I don't do drugs."

"Come on, where's your sense of adventure?" she asked.

"Oh, I'm sorry, I must have left it in my dorm room. Along with my brain." What, did she think I was an idiot? That I would actually take drugs from some chick I just met?

"But it's awesome!" Heather suddenly exclaimed. "Danni says it's called getting *vamped*."

I froze and locked eyes with Danni's cunning stare. The ghost of a smile played in the curl of her lips. She'd actually told Heather that the drug was vampire blood? Or had she merely said it was a drug? I didn't know, but something about the way she was looking at me, made me think she knew something she wasn't telling.

Instantly, I reached out with my power to feel her vibe. It was strangely faint, but I'd been drinking, so maybe that affected my power. What little I got from her was laid-back and bored.

"Take a hit," she offered. She reached over with one hand and held the charm bracelet hanging on her wrist. Among the colorful baubles was a slim vial in the shape of a fang. It was blood-red. She gave the vial a small twist and the body came off, leaving the top attached to her bracelet. The vial had to contain a tiny amount of vampire blood.

Cute.

Instead of immediately declining, I decided to probe a little into this business. Part of me was extremely curious—not that I wanted any. God, no. But I did want to know how the others did it, what they were willing to do for it and, most importantly, if they knew where the vampires were. It seemed likely if they were in contact with them.

"How much do I need to take?" I asked. "To get vamped?" I felt like such a dork saying it, but I was trying to use the lingo.

"A drop will enhance your senses; two gives you strength and speed. And three makes your brain work faster. Any more than that and you get all of the above, plus a serious high. It's euphoric."

I was thrown by her casual tone. It was almost apathetic. As if she was reciting the symptoms of the chickenpox out of a textbook.

"I've never heard of a drug that made you stronger," I said. "Or smarter, for that matter."

"I know about a lot you've never heard of," Danni said, flicking her auburn hair away from her neck.

Wanna bet?

"Where'd you get it?" I asked.

"A dealer," she said. "Just like everybody else."

Something in the overt nonchalance of her tone made me believe that Danni knew exactly what she had in that little bottle. "But that's not a regular drug. It looks like blood." *Don't give too much away, Faith.*

Danni examined the tiny bottle between her fingers. "It's dyed to make it more appealing. Like Gatorade."

I smiled despite myself. "Yeah, except Gatorade doesn't make you high."

Danni closed her finger over the end of the bottle and turned it over. She held her finger out to me. A bead of red liquid shone on the tip. A drop of poison. "Take it," she said, eyes never leaving mine.

"You first," I challenged.

Danni's mouth quirked. "Nah," she said. "I don't use. I just supply."

My smile hardened. "Then you'll have to excuse me. I don't think I'll be doing any drugs that even the supplier won't use."

This didn't seem to bother Danni at all. She held her finger out to Heather instead and said, "It's yours, babe."

Heather took Danni's wrist in an instant and stuck her finger into her mouth.

"Heather!" I exclaimed. "Come on, you're already high. Let's just get out of here." Forget this. Three of these blood bitches looked like they were going to go into a drug coma, and Danni was either too smart or too ignorant to tell me anything useful. It was time to go.

But Heather wasn't going anywhere.

"You can never be too thin or too high!" she said, eyes going in and out of focus.

I threw my hands onto my hips. "We're not going to wait all night for you," I warned, even though I would have if it meant her getting home safe.

"Okay," she said dreamily.

I stared her down as she turned the water faucet on and off, giggling inanely. I looked around at the dazed blood bitches and Danni smiling coyly. "Fine!" I burst out. "Come find me when you're done being completely idiotic!"

"'Kay."

I stormed out, cursing under my breath. This was the most ridiculous and frustrating night I'd ever had, and suddenly, I was sick of it—sick of all the supernatural bullshit. Of being paranoid all the time and always, *always* being the responsible one. Katie had gone and gotten drunk off her ass; Heather had just taken the first step to becoming a blood bitch; and Derek . . . he was too busy being an assbag to do anything dumb, but he hadn't listened to me about Paula and I was pissed.

I wanted to let loose, too. I wanted to forget about all the awful things that were going on around me—the things I had no power to change. That was the whole reason I'd gone out tonight. I wanted . . . I wanted to *dance.*

I went to our table and found Derek and Katie deep in conversation. They both turned when I came up. "Heather's not coming," I snapped. I tossed back one of the remaining shots and winced as it burned my throat. "I'm going to dance."

"But I thought we were leaving?" Katie said.

"Leave if you want." I stalked off to the dance floor.

I danced alone for a while, only semi-enjoying myself amidst my anger. Then some random dude came up and started dancing with me. I tried my best to be nice, but when his hand wandered to my butt cheek, I slapped it off, totally appalled and repulsed at his forwardness.

"Hey," he said. "What was that for?"

I started walking away and didn't even bother to turn around. *Why is everything a pain?*

I felt a hand on my shoulder and it spun me around. Random Dude was looming over me. "Why'd you hit my hand away?" he asked, slurring.

I pushed his hand off of my shoulder and said, "Because I don't appreciate you grabbing my ass when you don't even know my name."

"So tell me your name," he said, guffawing.

"No," I said with a sneer. "Go dance with someone else. I'm leaving."

I started to turn around but Random Dude grabbed my wrist.

Hard. I tried to yank it away and ended up wrenching it, which hurt like hell.

"Let me go, jerk!"

That's when a wall of white flew at us with the speed of an aerial missile. Derek. He drew back and punched Random Dude so hard he went flying through the air and crashing into the bar. His back splintered the wood and he was knocked unconscious.

For a moment I could only stare at Random Dude lying in a pile under the bar. I was unable to completely stave off the rush of vindication upon seeing him drooling uselessly on the floor. Then I realized that everyone else was staring—not at Random Dude—but at Derek.

Oh, fudge.

I grabbed Derek's hand and quickly towed him away from the stunned crowd.

"What the hell was that?" I screeched. "What were you thinking!"

"He was hurting you!" Derek said defensively. "You're my responsibility tonight. I wasn't about to let that guy break your wrist off."

"I'm not your responsibility; I'm Katie's. She's the one that's supposed to protect me if anything happens. And nothing *was* happening. You completely overreacted."

"I just defended you and you're yelling at me?"

I sputtered for a moment. "Couldn't you have at least *tried* to act like a normal person?"

"That *was* me trying. If I'd had it my way I would have changed right there and ripped his slimy skull off."

I gaped up at him.

"Sorry," Derek said, seeing my reaction. "I guess I should have been more subtle." He looked around, shoving his hands into his pockets. "Do you think anyone noticed?"

"Um, yeah!" I looked over at the exit and saw the bouncer on his cell phone. "We have to leave," I said. "Now. I think the bouncer is calling the police."

Suddenly Katie was at Derek's side. "What is *wrong* with you?" she all but shrieked.

Derek rolled his eyes. "Yeah, yeah I know. I lost it, all right? Like it never happened to you?"

"I never did it in the middle of a human club!"

"Where were *you* anyway?" I shot at her. "You're supposed to be controlling him."

Katie held her hands up helplessly. "He was gone before I could even react! How am I supposed to know he can move that fast?"

Derek looked a little too happy about that.

"Don't even start," I warned him, stabbing a finger in his face. I turned to Katie. "We can't leave Heather here, but I can't get her out of the bathroom."

"I'll stay with her," Katie said at once. She seemed to be trying to redeem herself for letting Derek slip through her guard. "You guys get out of here—quick. I hear sirens."

"Okay, but make sure Heather goes home with you. Haul her over your shoulder if you have to."

"Got it." Katie started to leave and then stopped short, giving Derek a worried look. "Maybe I should walk you to the car."

Derek looked ready to protest, but I nodded enthusiastically in agreement.

Katie waved us toward the back of the club. "This way."

Derek and I followed her, slipping in between the crowds like eels. People were freaking out all around us. I heard phrases like, *He came out of nowhere*, and, *Threw him across the room and then vanished!* As we reached the side door I saw a bouncer the size of a grizzly bear standing guard over it.

"Damn," I muttered.

"Come on," Derek said, striding forward.

The bouncer put his beefy hand on Derek's chest. He was at least three times as big as Derek and threw his weight out like a puffed-up gorilla. "Nobody in or out," he thundered. Derek grabbed the guy's hand and twisted it away, slamming him into the doorframe.

"Go," Derek said to us, and I scurried through the door followed by Katie. Derek trailed after us, leaving the bouncer staring after us in wonderment and rubbing his hand.

We entered into a slim, dank alley beside the club that smelled faintly of vomit. Katie began walking briskly toward the street, Derek and I keeping pace behind her, when suddenly she stopped. She turned to face us, and her eyes were like flashlights in the dark alley—iridescent yellow.

"Get back inside," she said.

"Why?" Derek asked, looking around.

Katie's body shook violently.

"Vampires."

HUMAN SHIELD

D erek pinned me to the wall in an instant. His arms braced against the side of the building like steel bars, his hard body pressed flush against mine.

He cursed as a rush of wind hit the side of my face and Katie yelled, *"Derek, get her inside!"*

I peered around Derek's waist and saw that three people had appeared at the mouth of the alley—all tall, beautiful, and distinctly vampire.

Derek's hand clasped to my arm so tightly I felt sure it would leave bruises as he hauled me toward the side door of the club. I ran and just barely caught sight of Katie angling herself between us and the vampires. In her hand was a wooden stake, much like the one Lucas had given me when we'd hunted together, but fancier and without the silver end. She crouched low, shaking and ready to fight or change—whichever came first. I'd never seen this side of her before, fierce and fearless. She was completely focused on the vampires, body tensed for the slightest sign of attack. I was in awe of her. She was ready to die right there defending us.

One of the vampires, a tall, dark guy with greasy hair, pounced on Katie and sunk his teeth into her arm. She grunted and raked the point of the stake across his face. He withdrew and she swept her leg out to knock his feet out from under him. He was too quick, though, and hopped her kick, only to make a fatal lunge for her throat.

"Katie!" I screamed, terrified. But she was amazing. She dodged the attack with impossible speed and rebounded off the wall to leap on top of the vampire like a lioness. She dug into his abdomen with her stake, and his angry hiss filled the night air. He shook her off, and she rolled away, coming to her feet in an ultrafast movement. Immediately, the vampire flew at her again.

Just then, Derek stopped dead, and I stumbled to a halt, hitting my head on his arm. I looked around and saw that the side door to the club was now blocked.

By Paula.

"You," Derek started, gaping at her.

Paula propped her hands on her tiny hips. "How observant," she said. "I thought I'd find you fleeing the scene."

"Get away from the door," Derek demanded.

"I can't do that." She pointed a silken finger at the vampires fighting Katie. The other two had joined in now and were helping to force Katie back toward us. We were going to be cornered. "They need to have a word," Paula said primly.

"Too bad. Move!" Derek swatted Paula away like a paper doll, and she fell to the ground. Katie tripped over her, almost falling, too.

Derek shoved me toward the door when one of the vampires— a slim dude with tawny hair—dove forward to snatch Paula out of the way. At the same moment, Katie spun around on him, taking the miniscule moment of opportunity as the vampire reached for Paula, and plunged her stake at his chest.

In a blink, the vampire picked Paula up by her arms and held her in front of his chest like a shield. The stake squelched into Paula's heart, and she let out a ragged groan. Blood gushed from the wound, and we all froze for an instant.

Was it vampire blood . . . or human?

The vampire eyes around us all blackened with the crave— even Derek's eyes were like inky pools.

Shit. Human blood.

But still, nobody moved. Derek was holding his breath—completely motionless and staring away from the body as though in pain. I could feel his vibe lashing at him like barbed wire—urging him to drink the blood in front of him. He only kept it at bay by thinking of me. How he *wouldn't* bite me. How he loved me.

It lasted only a breath of time.

And then the female vampire dashed for the bleeding corpse. Katie pried the stake from the body and whirled around on her with a vicious growl. The female stopped, eyes still locked hungrily on the dead body. Her vibe was ten times stronger than Derek's. She was *insane* with bloodlust—she could think of nothing else.

The tan-haired vampire who was holding Paula seemed more controlled. He released the dead body with a flourish and smacked his gloved hands together as if dusting them off. "Go on," he said to the female. "Take her."

Letting out an ecstatic yip, she slipped past Katie in a millisecond and clamped onto the dead body with her fangs. She sucked greedily as crimson liquid pooled down her delicate chin.

I clapped my hand over my mouth, releasing a small noise of repulsion. Derek's hands tightened on me, his vibe swelling protectively. I silently prayed that he would stay in control. Derek turning on me was the last thing we needed now. I would have told him to change and quell the crave, but I was afraid the vampires would kill him if he did.

Katie let her arm droop and looked helplessly at the gory feast going on at her feet. "Wait, she—she wasn't a vampire?"

The tan-haired vampire chuckled. "Goodness no. Merely a pet. I hadn't even gotten a taste yet—what a waste." He sighed, watching as the female vampire sucked the very last drop out of the body and left it curled and vile on the ground. The female wiped her gloved hand along her mouth and rose to stand next to the male. "At least *someone* got to enjoy her," he said.

Katie was speechless, staring at the exsanguinated corpse. Police sirens echoed in the background and walkie-talkies crackled with voices. If the police came storming down this alley, I was pretty sure we'd all get pinned as the serial killers. Wouldn't that be fun.

The tan-haired vampire turned on Derek and said, "Pardon Melissa." He nodded at the female, still licking her lips. "She's still young and *quite* the pig."

Melissa made an outraged noise.

"Well, you are," the tan-haired vampire said matter-of-factly. He gave Derek an apologetic face that reeked of fakeness. "This wasn't at all how we planned to make our first impression. Your human looks ready to faint. We apologize." He stepped forward and jutted his hand out for Derek. "Calvin Carnelian, at your service. And you are?"

"Derek," he said, refusing Calvin's gloved hand.

Calvin let it fall and his eyes locked on mine. Now that the crave had faded from them, they were astonishingly beautiful—*he* was astonishingly beautiful. Pale, even skin like fluffy marshmallow, blue eyes so saturated they were close to violet, and a dashing, pointed smile that would have melted any girl's heart.

Except mine.

To me, he was terrifying.

"And this?" Calvin asked with a smooth, saccharine voice.

Derek spoke for me, "Faith."

Calvin's pupils dilated slightly at the sound of my name. "A lovely pet," he said. "I see she is special like mine was. How fortunate."

Both Derek and I frowned, but neither of us said a word. Katie just continued to stare dejectedly at Paula's dead body. Calvin hadn't even bothered to ask about her.

"These are my comrades," Calvin said, indicating the other two vampires. "Silas Zircon and Melissa Jade."

They both inclined their perfect heads. Silas looked to be European; he had dark skin—well, dark by vampire standards— humongous brown eyes and a slanted jaw speckled with stubble. Melissa was flawless. She had alabaster skin, black hair like a sheet of obsidian, and a body to die for.

No pun intended.

Calvin stepped closer and leaned in, his hands clasped behind his back. "Again, we offer our apologies for the confusion, but my pet could not help but notice your outburst inside." He nodded at Derek significantly. "She alerted us and felt we should come and take a look-see. I must say she was correct, for there seems to be something amiss here." His keen eyes clamped onto Derek like vices. "Although you are clearly undead you reek of something different as well. . . . Something that reminds me very much of were-wolf." His tone had grown dangerous and his voice low. He cut a look at Katie. "My friends and I would be very interested to know why an unregistered vampire would reek of mongrel."

His smile was gone now, replaced by a cunning gaze that scared all the color out of my face. I caught eyes with Katie, who had finally broken her trance with Paula's body and gone very still, staring wide-eyed at Derek as though he might explode at any moment.

"I don't know what you're talking about," Derek said evenly.

"Do not lie," Calvin warned. "I could bring you in right now for a registration violation, but I won't. All I want to know is why you have been keeping company with the dogs." He jerked his head at Katie.

"What do you care if I'm with the werewolves?" Derek asked, sounding much braver than I felt.

Calvin's eyes glittered. "The monarch does not think much of race traitors. She would be quite put out if we let one slip by our notice."

Derek was silent, staring back into Calvin's eyes. He seemed to realize that they weren't going to let us go without explaining ourselves.

Katie was shaking her head frantically behind Calvin, eyes pleading. I could feel her vibe screaming *no, no, no!*

Derek ignored her. I heard him breathe deeply and then say, "I hang around them because I'm part werewolf."

Calvin straightened. His eyes flared with something dangerously close to rage. "What do you mean you are part werewolf?" he spat. "You are either a mongrel or you are not."

"I'm both werewolf and vampire. I've been infected by both races."

Now the other two vampires started forward. I began to scream, but Calvin threw his arms out, stopping his friends from attacking.

"He lies!" Silas hissed. "What he says is impossible."

"It's not," Derek said calmly. "I can change."

Silence bit through the night, punctuated only by the sounds of the police sirens fading into the night. I guess we were off the hook there.

"Prove it," Calvin said.

Derek shifted his weight. "Not here."

"We will ensure that your pet is safe whilst your mind is wild," Calvin said, leering at me. "Now, prove yourself."

Katie was shaking her head again.

"No," I whispered to Derek. "Don't leave us with them."

Calvin's violet eyes hit mine. "Then we'll take him with us. He can prove himself to us in the safety of our lair."

"No!" I yelled before I could stop myself. "You're not taking Derek anywhere!"

Melissa giggled behind her gloved hand. "Come on, Cal," she said, sounding bored. "Let's just kill the little liar and have his pet for lunch. I'm starved."

"Shut up," Calvin spat. "Christ, you *just* ate!"

She sulked.

"If what he says is true," Calvin said, "he will have no issue proving himself." Then he began speaking what sounded like Russian, and Melissa and Silas's eyebrows twitched up as they surveyed Derek with renewed interest.

"Okay, fine," Melissa said. "But let's get out of here. All of these warm bodies are making my tummy hurt."

Silas rounded on her. "How can you still be hungry?"

"Shut up the both of you," Calvin said. He turned to face Derek. "Come with us to our lair and prove what you claim. If we are satisfied, we will allow you to register with our brood and then leave. If not, well . . ." He licked his lips. "We will just have to find *some-*

thing to do with you."

"And you'll let Faith go?" Derek asked.

"Indeed," Calvin said. "We do not prey on pets that are not our own . . . often."

"And Katie?"

Calvin waved his hand dismissively. "Whatever."

For a moment Derek didn't say anything. Then he turned and pried me from his shirt. He held my hand open and pressed his car keys into it, closing my fingers over them.

"I have to go with them," he said softly.

"No!" I screamed and Melissa snickered again. "No, Derek," I said softer, but still firmly. "They'll kill you."

"I don't have a choice. We can't fight them all. Not with you here."

"Yes, we can," Katie spoke up. "Come on, Derek, we can take them."

The tension in the air ratcheted up a notch, and the vampires closed their ranks; Silas let out a low hiss.

"No," Derek said loudly, warding them off. "I'll go peacefully."

I started to protest again, but Derek shushed me, sweeping his frozen hand across my cheek. "I'll change for them, show them what I am, and then I'll see you tomorrow night. It'll be fine." He pushed my hand against my chest. "But you have to go. I can't have you getting hurt. I don't want to give Lassie a reason to kill me." He grinned ruefully at me, but his jokes were wasted. I couldn't even berate him for calling Lucas names.

"No," I said desperately. "Please don't do this."

"I'll see you tomorrow night," he said, embedding his wintry eyes into mine. He took my face and kissed me softly, his lips just barely touching mine on the way to my cheek. "I love you." He said it so whisper-soft I wasn't sure I'd actually heard it.

He let go of me and turned toward the vampires. Calvin slung his arm around Derek's shoulders and gestured to the opening of the alley where a sleek silver car had pulled up. "Your chariot," he said. He turned and regarded Katie coldly, nodding at the body lying mummified at her feet. "Take care of that, would you, doggie?"

Katie's lip curled.

Melissa and Silas laughed as they slipped into the car. Calvin escorted Derek to the passenger's side and pushed him inside. He blurred to the driver seat, threw me and Katie a sardonic salute, and skidded away on the wet street.

They were gone.

It was a long time before either Katie or I spoke. We stood there quietly, listening to the *thud, thud, thud* of the club music and the beat of my heart dwindling. Tears flowed fast and hot down my frozen face, and the bitter metal of Derek's keys cut into my clenched fist as a silent reminder of his departure. At last, Katie turned to me and said, "I have to take care of this." She indicated the dried-up body of Paula Tourmaline.

I cringed, feeling a few more tears escape. "How long will it take?"

Katie shrugged vacantly. "Hour. Two tops. I have to ah . . . call someone to help. I don't really know . . ." She trailed off, staring at the body with something close to horror.

"It wasn't your fault," I said. "You were acting on instinct. He used her as a shield for God sakes."

Katie nodded, but I could tell she wasn't convinced. After a while she said, "I'll walk you to the car."

She saw me to the parking lot and kept an eye out as I unlocked Derek's frosty car with shaking hands. I sat in the driver's seat and realized, "Heather's still inside. We can't leave her."

"I'll get her on the way back," Katie said.

I let out a relieved breath. "Thank you. You'll come back to my room after . . . ?"

"Yeah." She shifted her weight as she stuck her hand into her pockets. "You'd better call Lucas."

I felt a stab of dread hit my gut like a sucker punch. "'Kay," I croaked. "Bye."

Katie gave me a silent, melancholy wave and watched as I shut the car door and started the ignition. I pulled out of the parking lot, feeling like every inch I drove was one inch farther from Derek. He'd just sacrificed himself to keep me safe. Again.

And, once more, I'd done nothing to stop it.

• • •

Dawn took millennia to arrive. I'd called Lucas and told him what happened. He'd offered to alert the pack, but since there was nothing they could do to find Derek without any leads on where the lair might be, I declined. And I'd rather the pack didn't know Derek was with the vampires. As much as I hated to admit it, their fears about Derek threatening the pack were warranted. He was unimaginably strong, and if he was wooed to the wrong side of the upcoming war, he could potentially tip the scales in favor of the vampires. The werewolves deemed the uprising an impossibility as of now, but throw Derek into the equation? They might take a second look at the situation and realize they weren't the biggest kids on the block anymore. Derek was. And if he began helping the vampires, we were all screwed.

Katie drifted off to sleep somewhere around four in the morning (she got back well after curfew, and I'd had to sneak downstairs to let her in), so I'd braved the night, and ran across the courtyard to Derek's room to wait for him in case he came home.

He didn't.

I sat on the floor next to his door, watching the sunlight from the window near his room creep along the dirty brown carpet. When the light hit my feet, I knew Derek would be gone until nighttime. I stood and went downstairs to Lucas's room. Lucas wasn't there yet, so I cuddled into his bed and attempted sleep.

Just as I was beginning to succumb to my eyelids, the door banged open and Lucas came in. I bolted upright, blinking groggily.

He strode across the room and pulled me to him with a rough jerk.

"You okay?" he asked.

I managed to nod.

"Remind me never to leave you alone again," he said. "That was a dumb thing to do, Faith. Taking a runt around all those people? Knowing there were vampires in the area?"

"I know," I said. "I screwed up, okay? Again. Big surprise."

"Look, I'm not trying to be a jerk. I just don't want you getting hurt. I'm just frustrated that you were so careless with your life, when I'm always trying to be so careful with it."

I couldn't help but smile at him in thanks. For caring so much. Even if it was in his backward pain-in-the-ass way. Lucas drew back and thumped down on the couch.

"So I guess he didn't come back?" he asked.

"No. I waited up all night." I ran my hands through my hair. "If he's with the vampires now, the pack is going to kill him."

Lucas nodded slowly.

"He could be murdering girls right now for all I know."

"Well, not *right* now," Lucas drawled. "Right now he's asleep."

I threw him a look, to which he crooked a grin.

"What did Rolf say about the uprising?" I asked. "You didn't tell him Derek might have switched sides, right?"

"Nah." He propped his legs up on a stack of books. "But he thinks we might be right. Finally. He's not going public with it, yet, but he's opening fire on the vampires, like Julian said. And if Derek registers with the vampires, the werewolves will kill him on sight. No questions asked."

"But—that's not fair. We don't know for sure that he switched. What if he's neutral?"

"Nobody's neutral. Least of all Derek. If you want me to keep him safe from the pack, then you gotta convince him to stay with us. I can't do a damn thing if he sides with the leeches."

"I'll talk to him if he comes back tonight. I'm sure I'm just overreacting."

I sighed and joined Lucas on the couch. Just as one problem had been lifted from my shoulders—convincing Rolf to believe us about the uprising—another had been dumped on me. Now I had to keep Derek away from the vampires so the pack wouldn't "accidentally" murder him.

"The vampires were talking about registering last night," I

said. "What is it?"

Lucas leaned back against the couch, looking exhausted. "Vampires are real formal about things. And the monarchs are the worst."

"Monarchs?"

"That's what they call the leader of a brood. They're basically just the biggest pansies of the group."

I snorted.

"Anyway," Lucas said, crooking a grin, too. "A vampire that travels into another's territory is supposed to greet the monarch of that area and request permission to stay in their lair or whatever. It's all a bunch of political crap. The monarchs only enforce it so that they can keep track of who they have around to manipulate."

"Great," I said. "So now Derek's going to be on that list?"

"Hopefully he'll know better than to register."

I shook my head, staring across the room at one of Lucas's artworks. The twisted, tortured form of a human body screamed in silent agony, skin wrinkling and folding like a balled-up piece of paper. Blood poured over everything. I closed my eyes from the gore, praying silently that Derek came back safe tonight.

REPAIR

U nable to sleep, Lucas and I shuffled over to Spoons for breakfast and then met Katie to help her settle into her new apartment just across campus. Afterward, Lucas said he had to meet up with some pack member to discuss "wolf business," so I decided it was time for me to really try and make amends with Heather since last night had, admittedly, been a complete disaster.

After calling three times, she finally picked up and agreed to meet me in the Oval, which was basically a glorified front lawn with an oval walkway encasing it and gorgeous old elm trees speckling the perimeter. In the fall, the Oval had been colorful and vibrant as the leaves changed to brilliant ambers and rusts, but now the lawn was frozen and barren. The trees were leafless, and the ground—snowless at the moment—was a sad shade of brown. Still, the sun was out and the sky was a spectacular shade of blue, so it was a perfect day for hot lattes on one of the many wooden benches. As I waited for Heather to, hopefully, show up, I watched a couple jogging together along the walkway. It made me miss running, so I decided to drag Lucas out with me later on, no matter how tired I was.

A few minutes passed before I spotted Heather coming toward me from the library, books in her hands and a scowl on her face. When she approached, I stood and offered her the latte from Spoons as though it was a peace offering. She stared at it for a moment and then sighed, placing her books on the bench. She took the cup and sat down.

Score. She was at least going to hear me out.

Not that I knew what to say.

"So what did you want to talk about?" Heather asked, testing the coffee.

"Well, ah . . . first I wanted to apologize for being MIA for the past few weeks. I had some . . . family issues going on and I . . ." Derek was pretty much family, so I didn't consider this a lie.

"Stuff with your dad?" she asked quietly.

I swallowed hard. "No," I said, keeping my voice measured. I never even spoke to my dad. I'd almost forgotten I'd told Heather about him. It was a testament to how much I trusted her that I ever did.

"I don't really want to get into the details," I said. "But I just want you to know that I'm sorry, and that I hope we can still be friends. Or at least try to be."

Heather's smile was warmer than the coffee in my lap. "Sure," she said. "I understand. Things happen. I just wish you'd told me what was going on at the time. I was worried about you. I couldn't even get you on your phone."

Because I'd been ignoring her calls. I'd just had no energy to lie to her, and no idea how to tell her the truth. I still didn't.

"Sorry," I said again.

She shrugged. "I'm just glad everything's okay." She hesitated. "Everything *is* okay, right?"

Something inside me wrenched at the thought of what might have happened to Derek last night, but I managed to keep it off of my face. I nodded.

"Good." She smiled wanly and took a small sip of her coffee. "This is excellent," she said.

I nodded silently again as I composed what I'd come here to

say. Asking Heather to give me another chance had been the easy part. Now came the real issue.

"So," I started, not knowing how she'd take this. "About last night."

She averted her eyes, looking out onto the yard.

"Heather, you should really be careful," I said gently. "I'm not your mom or whatever, so I can't tell you what to do, obviously, but, it worried me to see you so . . . upset." And high.

"It was just fun."

"But do you even know those girls? They could be trouble." They could also be involved with murdering vampires. Damn, I wished I could tell her!

She remained silent. I knew my argument was lame, but I didn't know what else I could tell her without revealing the truth.

"Pete is garbage," I said. "He's lower than low."

"I know," she mumbled.

"So why are you letting him have this power over you?"

"Because I still love him."

"You love garbage?" I asked, letting a little levity into my tone. She snorted. "I guess so."

I sighed and slung my arm around her shoulders. She leaned into me, sniffling and smiling at the same time. "We're both messes," I said.

"How are *you* a mess? You always have everything so together."

"Ha!" I laughed and shook my head into her shoulder. *If only she knew.*

"I feel so stupid," Heather said. "That I let him get to me that way." She groaned and covered her face in her hands. "Thank you for having Katie stay to take me home. Who knows what could have happened otherwise."

I shrugged. "So you won't see them again?"

She pulled away, wiping her eyes with her gloves. "God, no. If my parents ever found out, seriously, they would send me to a nunnery or something."

I giggled.

"Plus," she continued. "You know with the serial killer still out there, we should all be extra careful, not extra stupid."

Heather stood and tossed her empty coffee in the trash beside us.

"Well, I have to go buy my books for this semester," she said, pulling her gloves on. "Do you want to come? We can talk about dickhead boys—like Pete—" She smiled ruefully and I puffed a laugh. "And then go shopping for new clothes. I don't know about you, but I need some heavy-duty boots for this arctic weather."

I'd planned on spending the rest of the day with Lucas, but suddenly, spending it with Heather sounded like the best idea in the world. I'd wanted more normality in my life, and here it was.

• • •

When I returned to Lucas's room—carrying several shopping bags and a smile I felt down to my soul—it was almost dusk. He was at his desk registering for classes. When I told him where I'd been, he seemed genuinely happy that I'd taken time to be with Heather. Secretly, I think he liked my little human things. Not-so-secretly, I did, too.

I joined him at the desk and registered for classes with him. We tried to arrange our schedules so that we'd have some of the same classes—all in the late afternoon so we'd have the mornings to sleep.

I decided to take a photography course in addition to all of the math and history and other boring crap I was forced to take. Lucas registered for it too, even though he didn't care much for photography. I think he was mostly concerned about keeping me in sight.

Afterward, we sat on the floor playing Slap Jack and waiting for the night to come, when I thought of something that had been bugging me since Calvin had said it. "Lucas, what does 'pet' mean?" I asked as I put down a king of diamonds. I decided to just blurt out the question without preamble with the hope of startling the answer out of him.

But werewolves, as I'd learned, weren't so easy to scare.

He threw down a three of clubs and paused, looking up at me. "You mean a vampire pet?"

"Yeah," I said and tossed my card.

"Some vampires are assigned humans to quench their thirst. They call them pets."

"What do you mean, *assigned*?"

"The monarchs will give humans out to their subjects if they do something that pleases them."

"And the vampires force the humans to stay and be bitten? But won't that kill them?"

"They have ways around biting," he said. "Sometimes they siphon the blood out with needles, sometimes they cover their teeth, or use their nails to make the incision. And yeah, sometimes they just kill them."

"That's so horrible," I said, rigid with disgust.

"Yeah, well. You asked." Lucas slapped the pile again, drawing the cards up into his hands.

"So how is a pet any different than a blood bitch?"

Lucas flicked down a four of clubs. "Well, first off, blood bitches don't give blood to the vampires. And blood bitches are free agents. They can come and go whenever they want—for the most part anyway. But a pet is like a slave. They're stuck with their vampire for as long as they want them."

I listened to the music playing in the background, taking in a soft rock melody I'd never heard before. "So are there any were-wolves that drink vampire blood?" I asked.

Lucas's face shadowed. "Are you crazy? It tastes like shit."

I felt my eyebrows shoot up with a smile tugging on my lips. "What? You've tried it?"

"Not *tried* it. When you've killed as many vampires as I have, it's only natural that their blood's gonna get in your mouth. It's disgusting and wrong. Our blood isn't meant to mix. But even so, there's no reason for us to drink it. Vampire blood doesn't give us any abilities like it does for humans. And it doesn't make us high no matter how much we ingest, and believe me, I've had a lot."

"Ew. Remind me not to kiss you anymore."

He leaned over and pressed a kiss on my lips so swiftly I hardly knew it happened.

I smiled at the roguish look on his face. "So no werewolf blood bitches?" I asked.

"I'm not gonna pretend like it doesn't happen. But it's rare and usually only occurs when both parties have something to gain. Like a trade-off kind of thing. And no blood is exchanged, since we don't have any use for it. They trade other stuff. Well, were-wolves aren't allowed to kill humans, right? So the vampire might say, okay I'll murder this dude for you, if you go out during the day and get this thing for me. Get it?"

I nodded. "But, that's not allowed is it? Rolf wouldn't let you guys work with vampires."

"Damn straight he wouldn't. Any werewolf that's found aiding the vampires is sentenced to death." He slapped the deck and gathered up the cards.

"Calvin said something about me last night," I said cautiously.

Lucas looked up, alarm written all over his face. "What'd he say?"

"That I was special like his pet." I dropped a card and slapped it, taking only two measly little cards into my pile.

"Oh, he was probably referring to your otherness," he said, relaxing.

"They can sense that stuff?"

"Some of them."

"So Paula had a gift then," I said. "Maybe she was like me!" But as quickly as the excitement came, it passed. "Oh, no. I could feel her energy. With Yvette I can't read her vibe. And anyway, she's dead now."

"Might've been a telepath," he said offhandedly. "Mind reader."

"Those exist too?" I said, equally nonchalant. Nothing sur-prised me anymore.

"Sure," he said. "Met a few in my time. Granted, that was mostly in the seventeenth century, but still. They must still exist. *You* exist, right?"

I looked down at myself as though checking to see. "Seems like it. And besides, I can sort of read minds. Like, when an emotion is really strong, I can sometimes hear a thought behind it, or figure out the reasoning."

"Okay, so what if I try to send you a thought. Can you hear it?"

"I don't know. Sometimes I get complete thoughts, but I don't know if you could *send* me one. Try it."

Lucas met my gaze levelly, expression calm and intent, but masked, which made me really want to know what he was sending me. I let the sparks between us fuse, hoping I'd be able to hear something, but all I got was a whiff of curiosity and amusement. I pushed deeper, willing myself to hear something.

Frustrated, I shrugged, breaking off the connection.

"We'll keep practicing," Lucas said. "What about the blocking thing we talked about? We haven't even tried it."

"Try it now." Maybe this I could do, at least.

"I, ah . . . don't really know . . ."

I'd never seen Lucas flustered, but it was terribly cute. "I don't know how you do it either," I said. "With Derek it feels like a wall in his head. Completely impenetrable. Maybe just visualize a brick wall, or something."

"I can do that."

I sucked in a deep breath. "Ready?"

"Yeah."

I ignited our connection and felt Lucas's emotions consume me like a category five tornado. Determination. Confusion. Disappointment.

Nice try, babe.

I released the connection, wondering if he'd heard me.

"Damn," Lucas grumbled. "Do it again."

We did the exercise over and over again for fifteen minutes straight. Finally, on the last time, Lucas managed to keep me out. It was a weak form of the block in Derek's head. More like a chain-link fence than a brick wall, but it kept me out and I let the connection drop.

"Yes!" Lucas shouted triumphantly, flinging his card across the room.

I laughed. "Pretty good."

"*Pretty* good? That was an impenetrable wall if I ever saw one—felt one. Whatever."

I laughed again, shaking my head. "You're right. It was impassible. I never could have gotten in if you hadn't let me."

He sent me a skeptical look. "How'd Yvette and Rolf figure this out, anyway? What a pain."

"She probably tried to make him do something and he didn't want to so badly that he blocked her out of instinct. Yvette said it takes practice."

"Yeah, well, at least they're the only ones who know about this, right? Could you imagine the whole pack blocking you out while they were changed?"

I nodded, but felt a frown between my eyebrows. "I don't know if Yvette is the only one who knows, though."

"What do you mean?"

"Remember Kevin? The other dude with the sense?"

Lucas nodded.

"Well, the vampires kidnapped him and probably tortured all

of his secrets out of him before they killed him. There might be some of them who know how to block me."

"But you can't control them, anyway so don't worry about it."

I wasn't so sure. I didn't like the vampires knowing about my powers. Even if I couldn't control them, the werewolves were susceptible, and I didn't want this blocking info to get out.

"Let's try it again," Lucas said.

"No, let's forget it for now. I'm tired." Really I was just keen on talking about vampires some more. "So about Paula," I said.

"Back to this . . . ," he grumbled and crossed the room to collect his cards.

"Yes. Back to this. Melissa drank like, all of Paula's blood. If she did have a power, does that mean Melissa will get them now?"

"How the hell would I know? Do I look like a vampire?"

I ignored him and worked it out in my head. "Well, I guess not," I said, answering my own question. "Vincent had some of my blood, and he couldn't use the sense or control you."

We were both silent for a while as Lucas continued to destroy me at Slap Jack.

"You know when I first started feeling them?" I said softly. "The vibes, I mean?"

"Hmm?" Lucas slapped the pile, leaving me with one lonely little card left.

"It was right after the surgery when I had to remove the bullet." I looked up at him and he put his hand on my thigh, right over the scar. He knew the bullet I meant. The one my stepdad sent flying into my flesh in a drunken rage. "I was lying in the recovery room," I said, "all doped up on morphine and Derek walked in. As soon as he got close, I felt this warm energy smother me. It was so sweet and bright . . . like something golden, I don't know. I told him about it and he just smiled at me and told me I was loopy from the drugs. I believed him at first, but the vibes stayed even after the drugs wore off."

I glanced up and saw that Lucas was nodding like this all made perfect sense. "You were thirteen right?"

"Yeah."

"Most supernatural abilities manifest at puberty. It was probably a coincidence that it happened after your surgery."

I put down my last card, and Lucas slapped it up. I slumped, defeated, and he gave me a smug smile as he reshuffled the deck.

I looked out the window and saw the ashen sky smothering the sun. "It's close to dusk. We should go up to his room to wait for him."

"Why don't you just call him?" he suggested stiffly. He stood and tossed me my cell phone.

I gulped and pressed the speed dial, hoping against all the hope in the world that Derek's mellow voice would sound through the receiver.

It didn't.

Instead, I heard the bold, slightly accented voice of Calvin Carnelian.

JUST A PULL

D erek Turner's phone," Calvin said, sounding a lot like a hotel receptionist. I expected him to ask me if I wanted a mint on my pillow next.

"Where's Derek?" I asked.

Lucas's gaze was like a razor blade slicing through my throat as he whipped around on me. My breath caught.

"Oh, is this Faith?" Calvin asked, seemingly overjoyed to hear me. "How sweet! Derek is lucky to own a pet so eager for him that she cannot even wait for him to wake."

I sneered at the phone and opened my mouth to say something snotty, but Lucas motioned for me to be calm. Although I could feel the spark of anger he felt at hearing Calvin's words.

"Can you please tell him to call me when he wakes up?" I asked in the nicest voice I could muster.

"Certainly," Calvin said. "Anything else you wish me to relay to your master?"

Again, I started to say something bitchy, but Lucas put his hand on my knee.

"Just tell him I'm waiting for him in the courtyard."

"It shall be done. Farewell, Faith Reynolds." He hung up, leaving me staring at the receiver and wondering how he knew my last name.

Lucas and I went downstairs into the snow to wait for Derek. It was freezing and I let Lucas wrap his coat around me and button it up. Snowflakes buzzed around our heads like gnats, landing on my head and cheeks.

Before long, a silver car pulled up beside us. Lucas unbuttoned me from his coat and clasped my hand.

"That's them," I said, recognizing the car.

"Stay behind me. If anything goes wrong, run inside and don't let anyone in. In fact, maybe you should just wait in—"

"No," I cut him off firmly. "I want to be here."

Lucas made a low annoyed sound in the back of his throat and pushed me behind his body.

I watched from around his waist as the back door of the car popped open and Derek emerged. His face was flushed, and he wore a giant smile, fangs glistening. He leaned down and said, "See ya later, guys."

He shut the door and strutted toward us as the silver car buzzed off.

Lucas relaxed slightly, but remained stiff—as though he was holding himself back.

"Hey," Derek said lightly. "What's up?"

I stepped around Lucas. "How was your *night*?"

"Great!" Derek said. "The vampires are really cool. Way nicer than the werewolves, no offense."

Lucas shot me an I-told-you-so look.

"Derek," I said. "What are you talking about? They practically kidnapped you!"

"Yeah, but once I showed them that I wasn't lying, they were really, really cool. They took me to their house—lair, whatever—which is basically this huge underground mansion that looks like a dump from the outside, but is really sweet inside. And everyone was so—"

"Ugh, Derek!" I yelled. "Vampires are not cool or nice or sweet. They're evil, bloodsucking murderers!"

"Not all of them," Derek said. "Some of them are nice. Melissa is so—"

"No, they're not," I cut in. "They just want to get you on their side."

"*Side?* What side?"

"There's an uprising about to start and they want you because you're powerful and unique."

Lucas put his hand on mine and shushed me, probably because I sounded slightly hysterical.

"Yes," Derek said to Lucas. "Thank you. She's being crazy, right?"

"No," Lucas said. "You're crazy if you think the vampires are your friends."

Derek scoffed. "Whatever. You guys don't know what you're talking about." He began walking away. I started after him, but Lucas held on to my hand, preventing me from moving.

"Don't bother," Lucas said. "He's chosen his fate."

I pried my hand away. "I can't let him become like them."

"He's a leech," Lucas said. "When are you going to accept that?"

I squared my shoulders against him.

"I'll accept it when it's true."

And I spun away from him. As I walked away, I could feel his vibe roiling with a tangle of mixed-up emotions. Jealousy being the major one. But there was hurt too, and of course my power chose this moment to kick in and allow me to read the reason why: I'd chosen to go with Derek over him. Frustration. He was being controlling again and he hated it, but also feared for my safety with Derek. Stubbornness, as he warred with himself to go after me.

I pulled out of his head, gasping. For once, I was glad he kept his distance. I needed to concentrate on Derek right now. His involvement with the vampires had to end if we had any hope of stopping the uprising and the murders. I went inside his building and knocked on his door. He answered immediately, looking less than happy to see me.

"Come to yell at me some more?" he asked.

I wrinkled my nose at him and went inside. "Only if you're going to be an idiot some more."

Derek shut the door and rounded on me, putting his hands on his hips.

"I don't see the problem with the vampires," he said. "You all had me so scared of them, but they're really nice—especially Melissa." His lips tilted up in a goofy grin and I swatted him.

"Always a sucker for the Megan Fox look-alikes," I said.

Derek wiggled his eyebrows at me and said, "That's why I like you so much."

I swatted him again and sat cross-legged on his bed. "Seriously, though, you can't hang around them anymore."

Derek rolled his eyes, and I caught his sleeve as he moved past me.

I dipped my head down to catch his gaze and said, "One of them tried to kill me, in case you forgot."

"I didn't forget. But they're not all like Vincent. Calvin is like, supersmooth. I swear he's like James Bond. And Silas knows how to speak every language known to man. Ancient Egyptian!"

"I don't like it, Derek," I said, unimpressed. "They're danger-ous. They *kill* people—think about how many girls have been found dead even since we got here. And they'll keep killing."

"They kill to survive. It's not like they want to."

"Please," I scoffed. "Now you're going to paint them as martyrs? Did you forget about how Vincent tortured us outside the barn? How he tossed that car around and watched us scream? If he'd just been having a meal, why didn't he do it quickly? Spare us the pain?"

He looked away.

"Promise me you won't see them again," I urged.

He looked away with a noncommittal grunt.

I grabbed his face and made him look at me. "Promise me, Derek. If not because they're murderers, then because one of them might hurt me. Even if it's just by accident."

"I might hurt you," He said quietly. "Lucas might too. Do you want us to go away?"

"That's different." I let my hands fall and folded them across my chest. "I know you guys wouldn't hurt me."

"I can't speak for Bingo, but I would never hurt you."

"Stop calling him names."

Derek's lips drew up around his fangs in a victorious leer. He moved to stand by his boarded-up window, leaning against the frame. "Derek," I said, fixing him with a penetrative stare. "You didn't register with the vampires, did you?"

He scratched the back of his neck. "Why?"

"*Did* you?"

"No," he said. "They tried to make me, but I told them that I wouldn't because I wasn't a true vampire. They weren't happy about it, but they didn't press the issue."

"Good," I said, exhaling. "Lucas said that his uprising theory has finally caught on with the pack and they're stepping up their hunting to cut the vampires' numbers back."

"Faith, there *is* no vampire uprising. You guys are just being melodramatic."

"How else do you explain all the dead girls?" I challenged. "And Vincent specifically mentioned an army of undead."

"Maybe he was lying."

"He wasn't."

"Well, even so, what about the humans? They'd just let the vampires start eating them?"

I sighed, exasperated. "I don't know their exact plan, Derek! I just know that they're planning a war on the werewolves and that you're going to get yourself caught up in it if you're not careful. You side with the vampires, and it's over. The werewolves won't stand a chance. Which is why they'll murder you first chance they get."

Derek went and flopped down on the couch. "Yeah, well, do me a favor and stop worrying about it, all right? I'll be fine. I can handle myself."

Everything inside me shouted to keep pushing him, but I knew doing so would only make him dig in harder. Derek was like that. My best chance at getting him to change his mind was to somehow make him see for himself that the vampires were evil.

"Do you have to leave?" Derek asked.

I forced a smile and said, "I'm yours for the night."

Derek beamed like the sunshine. "We should go out and do something. Something fun."

"I don't know," I said. "Last time we tried that, you almost ate a club full of people and smashed a dude through the bar. Maybe we should just stay in. We've got class tomorrow anyway."

"Well, my classes aren't until after dark, but I'm fine staying in," Derek said. "Just so long as we're together."

I nudged him with my shoulder. "Always."

He scooted closer to me on the couch and I shivered as his leg touched mine. "Wanna know something cool?" he said, his eyes lighting up like neon.

"Sure," I said, though I was a little wary.

"Silver doesn't bother me like werewolves. And if you try to stake me, it just goes right through like nothing. Hardly even hurts."

I gaped. "They tried to kill you?"

"No," Derek said, shooting me a look. "I'm not talking about them anymore. This is stuff I've tried on my own."

I rolled my eyes. "Great. Attempting suicide. That's awesome, Derek."

He ignored me. "I've just been testing myself like we did in California. Discovering my limits. I have to tell Rolf everything I find out, but it's fun to do anyway. And sometimes Katie helps me."

"Katie?" I asked, thrown.

"Uh-huh, we meet up sometimes and run and talk. She's a chemist, did you know that? I gave her some of my blood, and she took it to the CSU lab to test. Actually, I have to give her another sample soon, because that one got lost or broke or something." He shrugged. "She's funny anyway . . . helps me forget about the bad stuff. Helps me figure myself out."

Something here didn't make sense. "When did you meet with Katie? We were in California for five days and before that you were sleeping. I don't get it."

Derek's eyes shifted toward me. Something was hiding in them. I tested his vibe and instantly felt the stink of deception.

"Derek, what aren't you telling me?"

He bit his lip, which was actually a scary sight because of his fangs.

"She flew out to California," he said. "I—I called her."

"You *called* her?" I let this sink in for a moment. "Then how was she there to pick us up at the airport?"

"She left early," he said simply. He took in my open-mouthed face and placed his fingers under my chin, closing it. "It's no big deal. She was just helping me out."

"I could have helped you."

"Believe me, I would have rather it was you, but you were kind of busy with the boyfriend. Plus, I didn't want you getting hurt. Katie's more resilient."

I was put out for a moment and then I regrouped.

"What else have you found out?" I asked.

Derek played with a strand of my hair. The blackish-brown of it was abrupt against his albino fingers—like he was holding a tiny black snake.

"We haven't really discovered any new abilities, but we've been testing my limits on the ones I know I have. Like, with running, I can sprint at close to two hundred miles per hour for a good fifteen minutes before I start slowing down. And I can throw a pickup truck about the length of a football field or I could hold it for a couple hours without weakening. I can see in the dark even without changing, I can smell things from miles away, hear through the phone." He winked deviously. "And some other stuff," he said smiling proudly at my astounded expression.

"Wow," I said weakly. "When did you figure all this out? We usually spent the nights together in California."

"Not all night. I got bored when you went back to him. Plus, I needed someone to ring in the New Year with. We killed a cougar."

I laughed weakly, not entirely sure he was joking.

Derek smiled and bent his head to inhale the lock of hair he held in his hand. He moved closer, sniffing down my neck. He groaned.

"Derek," I said. "What are you doing?"

"Breathing."

I put my hand up against his face, pushing him away gently. "Well, stop it," I said, unnerved.

"No way," he said, inhaling deeply. "You smell fantastic."

I pulled away from him. "Stop it. What's gotten into you?"

He looked away, suddenly ashamed. "I—I drank blood last night."

I gasped. "What! You *killed* someone?"

"He was already dead."

"Derek! How could you?"

"Don't judge me," Derek said, fire in his tone. "You don't know what it was like over there. They were all staring at me, asking me if I had the blood crave. I told them I didn't want to do that, but they held the body right in front of me. I didn't need to smell it to know how bad I wanted it. And after seeing Paula last night, too, I was already revved-up."

"But you controlled yourself then," I argued, aghast.

"That's because you were there," Derek said. "I had to control myself to keep you safe. And I didn't look at the body, didn't smell the blood." He swallowed hard, and I watched his Adam's apple bob up and down. "At the lair I knew it would be all right if I let my guard down. Nobody would get hurt, and the human was already dead. If I drank from him, it would be . . . accepted."

"How could you?" I whispered again, but he didn't seem to hear me. His eyes had gone all funny and his voice was deep like the strum of a cello.

"I inhaled," Derek said. "I smelled the blood and it was like . . . like nothing I'd ever experienced. Hunger times a million and I just . . . snapped. I felt something take over inside of me. I had to drink it. I *needed* it. Not just because it tasted so good, but because it made me feel better—stronger."

I shook my head, unable to believe any of this was actually happening.

"We have to get you help," I said. "We have to get you to Lucas—he'll know what to do." I jumped off of the couch and headed for the door.

"I don't want help." He was in front of me before I'd taken a step. I jumped back and tripped over my feet. "I just need a little sip." His voice was sweet, cajoling. "I won't take a lot. Just a swallow and I'll be satisfied."

"Don't even think about it," I warned. "Lucas will kill you."

"Only if he finds out. And he'll only find out if you tell him."

He came closer and stroked my throat with feathery fingers, breathing me in like a starving man with a steak.

"You'll turn me," I said, thinking fast. "How're you going to explain that?"

"I don't have venom," Derek reminded me calmly. "I can take a pull. . . . The dog will never have to know."

"He'll know because I'll tell him!" My fingers touched the doorknob and I yanked it, but Derek's hand closed over mine. I was trapped. Trapped in a room with a bloodthirsty viran. His face was a breath away, eyes so hungry they were almost hypnotizing. So I did the only thing I could think of. I lurched forward and kissed him.

At first, he recoiled with the shock of it, but then he grabbed me up, clutching me close to him and kissing me back fiercely. It was a horrible thing to do. I was basically cheating on Lucas, but he had to understand. I was distracting Derek's blood crave with an entirely different craving.

Or so I thought.

Derek's fangs scraped against my lips and along my jaw as he made his way down to my neck.

"No," I said. "Derek, stop it."

He was breathing hard now.

"Just a pull . . . ," he begged. "I can't stand it. . . . I have to."

BLOOD BANK

D erek put his hand at the nape of my neck, holding me immobile as he tilted my head to the side. My pulse stuttered as he bent his head toward my throat. I swallowed hard, closing my eyes tight as if that would help. I felt his lips, his breath cooling my skin. My heart pounded faster and faster, practically buzzing in my chest.

Then he spread his lips and pressed his teeth against the vein at the bottom of my throat. Without any preamble, his teeth sunk into my flesh.

There was no pain. None. It was so odd. My brain was telling me there should be pain, but there was nothing but dull pressure. His mouth moved, and I felt him pull on the wound.

Something stirred inside me, something vaguely pleasing, but frightening at the same time. Like the feeling of riding a roller coaster. Vertigo.

It was like kissing times a thousand. My legs went numb, and I held on to Derek as he dragged. Everything went away. It was euphoria of the sweetest kind, and the longer he went on, the more I wanted. *Drink it all, take everything, just never let this stop....*

Stop....

Stop.

Stop, stop stop! I thought frantically, coming back to myself. He was taking too much. He was going to kill me! I tried to ignite the connection, but there was that wall again, blocking me. *Help!*

I beat my fists against his back, yelling because I was so angry and scared and lots of other things I couldn't really understand.

I dug my fingers into his face, but they were going numb from blood loss and fell ineffectually against his shoulders. He gathered me closer in his strong arms, growling deeply, words I could no longer hear. It felt so good, so perfect. . . . It was almost worth death. This must have been how his venom worked. It wasn't a paralyzing agent; it inoculated the victim so they didn't even know they were being killed. And it was working spectacularly. I was almost about to say to hell with it and just let him get it over with, when the door banged and splintered.

Derek unstuck himself from my throat and looked up, letting out a sound that might have been a hiss. His cheeks were light pink, almost the color of actual skin and his chin dripped with my blood. His razor teeth were coated with it, eyes completely blackened with the crave. I'd never been more afraid of him.

The door banged again and flew open. Lucas stood in the doorway, his face livid. He lunged at Derek just as he threw me to the floor. Lucas punched him straight in the nose and sent him sprawling. Derek was up in an instant, bleeding from his nostrils. His eyes went from black to white in hyperspeed and then his body shook violently. I clapped my hand to my bleeding neck and began inching toward the open door. God help us all if anyone saw this.

"Don't you dare change," Lucas warned. "I swear to God, I'll kill you."

Derek's white eyes flickered around the room, maybe looking for a way out. I clambered up from the floor and pushed the broken door shut.

"You could have killed her," Lucas yelled. "Do you get that, runt? Killed her! For your disgusting blood crave! I oughta snap your leech neck right now." He started forward and Derek cringed. His eyes had grown bluer again. They filled with anguish—regret.

He looked to me, ashen. "I'm so sorry," he whispered.

"You don't talk to her anymore!" Lucas roared. "You don't even look at her. You can't be trusted."

Derek looked as if he was about to cry.

"Lucas," I said quietly. I swallowed because my voice was hoarse. "It wasn't his fault. They fed him blood last night. The crave was too much for him."

Lucas spun around and gaped at me, aghast. "You're defending him? After he all but killed you?"

Derek's body seemed to deflate as he looked at me. I saw a few tears leak out of his eyes as he shook his head, denying Lucas's accusations. That he was actually *crying*...

I wasn't thrilled with what Derek had just done and it definitely crossed the line, but when he was looking at me like that, the anger just melted away. He'd only just woken up with this new body and its sick needs; it only made sense that he would have some weak moments. "Derek would never kill me," I said firmly. "He just lost control for a second. You lose control sometimes, too."

Lucas looked like he couldn't quite believe what he was hearing.

"We should take him up to Gould," I said, getting to my feet. "He needs help. Rolf said that if the crave got to be too strong, we should take him to Gould, so that's what we're going to do."

Lucas was still unconvinced. I could feel the raging energy coiling out from his body like flames.

"Look," I said calmly. "I'm not hurt. His bite didn't affect me." Besides the whole arousal thing. "But we have to get him help. I'm not going to abandon him just because he's having a hard time."

Lucas cursed and kicked a piece of the doorjamb across the room.

He turned on Derek and got in his face.

"This is the last time I forgive your ass for trying to kill her," he growled. "Once more, and you're mine." He grabbed Derek's shirt and jerked it. "Got it?"

Derek looked up, hate radiating from his every pore. "Got it."

• • •

The ride up to Gould was a silent one. Nobody spoke the entire two hours. I could feel the tension vibrating in the oppressively miniscule space of Lucas's car like a level ten earthquake.

Or maybe that was my leg jiggling against the seat.

Or maybe it was the two boys in the car repressing the urge to change and kill each other.

Or maybe it was my heart trying desperately not to break in two.

Regardless, I'd never been happier to see the werewolf mansion, even if it was at one o'clock in the morning. Together, Derek, Lucas and I, walked up the stone steps and stopped in front of the tall polished doors.

"Let me do the talking," Lucas said. He rounded on the two of us. "Okay?"

"Fine," I said. Derek just nodded with a jerk.

We went into the cozy living room and found Yvette sitting by a low fire, reading. I was a little thrown by this. I'd expected everyone to be fast asleep. And where was Rolf? Yvette folded her book in her lap and looked up when we entered.

"Lucas," she said. "What brings you and your friends so late?"

"Where's Rolf?" he said roughly.

Yvette's smile fixated. "Hunting." Her eyes flickered very briefly to Derek, and I wondered if he was actually planning something to do with him. "I was waiting up for him," she said. "Is there anything I can help you with?"

Lucas debated for a moment and then said, "Derek needs blood."

Yvette's black eyebrows rose, and she nodded slowly. "I wondered how long it would take for the crave to consume him."

"It didn't *consume* him," I said before I could stop myself.

Lucas shot me a look, and I quieted down.

"Please, don't fight," Yvette said. "It's nothing to be ashamed of. He cannot control what he is." She turned to Derek and said, "Tell me what you feel. Is it a constant nuisance, easily overcome? Or is it a full blood crave?"

Derek cast a look at Lucas and then said, "More like a nuisance, I guess. I can control it until I smell the blood. Then I can't anymore."

"I see," Yvette said. Her eyes turned sharp. "How many have you killed?"

"I never killed anyone."

"Then how is it that you have tasted blood? Are you able to control yourself once you have tasted it?"

"No," Derek said. "I mean, yeah. I can stop if I want to. I don't need much, but having none is like torture now that I've had it." He threw a look at me and winced.

Yvette's eyes swept me up and down, taking in my blood-stained shirt and the puncture wounds on my neck.

"Oh my," she said sadly. "Yes, you do require aid." She stood and put her book on the table beside her. "Faith, would you like to come with me into the kitchen to get cleaned up?" The way her eyes blazed into mine made it clear she wanted me to say yes, so I nodded. I did want to get cleaned up, after all. "Lovely," Yvette said. She turned to Lucas. "And I'll call Nolan. Both of you wait here."

She ushered me into the kitchen, leaving Lucas and Derek to glower at each other in the living room. The kitchen was gigantic—about the size of my mom's apartment in San Diego. A low light filtered in from the breakfast nook in the back, making the granite countertops sparkle in shades of yellow.

I leaned my back against the center island, folding my hands behind me self-consciously. "Who is Nolan?"

"Nora's brother. He works at Poudre Valley Hospital. He is our blood contact."

"Blood contact?"

"He works in the blood bank," she clarified. "He smuggles free blood to us when we are in need. We usually only use it for injured humans we can't bring to the hospital. This is a little unorthodox, but if Nolan is willing, I'll have him send you a suitable supply for the times when Derek's craving overcomes him."

"Thank you," I said, meaning it completely. This was such a sensible solution to what I'd seen as an impossible problem. Donated blood. Perfect.

Yvette went to the pantry and produced a bottle of cleaning agent and a towel. "Shirt off," she directed and went to the sink to wet the towel. I obeyed, feeling rather odd without my shirt, and handed it to her. She began spraying it down, eyes intent on her work.

"So," I said, wondering why she'd brought me in here. "What's . . . ah, what's up?"

"You let the hybrid bite you. Are you sure that's smart?"

"I didn't let him," I said, outraged by the accusation. "He kind of forced me."

"I see. And his bite had no effect on you?"

"No," I said, feeling the wounds on my neck absently. "I guess not." I wasn't about to admit to the part where I'd actually liked it—not even to myself.

"Interesting," she mused. She rinsed my shirt under the sink, staining the water pink. "Rolf will be interested as well."

Right because, Rolf needed to know absolutely everything about Derek so he could try to find some reason to kill him. He wasn't going to be thrilled about this development, but since I was relatively unharmed, I didn't think he'd find cause to hurt Derek.

"Here," Yvette said, handing me back my damp, but clean, shirt.

"Thanks," I said, tugging it on with a shiver.

"You'll want to be more careful around the hybrid," she said. "I know he seems tame, but he is still young. Their mood swings are quite abrupt."

"Okay," I said. Then I smiled, remembering something. "He wants to be called a viran, actually."

Yvette smiled as well. "All right." She handed me a gauze strip soaked in hydrogen peroxide for my neck, and I pressed it to the cuts, wincing. It was a small wonder that I'd only now been bitten by something. "Hey, Yvette?" I asked slowly.

She settled herself on one of the barstools across from me and leaned her cheek on her hand, regarding me warily. "Yes?"

"Why didn't you ever let Rolf infect you?"

Darkness crossed Yvette's face, and she hugged her arms around her slim body. "He never infected me because I didn't want the curse."

I leaned in closer. Finally, someone else who shared my views on this. "You didn't want to live with him forever?" I asked.

Yvette smiled softly, but it didn't seem genuine. "Who wouldn't want to live for eternity with the love of their life?"

The same argument I'd been having with myself. I decided to play devil's advocate and asked, "Then why didn't you have him infect you?"

She sighed as if she'd been through this a thousand times. But, then again, maybe she had. "Because I don't want to lose my mind," she said firmly. "I don't want to kill and fight and live in torment."

"But, everyone says it only lasts a few years and then it gets better."

"Better, but not gone."

I pressed my lips together, nodding. "I get it," I said. "I don't want Lucas to infect me either. It's not a life I want for myself."

Yvette's defensive demeanor relaxed. She leaned forward on the countertop again. "And have you discussed what Lucas wants?"

I almost laughed out loud at that. "Oh, no way. He'd freak out if I even mentioned it."

"Are you sure that's how he feels?"

"I—I guess so." I hadn't really thought he'd be all 'werewolves rock!' like Katie. He got supermoody whenever we even mentioned the supernatural, so talking about me becoming one? Not on the menu.

Yvette leaned in even closer, voice low and fervent when she spoke. "Tell him to try living without you for a few weeks. Tell him to imagine all the while that you're dead. That there will never be another kiss, another smile . . . another night together. Tell him to picture your funeral, your body reduced to ashes and scattered in the wind. Tell him that this will be his life forevermore: a broken entity whose other half will never return to him. And once he's done all that, ask him again if he wants to infect you." She looked down at the counter. "I think you'll be surprised by the answer."

So that was Yvette and Rolf's existence. I studied her profile as she stared away from me, feeling tremendous pity for her. But as sorry as I felt for her, I felt even worse for Rolf—which was surprising, since I pretty much detested him. Yvette was the one who got to live out her life with her match. Rolf, on the other hand would live endlessly without her.

It hit me then, that *Lucas* would be the one tormented forever. He would be the one without his match. Once I died, I would be released from the pain of losing him.

But my Lucas . . . how could I ever do that to him?

"Go," Yvette said suddenly.

I jerked out of my thoughts, surprised by the harshness of her voice.

"I must call Nolan," she said, clearing her throat.

I left the darkened kitchen, giving one last glance at Yvette's hunched form, her eyes faraway and dripping with silent tears. As I stood in the doorway, I had the surreal, terrifying sensation that I was watching myself twenty years from now, crying alone in a kitchen. Knowing with unerring certainty that one day, I would lose my match to death. And he would lose me.

I went out into the living room. It was all I could do to keep myself from rushing over to Lucas and having him bite me right there, I felt so bad for him. But deep inside, I still knew it wasn't what I wanted. The whole thing was confusing and terrible. Becoming a werewolf just to keep my boyfriend happy wasn't a good reason to do it. But the thought of how sad he'd be when I died . . .

A sudden thought washed over me like a bucket of ice water as I stood watching Lucas stare vacantly out the large window of the living room.

What if I was giving myself a little too much credit, here? What if Lucas *wouldn't* be all that broken up when I died? Sure, if the tables were turned and I had to live for eternity without my other half, I'd turn into a walking pity party. But would Lucas? He was the one who always said that relationships weren't meant to last for eternity. Maybe he'd be sad for a bit and then get over it; move on with some newer, younger chick.

The thought should have made me feel better, but only made me angry and jealous of this made-up young chick (whom I pictured looking very much like Heidi Klum). I visualized myself in sixty years lying in a hospital bed, too old and sick to even feed myself. And there was Lucas. Still as gorgeous as ever, flirting with Doctor Barbie right in front of me because I was too blind and too deaf to notice.

I glowered at his back, knowing somewhere inside that I was being ridiculous and petty, but I was unable to stop the fantasy from playing itself out. There I was, dying, and Lucas already had his next girlfriend lined up.

Bastard.

"Are you trying to use the Force?" Derek asked, slight amusement in his tone.

I started out of my inner Lucas hate-fest and shot Derek a sardonic look. Lucas turned and glanced at me. Though he appeared curious about my furious glaring, I could tell he was still seething over Derek biting me. He made no move toward me, nor did he beckon me over, so I thumped my butt against the back of the couch and proceeded to silently hate him for no reason.

Yvette came back into the living room minutes later, looking once more her calm, composed self.

"Nolan is agreeable," she said. "He will have the supply sent to Derek's dorm room once a week." She turned to Derek. "Keep it refrigerated, not frozen."

Derek nodded, looking repulsed.

"Is there anything else I can help you with?" she asked, returning to her seat by the fire.

"We need to sleep here for the night," Lucas said. "We can't make it back before dawn."

"You are always welcome here." Yvette bowed her head and picked up her book. "Goodnight to you."

Derek stood and we all left the room. Lucas trudged to the door that led to the basement, flung it open and pointed.

"You sleep down there," he told Derek.

Derek ignored him and turned to me, coming closer than was really necessary. "I'm so sorry," he whispered. His fingers brushed over the bandaged wound on my throat.

I nodded, glancing nervously to Lucas. "It's okay. I'll see you tomorrow night and we'll talk."

Derek looked as though he wanted to say something, but just kissed my forehead and ran full speed toward the front door.

"Derek!" I yelled after him. Lucas ran behind him, and I reached the doorway just in time to see Derek's form vibrate violently and shift into the slender white wolf. He flitted into the woods, a ghost in the trees.

Lucas stood in the front yard, trembling with the change. I ran past him, yelling for Derek. I didn't want him to leave like this. Not without talking about what had happened. What if he went back to the vampires?

"Faith," Lucas called out. "Let him go!"

But I was still irrationally angry with Lucas so I ran into the woods, following Derek's snowy paw prints.

"Derek!" I yelled again, coming to a stop. It had gotten dark extremely fast within the trees and I wasn't stupid. I knew what lurked inside the woods as night. I cursed, slamming my hand against the bark of an evergreen. My palm burned, the pain bringing me back to reality. Derek wasn't going to listen to me—especially not now that he was a wolf. And maybe running would do him some good—help him gain control over his blood crave.

I turned to leave, when I began to feel a hum in the back of my head. Someone's vibe. I looked around, hoping it was Lucas, or even Derek. But there was nobody—just the slowly shifting branches of the trees and the mysterious creatures lurking within them. My heart began to pound, even though there was nothing to be afraid of.

I took a step back, my foot crunching loudly through the snowy, silent night.

Another step, my hand came away from the tree. The hum became louder. Someone was out there with me. I began to breathe heavily, making it difficult to hear. The opalescent moon above me peaked from behind a murky cloud, illuminating the woods in patchy, white light.

That's when I saw it: a dark form crouched behind a tree, not five feet away from me. Two glowing eyes peered out of the darkness, a low bubbling sound swallowed the silence.

My entire body ignited, becoming both numb and hypersensitive. I could only stare. Nothing seemed to work. No legs to carry me away, no voice to call for Lucas . . . only eyes to watch the beast as it killed me.

17

THE STALKER

I knew it was a werewolf, knew it with every ounce of brain function I had left. It slowly stepped into the bluish light, its heather-gray body slim and powerful—eyes deadly alert and unblinking. Its glistening nostrils flared as it sniffed the air, staring straight at me.

I knew it was identifying me. But why hadn't it attacked yet?

Slowly, I began to function again. Ears began to hear, breath began to heave. I had to get out of there before the werewolf decided it was snack time. Werewolves weren't supposed to attack humans, but that look in its eye and the taint in its vibe . . . *hunger*.

Another brainwave—my power! Immediately, I ignited the connection and felt the animal's emotions swath my brain: malice, hatred. This werewolf, whoever it was, meant me harm. *No*, I said with my mind. *Stay where you are.*

I could feel a slight resistance, much as I had when I'd forced Lucas to let Derek go in California. But I swatted away the reluctance and forced in my will. *Stay. Don't attack.*

The werewolf lowered its head, submitting to me.

I turned and ran. The fear and lack of eye contact splintered the connection, and it died within seconds. I broke through the tree line, ready to scream for Lucas when I realized it wasn't following me. I stopped in the snowy lawn, shivering and staring into the rustling trees. No snarling, no paws breaking the snow.

It had worked.

I ran the rest of the way into the mansion and slammed the door shut behind me. What had that been about? It could have been a coincidental run in with a werewolf, sure. Or maybe a curious family member? A runt out hunting? Any of these options made sense, since I was at a house stocked with werewolves. But something about the way the heather-gray wolf had stared at me made me think it hadn't been a coincidence. Its vibe, too, had been saturated with ill will toward me. *Me*, in particular. I had ticked off a lot of pack members during the whole Derek ordeal in December, but I didn't think anyone actually wanted me *dead*. There had been a purpose in that meeting. I just didn't know what it was—or *who* it was.

But there was one person who might. I had to tell Lucas about this. I came away from the door and realized that he had left the living room. Yvette, too, had retired for the night. I frowned, thinking that it was pretty jerky of Lucas to just leave me on my own in the woods—especially in light of what had just happened.

I assumed he had gone to his room so I went upstairs and found his door closed when I got there. I didn't bother knocking and went in.

Lucas stood leaning against the windowsill, his back to me. He glanced briefly at me from over his shoulder, and his furious vibe was so oppressive I felt like someone had stuffed a damp washcloth into my lungs. I couldn't breathe.

I forced myself to go to the window and stand across from him, folding my arms across my chest. I felt a palpable rift between us, and I hated it. I needed to seal it and make my way back into Lucas's arms. But I didn't know how. My mind was a blur with everything that had just happened. Derek's bite, Yvette's talk, the heather-gray wolf.

We stood that way for a long while as I felt Lucas's vibe begin to smooth like ripples fading in a pool of water.

At last, he turned toward me and placed his fingers under my chin. He tilted my head to the side, sweeping my hair back behind my shoulders. His fingers slowly peeled back the bandage as he bent and touched his tongue to the wound on my throat.

I jerked away, a little disgusted, but then I felt the skin around the cut tighten and pinch and I realized he'd closed the wound for me.

Without saying a word, this was his apology. Silently, I wound my hand in his.

"I didn't know you could do that," I said.

"Only small things," he said huskily. "I would have left it, but I didn't want to see it on you anymore."

I let him draw me closer. His lips traveled up my throat to my jaw, searing along my cheek toward my lips. He paused before them, inches away. I longed for him with everything inside me and started to rise onto my toes to close the distance between our lips when Lucas pulled back.

"I can't do this," he breathed.

"What are you talking about?"

"You smell like him."

My stomach plunged to the floor, vision spinning.

"I'm sorry," I gasped. *For everything. God, I kissed Derek tonight. . . .*

"Don't be sorry," he said. "I know it's not your fault that he bit you, it's just . . . I'm just not good at this stuff. I don't like to share."

"What? Like I'm a *bone*? Like I'm property?" I pinned him with my most withering glare and, surprisingly, it worked. He looked just about as ashamed as it was possible to get. And, good. He should feel that way. I didn't belong to him or to Derek or anyone.

I was my own person and I could choose to do what I liked.

"You have to accept that Derek is a part of my life," I said. "He's my *friend*. And, believe it or not, I had friends before I met you. I had Heather and Pete—well, Pete sort of—but anyway. That's not the point. I used to do track. I used to see movies with people other than you. Not that I don't like seeing movies with you . . ." I tugged my fingers through my hair, frustrated that I couldn't voice what was bugging me. "You can't pitch a little baby fit every time I go see Derek," I said. "He's in my life. You have to deal."

He looked irritated by the baby-fit thing, but he blew out a long breath, raking a hand through his hair. "I'm a controlling jerk."

"Only because you care," I said, and it was true. He didn't think of me as a bone or as his property. He was just a big jealous idiot.

He cursed. "I'm trying, okay? You gotta understand, Faith, I've been alone for centuries. I don't deal with humans on a regular basis. With werewolves, when you got a problem, you just fight it out. That's how I function. I shut down emotionally and save it for the moon. But I can't do that with you, obviously, and honestly I'm struggling, all right? I mean, I've had human girlfriends sometimes, yeah, but I never let anybody in. Not really. Not since before I was infected."

I blinked, taken aback that he was talking about his human life, since he almost never did so. In my head, I could see what I saw on New Year's Eve—his sister screaming for him as she was killed just out of his reach, the countless fights he'd drawn in the building windows, the deaths he'd caused, the pain he endured every month for over three hundred years. And all those months we'd spent together as he tried to keep from killing me.

Then Lucas went on, his voice like a calming lullaby in my ear. "My family and Vincent were probably the only people in existence that understood me," he murmured. "They were the only people I ever let in. And they're all dead now. Ever since Vincent killed Reece, I've been closed off. Not because I want it that way, but because that's how it's gotta be. To keep people safe. I'm not used to being open. Being honest about what I'm really feeling. Am I gonna screw it up sometimes? Yeah. But, believe me Faith, it's not some territorial you're-mine-not-his dog shit. It's because I love you and I don't want you to get hurt."

I looked up and met his eyes. "Okay," I said, not really knowing what else I could say. He was trying, right? And that was all I could really ask for.

• • •

I missed my first day of classes—not a good way to start the semester. I was behind before I'd even started. But first days were usually pointless so . . .

No. I sucked.

Derek showed up at the house when night fell, with Katie hot on his heels. Apparently, he'd asked her to come up to the mansion and they'd run together, which I'd thanked Katie for profusely. She was surprisingly weird about the whole thing—defensive and flippant. I was just glad she was out there to watch over Derek and help him through the things I couldn't. Although, it did kind of hurt my feelings that Derek now took solace in Katie's company when he used to take solace in mine.

We made it back to campus sometime around midnight. Lucas

and I slunk out of his car and began shuffling to his room with Derek traipsing along beside us, wide awake and chipper as ever. He was actually whistling.

I suppressed the urge to plug his mouth up with my fist.

This being-awake-twenty-four-seven thing was starting to get old. I was turning into a major grouch. We walked through the abandoned courtyard, heading for Lucas and Derek's building, when a rush of wind like a Mack truck on the highway passed and three slim forms materialized before us.

It was Calvin, Silas, and Melissa leering at us like a trio of demonic supermodels.

Lucas immediately began to tremor and shoved me behind him.

"Tighten your muzzle, dog," Calvin said. "We come in peace."

Lucas let out a low guttural sound, and Melissa laughed, displaying her sharklike teeth. "Maybe he *wants* us to neuter him."

"You look a little pale, honey." Lucas growled. "Maybe you'd like a tan. I can strap your skinny ass to that tree there and watch you burn till noon." He barred his teeth in a half snarl, half grin. "I love a good vamp-roast."

Melissa paled further, but her eyes glittered like squirming beetles.

Then Derek shoved past Lucas, effectively stopping the showdown, and slapped Calvin's hand in greeting.

"Ready to go?" Calvin asked Derek, leering openly at me.

"Yup," Derek said.

My eyes flipped to him, and I tried to get past Lucas, but that was like trying to get around a brick wall that constantly moved wherever you moved.

"Derek," I said, peering around Lucas's waist. "What do you think you're doing?"

"Going out," he said airily.

"Aww, Derek," Melissa cooed. "Your pet is worried about you. Look at her pink little face." She licked her lips. "Maybe you should bring her with you. I'll let you bite mine if you let me bite yours." She wiggled her hips suggestively.

Lucas quaked violently, and I thought for sure he was going to change, but he remained under control.

"Now, now," Calvin admonished, shaking a finger at Melissa. "Friends don't let friends drink blood."

"Meanie," she pouted.

Calvin snickered, watching Lucas keenly. "And anyway, I don't think Faith is Derek's pet after all, Mel. I think she's the dog's bitch."

Lucas started forward, snarling. Silas and Melissa hissed back, fangs barred.

"I'm nobody's anything," I said, realizing too late how stupid that sounded. "And you're not going anywhere with Derek."

Calvin was unconcerned by my ire. "Well, that's really up to Derek, now isn't it? We had a lovely evening planned for the four of us. Box tickets to the big game in New York tomorrow night, private jet. First class all the way." He threw his arm around Derek's shoulder and shook him a little, grinning hugely.

Derek looked swayed already.

"You can't go," I told him. "You have class tonight."

"You need to put some slack on that leash, human," Melissa purred as she snaked her hand up the back of Derek's neck.

Derek seemed to deliberate for a moment and then shrugged.

"I'll catch up," he said.

"Excellent!" Calvin said. "Well, off we go, then. Farewell, Faith, my dewdrop."

I made a noise of repulsion, which was quickly accompanied by Lucas. I rounded on him. "Lucas, you're supposed to be guarding him," I hissed. "How can you just let him leave with them?"

"I'm protecting the humans from him," Lucas argued. "Not protecting him from the vampires. There's a difference."

"They're vampires!" I yelled. "You're supposed to kill them on sight, so kill them!" Power writhed inside me, threatening to force Lucas into doing what I wanted. "Please," I said instead.

Calvin, Silas, and Melissa had gone very silent, eyes trained on Lucas and bodies tensed to attack at any second.

Lucas's jaw flexed, and his gaze flickered to mine for a moment. "Not with you here," he ground out.

The vampires relaxed, all leering smugly. "Well, now that that's all cleared up," Calvin said with a cocky salute. "We're off."

"Ciao," said Melissa and made a kissy face at us.

With that, the three of them blew out of the courtyard.

Derek remained for a moment and shrugged at me. "Now you guys will have the nights to yourselves, too." And he blurred out of the courtyard.

JEALOUSY

February arrived in a flurry of homework, track practice, and vampires. Derek hung out with them pretty much constantly no matter how much I tried to warn him against it. Making things worse—or better depending on how you looked at it—was that the murders had actually slowed to a near halt since Derek took up with the vampires. It was great because people weren't dying, but it made convincing Derek to stay on the werewolves' side even more difficult. The only bright spot amidst it all was Valentine's Day. Lucas and I had a perfect night—the first one since . . . well, probably ever.

After dinner at a yummy Italian restaurant in Old Town, Lucas drove us back to CSU and stopped in the drive to give me my present. It was snowing lightly and the sky was this gorgeous violet color as Lucas reached into his coat pocket and handed me a little white box. "This is the most ridiculous holiday known to mankind," he said, putting the box into my hands. "But I know you girls like it. So here. Happy Valentine's."

I smiled triumphantly. He rolled his eyes, hiding a grin, and I opened the box. Inside was a silver necklace.

"Silver?" I asked, frowning. "Why would you get me a silver necklace?" I'd had to put all my silver jewelry away months ago to keep from accidentally putting it on and wearing it around him. Apparently, it "burned like all hell."

"I thought it was nice," he said evasively.

I narrowed my eyes at him, unconvinced. "But I can't wear it," I said. "Not around you."

"Obviously," he said. "It's for when I'm not around. It might give you a few extra seconds to get away if you need it."

I looked down at the delicate silver chain and the little rose on the end of it, thinking that Lucas was always giving me things to protect myself. The stake. This necklace. Both so that I could have a better chance of living in his world. It should have been romantic that he cared so much, but somehow it just felt cold. Like he was arming me for something.

I picked up the necklace, letting it dangle between my fingers. A little plaque hung on the clasp. I brought it closer and cursive script etched into the silver gleamed at me in the yellow light of the courtyard lanterns.

I'll always come back to you.

My heart fluttered with pleasure, and I looked up at Lucas again, feeling the smile that must have been all over my face.

"Promise to wear it every full moon, all right?" he said, chocolate eyes earnest and a little vulnerable, which was just way too adorable for words.

I nodded and put the necklace down to fold myself into his arms.

"Look, I wanna say something else," Lucas rumbled. "We've been at odds a lot lately, ever since I bit Derek. But I just wanted to say I'm gonna try not to let it bother me as much anymore. You hanging out with him, I mean. If you say you're just friends, then you're just friends. And I have no place trying to get between you two."

I met his gaze. "Thank you. I hate all this fighting. If I just felt like you had my back, it'd make the whole Derek thing easier to take."

"Hey," he said, looking firmly into my eyes. "I'll always have your back."

I twisted my lips to the side. "Not lately. Not about Derek. You were more than happy to write him off at the first sign of weakness. But, I don't think you really remember what it was like being new. To not know your body and its limits. Derek's confused. But I know if I can just get him away from the vampires, he'll be able to see how wrong he is about them. Just give me some time, okay? I can fix this."

It seemed to take Lucas a long time to manage his thoughts on that one, and I could feel the turmoil raging beneath him. But then I felt something click in him, and he nodded slowly. "Okay. I trust you."

He must have seen the relief on my face because he smiled and said, "Is that all it takes to make you happy? I should tell you I trust you more often."

"You don't have to say it. Just show it."

"I will."

And I could tell he really meant it, which was more precious to me than any gift he could have bought.

"Now this makes my gift look lame," I said. I shivered and cocked my head toward his building to indicate it was time to get my human butt inside and out of the cold.

"Why?" he asked as we began walking up the lane to his building. "What is it?" He took up my hand and brought it to his mouth to blow hot air all over it, which made goose bumps ripple down my spine in the most tantalizing way.

"Well, it's kind of an interactive present," I said, casting him a sidelong glance to gauge his reaction.

He looked more than a little intrigued, but for all the wrong reasons. His eyes smoldered into mine, and a roguish grin quirked his lips to the left.

"Not *that* kind of interaction!" I said, flushing. "I asked my mom to send me my grandma's famous chocolate-banana cake recipe. It won awards and stuff, and it's ridiculously delicious. My mom bakes it every Christmas."

"So you made it for me?"

"Actually, I thought we could make it together. You know, for fun."

"Fun?" he asked, as if it was some kind of foreign language. "What is this thing you speak of?"

I swatted his arm lightly and ignored him. "And I got a movie to watch, so we can eat cake in bed."

"I'm liking this more and more as you go."

"I thought you might."

We went upstairs to Lucas's room, where he had just enough kitchen appliances to facilitate cake making. The oven was tiny, the counter space minimal and the sink even more so, but it only made it more fun. Unfortunately, Lucas turned out to be just as useful in the kitchen as I was, and between the two of us, the only thing we were making was a mess.

"I think I found something werewolves are bad at," I said.

"You're one to talk." He looked down at my congealing lump of mushy banana. "That's supposed to be light and—" He checked the recipe. "Fluffy."

"I'll show you fluffy." I took the spoon and thwacked a big lump of it at his face. Which he dodged easily.

"Nice try, babe." He looked behind him at the mess I'd made on his desk. "I believe that was my statistics homework you just ruined. You owe me two hours of laborious studying. I just don't know how you're gonna make it up to me." He leaned in close, kissing the smudge of chocolate on my cheek.

"Don't even try," I said. "You probably spent five minutes on that."

"So five minutes of compensation are in order." He nibbled on my ear. "Plus interest." He began snaking his hand up the bottom of my shirt, and as soon as I was sure he was sufficiently distracted . . . I dumped the bowl of banana goo over his head.

I shrieked, giggling madly as I ran across the room to get away from him.

He just stood there. Dripping in grayish goo. Staring at me with an appalled half smile.

I put the rolling desk chair between us, still laughing uncontrollably. I watched him as he straightened and walked slowly toward me, a mischievous glint in his eyes. I backed up, climbing onto the couch, still gripping the chair between us to ward him off.

"Lucas," I warned. "Don't you dare."

"I hope you like banana."

He shook his head like a wet dog and sprayed absolutely everything—including me—with mushy banana. I screamed. He tackled me. And we spent the rest of the night in bed watching a chick flick and eating store-bought cookies straight from the box.

• • •

All too soon, it was the night before the full moon. It was Derek's first full moon since he'd woken up, and the tension between the three of us was almost blindingly intense. Lucas and Derek were supposed to go up to Gould together in a few hours to spend the night in the woods, but with the two of them barely on speaking terms anymore, I'd never been so scared that my boyfriend and my best friend would kill each other.

I was sure I'd be allowed to tag along and play my usual role as referee.

Not so.

"I don't see what the big deal is," I said as I stared out the window of Lucas's room. "I've been up there for the full moon before and everything was fine."

"That was different," Lucas said. "I was . . . well, you know where I was, and you were locked in there with me. No werewolf was gonna go within twenty miles of that room. You were safe. This time, you're just a hunk of fresh meat."

"Do you have to say it like that?"

"It's the truth." I turned to watch him stuff clothes and toiletries into a duffel bag. He paused when he saw me watching him and said, "I know you have your connection and everything, but what if it doesn't work? Or what if Rolf usurps you again? I'd just feel better if you weren't around us. Even Derek won't be himself."

"I want to be wherever you are."

His face softened, and he stepped toward me. "It's not that I don't want you to be with me. It's just not safe. Can you get that?"

I shifted my jaw, looking away as I tried to stave off tears.

"I'm scared," I admitted. "Promise me you and Derek will be safe up there. I don't know what I'd do if I lost you—either of you."

Lucas's mouth tightened infinitesimally, but he said, "I promise."

I looped my arms around his neck for a hug, but he pulled them away and took a step back.

"Not tonight," he said. "It's too close. I don't wanna chance it."

I let my arms fall along with my mouth, outraged. Lucas was totally in control of himself when it came to us, and with my power to back him up, there was no reason he couldn't touch me, even tonight. He was pushing me away for another reason. I tested his vibe and found what I had suspected.

Jealousy.

Over nothing.

• • •

Lucas finished packing and we headed down to the driveway, where Derek already stood with a bag slung over his shoulder. He was covered in a layer of sleet, and his hair was blown straight back from the wind. It was shaping up to be a blizzard.

"You're late," Derek called as we approached, shaking his coat free of the snow.

"Sorry," I said loudly over the wind. I gave him a brief hug and looked him sternly in the eyes, which was difficult given the sleet. "You be safe. And don't hurt anyone."

He only smiled halfheartedly and started off toward the parking lot.

Lucas came up beside me and put his hand over mine. I felt it shaking slightly.

"Come back safe," I said, curling into his warm arms.

I heard him heave a sigh. His voice was buttery-soft in my ear. "I'll always come back to you."

He placed a kiss on the top of my head and sauntered off after Derek. His words, while sweet, were probably just a reminder to wear that necklace he'd given me. I took it from my coat pocket with numb fingers and fumbled the clasp around my neck. The swirling snow created a hazy film in the air, like looking through a fogged glass. All I could see of Lucas and Derek were their silhouettes as they dipped into his tiny car. Over the wind, I listened to the engine rev as they drove out of the lot and faded from sight.

Fitful snowflakes wilted on my eyelashes, but I didn't blink and let them drip down my cheeks.

What if they kill each other out there?

What if I never see either of them again?

In my mind's eye I could see them fighting, tearing at flesh and keening those high-pitched shrieks into the night. If it happened, the pack would defend Lucas. A deep coldness rang through my bones as I imagined the fury of the pack descending upon a lone white wolf—my Derek. If tempers got out of hand tomorrow night, there was no telling what would be awaiting me when day broke.

Finally, I shook myself, feeling the thin layer of ice that had accumulated over my body crackle and shatter. I had to do something besides this or I'd drive myself crazy. I was about to go up into Lucas's room to grab my phone and call Katie, when I realized she'd probably be heading up to Gould, too.

Why are all of my friends werewolves or a viran?

Wait, I still had a human friend. The thought of spending the night with Heather watching chick flicks and studying for classes brought a warm, brownies-straight-out-of-the-oven feeling to my heart. We'd spent precious little time together since making amends, but that wasn't because we weren't close anymore. Between Heather's concert schedules for band, and my running around trying to stop a vampire uprising, we just hadn't found the time to hang out. Sure we talked on the phone a lot, but that didn't satisfy the craving for a connection—especially a connection to someone human—that I longed for.

Nobody else was outside in this weather, so I was alone in the courtyard. There were lamps to illuminate the area, but the snow smudged out the light and turned everything a murky navy blue. I made it to Heather's building without turning into an ice sculpture, but I didn't have a key to get inside. I'd also left my cell phone in Lucas's dorm room so I couldn't call her to let me in.

And, I realized a little too late . . . it was full-on nighttime. A very bad time to be loitering in the open, totally unprotected. I was about to go back to Lucas's room and forget visiting Heather, when suddenly, a vibe hit me hard like a slam to the back of my head.

A feral, crazed vibe that could only mean one thing: a werewolf.

A *changed* werewolf.

BLOOD BITCHES

I froze in the doorway, too frightened to move. It couldn't be Lucas or Derek; they were long gone by now. And why would they change?

"Julian?" I whispered. "Katie?"

Then a shadow materialized in the distance. Its hulking midnight form drew closer, eyes glimmering in the phantom light of the moon. I pressed myself against the wall next to the door, unable to even think.

It was the heather-gray wolf. The vibe was so familiar, the unique mix of hunger and malice. I tried to connect to it as I had before, but this time there was something in the way—something impassible. I tried again and again, panicking, but each time something shoved me back out. *Why? Why can't I connect?* Finally, I'd used up all of my power and all I could do was watch the werewolf come closer and closer, so very slowly, as if reveling in this quiet moment before the kill.

Then a miracle. Someone opened the door. A boy started to come out, but as soon as the yellow light of the hallway illuminated the stoop on which I stood, I darted for it. I slammed into the boy, forcing him back into the hall. I yanked the door closed behind us, holding on to it with all of my strength.

The werewolf could easily overpower me, break down this flimsy glass door and kill both me and the startled boy beside me. But it didn't. I squinted out into the whirling snowstorm and found the looming body of the beast gone.

"Are you okay?" the boy asked, putting a hand on my shoulder.

I jumped and released the door handle with a jerk.

"Yes," I said, panting. "I—ah, I was just . . . cold." I turned toward him, watching his face crumble in concern. "It's really cold. Out . . . there . . ." My cheeks flushed as I realized how crazy I sounded.

"Okay . . . ," he said, moving to brush past me.

"Be careful!" I said, jumping after him. He turned to look at me, confused. "Of . . . the cold." *And werewolves.*

The boy made a she's-a-psycho face and said, "Okay." He left, probably wondering whether or not I'd gone off my meds.

I stood in the hall for a moment, trying to gather myself. There was a werewolf stalking me. That much was obvious. But why? And who was it? I didn't have a feud going with any of the were-wolves to my knowledge. Julian had said they were scared of me, but somehow I didn't think that was cause for murder. Rolf may have wanted me dead if Yvette had broken her promise, but I knew Rolf's vibe. And that werewolf was *not* Rolf. Rolf was strong and poised, even when changed. This werewolf was unstable.

Part of me had been convinced that the last encounter was a fluke. A random run-in with a runt or some other family member. But now, it was clear that there was definitely something going on.

I was pretty much stuck in Heather's building for the night since there was no way I was entering the courtyard again to get back into Lucas's building. I hoped Heather would let me crash in her room, because those lounge chairs in the common area didn't look too comfy.

I took the stairs to the fourth floor and went to Heather's room at the end of the hall. I hoped I'd remembered the room number correctly, since she had only mentioned it once a long time ago. I knocked, and to my relief, Heather answered.

sked, trying

t with them

ard that hit.
ut with her.

to that—that
ow it sounds
or, and—"

e she meant
n having fun,
staying. You

as so not my
These chicks
y real danger.
d she needed

fact, she looked a little scared.

ly so I could only see her face.
guy in there, or something?"
eather needed to get over her
m be gorgeous and sickeningly

the squeaky hinges of a door,
you okay?"

you wanted to do anything
work—" This was usually my
vhile I was stuck at the were-
k gnawed on. "And you don't
eone in there with you."
er room and then cackled—

it didn't sound like a dude.
eyes.
" It was kind of hurtful that
her friends, but that was def-
er.
. "It's just—"
ed from inside. "JOSH IS
osion of laughter followed as
ms.

g anything but looking at me.

"Are those the same girls we met at Zydeco's?"
to keep the accusation out of my voice.

She nodded reluctantly.

"I thought you said you weren't going to hang
anymore."

Man, I sounded like her mother. This sucked.

She remained silent.

"What happened?" I asked.

She just shrugged. "I got lonely."

She could have slugged me in the gut for how
She'd been lonely because I'd been too busy to har
Well, that was all going to change. Starting now.

"Look, let's get out of here," I said. "We can g
Career Night thing they have going on in the Union. I
lame, but maybe not, right? I still haven't picked a m

"I can't," she said stonily.

"Can't?"

"I mean, I don't want to. I'm fine here."

"Heather—"

"No." She finally looked up at me and I could
business. I could also see her pupils were dilated. "
which is pretty hard to come by these days, so I'
can stay, too, if you want."

My first instinct was to refuse her, since pot
thing, but then I couldn't exactly leave her, could
were blood bitches with the potential for some ve
Heather, God love her, was being a little dumb, a
me to keep her from taking dumb to death.

"Take it easy," she warned. "You might need those brains one day."

I smiled despite myself. *Serves you right, you big idiot.*

"Hey, Danni?" Heather asked. "Do you have any of that stuff from the other night?"

"I already gave you some. Free of charge, no less. Don't tell me you used it all?"

"No," Heather said, picking at the pilling fibers of a purple throw pillow.

"Well, go use your own stash," Danni said, waving her off. I watched her wrist peek from behind her leather jacket and saw her charm bracelet. The bloody fang glittered among the beads.

"What's it called?" I asked. "That drug you all were using?"

Danni's piercing stare turned on me, studying every inch of my face, as if trying to find ulterior motives. I strained to keep my expression innocent. Finally, she said, "Anything you wanna call it."

Hmm, how convenient.

"So why don't you use?" I asked.

"Doesn't gel with me." She fiddled with her nails, which were surprisingly filthy.

"Why not?"

"Just doesn't do anything for me."

I eyed her profile, trying to figure out whether she was lying.

"If you're so curious, you should try it," Danni said.

"Why is everyone so intent on me trying this junk? I don't want it, all right?"

Danni's smile fixated. "Got it." The finality in her tone made me believe she wouldn't offer it again. "You're missing out, though. It's a hell of a ride, so I hear."

Heather snickered into her pillow.

"So do you go here?" I asked Danni. "To CSU?"

"Nope. I work at a restaurant in Old Town."

"So you're graduated?"

She shook her head. "Dropped out."

"And turned to drug dealing?" *Oops, that slipped out.*

Danni's petite jaw flexed; her gaze slowly turned to mine, and I felt a flare in her vibe, making it stronger for just an instant. But her expression wasn't angry or offended, merely interested. "Is that a problem?" she asked.

"No," I said, covering. "I bet you make a lot of money doing it. Especially on a college campus."

"I do it more for the connections than the money."

Connections to the vampires? Why would she want to get closer to them, especially if she didn't actually do vampire blood?

I watched Danni as she picked at her nails again. What was her deal?

"So who was that dude you were with the other night?" Danni asked. "Boyfriend?"

I faltered, not wanting to discuss Derek with someone I suspected of involvement with the vampires. But if I didn't answer, Heather would, so I said, "Just a friend. His name is Derek."

Danni grinned, exposing pearly white teeth. "Friend, right. He's a little too drop-dead gorgeous to be just a friend." She shot me a wicked look. "Is he available?"

"No," I said instantly. *Not for you.*

Her smile faded, gaze like needles into my skin.

"You should see her boyfriend," Heather chimed in, taking a

drag off a joint and choking on it.

Yeah, that's real sexy, Heather.

"Oh?" Danni said, hiking up a spindly brown brow. "Spill."

Damn it. I didn't want to talk about Lucas either. I threw Heather the stink eye, but she wasn't paying attention. "There's nothing to spill," I said, dodging.

"He's like, the hottest thing on the planet," Heather said, still gagging. "I couldn't believe it when they started dating. He looks like the cover of a romance novel."

"Oh, thanks," I said flatly.

Danni let out a soft chuckle. "So have you and Fabio been together long?"

"His name's Lucas," I corrected without thinking. Why was everyone always calling him names?

"Right, sorry," Danni said and turned away to say something to Heather. I thought I felt another small flare of her vibe, but I couldn't be sure. All the smoke in the room was giving me a headache and numbing my power. I was also fairly certain I was getting high off the secondhand smoke. I wanted to go downstairs and brave the uncomfortable lounge chairs for the night, but I just couldn't bring myself to leave Heather here alone. These people didn't look dangerous, but I so didn't trust them. Heather was in distress, and everything inside me said I had to protect her. Maybe it was because I'd been hanging out with overprotective were-wolves and a viran for so long, but I just felt I had to stay with her tonight. And in the morning, I could try and fix everything.

20

NEGOTIATION

I ended up sleeping over at Heather's place, and woke up to find the blood bitches gone and Heather conked out on the bathroom floor, where she'd spent the latter part of the night throwing up.

It was a *super*fun night.

I'd fallen asleep slumped over on her desk in between helping her keep her hair out of the vomit-filled toilet and trying to get a hold of Lucas on his cell. The reception was garbage in Gould, so it wasn't surprising that I'd failed, but I missed him and Derek. I didn't even want to think about tonight.

Instead, I wanted to . . . I sighed to myself. As much as I loved and cared about what happened to my boys tonight, today, well, today I just wanted to be human. I'd made a promise to myself that I'd take time to do the things that were important to me—like school and running and photography—but I hadn't held true to that promise. I had good reason, sure, but that didn't make it right. Today, I had the rare opportunity to do whatever I wanted. And damn it, I was going to do it all.

Starting with a morning run.

I sat up from the desk and stretched, heading for the bathroom. Heather looked *literally* like roadkill, and smelled even worse. I glared down at her prone form, both worried and irritated at the same time. I was about to throw a blanket over her and wait until she woke to deal with her, but then . . . I had a better idea.

It was something my mother had done to me in high school when I'd come home late from a party totally wasted. It was, in fact, how I began running in the first place.

I dragged Heather into the shower and started it. She woke up immediately, screaming profanities. I slammed the glass door shut and threw my weight against it as she tried to pry it open.

"Faith, oh my God, have you lost your mind?" she shouted.

"No, but you seem to have," I said calmly. "And you smell, seriously, like something dead."

"Screw off," she said, banging on the glass. "Let me out. Come on, my head is killing me. I feel like I'm going to puke again."

"Okay, then I'm *really* not letting you out."

"You're such a bitch!"

I smiled. "But I love you. Now use that soap until there's nothing left, and get dressed. I want to go out."

She groaned, wiping her hair out of her face. "What *time* is it?"

I checked my cell phone. "Six a.m."

"You psycho."

I grinned devilishly. "You think this is crazy? Wait until you see what we're doing."

• • •

Last night's storm had passed, and left in its wake a layer of snow half a foot thick. The campus workers who cleared the snow away for everyone had yet to get to the Oval, so Heather and I headed for the gym. Heather groaned and muttered at me the entire way over, but I ignored her. If she felt half as bad as she looked—and that was pretty terrible—she'd think twice before smoking pot again.

I know it worked on me when my mother did this. Only with me, it had been about a hundred degrees outside, and she'd made me run in the sand. Heather had it good by comparison.

"I hate you so much right now," she grumbled as we trekked through the snow. The sweatpants she'd leant me were already soaked through, and my shoes felt like ice cubes. Admittedly, I was beginning to rethink my little plan, but there was no going back now.

"I know," I said. "But you deserve it."

Once at the gym, I did some stretching to warm up my frozen muscles and then ran around the track three times. Heather, on the other hand, made it halfway around and then sprinted to the bathroom to puke some more. Once I'd finished my workout—and wow, it felt amazing to run again—I collected Heather from the bathroom and dragged her downstairs to the café for some sustenance. I treated her to a strong cup of mocha latte and a chocolate croissant as a peace offering and contented myself with a low-fat muffin so I wouldn't ruin my workout.

Having sufficiently made my point about the drugs, I decided there was no more need to harp on the subject. Instead, Heather and I talked about normal stuff. Her family, school, this hot guy in my photography class I wanted to set her up with, and a million other things. When it came to this stuff—normal stuff—I felt she was the only one who truly understood me. Lucas tried to, sure, but I think he'd been a werewolf for so long, he'd forgotten what it was like to be human. Heather, thankfully, did not have the problem.

"I get to start my internship next year," she said. "At Bennett Elementary, you know that one right down the road? I'm teaching first graders to read music."

"That's really amazing," I said.

"So you're still undecided as far as you major goes?"

I shrugged. "I guess so. I really love the photography thing, but I don't know how I'd make a living doing it."

She chewed on a bite of her croissant. "You could do graphic design. I have a cousin who does custom wedding invitations and stuff. She gets paid a lot of money for it, too."

I made a face. Weddings weren't really my thing. And as I thought about it, I still couldn't exactly pin down *what* my thing was. When I thought about the future, it was difficult to imagine a normal life with marriage and a job and kids. What with everything I'd been through, I just felt I'd be lucky to be alive to see my future at all.

Heck, if the werewolves didn't stop the vampires from proceeding with the uprising, there might not even *be* a future.

• • •

After our brunch, Heather and I spent the day studying in the library. I'd been slacking on my human duties (like school), so I had a waist-high pile of homework to get through. By midafternoon, however, my brain was mush. Heather said she had band practice, so I went back to Lucas's room to finish homework, watch some TV, and call my mom. By dusk, I'd snuggled into Lucas's bed for some much needed sleep.

Not that I got any. I spent the night staring out at the luminescent full moon, wondering what Lucas and Derek were getting into, and whether they'd still be civil to one another as wild beasts. I fingered the cold silver at my throat hearing Lucas's soft, grating voice in my ear saying the words *I'll always come back to you* over and over again until finally, sometime around dawn, I fell asleep.

It was my phone that woke me, hours later, from a nightmare involving Lucas eating Heather.

"What's wrong?" I asked, not bothering with a greeting. I saw Lucas's name on the caller ID. My heart was already going haywire from the dream, and it only intensified at Lucas's next words.

"We have a problem," he said. "Rolf knows Derek has an in with the vampires."

"What?" I blurted, sitting up. "How?"

"It wasn't anybody's fault. Derek reeked of them. I guess I'd just gotten used to it or something, but the others smelled it immediately. And ah . . . there's another problem."

I groaned, throwing my head in my hand.

"Derek has the blood crave on the full moon. He went nuts last night. It took six of us to corral him up into the mountains, and then five more to keep him from escaping into town."

"Christ . . . ," I whispered. "Is he okay? Did he hurt anyone?"

"Few bumps and bruises on our end, but he didn't kill anybody, and that's the most important thing." He heaved a sigh. "That's not even the bad part."

"What's the bad part?"

"Rolf's out-of-his-mind pissed. He thinks we knew about this and were keeping it from him. I tried to tell him we had no way of knowing since, this is the first full moon we've been with him since he woke up, but he's such a stubborn bastard. He won't listen."

"What do we do?" I asked. "Where is Derek now?"

"He's at the house. In the silver room. The silver didn't do anything to him, but it kept him inside, anyway."

"What are you going to do when he wakes up?" I got out of bed and began getting dressed, already thinking up ways to break into Derek's room and snag the extra set of keys to his car.

"Well, see . . . that's the other problem. When everyone smelled the vampires on Derek, they freaked out. And this was before the full moon hit us, mind you. Derek was asleep in the basement while this was going on, so he pretty much has no clue what's about to happen."

"What's about to happen?" I began packing an overnight bag, throwing in clothes and toiletries as fast as I could.

"Rolf wants to use Derek as a spy for the pack."

"*What?*"

"Thought you'd say that."

"How can he do that? He promised he wouldn't hurt Derek, and this is going to put his life in danger."

"Not the way Rolf sees it."

"Who cares how he sees it, he's breaking the Blood Pact!" I slammed the door to Lucas's room behind me as I jogged toward the stairwell. "You have to stop him."

"Well, see," Lucas said, sounding slightly pained. "That's the problem. The Council doesn't see it as a breach of the Pact either, so really, he's got no choice."

I took the stairs two at a time. "That's bullshit! What about a trial?"

"He can't have a trial because he's not a pack member."

"Well, can't he just leave the mansion and never go back? If he has no allegiance to the pack, how can they force him into this?

Wait. Don't answer yet." I'd come to Derek's door and had no way of entering. "Tell me how to pick a lock."

He puffed a laugh, and told me how to get in, which was disconcertingly easy to do.

"Thanks, babe," I said once inside. "You're useful for something besides eye candy, after all."

"Glad to hear it."

I went straight to Derek's desk and found the keys to the Bentley the vampires had just given him as a "gift."

"So what do we do?" I asked, going back out of the room at top speed. "We run, right?" Something painful clenched inside me at the thought of leaving CSU and the life I'd built here, especially after yesterday with Heather, but I'd do anything to keep Derek safe.

"We can't run," Lucas said. "Not forever, anyway. And, Faith . . ."

I halted at the front door of my building, panting. "What?"

"I'm not sure we shouldn't go through with Rolf's plan."

"Are you insane, I—"

"Hear me out," he said. "You want the pack to accept Derek, right? You want him to be on our side?"

"Yes," I said slowly.

"Well, maybe this is the perfect way for him to prove himself. Maybe if he does this, they'll forget about the whole blood-crave-on-the-full-moon thing."

Something cold slipped through my veins as I caught his tone. "Are you saying they're going to blackmail him?"

"I wouldn't put it past them."

"And what if Derek refuses?"

"I'm not sure. That's why I called you. I know you're gonna

hate me for this, but I want you to convince Derek to do it."

"No." Not even a possibility.

"Faith, it's better than the alternative."

I swept out of the front door, heading for the parking lot. "We don't even know what the alternative is, yet, so why don't we just hear Rolf's proposal first?"

"He's going to execute Derek," Lucas said.

I stopped short of Derek's car, frozen. "You don't know—"

"Doesn't take a genius to guess Faith. I can just hear him now, 'the danger he presents to the human race on the full moon . . . he cannot be easily controlled' . . . blah, blah, blah. I know him, and he'll manipulate the system until he gets what he wants. It's what he did when he offered the Blood Pact. All he had to do was wait for the right opportunity, and here it is."

I unlocked Derek's car and slowly lowered myself into the seat.

"Faith, if Derek doesn't do this, he dies, all right? I don't like it any better than you but—"

"Oh, like hell you don't!" I exploded. "You're just like Rolf, biding your time until you can get rid of him."

He was silent, and I wished I could see his face to see whether I'd misjudged him or called him out on the truth. Either way, fighting with Lucas wasn't going to help the situation. Lucas was my only ally in the pack besides Katie and maybe Julian, but neither of them had the power to sway Rolf. Lucas was my only chance at saving Derek, and if anyone could change his mind, it was me.

Only, it turned out that I didn't need to convince anyone of anything.

When I arrived at the werewolf mansion, Derek was already

awake and Lucas, probably having foreseen my plan to wheedle him into submission, got the jump on talking to Derek.

"It's honestly not such a terrible idea," Derek said as he stretched out on his cot, looking totally at ease. "The vampires are pretty chill, always sharing their stuff. Heck, Silas gave me a new *car*."

Well, that explained the Bentley.

"But they're all really self-absorbed," Derek continued. "So they probably won't pay much attention to me prying into their affairs."

Lucas looked smugly in my direction, but I ignored him.

"Don't you realize what will happen to you if they figure out you're a spy?" I asked.

"No worse than what'll happen to me if I refuse Rolf."

I sputtered, appalled that he was taking this all so easily.

"Look," Derek said, sitting up and turning to Lucas. "The truth is that I don't think there is a vampire uprising. I think you werewolves are a bunch of paranoid losers with nothing better to do than pick on vampires for fun. But if 'spying' on the vampires is what it takes to convince you that they have nothing planned, then fine. I'm hanging out with them anyway, right? What does it hurt me?"

I began to protest again, but Derek stood in a superfast motion and towered over me.

"It's not your decision, Faith, it's mine and I'm doing it. I'm telling Rolf now. Deal with it."

He strode out of the basement, and I watched him wave Katie—who was lounging on the couch, playing on her phone—over to him. Together, they made a beeline for the backyard.

For whatever reason, it hurt to watch him go off with her.

"Probably going to go for a run," Lucas said.

I nodded vaguely.

"You okay?"

"Whatever," I said. "I can't control everything. Or anything."

"He's a big boy. He can take care of himself."

I sniffed bitterly.

"When he comes back, you should all go back to campus. You've got class tomorrow and stuff."

At first I began nodding, and then gradually realized what he'd said.

"What, you're not coming with us?" I asked.

"No," he said, clearing his throat. "Rolf's concerned by the reduced number of murders lately. He thinks it means they're planning something big. We've got a raid planned for tonight. Largest one we've ever done. I gotta stay and help."

I searched his face as I decided how to react.

"Shouldn't Derek stay and help?" I asked. "He might have clues to where the lair is."

"He says he doesn't know anything, and I believe him. The vampires wouldn't be dumb enough to show an unregistered mutant where their lair is."

"Viran," I corrected.

He waved me away. "Besides, Derek isn't a pack member. He'll only get in the way."

I bristled at that, but ignored it. "Can't I help at all? Like I did when we caught that vampire together?"

He shook his head with one of those you're-being-silly looks he often gave me.

"I appreciate it," he said and cupped my cheek. "That's really brave of you, babe, but you're better off just letting us do our thing."

I shook his hand away. "I want to *do* something. I hate being powerless. Do you understand what that feels like? To constantly be at the mercy of creatures stronger than you?" I curled my lip. "No, I guess you don't, right?"

He looked up at the ceiling, dragging his hands down the sides of his face. "Why are you giving me a hard time? You know I have to stay and do this, and you know you can't help."

I whirled away from him, folding my arms across my chest.

"I don't know," I said. "It just . . . kind of hit me yesterday that if we don't stop the vampires, my entire future will be nonexistent. I mean, why am I even *in* college? To prepare for something that's probably not even going to happen anymore? I should just face it: I'm going to be some vampire's dinner and nothing else."

An iron hand clasped my arm and spun me around. Lucas stood over me, shadows masking his face, but with eyes glowing bright silver. "Don't you ever say that to me again. Don't say it period. Don't even think it." He shook me slightly on the last word, and I jerked my arm away.

"I want to help stop this," I whispered fiercely. "It's my race they're trying to eliminate. I have a right to help defend it."

"*We* defend you," he said, spreading his arms wide. "It's our whole purpose. So just let us do our jobs, okay?"

"And stand by idly while people are killed night after night."

"It's been slowing."

"Only so they can plan some new form of terror against us."

He swore and began pacing around the room. When he

returned to me, he was calmer, but I could still see something twitching in his temple.

"I get it," he said. "If it was me, I'd want to do something, too. But you gotta face the reality, Faith: you're human. And these are vampires. They *will* kill you if they get the chance, and the only advantage you have over them is the fact that you know they exist. You can hide."

"So that's all I get to do, hide like a little child?"

"Unfortunately, yes."

"I'm not some stupid damsel, Lucas. I don't need you to save me all the time!" I knew this wasn't true. And that was the frustrating part. I knew I needed him to save me, I just didn't *want* to need him to save me. I wanted to save myself for once.

To my surprise, Lucas's face tightened into a small half-concealed smile. He held my face in two hands and said, "Three months ago, I never would have heard those words come out of your mouth. You would have been more than happy to let me save you."

"Three months ago, I was powerless."

"But your power is useless against the vampires."

I ground my teeth and looked away.

"It's okay to have weaknesses," Lucas said softly. "You taught me that."

I looked up at him again.

"It's okay to need people," he whispered. "If you need me, it doesn't mean you're powerless. It just means you need help." He shrugged and smiled. "And it's okay. Because there's gonna come a time when I'll need your help, too. And I can promise you this, Faith: I won't be too proud to accept it."

I swallowed hard to keep the tears back and nodded. "Okay," I whispered.

He relaxed. "Now will you please go back to CSU where it's safe?"

I sighed heavily and shrugged. "I have no choice."

· · ·

D erek and Katie returned an hour later, both flushed and windblown, and looking too happy to be allowed. By that time, the pack had already left for the raid, leaving only me and a scattering of human guards and children in the mansion. It was getting close to nine p.m., which meant we'd never make it back to CSU before the curfew. Meaning we'd have to either sneak in or get a pass from one of the many policemen standing by at the entrances to the campus.

I was in no rush to get back to school and deal with that. Katie and Derek seemed content to stay a while, too, since neither of them had come in from the back porch yet. I debated on joining them, but they both looked a little too hyper for my taste. I was in the mood to be angry, not make doggie bathroom jokes.

I shoved off from the sofa and began making my way into the kitchen. With the werewolves gone, everyone else had scattered into their private quarters, leaving me alone on the bottom floor, which effectively creeped me out; the mansion was spooky at night without the rowdy werewolves to fill the silence.

I went into the kitchen, hoping to find some leftover brownies or something. The lights were off, but I couldn't find the switch in the darkness, so I rushed to the fridge to light the room. I rooted around inside it, finding nothing appetizing. Glass bottles clinked together, tinfoil crinkled as I pushed it out of the way and—

I straightened, ears pricked. I couldn't bring myself to turn around, but I stood stock still, listening for the sound I was sure I'd heard.

There it was again. I stepped away from the fridge, and it closed behind me with a small thud, plunging me into total darkness. I swallowed hard, trying to be brave. I'd heard someone moving around in the back hall. It was a distinctive kind of scraping sound, like bare feet on hardwood. It had started then stopped. Waited. Then started again.

Now whoever it was had stopped, probably realizing I'd heard.

I edged around the counter toward the knife block. Why would someone be sneaking around in the mansion? Spying on me? No, that was too narcissistic. Maybe they wanted to get to Derek? To kill him for last night's disaster?

Slowly, I pulled a chef's knife from its sheath and held it by my side. It had only made a soft whooshing sound, but if the person sneaking around in the hall was a werewolf, he'd have heard it and known I was armed.

I waited in the corner between the island and the back counter, trying to become invisible. Part of me tried to play this off as paranoia, but there was this irrepressible feeling inside me that insisted whoever was in the hallway was there with malicious intent. Cautiously, I reached out with my power to try and find the being in the hall.

It was a faint vibe, but it was there—

I frowned. It wasn't a werewolf. That made me relax my hold

on the knife somewhat. He or she was human. And he or she was hiding. From me. I strained to hear the person's exact thoughts, but I must have been too nervous. All I got was a name.

A name that froze my heart to solid ice.

Calvin.

21

FAIR WARNING

I couldn't stifle a gasp. But I immediately regretted doing it. I barely got a second's warning in the vibe before he was exploding out of the hall at top speed—a mammoth of a man with agility that shouldn't have been possible. He darted around the countertop and was almost on top of me before I could scream. I dashed out of his grip and rounded the island, throwing a stool down behind me. He tripped over it, and I sprinted for the back door—the only place I could think to go.

It was locked. I tugged on it, crying out, but it didn't budge. I spun to see the man crawling toward me as he got up. Panicking, I chucked the knife at him and tried to squirm away past his bulky body. He dodged the knife as though this was just a game of dodgeball and then lunged for me. He caught my foot as I made to jump around the island again, and we both hit the tiled floor. My head slammed into the tile, dazing me, as the man got a good tight hold on my shoulders. He straddled me, weighing about as much as a full-grown horse might and pressed the knife I'd thrown at him against my throat.

"Shut up, shut up," he whispered.

When your attacker says to shut up, that's usually a good time to scream.

I inhaled deeply to do just that when he took the knife and slashed my cheek.

I gasped and he replaced the knife to my throat.

"Next time I'll make it scar," he said.

"Fuck you," I snarled, half crying.

"Not interested."

I squirmed beneath him, but that did pretty much nothing. This guy was a tank. He was probably one of the men who'd taken

Lucas down to the silver room, but I couldn't catch a clear glimpse of his face to be sure.

"What do you want?" I demanded.

"I want to tell you something."

"And you need a knife to do that?"

"I need a knife so you won't scream. I was going to try and do this telepathically, but you're still too new."

"What?" I asked. "What do you mean? Did you talk to Yvette?"

"No. My brother."

"Kevin," I whispered. By now all I could *do* was whisper, since he was sitting on my chest.

I saw his silhouette nod in the darkness.

"I had suspected you were one of them for a while," he said. "But when Lucas came out of that room with his sanity, I was certain. Listen, Faith, you must know something. It's about the uprising."

"What?" I asked breathlessly.

"Rolf will not listen to me because I am human, and nobody here trusts me, so I need you, Faith."

"Why doesn't anyone trust you?" I could make a few guesses based on my current situation, but I wanted to know more.

"That is a story for another time. What you need to hear, you must hear quickly and then convince Lucas to take action."

"Okay . . . so tell me."

"The vampires want Derek. They want him badly, and they will do anything to have him."

My stomach plummeted. "Why?" I croaked.

"I know not. But they want him. Faith, there is talk of kidnapping him, or keeping him hostage. Of keeping *you* hostage so he will comply with their wishes. My insiders can keep their plans at bay for now, but it will not last forever. You have to leave here. Go someplace where the vampires cannot find you."

I gasped for breath. "I can't leave. My whole life is here. Lucas is here."

"Do you not think Lucas will follow you anywhere?"

"He needs the pack to stay sane, I can't ask him to—"

"So you would rather your best friend die? Or yourself?"

I struggled again to get away, furious. "Who are you? What do you even care about us?"

"I am closer to you than you think," he rumbled. "Please, Faith, heed my words."

Heed his words? What a loser. "What am I supposed to do with this information? I can't leave. I won't."

"Then for Heaven's sake, at least take precautions. You cannot run amok through the night and not expect evil to find you."

"I don't run amok anywhere; I have protection. And I'll tell Lucas and Derek what you said about them wanting him for something, but beyond that there's nothing I can do. In case you haven't noticed, I'm just a human."

He slid the knife slowly away from my throat and said softly, "Some of the bravest people I've ever known have been human. Your mother among them."

"My mother?" I asked. "What do you know about my mother?"

But he ignored me and said, "Just because you are human, doesn't mean you are inferior. It just means you must be careful. So be careful, Faith. I'll be watching." And with that he was gone, vanished like a ghost.

"You slimeball, what do you know about my mother?" I screamed to no one. "Tell me, damn it!" I rolled over and slammed my fist into the ground, effectively shutting me up. I sat back on my haunches, cradling my hand to my chest. Suddenly, the light popped on, and I heard voices coming in from the living room. It was Derek and Katie, the dynamic doggie duo, complete with wagging tails and drool slathering from their grinning mouths. Man, I was not looking forward to spending two hours locked in a car with those two. I loved them, yes, but chipper was so not me at the moment.

Derek all but stepped on me as he made his way to the fridge.

"Oh—what the hell? Faith?" he asked, stooping down. "Are you okay?"

"No," I whispered. "I am not okay. Some dude just attacked me and held a knife to my throat."

"Oh, my God," Katie whispered and did a quick sweep around the room. "I don't smell anyone weird. Who was it?"

"I have no idea. I couldn't see him." Derek helped me up onto a stool and held a damp cloth to my cheek to staunch the blood flow from the wound my attacker has given me. Derek noticed my swollen hand and quickly got a bag of frozen peas.

"Did you hit him?" he asked.

I swallowed. "Yeah," I said, not wanting to go with the truth, which was much more embarrassing.

"Way to go," he said and winked at me. "Well, are you sure you're okay? What did he want?"

"I'm fine. And he said he just wanted to tell me something— something about you, actually."

"What was it?"

"He said that the vampires need you. And that they'll do anything to get you to work with them. He said that they'd use me to get to you."

Derek appeared worried for a moment, and then he frowned. "Wait—how did this guy know all of this anyway? Maybe he's screwing with you."

"I thought that, too," I said. "But he said he had an insider. And something in the way he said everything . . . I don't know. I believed him."

"So what does this mean?" Katie asked, handing me a glass of water.

I took it gratefully, realizing as I did so that my hands were shaking.

"Well, I'd say Derek has to stay away from the vampires, but since he's got to spy on them for the pack, it's not an option."

Derek nodded gravely. "I'll just be careful. Besides, I'm sure this guy is just trying to scare you. It'll be fine."

I gave him a flat stare. "Famous last words."

• • •

Over the next two weeks, I barely saw Derek at all. The more time he spent with the vampires on spy duty, the less he hung out with me and Lucas. But it was my personal opinion that Derek wasn't hanging out with them because he had to—he did it because he genuinely liked them. No. Scratch that. He was crazy about them—their money and charms drew him in like blood through veins.

The only thing Derek *didn't* seem to like about the vampires was their diet. And not just that—he couldn't really judge them when he had the same needs—but the way that they took it. Their sick little pets.

That didn't stop him from accepting more of their fancy gifts, though. Cars, designer clothes, an expensive phone, and a watch that cost more than my spring tuition were just a few.

Since my mystery attacker had said the vampires wanted Derek for their uprising, I could only assume they were giving him these things to woo him. They wanted him on their team, and they were doing a fine job of luring him in. It seemed that with each gift, Derek released less and less information about the goings-on inside the lair.

He'd been required to give nightly updates since the last full moon, but lately, the information was scarce. In fact, Derek fought us tooth and nail on the very existence of an uprising.

It was after they'd given him VIP concert tickets to see Paramore—one of my favorite bands—that I finally confronted him about it.

We were walking to his room after one of his oh-so-fantastic nights with Calvin, Melissa, and Silas. It was close to five a.m., so I wasn't in the best mood anyway, but when he pulled out the tickets, it was like he rubbed my nose in his smelly socks.

"There are two tickets," Derek said. "We can both go if you—"

"I don't give a crap if you have a thousand tickets!" I exploded. "Can't you see that this is all a ploy? They're being way too nice to you!"

"What?" He let out an exasperated noise. "Can't you just be

happy for me? I have some friends again. I'm not going to apologize for wanting people to talk to besides you."

"I'm not asking you to. I understand you wanting to have friends, but if you'd open your eyes, you'll see that you already *do* have friends. What about Katie? She's been calling me and asking where you are. She says she hasn't heard from you in weeks and you barely speak to her in your classes."

Derek's jaw tightened, and he looked away.

"Did you guys have a fight?" I asked.

"No," he said. "Katie is just . . . the werewolves aren't like me. I don't fit in around them."

My heart sunk. I think part of me knew it was true.

"You just have to spend some time with them," I said, as I put my hand on his arm. "They're actually really nice . . . some of them."

"They only want me to spy for them," he said dismissively. He shook his head with an eye roll. "For a second that night . . . for a second, I actually thought they wanted me around. *Me*, not my powers. I thought helping them might be my way to finally connect with the pack. But then Rolf made it clear that he'd have me killed if I didn't help. He said that because I have the crave on the full moon, I'm too dangerous to have around. But if I proved useful, they'd be willing to take the 'appropriate cautionary measures.'" He sneered.

"You see, Faith, they're all like Lucas. They can't stand to be around me, want nothing to do with me because I'm not a pureblood werewolf. I'm just a dirty mutt to them. And I know you think I haven't but I've *tried* to connect with them, feel something when I'm around them, but it just doesn't click. The only time I feel anything like them is when I change. Then . . . like when I run with Katie." He swept his hand through his hair and sighed. "Man, it's like we're the same person. Like we have the same heartbeat. I've never felt closer to anyone in my life." His smile was far away as though he saw some unseen vision I could never understand. But in a breath, it disappeared. "Then I turn into me again, and it's gone. I can't connect to anyone. . . . I'm like one of them. A vampire."

Derek sniffed bitterly and flopped down on the bench outside his building. I stood between his feet with my hands in my pockets. He was so desperate to connect to someone that he was latching onto the only people who were nice to him, regardless of the fact that they were murderers. I had to make him see that they only wanted to use him as a weapon in their uprising and that siding with them would pretty much mean the end of civilization. I'd tried repeating my mystery attacker's warning, but he didn't seem to believe that guy. Frankly, I wasn't sure if I did either, but I didn't want Derek around the vampires anyway, so I'd use whatever ammo I had.

"Have you heard them mention anything about their plans?" I asked. Since the massive raid had been a total bust, the pack was more desperate than ever for info. If they didn't get it, I worried they'd come after Derek. He didn't like when I pried into what he called "his business" but I didn't have a choice anymore. It was either annoy him or risk the pack's fury.

Derek dragged his hands down his face and regarded me flatly.

"I haven't heard anything. But that's because there *is* no uprising, Faith. You're being paranoid, I'm telling you. The vampires aren't interested in the werewolves aside from staying away from them."

I kicked his shoe absently. "What if there *is* an uprising, but they're just not telling you about it because they want to use you?"

Derek made an aggravated sound that sounded suspiciously like a snarl and stood.

"Using me for what?" he asked. "Half the time I don't think they even want me around. They think I'm a freak. They tell me every night what a wuss I am because I don't kill people to satisfy my crave; they laugh at me when I get upset and tremor. They don't want to use me; they probably want to get rid of me."

Derek started walking toward his building.

"Derek!" I shouted after him.

He blurred through the door, leaving me looking around to make sure nobody saw him moving at the speed of light.

I thumped down on the bench, reeling. He was like a bratty child, fit to explode at the first sign of upset. I supposed it was the split magic affecting him again, but that didn't make it any easier to deal with. And worst of all, he seemed hell-bent on staying with the vampires.

I kicked a pinecone across the yard, cursing to myself.

Why was he being so stubborn? So—I puffed a laugh. So like a werewolf.

It was clear he was not going to listen to me or my mystery attacker's warnings, so that meant I had to somehow prove that the vampires were, indeed, using Derek for their upcoming revolution. *But how can I prove it to him?*

The answer came to me in a rush of terror and, oddly, excitement: I had to make them admit it. Which meant I had to get closer to the vampires and work it out of one of them. I could use my gift the way I had with Lucas when we interrogated that vampire in the barn so I'd know what information was true and what was false. Plus, now that I was getting better at picking out actual thoughts from peoples' heads, sneaking out information would be even simpler. I could even get info out of them for the pack.

If Derek wasn't going to spy for the werewolves, I would. Only when the time came to hand the pack information, I'd make sure Derek still got the credit. They needed to know that Derek was upholding his side of the bargain. If everything worked out and the pack was able to eradicate the vampire brood, they might be more willing to accept Derek.

But I couldn't just go up to the vampires all willy-nilly and start spouting questions. I had to have a game plan. I had to be slick—not my strong suit.

And I had to break the news to Lucas.

So, with the moon waxing over my head, he and I sat on the very bench where I'd first seen him those many months ago. The massive evergreen loomed over us, blocking the snow from reaching our heads. We sat in silence after having returned from a date in Old Town. We went to see *Cursed*, this ridiculously scary horror flick, which made me feel even antsier than I already was. Lucas began humming something that sounded vaguely like an Incubus song. I listened, jiggling my leg frantically as I tried to get up the guts to start this harebrained conversation, even though it would probably lead to a fight and maybe the loss of one of my arms.

"You're shaking like crazy," Lucas said, putting his hand on my knee. "Nervous much?"

"Sort of. The movie got me all spooked." I tried to smile up at him, but my face felt stiff. I might have looked psychotic.

"You're such a wimp."

Again, I tried to act normal and laugh, but it really sounded frightening, so I stopped. Apparently nonchalance was not my strong suit, either.

I sucked in a deep breath, trying to make my voice even. "Lucas?"

"Yeah, baby?" He hugged me close and kissed the side of my head. Would I ever *not* get chills when he touched me?

I'd already decided it'd be better to ask Lucas if he minded me going with Derek rather than telling him. Giving him the illusion of a choice might make all the difference. Although I still resented the notion that I had to ask permission to hang out with my friend.

"I have a question," I said, wincing.

"Well, don't sound so low about it. Like you can't ask me a question?"

"I just—I don't want you to get mad when I ask it. It's something you won't like."

"It's about Derek, isn't it?"

I swallowed. "He asked me if I wanted to go night skiing with him. It's supposed to be really cool, and he said he missed skiing. And I do too, sort of. It was fun minus the face-plant into the tree. Anyway, I thought I'd make it nice for him and go with."

It was sort of the truth. Derek and the vampires *were* going night skiing tomorrow night on Keystone Mountain. They were taking their private jet to some five-star resort in the mountains and spending the weekend on the slopes. Derek had been talking about it for days.

Lucas pursed his lips and regarded me critically. "You're just going because Derek asked?"

"Well," I said carefully. "I also thought it might be a good chance to really talk to him about the vampire uprising. He's still skeptical, but I don't know . . . maybe going off alone together will clear his head—help him see clearly what they're doing with him."

Lucas was nodding throughout this, so I figured he was convinced. It also played in my favor that I wasn't totally lying about that last part.

"The vampires won't be there?" he asked.

"No," I lied.

He narrowed his eyes at me, trying to see if I was lying, no doubt, and I looked away. I was such a bad liar.

"Okay. I guess I'm cool with it." He grabbed my chin and made me look at him. "*No* biting. If I see even a scratch on your neck, I'll pulverize that kid."

I gulped. "No problems there."

He kissed me briefly and then stood up. "Speaking of food, I'm starved. Let's jet."

· · ·

The next phase of the mission was considerably easier, even though I was still surprised by how readily Lucas accepted my little lie. He must really trust me. Or maybe I was a better fibber than I thought. I hoped it was the latter because I was about to do a load of fibbing this coming weekend.

Just after dark on Friday night, I called Derek from right outside his room.

"Derek Turner at your service," he said, when he picked up.

"I have a surprise for you," I said.

I heard him yawn. "You dumped the dog?"

"No." I made a face at his door. "Come outside."

"Is that you I hear out there? What are you doing here?"

"Just come here!"

Derek whipped the door open with the phone still stuck to his ear and took me in, standing in his doorway with a suitcase and a parka slung over my arm.

"I'm coming with you!" I said.

Derek dropped the phone and pulled me into a backbreaking hug, saying something that sounded very much like, "ohmygoshyay!"

• • •

That was, by far, the simplest and most enjoyable phase of the mission. The next ones were entirely too dangerous and destined to fail miserably. As Derek and I stood on the airplane hangar, waiting for the vampires to show up, I let my foot tap against the asphalt—the only clue to my inner turmoil I let show. On the outside I remained calm, channeling my inner Lucas and repressing every wave of panic that bubbled up in my chest.

Derek didn't seem to notice, which was somewhat disappointing, because Derek usually noticed everything when it came to me. He kept his eyes fixed into the distance, his face unreadable. His vibe was thrilling with excitement, but tinged with something else. Worry. I wondered what he was thinking.

"You're early!" said a smooth voice from behind us. We both

turned and saw a group of people sauntering toward us, their mountains of baggage being towed behind them by airport employees. Calvin walked in front wearing an all-black suit that showed off the slimness of his body in the best way.

Even I, who hated this slime bucket more than anything else in the world, had to admit he looked very much like a young Brad Pitt.

Silas and Melissa flanked him on either side, each one with a human on their arm. Their pets, I guessed.

Calvin clapped Derek on the shoulder.

"Ready, buddy?" he asked jovially. He turned to me and his eyebrows shot up. "The dog let you borrow his bitch?"

Derek shrugged Calvin's hand off. "Don't call her that."

"Merely a jest, Derek. Merely a jest." His violet eyes were striking as he surveyed me head to toe.

With a cocky smirk, he turned and waved everyone up to the jet.

The inside was like a really expensive hotel room. Luxurious leather armchairs lined the beige walls, where there was a small flat screen for each one. There was a bar in the back that glittered with champagne bottles and decanters of dark liquid that had to be blood. A plump flight attendant stood next to Calvin's chair, pouring some into his wine glass. I wondered if all the humans were blood bitches or just oblivious.

Probably the former.

Calvin took a sip of his drink, and I gagged as his teeth glistened with wet blood. Color flowed into his cheeks.

"Ahhhh," he sighed, smacking his lips. "Lovely. . . . The boys are so sweet this time of year."

More gagging from me.

Derek squeezed my hand and led me to the armchair next to his. Melissa and Silas began conversing in something that sounded like Chinese and shot furtive glances at me several times. I swallowed hard and tried not to look as suspicious as I felt. Calvin and Derek began talking about something having to do with football, but I couldn't concentrate. I was utterly terrified and wishing with every bone in my body that I hadn't gone through with this. I wished Lucas was with me.

As soon as we were in the air, the flight attendant approached me.

"A drink?" she inquired. She was a curvy lady with a tiny red-painted mouth and piggish eyes. She tilted her head to the side, and I realized she meant from her.

"No," I squeaked.

Melissa giggled hideously from the armchair next to Calvin's. She was pointing at me. Silas's mouth ripped into a sneer as well.

They were playing a joke on me.

Nice.

Calvin looked up and said, "Now, now. Be nice to our guest or I'll have the pilot turn this plane around!"

Derek's smile was apologetic as he held his arms out, inviting me to sit on his lap. Normally, I would have refused, but I was too freaked out to worry about leading him on. I clambered over and leaned my head against his glacial chest. I shivered, and Derek looked up, snapping his fingers. The flight attendant hurried over with a thick woolen blanket, and Derek wrapped it tightly around me so that I felt like a baby kangaroo, all warm and safe in my pouch.

Except that it was possible that I might be eaten at any moment.

"How did they do that?" I asked, gesturing to the flight attendant.

"Make her offer herself to you?"

"That sounds so nasty," I whispered. "But yeah. How do they mess with our minds? Is it magic?"

"It's like hypnotics. They can make you see stuff or do stuff. Only the really old ones can do it. It takes a lot of practice."

"So if they can use hypnotics, why do they bother with all the blood bitch stuff?"

Derek rolled his eyes. "It figures you'd call them that."

"That's what they are, aren't they?"

"The 'blood bitches' aren't like what Lucas says. They're not all crazy drug addicts. Most bloodies—"

"*Bloodies?*" I spurted.

"Blood buddies," Derek said smiling. "Not bitches."

I recomposed myself. "Same difference. They're drug whores."

"No, no," Derek said. "That's just some of them—the radicals. Most bloodies use the stuff inconsistently and only in small doses. They know how . . . ah, temperamental some of the vampires can get, so they don't stick around for long."

"You mean they know that the vampires will eventually kill them?"

Derek just shrugged. "Anyway," he said. "The vampires don't like using hypnotics unless it's unavoidable. It takes a lot of their strength when they do it, so it leaves them vulnerable to attack."

"So why'd they just use it for me?"

"Because who's going to attack them here?"

"True," I said. "So can you do it, too?"

"Nope. Not yet, at least." His eyes twinkled at me, but I wasn't impressed.

"What about Calvin?"

Derek frowned. "I don't know. But I know Silas can do it. He's almost three hundred years old, can you believe that?"

"Yes," I said, thinking he was younger than Lucas was. "I wonder if it works on me."

This last statement was a lie—my first of many. I knew hypnotics worked on me. Vincent had made me see Derek bleeding that night in the woods. I'd told Derek about it when I'd given him the Vincent rundown many weeks earlier. So, I fake-wondered this aloud to get Derek to bring up Vincent, which would, in turn, allow me to bring up the murders without looking suspicious. But he didn't bring Vincent up.

Instead he gave me a funny look and said, "Why wouldn't it work on you?"

This threw me. "Be-because I'm special. Maybe hypnotics don't work on me."

Derek sighed like I was being difficult on purpose.

"Calvin said I was," I argued. I didn't want to go into what Yvette and Lucas knew about my power, so I just stuck to what Derek knew.

Calvin's voice rang through the cabin, "What did Calvin say?"

I blinked and he was sitting on my armrest. "You said I was special," I muttered. "Like Paula."

"Ah, yes. Indeed, you are!"

"Derek doesn't believe me," I said, sounding too much like a sullen child.

Calvin gasped and threw his hand to his chest. "Derek, how could you debate such a thing, when she is so obviously unique?"

"Come on," he said. "Quit playing around and tell her the truth. There's nothing special about her."

Ouch . . . that was a tad harsh.

He must have seen my face and said, exasperated, "You know what I mean. You don't have powers or whatever."

"Oh, but she does," Calvin said. He turned to me. "What exactly is your little gift, Faith Reynolds?"

For a moment, I debated over telling them the truth, but my "little gift," as they were calling it, was useless around them, since I couldn't control their emotions. They'd supposedly killed the last person with this gift, but I had Derek with me so I felt sure they'd never try anything. Besides, I didn't have to tell them I could control the werewolves.

"I feel emotions," I said. "Like vibes rolling off of people."

Derek snorted derisively.

"Don't laugh," Calvin admonished. "This is a serious matter. You must help her to hone her skills. As her master it is your duty." Then he paused as if remembering something. "But, oh . . . she isn't your pet at all, is she? She belongs to the dogs."

Derek's body tensed.

"I don't belong to anyone," I said hotly.

Calvin snickered. "Yes, you keep saying that, but sooner or later, darling, you're going to have to pick a side."

I just glared at him as the fasten-your-seatbelts light came on overhead.

"Oh, my," Calvin said. "We've arrived already. Lovely, lovely." He returned to his seat and took a sip from his glass. He saw me watching him and toasted me, taking a long gulp from the glass as if he wished it were me he was drinking from.

In his dreams.

I huddled into Derek, not bothering to go back to my seat. I was safer in those iron arms then I'd ever be with a strap of fabric over my waist. The plane landed and we filed out and into a shiny black limo. We drove up into the mountains, winding through the roads like a short black snake sliding down a river. Derek and Calvin talked the whole time, mostly about sports, and the other two vampires conversed in foreign languages. With the other two humans mute, I contented myself with staring out the tinted window.

Tucked into the craggy folds of a humongous white capped mountain, which could only have been Keystone Mountain, was the resort we would be staying at. In the dark, it glittered and shone in pink and blues, reminding me of Cinderella's castle but made of wood. The ski paths lit up the mountain in bolts of lightning. I saw little dots flying down the pathways and felt a thrill of anticipation. The dots were people night skiing.

The limo pulled up to the overhang, which led to the lobby, and we all filed out again. I saw a lot of people gaping at the vampires and some at me, too—probably wondering what an averagely attractive girl like me was doing among these godlike—okay, and slightly creepy—creatures.

Calvin loped to the reception desk and leaned against it, flirting with the concierge.

The lobby was like an opulent wooden cabin, complete with ceilings that reached heaven, big furry armchairs stuffed into every nook and cranny, slate fireplaces roaring with fires and windows as big and wide as minivans. It was lovely and warm and strangely quiet. Peaceful, even.

Too bad my insides were screaming.

Calvin returned, jiggling his keys around.

"Penthouse," he said grinning like he just saw a vat of blood with his name on it. He was looking at me when he said this, so maybe he did.

A couple of bellboys accompanied us to the fifth, and topmost, floor of the resort. We had the entire right wing to ourselves. When we went in, Calvin immediately hung the DO NOT DISTURB sign on the doorknob, which disturbed me to no end.

The vampires spread out to inspect the suite—all except Melissa, who sprawled herself out on the big brown couch, rubbing her pet's thigh seductively. The guy looked ready to wet his pants, and not with pleasure.

"Where will you guys sleep during the day?" I whispered to Derek.

"Under the closets," he said. "Calvin said they've rented this hotel room out before, so they have it customized."

Probably the work of another blood bitch.

Melissa and her pet were engaged in what looked to be some sort of silent battle for neck-possession. Every time Melissa touched his throat, the man cringed away and fought to cover it up. Then she'd giggle and taunt him again. Her vibe boiled with hunger so strong it almost made my stomach rumble, too.

As her perfect red mouth inched slowly toward his thick, stubbly throat, Derek suddenly grabbed my hand and sequestered me between the wall and his body. I frowned up at him and he nodded significantly toward Melissa.

Her eyes were blackened with the crave, and a wave of terror flew down my spine. I really wanted to somehow hide all of my blood.

But Melissa seemed to have no interest in me whatsoever. She slipped her gloves off with her teeth and pressed a pointed nail into his neck. The man cried out as blood flowed down his throat and chest. Melissa licked it up and took long, noisy draws.

It was like watching a car wreck; I couldn't tear my eyes away.

"Derek, you want a pull, honey?" Melissa cooed.

I whipped around to look up at Derek. His pupils dilated, eating up all of the blue.

"No," I said firmly, glowering at Melissa. "He doesn't do that."

Melissa tittered. "That's what he *tells* you."

Liar.

Derek swallowed hard and I noticed his nostrils flare, like he was trying especially hard to keep from breathing.

Calvin came out of one of the bedrooms, tossing a tiny bottle of hotel shampoo between his gloved hands. "Stop your nettling, Mel," he said. "Derek prefers the plastic-tasting stuff." Then he spun around and clapped his hands together, eyes wild with excitement. "Who's up for a dip?"

"Dip?" I asked bemusedly.

"In the hot tub!" Calvin exclaimed. "Last one in has to drain an old lady!"

CONFESSIONS

The vampires zipped outside onto the balcony immediately, while I threw a murderous look at Derek and swept into the room he and I were sharing.

"I'm not going," I said firmly. I stood facing the darkened window, refusing to look at him.

"You have to go," Derek said from behind me.

"I don't *have* to do anything," I said acidly. "I signed up for night skiing, not hot tubbing."

"We're going skiing tomorrow night. There's not enough time before dawn tonight."

I spun around. "And that was *vile* out there, by the way. God, she was sucking his blood right there in the living room!"

Derek stuffed his hands into his pockets. "Melissa's still kind of young, and she needs more than most."

"I know that, but it's not an excuse! She could drink donated blood."

"That stuff tastes like plastic. I don't blame her for wanting the fresh stuff."

"You don't *blame* her?"

"Aw, Faith, do we have to get into this? I thought we were here to have fun."

I dug my fingers into my eyes, trying to reign in my temper. "Okay," I said. "Sorry. That was just . . . gross."

Derek's mouth tightened, and I realized I'd hurt his feelings.

"Sorry," I said again.

He just shrugged and flitted into the bathroom. He emerged seconds later in a pair of light blue Lacoste swim trunks and a bare chest.

As I was busy gaping at his rockin' bod, Derek tossed something at me.

"What's this?" I asked.

"Bathing suit. Duh."

I untangled it and saw that it was a black Victoria's Secret bathing suit with barely anything in the butt department.

"No way," I said. "I'm not going."

"They'll be insulted if you don't."

"Like I care." I turned away from him.

Then Derek came up behind me, putting his cold hands on my arms. "Please, Faith? I just want to have a good time this weekend. It's been so long since we've been able to just be together without any drama. I miss us." His hands traced lightly down my arms, coming to a stop at my wrists. He bent his mouth close to my ear, giving me chills. "I'll make sure the others behave. They listen to me."

Because they want to use you, I longed to say. But I'd been defeated. I was always a sucker for his sweetness.

So I put on the tiny swimsuit and forced myself to go out onto the balcony with Derek strutting along beside me.

The hot tub was inset into the lacquered oak planks of the deck, making it flush with the floor. The view behind the balcony was the dark form of Keystone Mountain, so close it blocked out the sky. Blue and red lanterns hung along the balcony and cast us all in a creepy purplish glow. Wine glasses filled with dark liquid dotted the edge of the hot tub and music played in the background. It might have been romantic if I hadn't been scared out of my mind.

The vampires were already inside the roiling water of the hot tub, and I was willing to bet that none of them had any clothes on.

Not that I was about to look.

Not that I noticed Calvin had the pecs of a Greek god.

Or that Melissa's bathing suit was twice as tiny as mine, and it was hanging over the edge of a wooden chaise lounge.

Thank God for bubbles.

I sank in next to Derek and tried to become as small and insignificant as possible, which was, sadly, not as easy as I had hoped. Across from me, I tried not to watch Melissa sexually molesting her pet.

"Hey, Calvin," I said, nudging his arm.

He turned with a giant smile on his face, and for a moment, I was distracted by his supreme cuteness. *Damn vampires....*

"Do you know Vincent Stone?" I asked.

I felt Derek go rod stiff next to me.

"Why yes," Calvin said pleasantly. "I know him quite well. Lovely fellow, Vince. A smidge vengeful over some feud he had going with a werewolf, but I hear that's all done with." He frowned, looking off into the distance as if trying to recall something. "I wonder what's become of him now." Then he shook himself and said, "Why is it that you ask?"

"Because I was curious about whether he ever got punished."

"Punished? Well, whatever for, dear Faith? Vince never committed any crime to my knowledge."

"I heard he did."

I was being careful not to outright accuse their friend of murdering girls in Denver, but that was exactly what I was trying to get at. If Vincent wasn't the only one killing girls—and it was pretty obvious that he wasn't because he was dead and girls had been murdered afterward—then I wanted to know who else was.

"What did you hear?" Calvin asked.

Derek's foot stomped on mine, and I winced, tears springing into my eyes. I looked down and pretended to sneeze.

Derek cut in while I was enduring the severe pain he'd caused my baby toe.

"She heard he'd never registered when he came to Colorado," Derek said. "I told her."

Calvin smiled tightly. "You tell your pet a lot, Derek. That may not be the smartest move considering her ties with the dogs. One might deem that as treachery."

"I don't cross information," I said. "What Derek tells me stays with me."

Calvin dipped his head into a bow. "A loyal pet. Such a rare exception."

"But that's not what I heard about Vincent," I said before Derek could stomp on me again. "I heard he didn't hide his, ah . . . prey properly a time or two and that he was going to be punished for it."

Calvin narrowed his eyes and scratched at his ear, internally debating something. Silas, listening in to our conversation, seemed totally bored, while Melissa, on the other hand, had mounted her pet and was doing . . . something to him under the water. I didn't think she was listening.

"Where did you hear this?" Calvin asked.

"I kind of figured it out. I knew Vincent. We went on a few dates." Technically not a lie. "I know what you're talking about when you say he was involved in a feud. It's all he ever talked about. Except once. Once he told me he was turning people. A lot of people. He said that girls were harder to turn because of their souls or something. With all those dead girls on the news it didn't take long for me to figure out it was him, and to figure out that he would be punished by his superiors."

Calvin's expression was completely masked as he listened, so I tested his energy to see whether I was getting anywhere. He knew I was angling, but he couldn't tell why. I heard a few stray words, *traitor* and *lying* among them.

I focused on the water and played with the beading on my bikini top, trying to go for sexy little vampire pet, rather than werewolf informant. "I—I just wanted to know if something bad happened to him," I said mournfully. I risked a look at Calvin and saw that his gaze has softened.

He scooted closer to me and wrapped his frosty arm around my shoulders. "Regrettably, I know not what happened to Vince. He was an excellent vampire, quite a few years my senior, if I recall. I shall send word out to our neighboring sectors for you, if you like. Perhaps he would return if he knew your concern for him."

"Ugh, no way," I said before I could stop myself. Derek stomped me again and I let out a noise that sounded like a trampled Chihuahua. I sniffled trying to pretend like I was crying. "I mean, no—no," I fake sobbed, secretly rubbing my toes. "No, don't bother him. He's such a busy, busy man."

Calvin rocked me side to side. "Ah, the love of a loyal pet is such a beautiful thing. It is such a shame so many of you have to die."

I sniffled and shivered underneath Calvin's icicle of an arm. I shot the evilest of all evil looks at Derek and mouthed the words, "I hate you."

"Tell me, Faith darling," Calvin crooned, "what does it feel like to be bitten by a vampire? I must admit, I am quite curious. Sadly, I cannot remember the experience for myself." He leaned back, tracing his chilly finger over my shoulder.

"I've never been bitten by a vampire," I said, evading.

"Oh yes," Calvin said. "But Derek has bitten you. He told us." He threw an approving smile at Derek, like one a father might give his son when he won a soccer game. "A viran's bite cannot be so different from a vampire."

"It—it feels like a bite," I said reluctantly. I didn't want to admit that it was pretty much the best feeling in the entire world.

"Oh, come now," Calvin coaxed. His voice was soft and slippery as butter. "You must be more descriptive than that."

I glanced around nervously and saw that the entire hot tub had gone silent. Only the bubbling of the water and the soft lull of music floated through the air. They were all staring at me, even Derek.

"I was mostly just scared," I muttered.

Derek looked away, shame raking through his vibe.

"Of what?" Calvin pried.

I bit my bottom lip, wishing the subject would change. But the vampires seemed genuinely interested in this. It was so weird. Maybe they got off on talking about it.

"I was scared that—that he would take too much and kill me."

Derek's profile crumbled into a grimace, but he remained silent.

"And when he pulled," Calvin said eagerly. "What then? Only fear, or was there . . . something else?"

I drew in a shuddery breath. It was like they *knew* I was holding something back. But how could they know that?

"It wasn't bad," I admitted finally.

"Good?" Derek asked.

"I don't want to talk about it."

Melissa's face ripped into a grin. "The dog girl likes to be sucked!" she shrieked wildly.

I glared off into the distance, hating Melissa. Hating Calvin. Hating myself because her words were true.

Calvin splashed Melissa, and she quieted, stroking her pet's wrist as if she was about to start drinking from him again.

"Do you?" Calvin asked. "Do you like it?"

Derek cut in, saving me.

"She doesn't want to talk about it," he said. "Lay off."

Calvin straightened and a sound bubbled in his throat as he glowered at Derek.

Derek didn't back down, and soon Calvin dissolved into his debonair self. "I think it is clear that the experience was not displeasing. I daresay she might have enjoyed it, but that remains to be seen."

Melissa scoffed. "Does it matter? That whole thing is so idiotic anyway. You men and your libidos."

I frowned. "What do you mean?"

Melissa licked her pet's wrist obscenely and said, "The male vampires have this . . . *other* need. You know the one I'm talking about?" She leaned in and winked slyly.

Oh . . . *that* need.

She smiled. "Something to do with how the magic reacts to the testosterone or whatever. They keep their sexual desire and we don't." She waved her hand around idly as if that was all irrelevant, but I found myself thinking that was totally unfair. Why should the male vampires be the only ones to have sex?

"But anyway," Melissa continued, "that particular need is too closely related to the blood crave, so it's too hard for them to do it without killing every girl they f—"

"Melissa!" Calvin cut in, standing up suddenly. "That is enough."

"What?" she said. "It's true. You all just can't get over it. Like it's such a big deal. The feel of a freshly deceased corpse around your lips is twice as good as any of that." She rubbed her teeth along her pet's arm and he flinched. "As if any human would want to do it with you if they knew the truth anyway. What human wants a dead guy to sleep with?"

Calvin sat down again, his back stiff.

"Melissa," Silas warned, his deep voice rolling through the night.

She snickered viciously. "And they don't want *us*," she went on, looking at me with a coy smile on her flawless lips. "The girl vampires, I mean. Like we want them either." She made a gagging motion with her finger. "They only want the warmth of a human body so they can feel close to the living again."

Calvin looked as though he was about to rip Melissa's head off. "That's not true," he ground out, though his vibe proved to the contrary.

"Methinks thou dost protest too much," Melissa sang.

Silence stretched through the hot tub until finally, Calvin turned to Derek, seeming to have quelled his anger with Melissa. "Have you given any thought to what we spoke about the other night?"

Derek's throat moved as he swallowed.

"I . . . I'm still thinking," he said after a long while.

"Well, you'd do well to speed it up," Calvin said briskly. "With our numbers growing so rapidly, the death toll on the humans is becoming increasingly noticeable. We don't have much time left."

Whoa. Were they talking about the murders? And what did Derek have to do with that? I was about to ask, when Calvin and Silas began an exchange in some other language, which ended in Calvin shouting, "The Ancestors won't do a thing, Silas! They encourage it!"

"Ancestors?" I jumped in. "Who are they?"

"Hmm," Calvin hummed speculatively. "It seems the dog girl is not all-knowing after all."

"I never said I was," I said. "But I am curious. Are they, like, your sires?"

"In a way," Calvin said. "It is said that the Ancestors are the very first vampires. That their blood began the vampire race as we know it today. They are indeed ancient, but there is no way to tell if they are the first. Vampire lore says that we are all connected, that we all came from the Ancestors—hence their name." Calvin's tone was skeptical and I got the feeling he didn't believe.

"You don't think so?" I asked.

Calvin let out a puff of laughter. "Hardly."

"That's treason," Silas said at once, his dark eyes blazing. "They are the one true authority." He turned on me. "No one crosses them."

"They're lunatics," Calvin said dismissively. "Don't look at me that way, Silas, you know what happens when we age. Soon we will all meet the same fate as the Ancestors. We will lose ourselves entirely. It is a fate we must all accept. But pretending like the Ancestors are above that end is naïve. They have lost all ability to think or rationalize. Yet those of you who follow the old ways still think they're competent rulers."

"They *are* competent," Silas argued. "Their word is law."

"And when was the last time they made a law, hmm? Last I checked they remained sequestered in their *palace* in Florida, eating tourists."

"Florida?" I asked, thrown. That was the last place I would have expected. I would have pinned them for Romania or Iceland or somewhere chilly and barren.

Calvin turned back to me as if surprised I was still there. "Indeed. Vampires don't care for the cold."

I let out a skeptical sniff. "So what are you doing in Colorado? It's freezing here."

"I said we don't care for it, not that we won't endure it. Many do, but the older we become, the harsher it is on our bodies. With the Ancestors' ages raging from two to three thousand years old, naturally, they would choose to live in a warm climate. With Florida's tourist sites, they get many victims coming right to them. They hardly even hunt anymore—just wait for their prey to come to them. They are mindless shells."

"Treason," Silas mumbled.

"Maybe," Calvin said. "But Arabella agrees with me. This scheme they've cooked up is ludicrous. It will never work. We don't have nearly enough numbers, and we never will what with the precautions we have to take for the younglings. We have to find a way to—"

"*Stilte!*" Silas said suddenly. He continued speaking in whatever language that was, and I turned my power on high to try and get a clue to what they were talking about. Calvin's emotions burned hotter and hotter until I was sure the tub was filled with lava, and then it extinguished abruptly.

"Fine," Calvin mumbled. "But you know I'm right. And so does Arabella."

"You are sadly mistaken in that," Silas said. "Arabella's only use of the stuff is for the younglings."

"She *would* tell you that because of your support of the Ancestors."

"And she would tell you the opposite because you doubt them. She manipulates everyone. Do not be so foolish to think she cares for your opinion."

"She's my sire," Calvin hissed. "She cares for me more than any other being."

"Foolish," Silas repeated softly.

The hot tub fell silent.

That was weird. What stuff? What younglings? And who was Arabella? I was so acutely curious over what had been said there— or *not* said—that I almost brought the subject back up.

But I never got the chance.

There was a gasp from Melissa's end of the tub. I looked over and almost puked. Melissa had punctured her pet's wrist with her teeth and was sucking greedily from the wound. Horrible scarlet blood leaked out of the corners of her perfect mouth and snaked through the hot tub, turning the water frothy and pink. Calvin and Silas glanced at each other and then shrugged. They pounced on the body to enjoy the feast as well.

I vaulted to my feet and tried very hard not to scream. Derek stood and yanked me out of the tub. I struggled against him, afraid that he would bite me. He started to scoop me up, but then Calvin unlatched from Melissa's dead pet. He turned to us, blood dripping down his chin.

"Leaving so soon?" he asked.

ULTIMATUM

C alvin was on us in a millisecond and then I *did* scream—a high bloodcurdling scream that even made my skin crawl. Derek's body vibrated with the change, and he held me so closely I swore I was melting into his body.

"No," he said forcefully. "No one bites her but me."

I didn't know if I agreed with that exactly, but I was definitely willing to negotiate right then.

Calvin's eyes were black with the crave. "Just a pull," he said. "The man was sour. He left such a nasty taste."

"No one touches her!"

Melissa stepped out of the pool—totally naked—and skipped over, clapping her hands like a two-year-old at Toys"R"Us.

"Me first, me first!"

Only Silas remained in the red tub.

"He said no," Silas said dully. "Leave the kid alone."

Thank you, Silas!

But Calvin's crave was too strong for him to listen. He reached around Derek and snatched up my wrist with unearthly speed. He was centimeters away from biting me when Silas knocked Calvin back, and Derek trembled violently.

"He's gonna change!" Melissa yelled, pointing at Derek and backing up. "I'm getting out of here!"

She zipped back inside, shattering the French doors as they slammed shut behind her. I jumped at the sound and realized, yes, Derek was going to change.

I saw his fangs drop, and I dove to the side.

Calvin lunged for me, catching me while I was still airborne and rolling away with me pressed to his body. I screamed as his teeth gnashed together next to my ear. I struggled to push him away and then he was lifted off of me. I saw huge white paws on either side of my head and knew it was Derek. A shrill, almost hollow howl pierced the night.

I sat up and saw Silas staring straight at me with this creepy, hungry look in his eyes. So much for leaving me alone. I struggled to stand, slipping on the now icy deck.

Calvin clawed at Derek, leaving red marks all over his muzzle. He squirmed out of Derek's jaws and then flung himself onto Derek's haunches to sink his fangs into his throat. Derek yowled in pain. The two of them tussled, while I began backing away, keeping my eyes locked tight on Silas.

Too bad I backed away into the hot tub. I plunged in and got all turned around with the bubbles and the terror. I couldn't find my way up. Panic suffocated me . . . or maybe that was the water. I didn't know. But I did know that I was going to drown if I didn't figure out a way to the surface pretty damn soon.

Then something bumped into me. I looked up and saw Melissa's dead pet floating in the water with me. I screamed, which is a bad idea to do underwater because once you scream, you have no more air left. I sucked in bloody water and flailed around uselessly.

A hand grabbed my shoulder and tugged me out of the water. I coughed and drew in a humongous breath. The hand that saved me spun me around, and my body went limp for an instant.

It was Silas.

I pushed against him, knowing that struggling was futile, but I was unable to just stand there and let him bite me.

"Stop—it!" I screamed, pushing against him with all my measly strength.

"No chance," Silas said as his pupils widened.

Derek let out a loud frenzied bark that sounded very much like, *no!*

"Sorry, darling," Silas said. "But Arabella requires more vampires. And she does like the pretty ones."

Oh, I'd heard that before.

Silas lowered his mouth to my skin, but before I could feel the ice of his lips, something *huge* jumped up onto the balcony. The floor trembled and all of us were knocked back onto the floor.

Everyone stared up at the creature that had jumped five floors to the penthouse balcony. It looked like a wolf, but bigger and shaggier.

It was, of course, a werewolf. And not just any werewolf.

My boyfriend.

Lucas was here to rescue me. He didn't waste even a moment; he lunged at Silas and ripped his head off.

Just like that. Blood spurted everywhere, drenching me in poison, and I watched through my fingers as Lucas turned to charge Calvin, who was backing slowly away. Derek, who had just suffered a crushing blow to his ribs, struggled to stand. Then, clueing in to Lucas's plan he flanked him and proceeded to corral Calvin against the edge of the balcony. He was cornered, and knew it.

With a smug grin, he gave us his signature salute, and then leaped over the railing. The two wolves barked and started after him, but it was too late. Calvin was halfway up Keystone Mountain by now, and with Derek injured, they'd never catch him.

I exhaled heavily, not caring that Calvin and Melissa got away, not caring that there was a dead guy in the hot tub, or that Silas's venomous blood was all over me, or even that my best friend and my boyfriend were both in wolf form and liable to kill me at any moment.

All that mattered was Lucas. He was there. Somehow, he'd known to follow me on my stupid idiotic mission.

He'd saved me, yet again. And despite what I'd said to him earlier, I was glad he'd come to my rescue. I had to face it: I'd be dead right now if he hadn't. Thanks were most certainly in order, but before I could so much as stand up, the wolves turned on each other.

They began fighting, tearing at fur, yanking muscle, snapping and snarling. I was powerless to stop it. I'd promised Lucas I would never use my power against him again.

Then Lucas began to shake and he changed, unable to hold his form any longer without any vampires around. He dodged Derek's attacks, but something about seeing him human made him seem more vulnerable. Derek made to attack Lucas again and coldness swept through me: the thought of him killing Lucas.

"Derek!" I screamed, starting forward. "Stop it RIGHT NOW!"

Derek's big lupine eyes flickered to mine and creased into a frown. To my amazement, his body shook and he changed.

So of course, Lucas punched him. Or tried to. Derek managed to dodge at the last second and swung back, missing, too. Lucas tackled him and they went sprawling.

I shook my head and dragged my hands down my bloody face. *Men. . . .*

"Stop it!" I yelled with a little less enthusiasm than before. "Lucas, come on. This is dumb. You're not going to kill him, just stop it!"

Lucas held Derek down in a choke hold.

"Like—hell—I'm—not," he grunted.

"STOP! Don't hurt him. I don't want to use my power, but I will if you're going to hurt him, now *stop!*"

Lucas looked over at me incredulously and released Derek with a jerk. Derek drew in a strangled breath, hacking. Though he didn't need to breathe, Lucas had probably broken his windpipe.

Lucas strode up to me and pointed back at Derek. "You can't be defending him again," he warned. "How many times does this guy have to try and kill you before you realize what he is?"

Derek was standing now, his breath heaving through his body. He looked livid and ready to pounce on Lucas at any second.

I rounded on him. "Don't even think about it! Lucas just saved my life. Show a little gratitude."

Derek blinked. He seemed to have just realized I was still there—that I'd almost been eaten by his "friends."

"Faith, I'm so sorry," he said, stepping closer. "You were right all along, I guess."

I drew in a deep breath, sucking up my anger, and said, "It's okay. I forgive you."

Derek was hugging me within a second, but it only lasted about that long before Lucas ripped him off of me.

"God, you're relentless!" he shouted. "When are you gonna get it through your runt head that she doesn't love you, she loves me!"

Derek cringed as though Lucas had finally landed that punch.

"Lucas, stop it," I said, a little stricken by his outburst. "He feels bad enough without adding this on top of it. He said he was sorry. He's going through something terrible right now."

"That's all well and good," Lucas said, "but he's manipulating you, Faith. He's wheedling his way into your heart and lodging himself between us."

"No, he's not. We're just friends." I looked at Derek. "Right?"

Derek leaned against the wall, as casual as can be when you're buck naked. "Yeah, man. I really think you're being paranoid. Me and Faith are just friends." He smiled, baring his razor-like teeth. I winced as the light glanced off of them and blinded me for a moment.

I turned back to Lucas. "See? It's fine. I've told you a million times, you've got nothing to worry about here."

Lucas's vibe blasted with a million pent-up emotions. Anger. Frustration. Jealousy. Desperation. He was trying to keep them in, trying to repress them, but at last they grew so strong, the emotions almost swallowed me with it. He let out a loud roar-like sound and said, "Damn it, I can't take this anymore! I feel like I'm going crazy!"

I started to put my hand on his shoulder, but he jerked away.

"No," he said, shaking his head. "I'm not gonna pretend like I'm not jealous anymore, when I am. I'm jealous. I admit it, okay? And if that makes me a jerk, then fine. I'm a jerk, too."

Derek snorted and I silenced him with a look.

"There's nothing to be jealous of," I insisted.

"You think I don't notice the way you look at him? You think I don't see you flirting with him, holding his hand and playing footsie in the car? Did you really think I was that stupid?"

I attempted to protest, but Lucas cut me off with a slice of his hand through the air.

"No, Faith, I can't keep pretending to be this good person anymore, when I'm not. I'm a werewolf. An animal. And I thought, maybe you'd . . . I don't know, *softened* that instinct in me, but now I feel so crazy jealous that I know I'm still as horrible and jerky and—and whatever else you wanna call me as I always was."

"Don't say that," I begged. "Don't be this way. You know I love you." I reached out for him, but he stepped back.

"I can't do this anymore. You either gotta pick me, or you gotta pick him. But I can't watch you flip-flopping around anymore. I can't take it."

I felt like the world had just toppled over on itself, leaving me standing alone in the middle of it. Nothing made sense. I struggled to form words, but tears blocked me. I swallowed hard and made myself say something.

"Are you breaking up with me?" I gasped, still reeling.

Lucas didn't answer, but his expression was hard, bitter. "I'm telling you to choose."

"Don't—don't make me do that," I said. "This isn't just about Derek and you know it—the whole uprising depends on getting him back on our side. I thought you understood. I need to be with him."

Lucas stared at me for a long time. "That's your choice then?" he asked finally. I heard absolutely no emotion in his voice. The years he'd spent keeping his feelings inside were paying off. He was blank. Even his vibe was smothered.

"I can't," I whispered. "I'm not choosing. I won't."

Again, he said nothing for a long while; he just looked down at the floor, thinking about what, I could never know.

Finally, he looked up, determination hardening his features. "Look, this isn't going to work."

I shook myself, thrown by the change of his tone. "What?"

"We both knew this was coming. We both knew it would end one day."

End? What was he talking about? "But I thought—"

His voice was suddenly menacing. "What? What was your solution for this, Faith? Change you? That's never going to happen."

"Yvette and Rolf—"

"Aren't us. This was always our fate, Faith. Why prolong the inevitable? It's only torturing me more."

He could have slapped me in the face for how bad that hurt.

"Where is this even coming from?" I asked. "Just, please—let's talk about this."

"What's to talk about? I'm immortal. You're not. We don't have a future together."

"What about *my* future? Do I mean that little to you that you can just dump me without even talking to me first?"

Lucas's face tightened, his expression fluctuating between ambivalence and frustration. He seemed to wrestle with something and then said with a stony, forced voice, "Look, I changed my mind. Simple as that. I don't want to live in repression anymore."

Changed his mind . . . "What do you mean?" I whispered.

"Repressing the change is bad enough without adding what you do to me on top of it. It wouldn't be like this with any other girl. With someone else, I wouldn't have to worry about killing her all the time. We could be together. Fully."

At his last word, the meaning of what he was saying sunk in like a knife through my heart. I just stood there, unable to believe what I was hearing. It felt like a dream—a waking nightmare.

"That's how you feel?" I asked numbly.

His face was rigid, revealing nothing, and when he spoke his voice came softly in monotone.

"That's how I feel."

I stared him down, refusing to believe, but Lucas stared right back at me with empty, fathomless eyes. My world was caving in, crushing me beneath his black stare. It hurt so much, I could think of only one thing to do: hurt him back. Make him feel even half as awful as I did.

"Fine," I said. "Then I choose him. I choose Derek."

For the briefest instant, I thought I saw a flicker of regret. But then it was gone, and his mask of indifference was back.

"Good," he said.

Another blow to my heart. *Good?*

I was so busy trying to keep from sobbing that I didn't even notice Lucas walking toward me. He came very close, and I thought for one blissful moment that he was going to hug me, tell me to forget it, that he would stand by me like he always promised he would. But he just whispered in my ear, "We always knew there would be an end, Faith. I know you don't understand, but it's better this way." He reached up and touched my cheek. There was warmth for the smallest moment and then he said something so softly I wasn't sure if I'd heard correctly. His voice was low like the wind howling. "You'll always have my heart."

With that, he walked to the edge of the balcony and jumped over.

It was like there was a string connecting us because as soon as his feet left the floor, I dashed for the edge. The only thought in my mind was to follow him. I *had* to follow him, he couldn't leave.

Derek yanked me back.

He held me at the edge of the balcony as I screamed for Lucas. It was pathetic and desperate, but the only boy I'd ever loved had just left me. Left me wilted and alone, just like my stepdad had all those years ago. Left me just like Derek had when he'd told me he'd cheated on me. Left me crying, bloody and broken on the ground . . . like I was nothing.

SURVIVAL

I spent the next day alone. Not crying. Not thinking. I was in a state of numb denial. He couldn't have left. Not really. Not my Lucas—not my match.

I called him, must've been a hundred times.

He shut his phone off.

That night, Derek and I rented a car and drove four long hours back to CSU. Neither of us said a word the entire time, though I could feel his vibe shifting restlessly beside me. He wanted to comfort me, but didn't know how.

I thought, but didn't say, that the silence was enough.

When at last we reached the courtyard between the CSU dorm buildings—and after dealing with irritating curfew issues—I finally had a reaction. I wanted to run to Lucas's room. I wanted to bang on his door and scream at him, hit him, kiss him, make him hurt as badly as he'd hurt me. I wanted it so much I couldn't stop my legs from running up the stairs to his room, flying down the hall, raising my hand to knock on the door—

"Don't," Derek said, catching my fist before it hit. "It won't solve anything."

I sagged against him, my back colliding with his chest. I let my fist fall. He was right. Starting another fight would only make things worse. And make me look more pathetic.

So I let Derek drag me upstairs to his room where I spent the rest of the night crying.

I had class on Monday. I had track. I had a life to get back to. A life that now highlighted Lucas's absence with every agonizing minute that passed. From the moment I opened my swollen eyes to Derek's empty room to that last shuddering breath I took at night when I cried myself to sleep—I missed him. I missed his face in the morning and his voice in my ear before bed.

Living without him now was like trying to breathe with a hole in my lungs—impossible. But I forced myself through it. For two long, miserable weeks I made myself wake up, get dressed, go to class, come back, and slip into blissful silence with Derek at my side. I made myself live, because the alternative was not an option. I would take to wallowing alone in my own room with *P.S. I Love You* and a bag of chocolates. And while there were times during the day when that sounded like the best idea in the world, if I let myself fall into that pattern, I'd never resurface.

On the night of the full moon, when Derek went with Katie up to Gould, I'd called Heather again to keep me company, only to find out she was at Zydeco's with her druggie friends. I'd been in contact with her throughout the past weeks, but she'd never mentioned her return to drugs. Or maybe I'd been too upset to notice it. Either way, she made it clear that nothing I said was going to stop her from hanging out with the blood bitches, so the best option I had left was to join her. Try to make sure she didn't die.

So I began spending more and more time with her and her idiotic friends. It was both mind-numbingly stupid and euphoric at the same time. Convincing myself that I was somehow keeping Heather safe by being with them gave me a welcome distraction. So much so that I began hanging with them while Derek went to class.

When Derek returned from his classes, I left and said a small prayer that Heather could take care of herself. Derek and I did all of the old stuff together—late night TV, cold pizza, talking ourselves to sleep. Although he did most of the talking now.

The nights I spent with Derek healed the scorching hole in my heart, and I was okay until dawn. And then the daylight would break my heart all over again.

• • •

D erek and I got a visit from Calvin a few weeks later. We had just gotten out of a midnight showing of some action movie Derek had been dying to see and were meandering our way back to his car parked outside a restaurant in Old Town. Derek was plotting out how to sneak back onto campus and cheat the curfew, and I was trying my best to act interested. The town had seemed to relax somewhat since there hadn't been any murders in a few months, but the school had yet to lift that stupid curfew. I wouldn't have cared much, except that it made hanging out with a nocturnal creature difficult.

It was early April, so the weather should have been warming, but winter seemed to be giving us one last shove before spring took over. Flurries swirled through the purple sky above our heads, and I remembered the way Lucas had looked, so long ago, in the early morning snow, after Vincent had attacked Derek and me. I'd never been so happy to see him, bare chested, snow in his hair, and grinning at me.

I actually stopped walking when my gut wrenched. Derek looked down at me.

"What is it?" he asked, putting his hand on my arm.

I was about to tell him it was nothing when a rush of ice-wind smacked my face. I looked over and Calvin was there. I should have screamed, but I was too stunned. I just stood there. Petrified.

Derek was the one with all the reactions. Without a word, he sprang forward and tried to pummel Calvin, but he dodged the blow and they began to fight. Not physically fight, but there was a lot of yelling. I couldn't follow most of it because they did this annoying vampire thing where they talk ultrafast. Basically, Calvin tried to apologize and Derek told him to shove off.

For the first time in over a month, something other than pain and loss enveloped me. Relief. At least one thing had been accomplished by my suicide mission: Derek no longer wanted anything to do with vampires.

Calvin said something to Derek with a swift nod in my direction. I winced, watching Derek's body begin to quake violently. His eyes faded to clear and he said slowly enough for me to hear, "Go now, Calvin, or I'll show you the true meaning of death."

Calvin's perfect lips curled. "Big mistake, Turner. We've given you all the time you'll receive to get over the incident on Keystone. Refusing us now will mean death on your hands."

"I'll take my chances."

With a shake of his head, Calvin flitted away in another rush of wind.

Derek came to stand by me and put his arms around my waist, trying to comfort me. He murmured sweet things in my ear, telling me he'd never let anyone hurt me again.

I tried my best to believe him.

• • •

It was mid-April when I finally started feeling normal again, or at least seminormal. I still had a festering gaping wound in my heart where all the love I'd ever felt used to be, but you know, other than that.

My grades were abysmal, I was probably going to fail my final coming up, and I'd never been so tired in my life, but at long last the beginnings of recovery were creeping in on me.

April, however, was also when the murders started up again. Big time. Calvin had warned us it would happen, and boy was he right.

I was sitting in Derek's room, zonked out on the couch and staring blankly at the TV when the word *exsanguinated* filtered through my stupor. I sat up and hit the volume.

"Two more bodies were found," the anchorman said, "in an alleyway in Old Town, Fort Collins. The victims were both twenty years old and attended the Colorado State University. The police still have no leads on the killer. If anyone knows anything about the murders, we urge you to call the crime stoppers hotline on your screen."

I made a face at the TV. *Oh, right. I'll just call 1-800-CRIMESTOPPERS and tell them that the killer is a lair full of vampires. That'll go over well.*

The doorknob turned and Derek entered.

I clicked the TV off. "I thought you were picking up something to eat," I said, a little crestfallen. I hadn't eaten all day for lack of appetite, and now I was famished.

Derek grunted noncommittally as he locked the door behind him.

"You won't believe what was on the news just now," I said. "Two girls were murdered last night. Can you believe it?"

Derek swung around and cursed. "So much for 'we can handle this matter ourselves.' Stupid dogs." He snorted and kicked a stray book across the room.

Derek had been feeding the pack false information for the past few weeks and facing a lot of heat for not getting closer to the vampires as he'd been instructed to do. The pack had enough spies around us to know he no longer went to their lair, but Derek claimed to still speak with them via phone. The pack wasn't happy about this, but Derek refused to budge. He had offered to help find the lair in other ways, but they'd plainly refused him.

Majorly insulting.

It hurt his pride that the pack refused his help, and I totally got it. They'd refused me, too. I opened my arms for him, and he came to sit beside me on the couch, still brooding. I threw a blanket over us and cuddled into his side.

"They're only doing this because of what I told Calvin," he said. "You know that, right? It's like some sick little incentive to get me to go back to them. If I join up again, they'll stop killing. If not, people die. What the hell am I supposed to do now?"

I bit my lip. Derek couldn't go back to the vampires, not after everything I'd done to get him away from them.

"I guess we just have to trust the pack to take care of it," I said. "They swear up and down they don't need any help so . . ."

"So just sit around and pretend like it's not happening?"

I shrugged. "You'll get used to it."

He growled low in his throat and punched his fist into a pillow. The stupid thing exploded like a feather bomb and coated us both with down. I looked up at him, trying to keep from laughing because I knew this was a serious situation, but the look on his face—I couldn't help it.

I cracked up, crying with laughter like I hadn't experienced in months, and pretty soon Derek joined in. He threw the pillow across the room and shook his head. "No wonder they don't want my help. Derek Turner: Pillow Punisher."

I snorted.

"You know, we don't have to join up with the pack to help," Derek said. "We could do something together."

"Go all vigilante on their asses?"

Now he snorted. "Yeah, I guess."

"Except we're just as clueless as the pack is when it comes to locating the lair."

"Not if I get the vampires to show me where it is."

I looked up at him, narrowing my eyes. "That sounds dangerous."

"What, did you think we'd skip through the daisies up to their house and offer them a basket of muffins in exchange for laying off the murders?"

I elbowed him in the side. "Since when are you Mr. Sarcastic?"

"Since I started spending so much time with you."

I elbowed him again, only more lightly, since I'd hurt myself before. "I don't want you anywhere near the vampires again," I said. "That's not something I'm willing to risk. Not after . . ." I swallowed down the lump in my throat. "We'll just trust the pack. They swore to protect us, and we'll only end up getting in the way if we try to intervene."

"Well, that's very mature of you."

"It's called being smart. Try it sometime." I gave him a sly look out of the corner of my eye, and he brushed an affectionate kiss on my cheek, effectively stunning me into silence.

"Wanna see what's on?" he asked, flipping the remote in his hand.

"It's not like there's an uprising to thwart or anything."

Ironically enough, *Dracula* was on the classic movie channel, and we couldn't help but watch it given the circumstances. Halfway in, we were laughing at a corny bat-morphing scene when I said, "How sweet would that be?"

"What?" he said, still chuckling.

"If you could change into a bat, or something cool like that."

"Wolves are cool."

"Yeah, but bats can fly." I turned and smiled up at him, one of the rare ones I saved only for him. "You could pick me up and fly me away somewhere."

He bent and kissed my forehead. "Anytime, baby. Say the word and we're gone."

I looked away. "If only it was that simple."

"It is. We get on a plane and go. I can sell that stupid car the vampires gave me, and we'd have money to live off of for a year." He took my face, making me look at him. "Say the word and I'll do it. We'll get out of here, away from the vampires, the pack, Lucas."

I winced and he smoothed his thumb over my cheeks, shushing me.

"The pain would stop," he whispered. "You could move on."

I swallowed back a rush of emotion. Such sweet, tempting words. . . . I wanted so badly to take him up on his offer. Derek and I could travel, I could start taking pictures again, and we could be happy—best friends forever. Maybe even more than that someday.

But the thought of never seeing Lucas again broke the moment of felicity. To leave Colorado would seal our break-up in the most permanent of ways. There would be absolutely no chance that I would ever see him again.

It was a thought I couldn't handle.

I managed a weak smile for Derek's sake and said, "My mom would kill me if I dropped out of school."

Derek's face fell, but he picked it right back up. "Yeah, you're right. My dad would freak, too."

I turned back to the movie, watching Dracula seduce some chick and then crunch her neck up with his stick-on fangs.

Derek stretched next to me and said, "Be right back."

He got up and crossed the room, doing something by the fridge, probably getting a sip of blood. I turned the TV up and averted my eyes because I didn't like to watch him. He hadn't had any more cravings in a while, so he was definitely due. . . . But then again, I didn't remember the runt dropping off any more supply this week either.

Derek turned around and flicked the TV off. He came toward me slowly, something odd glinting in his eyes, something . . . hungry. His vibe, too, was serious. Determined.

"Hey," I said, nervous at his sudden flip of emotions. It was moments like these that reminded me how young he was in the supernatural world. "You okay?" I asked.

"Perfect," he said, still eyeing me intently.

"You seem a little hungry." I sat up, stretching my legs out.

"I am. Very."

It felt like someone had drilled a hole in my stomach. I stood up instantly. "We should go eat," I said. "We should go eat right now." The food wouldn't sate his blood crave, but it might hold him off if he was hurting. I started searching for my purse, but I had barely moved before Derek cut me off.

"No." We were inches away, his body so close, I could feel its coolness like a winter breeze. He swept his hands along my arms up to my throat, gathering my hair away from the skin. "I don't want food. I want you."

I gulped and tried to back away, but found I was already pressed against the wall. *How did that happen?*

"No, Derek. I don't want to. Let's just go get some food. It might help."

"I told you," Derek said, bending his face to mine. "I don't want food. I want you. Right now."

I shook my head, feeling tears creep into my eyes. I wanted to repay him for everything he'd done for me and to make up for all the wrong I'd done to him, but not like this. I was not his pet. "Please," I whimpered. "I don't want you to do this."

"I have to. I can't resist you anymore. It's too much. The dog isn't in the picture now. You have no excuses."

I began to protest, but he put a finger to my mouth.

"I'm going to kiss you now," he said, lips close to mine. "And I'm not going to stop. I'm not going to stop until I'm completely satisfied. . . . Until my hunger for you is finally sated." His pale pink lips curved up into a crooked smile, and his eyes sparkled.

He was joking. Playing like he wanted my blood when really he wanted . . . me.

"You jerk," I whispered. He smiled more broadly, that heart-stopping boyish smile that melted my heart. Every time.

I drew in a ragged breath, thought briefly of putting up a fight, and then said to hell with it. Lucas left me. He wasn't my boyfriend anymore. And Derek had always been my first love. Derek would be a good boyfriend. He would keep me safe, and I could certainly enjoy kissing him.

And somehow, the thought of kissing Derek felt like a first step. A step toward moving on. A step away from Lucas and the fiery hot coals I'd been dragging myself over. A step into the snow-covered ground, where it was cool and soothing over my singed skin.

Something to heal the wounds . . . or at the very least, numb them.

So I shut my mouth and closed my eyes, silently giving Derek the go-ahead to kiss me. I felt his frigid hands slip behind my head and down along my back. His cool breath tingled over my cheek and the tips of his teeth scraped against the soft skin beneath my jaw.

Suddenly memories of his bite swept over me in a rush of pure need. That sweet nothingness his bite had induced was exactly what I wanted—just a moment to forget about Lucas and everything I'd lost. To feel happy again . . . it was all I wanted. But I knew it wasn't right. . . . I couldn't use Derek that way.

"Don't bite me," I whispered, hating the words as I said them.

I felt his lips break into a smile along my cheek. "Oh, all right," he said. And he pressed his lips against mine, snarling his fingers through my hair and holding my body to his. Derek and I had kissed a hundred times before, but everything was different now. His lips weren't warm anymore; they didn't give when he pressed them to mine. They didn't taste of his sweetness. They were like unrelenting marble, bruising against my skin, yet somehow still pleasing. Everything was cold; my heart pounded as his lips parted mine and my breath came raggedly. I wanted him to bite me so badly. . . .

I knew it wasn't going to solve anything—but as we kissed, I could think of nothing else. I wanted to try it again, just once more. Just one bite.

I turned my head, and Derek kissed my jaw, moving up to my earlobe, pulling my hair back. I arched my body into his, willing him to do it. He kissed my neck, his hands clutching me ever closer.

I pressed onto my tiptoes, panting with anticipation.

But Derek pulled back, his forehead still touching mine. "Do you want me to?" he whispered.

I answered him with a nod, turning my head just slightly. A flicker of doubt played in his eyes, and then they darkened with the crave. I swept my fingertips lightly over his eyelids; he was so unearthly beautiful I couldn't look away. My old friend.

He bent over my throat, just underneath my jaw. His breath froze my skin, giving me shivers as I waited for my high to come, my moment of relief. His lips touched my skin, and I almost whimpered in desperation.

"Do it," I begged.

Derek kissed my skin tenderly. "No," he whispered, coming back to look at me.

"I want you to," I said. "Please."

But he shook his head, and his eyes dissolved into that ultra-light blue. "I don't want it to be like that," he said. "You're not food. You're my best friend. I love you."

I winced at the words, knowing how much he meant them and feeling a pang of guilt at not being able to say them back. I did love him, but not the way he wanted me to. I was about to push away from him, to forget this whole thing, when Derek took my face and kissed me so sweetly, so slowly and carefully it erased the broken feelings inside—just for a moment. It was almost as good as his bite.

And I kissed him back, becoming wrapped up in his wintry lips again. He was fantastic, almost good enough to make me lose myself. I wanted it to go on forever, and I suddenly realized that it could. This wasn't temporary the way it was with Lucas. There was no danger. Well, maybe a little danger, but if Derek bit me, he'd stop before he took too much. He didn't want human blood badly enough to *kill* me. Besides, he seemed very much in control. I'd all but begged him to bite me and he'd refrained.

The realization made my head spin and my body warmed beneath Derek's cold hands. *We don't have to stop.*

Derek seemed to be thinking the exact same thing because he scooped me up in his arms and lowered me onto his bed with one hand while his other tugged his shirt over his head. I gasped, taking in the gloriousness of his body. He couldn't be meant for me— not after everything I'd done to him.

But all he wanted was me. All he'd *ever* wanted was me. And now, finally, I could give myself to him. Somewhere inside, this thought shredded through me like a buzz saw, but I ignored it.

He left me. I'm not his anymore. I have to let it go. . . .

Derek unbuttoned my jeans and yanked them off with one swift tug; my body went wild with nerves. He lowered himself onto the bed and laid his long, hard body on top of mine, stroking the hair from my eyes with loving fingers.

"I can't believe this is happening," he said softly. "We always said we'd be each other's first."

I tried to say something, but the words were smothered underneath Derek's kisses. He was so cold; my entire body was frozen like I was buried underneath an avalanche. It was numbing—I couldn't feel anything, least of all what I was supposed to be feeling: that this was right, that this felt good.

Suddenly, I longed for warmth. I longed to feel two hot arms surrounding me, sweet dark eyes melting my heart away, and heat surging beneath every touch. I saw a pair of perfect lips behind my closed eyes. They creaked into this crooked little grin, and I smiled back without thinking about it.

Then my eyes snapped open.

This was *wrong*.

This wasn't going to happen.

Derek's hand crept down and down, his thumb hooking into the seam of my underwear. I snatched at his wrist.

"No," I said. "I can't do this."

"Sure you can," Derek said gently. "I won't hurt you. I don't even want to bite you, I really wasn't thinking about that. Believe me."

"That's not it. We shouldn't do this just because we can, just because we always said we would." I paused. What I was about to say would hurt him more than anything else I would ever say. But I had to be honest. "I miss Lucas," I admitted.

For a moment there was silence. Then Derek's face coiled into a snarl, and he sat up. I did too.

"I still love him," I blundered on. "I still want him, even after everything we've had to go through. And I love you too, it's just different."

"You mean, *I'm* different," he said. "Dead."

"No. I mean, I *feel* differently for you than I feel for Lucas. I love you like my best friend."

Derek let out a noise of repulsion.

"Yes, I *am* attracted to you," I admitted. "You're everything I should want in a guy. You're easygoing where I'm stubborn. You're sweet where I'm bitter. You're perfect for me, but . . ."

"But you still don't want me," Derek finished for me. His tone was hard as his skin.

Ugh, that sounds so mean. I had to try and fix this. "You were right about me. I did love you for all those years and I just couldn't let myself go, let myself feel it. But Lucas was the one who awakened me. And now, I'm in love with *him*, probably too in love. I've fallen way too far, and now he's left me. I think maybe I'm broken again. I feel broken inside." Tears crept up on me, and I looked away.

I felt Derek move closer to me on the bed. "I can fix it," he whispered. "I can fix it, Faith. You know I can. If you know how to let go now, just do it with me."

"No," I said firmly. "You can't replace him. Nobody can. My heart is his. All of it. Always."

"You feel that way now, but you don't have to love me right away. We could just try. We could go away together. Like you said, we're perfect for each other."

He didn't get it, he didn't get that I could never love him like I loved Lucas. Those loves were worlds apart. With Derek it was easy, effortless love—comfortable and calm like the sea breeze. But I loved Lucas like a thunderstorm in my soul—powerful, inescapable, all-consuming love. It was like my heart was staunched before him and when we came together, he opened the flood gates. Now I had this rush of *everything* pouring out of me.

Maybe I'd drown in it, maybe I wouldn't. I didn't know. All I knew was that I wanted Lucas to be the one I gave myself to. I wanted him to have me.

"I'm sorry," I whispered, pleading with him to understand. "I wish I could give you more of myself, but all I have is friendship." I swallowed hard and took a deep breath. "And that's all I'll ever have."

"But he doesn't even want you anymore," Derek spat. "He left you. It's been over a month, when are you gonna get over this guy? It's getting pathetic, Faith, honestly!"

I recoiled, feeling dryness in my eyes where the tears wanted to form, but couldn't. The tears were over. Done with.

I launched out of the bed and started shimmying into my jeans.

"What are you doing?" Derek said. "Leaving? Now you're leaving me?"

I zipped my jeans and swept into the bathroom to grab my toothbrush and other girly crap I stored in there.

Derek was in the doorway, his face a mess of pain and rage. I guess he didn't know which emotion to feel so he went with both.

"Don't leave," he said angrily. "I'm sorry—I just, I thought maybe now we could be together."

"Ugh! Derek!" I slammed the cabinet shut and brandished my toothbrush at him. "We're not going to be together, okay? Ever! I was wrong to kiss you. It was a mistake. I'm in love with someone else."

Derek's face ripped into a hateful grimace. "So what? If you can't have Lucas you won't have anybody, is that it? You're just gonna go the rest of your life never loving anyone?"

"Maybe!" I yelled and pushed past him. I grabbed my bag full of clothes and headed for the door. Derek stopped me when my hand touched the doorknob.

"Don't," he said, ragged. "Please, don't. . . . You're all I have."

I smacked his hand away. "Then you should have thought of that before you told me how pathetic I was. You want me to get over him? Get my own life? Well, watch me!"

I stormed out, leaving Derek in the doorway.

For once in my life, I was the one who did the leaving.

THE MISSING

I was officially through with any and all supernatural beings. I was pissed at every one of them regardless of whether or not they had actually done anything to me. I was through being all mopey and weak and pathetic. I was taking my life into my hands and healing my own wounds for a change.

I was strong. I could be alone and not be miserable. I could finish out this god-awful semester and move on with life.

I could.

At least that's what I told myself while I pored over textbooks, studying like mad before my final exams. It had been a week since I swore off werewolves and vampires and virans and whatever else was out there, and I was doing pretty well thanks to my coping mechanism, which came into play with a vengeance: running. I hadn't run seriously in a very long time what with all the drama I'd been dealing with. Exhaustion, and guilt, and trying to hold on to Lucas had taken the life out of me. What few meets I'd attended, I'd ended up losing in most or all of my heats. I'd gotten soggy.

But now I ran almost constantly, pushing myself harder than I ever had before. The steady pounding of my feet was the only refuge I had left. It was the only reliable thing I'd ever had in my life and I clung to it.

The downside was that it made me think of Lucas. We'd always run together in the afternoons and, at first, I thought I would never be able to run again without his presence beside me. But the first time I'd stepped onto the ice-hardened field, I imagined he was just behind me—that I was running *from* him, not with him. And I was unstoppable.

Through exercise and time, the sadness that had enveloped my every thought ebbed and white hot anger took its place. Every word he'd ever said to me turned into a lie. Why had he promised me forever if he didn't mean it? Had he been *trying* to hurt me? Was he really the monster he claimed to be?

Sometimes I thought so. Sometimes I was convinced that I hadn't fallen in love with a boy, but a heartless evil creature—a true werewolf. What else could inflict this kind of pain?

But then the memories of the way he'd look at me after we kissed washed over me like a warm ocean wave. I had *felt* his love in those kisses, and I knew there had to have been some reason why he'd done this. I pictured his face as he'd told me he wanted to break up—that cold, careless mask of indifference. He'd even choked off his vibe. It was like he didn't want me to know what he was truly feeling. And the last thing he'd said to me . . . *You'll always have my heart. . . .*

So had he really wanted to break up with me?

I could never know. I could only run.

School and track were a good distraction during the day, but at night, when my muscles screamed with fatigue and my brain had had enough of calculus and essays, there was little to keep me from thinking about Lucas. Derek crept in there too, though mostly I was just mad at him. I'd given up so much for him, and he'd thrown it in my face just because I didn't want to be with him. It was last semester all over again, and I was done with it all.

But I was terribly lonely, despite my try for independence. Ashley wasn't much company because she was usually out with her friends. We weren't all that close, which made sense, seeing as I'd hardly spent one night in my room since the beginning of last semester. Needless to say, she didn't invite me out with her.

With Heather hung up on Pete, drugs, and her new friends, she had veered away from me, hardly even taking the time to talk on the phone with me let alone catch a movie or meet up to study together as we once had. I missed her—the *old* her—almost as much as I missed Derek and Lucas.

Part of me had gone back to thinking that I was destined to be alone—that my fate was to ruin every relationship I made. But that wasn't true, at least not totally. I had someone I was meant to be with. I'd had a future with Lucas. Even if it wouldn't have lasted for eternity, it was *my* lifetime. My future. And Lucas was supposed to be in it. We were matched. That was supposed to be my destiny, but I'd messed it up. He'd been right to be jealous, I realized. I would have been.

• • •

By Saturday I decided I'd had my share of wallowing, and I needed someone to hang out with whether she wanted me around or not. With the murders raging on like an unstoppable wildfire, my nerves and will for independence were worn thin. The town was back on high alert. People rushing into their dorms before dusk, keeping their heads down as they walked determinedly through campus as though the murderer could be any one of us. Professors lectured on the importance of keeping to the curfew and carrying mace around in our purses in case of emergencies.

It seemed that every morning report brought an onslaught of gory details to wash down with my OJ and bagel. Bloodless bodies, unidentified corpses, and a growing body count that flew higher and higher at an alarming rate. And with every murder, my fury with the pack grew. They were supposed to be taking care of this! Or had they simply left us to defend ourselves as Lucas had left me?

Regardless, being alone had now become somewhat nerve-racking. Even staying cooped up in my room was unbearable. Once again, I needed my friend for comfort, only she didn't seem all too keen on being my friend anymore.

She knew I didn't approve of her drug use, so she pulled away from me. And for the most part, I'd let her, having been too wrapped up in my own drama to really make an effort. Granted, I'd tried, but it wasn't nearly good enough. If I was ever going to get her back, I had to get serious about removing the blood bitches from her life. I didn't make friends often, but when I did, I made them count. Heather was no exception. She was the closest thing I'd ever had to a sister, oddly enough. And now I might have lost her because of my selfishness.

If I could fix nothing else, I had to try and fix this.

So I sat on my bed with the phone ringing in my ear, staring out at the waning sliver of a moon that winked at me through my dorm window. I'd gone through two full moons now without Lucas in my life, and each night I wore the silver necklace he gave me and heard his words replay over and over in my head: *I'll always come back to you.*

I sighed wistfully at the moon. *Won't you?*

"Hello?" someone said, startling me out of my reverie. It wasn't Heather's voice, and for a moment, I thought I'd called the wrong number.

"Who is this?" I asked.

"What, you can't recognize my voice?"

"No."

"Give you a hint: I'm beautiful, funny, and always fashionably late. Oh, and my name rhymes with tranny."

I smiled to myself—my first real smile since Derek and I ended things. "Hey, Danni," I said. "Why are you answering Heather's phone?"

"She's indisposed."

"You mean too high to realize her phone is ringing?"

"Ding, ding, ding! Twenty points for Faith."

I sighed. "Why do you let her do that to herself?"

"Babe, I'm not her mommy. She can do whatever she wants."

I jumped up from my bed, pacing around restlessly. I wanted to get out of my room. "Where are you guys?" I asked.

"Zydeco's. Heather's obsessed with the notion that Pete will come back here. I don't have the heart to tell her he's probably getting it on with his skanky new girlfriend."

I swallowed, wondering if Danni knew Paula had been dead for weeks.

"We can leave though," Danni offered. "I'm sick of this cheese-ball place."

I let out a short laugh.

"We haven't hung out in ages," Danni went on. "I was about to barge into your dorm room and drag you out if I didn't hear from you soon."

"That would have been nice," I said with complete sincerity.

"Come to my place," Danni said.

"Your place?"

"Yeah, as in my home? My residence? My place of dwelling? You know, where I keep my bed and my closet full of Jimmy Choo shoes. Don't be jealous. I'll let you borrow."

I was smiling again. Not because of the shoes, but the thought of leaving. And it was a household, which no vampire could enter uninvited, so I wouldn't be in danger. The curfew would be a pain if I stayed out late, but the police officers usually let us through without a problem once we produced school IDs.

"Okay," I agreed. "But I don't have a ride."

"We'll pick you up. Ten minutes. Just let me peel Heather off of the bar."

I groaned. "Don't let her drive."

"Yes, mother." She hung up.

• • •

Danni lived in a small apartment complex across from campus. I found it a little odd that she lived so close to a school she didn't even attend, but decided it was probably because there were people her age around.

Danni, Heather, a couple of the usual blood bitches, and I all congregated in her cramped, yet sparse, living room. An old episode of *Californication* played on a run-down television, but nobody was really watching. Mostly, everyone conversed steadily, joking around and flirting. I stayed out of the conversation, only feigning laughter when everyone else did. As much as I'd wanted to come and "rescue" Heather from herself, seeing her here among her new buddies only made it all the more clear how much she'd changed in the past months. I barely recognized her with her sallow complexion; stringy, greasy hair; and unfocused eyes. This was not the Heather who wanted to be a school teacher. This was not the Heather who had comforted me about my dad and joked around with me about bad classes and football games.

I missed my friend—and I had no idea how to get her back again.

"Dude, you look like you just saw your hamster die or something," Danni said in my ear.

I looked over at her and faked a smile. "Sorry. I'm just . . ."

"Going through a break-up. I know. It sucks. But seriously, babe, it's been over a month. Don't you think it's time to get over Fabio?"

The sudden mention of Lucas only plunged another hole in my heart, practically making me gasp.

"I always thought he was a jerk!" Heather suddenly piped up. She ran over and flopped onto the couch beside is. "He was so grumpy."

Well, yeah. I had to give her that one.

"I had a boyfriend once," Danni said. "He'd totally flip out at any little thing. We broke up because I burnt his toast one morning, and I just couldn't take it anymore. I chucked the toaster at his head and put him in the hospital."

"That's normal," I said while Heather cracked up with near maniacal laughter.

"Who breaks up over toast?" Heather snickered.

"Me, apparently," Danni said dryly.

Heather leaned in and said, "Faith—remember that night we all went out to the La Poudre together?"

"Yes." Wow, that felt like ages ago.

"Well, I woke up in the middle of the night and saw Pete reading—" She dissolved into giggles. "He was reading a *romance novel* on his Kindle!"

I had to laugh at that.

"What a girl!" Heather shrieked.

I chuckled and looked between the two of them. This was actually kind of fun.

"Okay," I said. "Lucas used to do this thing every night before bed—he never saw me watching, but whenever he got out of the shower, he'd spend like, twenty minutes just staring at himself in the mirror. It was so bizarre. I think he was looking for wrinkles."

"Or pimples," Heather said, guffawing.

We all snickered.

"How self-absorbed can you be?" Danni grumbled. "My last ex used to make me go into the changing room with him when we went shopping. And not to fool around. No. He wanted me to tell him how his ass looked in every pair of pants he tried on."

"Pete wears tighty-whities because he thinks they make his package look bigger!"

Everyone—including some of the blood bitches who overheard—screeched with laughter.

When we calmed down, Heather ran into Danni's kitchen to cook some pizza snacks, and I leaned on the couch, sighing. As much as I hated being around these druggies, I had to admit, this was the best time I'd had since . . . well, since Valentine's Day, probably.

Danni, too, had turned out to be less threatening than she was irritatingly funny. I should have hated her for what she'd done to

Heather, but—and I totally loathed myself for this—I could actually see why Heather liked her.

Which gave me an idea. Danni was the ringleader here. Heather had made it perfectly clear that she wasn't going to listen to me, but maybe if Danni stepped in, she'd pay attention.

"Hey, Danni?" I asked. "Do you think you could do me a favor?"

"Sure, babe. Anything for you." She winked slyly at me.

I leaned in closer so nobody else would hear us talking. "Look," I said. "I get that you guys are into all—this," I gestured to the room at large. "But Heather isn't like this. At least, not the Heather I know. She's just—I guess she's still upset about losing Pete and stuff, so she's using the drugs as an escape. Which I get. But, really do you think this is *good* for her?"

Danni studied me with those emerald orbs of hers and said, "I'm not fit to judge anybody, man."

"I'm not asking you to. I'm just asking you to talk to her. Can you do that?"

She wrinkled her nose. "It might sound a little hypocritical coming from me."

"She'll listen to you, though." For some idiotic reason, Heather trusted Danni. I'd seen no evidence of trustworthiness in her, but whatever.

Danni watched the group below us with a calculating expression, before finally saying, "Sure, lady, I'll talk to her. What can it hurt, right?"

I breathed a sigh of relief. "Thank you. But make sure she doesn't know I asked you to."

"Why, you two having a fight?"

I shrugged. "Not so much a fight as a rift. I don't know. . . . We just aren't as close as we used to be. Most of that is my fault, but I can't seem to fix it."

"Well, just call me Dr. Phil. I'll fix it for you."

I shook my head at her, fighting off a smile.

"Hey, do you think you could take me home now?" I asked. "Curfew is coming up and . . . well, to be honest, this is kind of depressing me."

"Yeah, watching people get high loses its glamour after a while."

I watched her fish her keys out of her jacket pocket. "So why do you do it so much?"

"These are my clients, babe. I gotta be present or else they'll find someone else to buy from."

I eyed her as she stood. Now would have been the perfect time to oh-so-casually bring up the vampire blood again, but as I watched her say good-bye to her clients I just couldn't bring myself to do it. I was done with that world. Whatever Danni was into was her business, and I refused to get dragged back into that mess.

So I followed Danni out the door and let her take me home to my lonely dorm room.

• • •

I was totally going to flunk out of college. I was convinced.

Final exams were coming up, and I was completely unprepared. I'd basically bombed this whole semester thanks to Lucas and Derek, so for the next two weeks, I took studying to a whole new level. I lived in the library, drowning myself in useless facts and numbers until my brain felt like old cereal. It was lame.

And lonely. And sad. But it was better than agonizing over missing Lucas and Derek. And it would keep me from failing all my classes.

I did have one social event to look forward to, though. Danni had found me on campus a couple nights ago and cornered me into a double date with Heather and her new blood bitch boyfriend, Ryan. I was being set up with Ryan's roommate, Harrison. He was not a blood bitch, which was the only reason I'd agreed. Plus I wanted Danni to leave me alone about being so moody, and she'd claimed that this was the only way for me to move on.

The Sunday before exams was spent in the library for yet another marathon study session. As I trudged back to my dorm room, I tried to make myself feel something about my upcoming date on Friday—excitement, nervousness, anything. But all I could muster was dread. Imagining myself with anyone but Lucas was completely foul. I actually felt physically ill from it as I hurried through the courtyard, angry at myself for staying out past dark. I usually never did that anymore because I had no protection now and the murders were just as awful, and frequent as ever.

And it seemed that I needed protection because as I approached my building, a blast of wind hit me. I almost shrieked. But I regained composure long enough to see that it wasn't a vampire.

Quite the opposite, actually.

It was Katie.

I blinked for a moment, letting my bag fall to the floor as my body went limp.

"Hey," she said with a smile. Through the static of her crazy werewolf vibe, I could feel her phony niceness. I wasn't sure why she was being fake with me, but I wasn't about to confront her. I was too shocked and too happy to see her.

"I'm not here to talk," she said. "I have a message. From Derek."

More shock hit me like a hammer to the skull.

"Y-you talked to Derek?"

"Yep. He, ah . . . he called me when you left. He was pretty broken up, Faith. Really broken up."

I pressed my lips together and took a deep breath. I hated to hear that I'd caused him even more pain, but I didn't regret leaving him. "What's the message?" I forced out.

Katie shifted her weight and looked around for a moment, almost like she didn't want to tell me. Why was she acting so strangely?

"Just tell me," I said flatly.

"He says he wants to meet you," she said. "He wants to say good-bye."

I balked. "Good-bye? Is he going someplace?"

Katie tossed her short black hair out of her eyes with a flick of her head. "He wants to tell you himself. He said to meet him on the football field at midnight tonight if you want to say good-bye. Otherwise you won't see him again."

My face collapsed into a frown as I absorbed this. Derek was leaving. Leaving where? Why?

Katie and I stood there for a long moment, and when she spoke up, her voice was softer, almost pained.

"So are you going to go?"

I wanted to go see him, but if I did so, I would only end up asking him to stay. And that was wrong. If he was ever going to learn to be happy, it had to be away from me and the pain I caused him.

"No," I said finally. "I can't say good-bye to him. If he wants to go, then that's good. He should go. He should find a place for himself . . . someplace that makes him happy."

"He's happy with you," Katie said. "He wants you. He's practically human still, there's no danger with him if he takes your blood. He can't turn you. And he'd always love you. Just give him a chance."

At first I started to let myself believe Katie's words, but I forced myself to stay strong.

"No," I said. "No. I won't give him anything more than friendship. You—you tell him for me, that if he wants to be my friend, I'll always be here to help him. I'll always love him that way. Otherwise, this is that way it has to be."

Katie seemed to relax, as if relieved by my words.

"I'll tell him." She took a step and touched my arm. "Take care of yourself, Faith."

And she was gone.

• • •

Final exams just happened to fall on my least favorite time of the month: the full moon. I got through exams with passing grades, which was a humongous feat after having slogged through the semester with only sections of my brain in working condition.

Friday night, and three weeks since I'd last spoken to Derek, I stood outside of my building in the courtyard, waiting for Heather. After Katie's visit, Derek had tried calling me relentlessly for two days until I'd finally just shut my phone off. I couldn't say good-bye to him.

I fiddled with the silver necklace Lucas had given me as I waited in the scanty yellow light of the courtyard lamps. It had finally stopped snowing. I wasn't exactly sure when that happened, but now the ground was sprouting with fresh grass and the trees were starting to bloom waxy green leaves. The world was becoming alive again.

I checked my watch. Heather was late. I didn't like being alone at night even with the silver at my throat and the double-ended stake stuffed into my purse. I was still grossly vulnerable. And there had been so many murders this past week; two or three every night. It had me—and everyone around me—totally on edge. I only wished the stupid pack would find the brood already. If they couldn't manage it, not only would countless more die, but Lucas and the others would be entrenched in a war.

I winced as my body scorched, and then shoved the thought aside. *He doesn't matter. He doesn't even care that you're out here unprotected. You could be dead for all he knows. . . .*

I checked my watch again and then pulled out my cell phone. I called Heather and got her voicemail. I waited ten more minutes, fingering the stake in my purse and imagining the moves I'd make if a vampire came at me.

Feeling idiotic, I went back up to my room and called Heather to cancel. But she didn't answer. I tried her three more times, only to find that her phone had been disconnected.

What if something bad had happened to her? The vampires could have found out about her use of their blood and killed her. It was totally plausible. I called her about a gajillion times, but she never answered.

I couldn't sleep at all that night.

The next morning, seven o'clock on the dot, I flicked on the news.

Sure enough, there had been murders last night. A car full of people. I gasped as the news lady listed the names. Ryan Avery, Harrison Klinger, and Jessica Faust. That was Heather's boyfriend and his roommate! The girl was one of the blood bitches. But Heather's name hadn't been read. What did that mean? I flicked the news off and called Heather immediately.

No answer.

I started pacing to keep the tears from taking over. Heather wasn't just my friend, she was my *human* friend. And that meant something to me—it meant everything. If Heather died, it was almost as if my humanity died with her. I had next to no other human friends, no real ties to the human world besides perhaps school and my mother. For some reason, and maybe it was just because Heather was my age, I just felt that if she was gone, it wouldn't be long before I followed in her wake. It was selfish, but I had to face the facts: I attracted vampires. Whether it was because of my otherness or whatever, I had an uncanny ability to get mixed up in their world.

And I had zero protection now. I'd sworn off all supernatural creatures. Not a smart move for a vampire magnet.

I had this horrible, sinking feeling that the attack on Heather's car had been because of me. The vampires knew me, knew my gift. They had already tried to turn me twice—first Vincent and then Silas. What were the odds that the same car I would be getting into would also be the one that the vampires targeted? It was just too much of a coincidence.

I had to acknowledge the truth: the vampires were coming for me. Derek had refused to go back to them, and in order to lure him in, they were doing just as my mystery attacker said they would. They wanted to use me as leverage. Because they needed Derek. He was the key to the uprising, and without him they were doomed.

So if the vampires found me, the war was essentially over before it had even begun.

And here I was. A sitting duck.

Late that afternoon, I sat blankly at my desk, staring at the barren white wall until my cell phone blared through the silence. I dove for it, hoping to see Heather's name on my screen.

Not Heather, but still someone who might know something.

"Danni, hi," I said, exhaling into the phone. Why hadn't I called her sooner?

"So you heard?" she asked.

"Yes. It was on the news. I was supposed to be in that car, Danni. I was supposed to be there."

"Yeah, I know." Her voice was rough—haggard. "You're one lucky chick."

"They didn't say anything about Heather, but she had to have been there—it was her car. She's not with you, is she?"

"I didn't see her at all last night," Danni said. "So do you think it was the serial killer dude?"

No, I think it's the vampires.

"Yeah," I said. "Why wouldn't it be him?"

"Well, I mean, the victims were boys. He always kills girls."

"First time for everything," I said, running my hand over my tired eyes.

"Yeah," Danni said pensively. "Maybe he didn't have a choice but to kill the dudes. Maybe they saw him attack Heather and Jessica, and he had to kill them to keep them from talking."

I swallowed hard. "So you think he killed Heather?"

"Seems so, babe."

Suddenly I was furious at her casual tone. I knew it was just *her*, but it was so callous. "You don't give a shit about her at all do you? She was just another stoner to you, right?"

"Hey," her voice came harshly now. "She might have been a client, but she was my friend, too."

"Right. A friend you let get high out of her mind practically every night for the past four months. Her brain's probably scrambled eggs by now thanks to you."

"Heather makes her own choices."

"Yeah, and you facilitate them."

She was quiet for a moment. "I'll admit I shouldn't have let her have a taste that first night in Zydeco's. She was a mess and I played into it. That was my screw-up. But after the first time, there was no point refusing her. She was hooked. She would have gotten it from someone else if I didn't sell to her."

"So as long as she's turning into an addict, you might as well make some money in the process? Nice, Danni. I can tell you really care about her."

"That's not what I meant. Jesus, you're such a pain in the ass."

"Did you even talk to her like I asked?"

"I never got the chance."

I was tempted to throw the phone across the room, but something kept me holding it to my ear—I wanted her to apologize.

Wanted us to be friends, even though she was borderline dangerous. She was all I had.

Pathetic. . . .

"All I meant before," Danni said, and I could hear her forcing
her voice to be level, "was that if she was going to do the drugs
anyway, at least I knew they were safe. Relatively."

"Oh yeah, because this mystery drug you guys take is so safe," I
said, dripping sarcasm. "You still won't even tell me the name of it."

"Not the point," Danni said, avoiding giving me a name, yet again.

"Then what's the point, Danni?" I was tired of fighting. So, so
tired. . . .

"The point is that I care if Heather is dead or not, all right? I
know I come off all tough and shit, but when a friend dies—or
might be dead—it's enough to crack the shell. For anyone. So just
. . . just stop acting like you're the only one who cares about her.
And Ryan and Jessica, too."

I blinked at my white wall, as it finally sunk in that three people
were actually dead and that two of them had been Danni's friends.

She was silent for a moment. "It just doesn't feel real, you
know? About Heather, I mean. Like, it's not real until there's a
body, as sick as that sounds. I have a feeling Heather's probably
dead, but I don't know. Maybe she's not."

It was a possibility. If the vampires wanted me, then taking
Heather was a good way to lure me out of my room. Vincent had
done it before with Derek. And it had worked. Too well. If the
vampires weren't after me and the attack last night was a coincidence, they might have taken her so they could turn her for their
army. Either way, she could be alive. And if that was true, I had

until sundown to find her.

"We should go look for her," I said.

"For sure," she agreed instantly. "I'll be there in five. I'd say don't be late, but I know you will be anyway."

She hung up and I raced around the room getting dressed and pulling my hair into a harried ponytail. Ten minutes later, I met Danni at the driveway outside my building. The weather was beginning to warm up, but the sky was still that sheet of white instead of spring-blue. Danni didn't seem to mind the chill in the air, though, because the top on her convertible was down and she wore only a thin camisole in bright green.

I jumped into her car, giving her a brief smile.

She nodded at me and started off down the road.

"Where to?" she asked.

I gripped the edges of the leather seat, biting my lip absently. "I guess we should check out the wreck?"

"Nah. That'll be swarming with cops and news crews."

"Still? You think?"

"Oh, hell yeah. This case is top news. The public is in an uproar over it—they'll be all over that place for days. Nah, why don't we start wherever you were supposed to be going?"

"Zydeco's," I said reluctantly. I despised the place. Every time I went there something catastrophic happened. But then again, the vampires seemed to like it in that silly club—probably because of all the drunk, easy prey—so it was a good starting point.

Danni turned toward the club. "It's not open yet," she informed me as she turned on the radio.

"What time does it open?" I asked, checking the clock. It was five—two hours until sunset.

"Seven," she said.

I made a face. "We'll just look out back for now."

"You don't wanna wait for it to open? We could ask the club staff if they saw her or something."

"No. I can't, ah . . . stay out that late."

Danni chuckled skeptically. "Okay, granny, what aren't you telling me? Why the curfew?"

"No reason, I just need to do some studying."

"Liar. Exams were last week. You're officially on summer vacay."

I looked over at her profile, watching the creases along her almond-shaped eyes as she watched the road. "How do you know when my exams were?"

"Because I've been stalking you."

"Shut up."

"You told me the other day, remember? When I met you on campus?"

"Right—when you harassed me into this stupid double date in the first place."

"Harassed is a strong word," Danni said thoughtfully. "More like forced."

"I'm going to take a summer class anyway," I said absently. "So I can stay in my dorm room during the break." There were two weeks between the spring and summer semesters, and I seriously didn't want to go back to California for them. If I took a summer class I could stay. This place—this hell I'd come to call home—was my only tie to Lucas. I wasn't ready to leave it yet.

Danni didn't respond, so I stared out the windshield and saw that we'd come to Zydeco's parking lot on the side of the building. We exited the car and walked around the empty lot.

"Nothing here but the smell of coagulated vomit and exhaust fumes," Danni said, leaning against the trunk of her car.

I circled around the lot, looking for what, I didn't know. I glanced up at the side of the brick building and saw a security camera facing the lot. I pointed at it. "I wonder if that shows anything."

"Maybe," Danni said disinterestedly.

I folded my arms across my chest. "You could be a little more helpful."

"What do you want me to do? There's nothing here."

I shifted my weight, glaring away from her. "I know. Besides, it seems like they got intercepted by the vam—the killer before they came here. They were on the way to pick me up."

Danni shrugged making the afternoon sun flash on her silky shirt and leave a white spot in my vision. "So what'd you wanna do?"

I circled around the lot once more, thinking about the vampires—where they'd likely take their prey. If they'd killed her, they'd have just left her with the others, which made me think they'd either successfully turned her or were keeping her to get to me. Hopefully, it was the latter. And if so, they'd take her to their lair.

Well, the only lair I knew of was Vincent's and last I knew, it had been turned into a vampire-feeding-frenzy thingy. It seemed like a stretch that they'd still be there after the pack raided the place twice, but it was worth a shot. I had nothing else to go on.

"There's some place I want to check out," I said, going back to the car. "Come on, I'll direct you."

• • •

Twenty minutes later, I'd successfully gotten us to the barn. Without the snow surrounding it, the whole thing looked strikingly dull. On the night Derek had been turned, the barn had been a dark, foreboding structure stabbing a sea of white powder. Now it blended in with the deadened, green-mottled grass. It was old and filthy—lonely looking like a stray dog.

As Danni stopped the car in front of it, an assault of terrifying memories raced through my brain. Vincent's pointed leer, the flash of his knife as he killed that unnamed werewolf—his maniacal face just before he bit Derek. And more recently, those decomposing dead girls piled in the corner of the barn like a garbage heap. . . . I swallowed hard, shoving away the memories. Vincent was dead now—truly dead. He couldn't hurt me anymore. And with the sun firmly in the sky, no other vampire would either.

"So is this where you're going to kill me?" Danni said lightly.

I fought off a grin. She didn't know how close she was to the true purpose of this run-down barn. "No," I said. "I went to a party here once."

"And . . . you were hoping someone left some beer around?"

I cut her a look.

"What?" she said. "I could totally use a drink right now."

"Will you be serious for a minute?" But I was smiling now.

"Okay then, Sherlock. Why are we here?"

I cooked up a story quickly, trying my best to keep it sounding plausible. "I heard one of the murdered girls was found around here." Kind of true. Not only had there been a dozen dead bodies here, but Vincent had killed a girl on Halloween night—same night I'd found out what he and Lucas were. She hadn't been found here, but whatever. It made more sense than me telling Danni we were here because it had once been a vampire lair-turned frenzy house.

I prayed to everything I knew that Heather would be here. I had no other leads and no time to do any more searching before nightfall.

"Place smells like wet dog," Danni called as she poked her head into the barn.

I exited the car and came up behind her, following her inside. Everything was as I recalled it, minus the dead bodies.

"Empty," I said, voice hollow.

"There's a door here," Danni said, leaning over a place on the floor with her hands on her knees. "Basement, I guess."

I hurried over as Lucas's words echoed through my head—vampires liked to live underground. I pushed past Danni as I came up to the door. "Let me," I said and reached for the iron ring on the basement door. *They'll be asleep. It's still daylight.*

I yanked on the handle, feeling a puff of stale air smack my face as the door flipped past me. I darted back, terrified of what I might find. But nothing happened. No vampires popped out. No corpses rattled. No Heather.

It was just a small compartment filled with an empty beer keg and some cracked plastic cups—remnants from the Halloween party, no doubt.

"Damn," Danni muttered, kicking the door back in.

"Yeah," I looked out at the sky above the hayloft. It was turning the color of peach skin—sunset. "We should really get back."

"What about Heather?"

Something inside my stomach pinched, but I ignored it. I wanted to help her so badly, but staying out past nightfall wasn't an option. I'd only make myself available to the vampires and then I'd never be able to help her.

"I'll, ah . . . make some calls," I said. "To her roommates and stuff. Maybe they know something." It was a dumb excuse, but I couldn't think of anything else to say. I started walking out toward the car. But Danni stayed put, hand propped up on her trim hip.

"The police will have already done that," she said. "We should keep looking."

I spun on her. "Where? Where do we look, Danni? I have no idea where she might be, do you?"

Danni pursed her lips. "No, but we can't just leave. We should—"

"No," I cut her off, voice firm. "I need to get back."

Danni seemed to wrestle with something, probably the same guilt I felt over Heather's fate, but then reluctantly followed me to the car. We didn't speak for a long time on the way back to campus. I was on the verge of tears, and Danni's face was a mask of stone. She drove agonizingly slowly to campus so that when we finally got there, it was dark and my mind was swimming with fear. I practically flew out of the car when she pulled into the driveway.

"I'll call you if I hear anything," I said.

She just nodded, and I could tell by her face that she was pissed. But I didn't have time to worry about that—I could call her later and amend it. I waved and watched her take off down the road.

I cursed to myself as I hurried back to my room. Why had Danni driven so slowly? We could have easily been back before sunset. The temperature had dropped with the sun, and I shivered in my light sweater and tank top. It was one of those odd hours during the day when nobody seemed to be around, so I ran to my front door. I struggled with my keys as I tried to fit them into the lock, and they fell to the brick floor in a pile. I swore again as I bent to pick them up.

"You're a clumsy little bitch aren't you?" came a voice from behind me. I froze at the sound. I knew that voice.

I turned and faced Melissa.

She smiled, propping her hands on her hips, which were just barely hidden by an impossibly tiny miniskirt. Her hair was pulled straight back, and her face was painted in heavy makeup, making her even more stunningly beautiful than usual. But the deadliness glinting in her eyes was all I could focus on. Because it meant she was there to kill me.

26

SLIPPING BELOW
THE SURFACE

Although the sight of Melissa's gorgeous, coy smile sent ice water shooting through my veins, I refused to let her know she'd scared me.

"Where's Heather?" I demanded.

"Heather who?" I tested her vibe and was surprised to find genuine bewilderment. She didn't know who Heather was—not her name, but maybe she'd know about a new vampire or a hostage being held.

"The girl taken last night," I said. "What did you do with her?"

Melissa flipped her long tendrils of black hair over her shoulder, eyeing me with distain. "We didn't take anyone, you idiot. Why would we?"

"To—to get to me?" It sounded so narcissistic when said aloud.

"Oh, please. We don't need to take captives to get a hold of one measly human—especially one dumb enough to stand outside after nightfall. Alone." The greed shining in her eyes sent my stomach into a whirl. "Besides, if we did want you that badly, we'd just use a bloodie."

"Why didn't you, then?"

"You're dumb, Faith Reynolds. But even I know you're not *that* dumb. You'd be able to tell if a bloodie was trying to trick you with that handy little power of yours."

I held my head a little higher, happy that I'd gathered some semblance of a reputation among the vampires.

"Then again," Melissa said, "you were stupid enough to stay out after nightfall tonight. So maybe we should have used a bloodie, after all. It would have saved me the trouble of scuffing my new Manolos." She wiggled her spiky high-heeled shoes at me.

"Why now?" I asked. "Lucas and I have been apart for months, and Derek has been gone for weeks. Why wait until now to take me?"

"I wasn't told to come and get you until tonight. I don't know why Arabella waited so long. I don't ask questions. I follow orders."

"Like a good little bitch," I said swiftly.

Her eyes sliced holes in my head, and I immediately regretted my outburst.

"I'm not coming with you," I warned.

"Of course you are. Now come on." She held out a petite tan-gloved hand. "Or am I going to have to drag you?"

I planted my feet. "I definitely think it's going to be the latter."

Melissa sighed as if greatly inconvenienced. "I hate humans." She made to grab for me, and I screamed as loud as I could. Melissa stopped, glancing around to make sure we were alone.

"That's right," I said smugly. "There are windows all over the place. If you try to take me, someone will see. I'll scream again."

Melissa pressed her lips together as if trying to hide a smile. Suddenly she was on top of me—her arm slung around my waist—and she jerked me into the shadows. There was no time to scream; it lasted less than the length of a heartbeat. When she stopped on the shadowed side of the building, she let me fall hard to the ground. My head clashed against the brick pathway. We were sequestered within the thick foliage on the side of my building, completely invisible to anyone in the courtyard or the road beyond it.

I heard Melissa laughing above me as I struggled to my feet, disoriented.

"I guarantee *nobody* saw that," she hissed.

I knew she was right. And I also knew she was playing with me—she could have killed me, turned me, or taken me away by now. I leaned against the brick wall, head throbbing. "Didn't your mother tell you not to play with your food?" I said.

But Melissa wasn't listening. She came closer, her eyes glittering in the moonlight, pupils growing wider with blackness. It was then that I noticed a warm slippery feeling on the side of my head. I reached up and then held my fingers out, feeling warm wetness that filled my gut with dread. They were coated in scarlet.

I looked up at Melissa's hungry face.

"Shit."

She lunged at me.

I crouched low, covering my head in my hands and bracing myself for the bite that would end me forever. But it never came. Instead, I heard a grunt and a deep throaty sound. Melissa cursed and I looked up.

The heather-gray wolf was there.

My heart exploded with relief—and fear. I didn't know whether to be afraid of the wolf or happy that it was here. Was it there to save me or get at me first?

I wasn't going to stick around to find out.

The wolf pinned Melissa to the ground with its jaws, but she struck out with a silver knife she'd pulled from a band on her thigh and stabbed the wolf's side. It howled and cringed away, releasing its hold on Melissa long enough for her to fly at me.

I ducked again, but the wolf recovered in time, clamping its jaws onto Melissa's trim leg. She screamed and I ran.

I ran out of that pathway and across the courtyard so fast I hardly knew it was happening. I only refocused when I'd shut myself inside my building to watch through the glass door, trying to see signs of the fight still raging behind the wall on my right. But I couldn't see anything. There were no sounds. I stood there for a few minutes longer—listening.

Finally, I accepted the fact that they must have left.

I turned to go up to my room and was instantly confused.

I wasn't in my building. I was in Lucas's. I shook my head at myself, slapping my forehead. I winced at the pain, since my head was still throbbing from hitting the ground. I'd been so eager to get away that I'd run clear across the courtyard and into Lucas's building. I still had his key, so I'd been able to let myself in. I didn't know if it'd been habit to come here or if it was some subconscious lure to the safety that lay just one floor above me.

Lucas.

Either way, I was stuck in here. I wasn't going back out into the courtyard. If Melissa had won, she'd been waiting to take me. If the wolf had won . . . well, I didn't know what it would do. It seemed to be stalking me, and the malicious intent I sensed in its vibe indicated that it probably wanted to kill me.

But just now it had saved me.

Regardless, I wasn't going back outside until dawn.

So, I curled down against the wall and pressed the heel of my hand against the cut on the side of my head. It had stopped bleeding, thankfully, but I took off my sweater to mop up the blood on the side of my face.

There was no more denying it: I needed protection. With Lucas and Derek out of the picture, Katie was my first thought, but I just couldn't bring myself to call her. She'd made it clear that she wasn't willing to risk her reputation within the pack in order to help me.

So that meant I had to make up with one of the boys I'd pushed away. I looked up at the ceiling, imagining that I was directly below Lucas's room, even though I knew I wasn't. I closed my eyes, hoping that I could sense through the ceiling and feel his vibe; his wild, tumultuous energy that had become more of a comfort to me than anything else in my life. I missed him so much it was an actual physical pain—my body was on fire.

I winced and looked away. I couldn't ask Lucas to help me. I'd never survive the trauma of seeing him.

So that left Derek.

I drew in a deep breath, dragged my cell phone out of my back pocket, and punched the speed dial.

"Derek Turner at your service," his soft voice came through the phone.

"It's Faith."

He didn't say anything for a moment and then, "Yes?"

"I'm sorry," I blurted. "About . . . that night."

He was silent.

"I was just overwhelmed, I guess. By everything. And I didn't mean to cut you out of my life. You did that to me last semester, and I should have known how it would hurt you. I'm sorry."

"Whatever. It's fine."

I frowned at my shoes. "Did you hear what happened to Heather? It was on the news. The people she was with are dead and she's missing. I can't get a hold of her. I'm scared she's dead, too."

"Uh-huh," Derek grunted. I heard glasses clinking in the background and music playing. Someone released a slimy sallow laugh—Calvin's laugh—and a chill skittered down my spine.

Derek hadn't left, after all. He'd gone back to the vampires. After everything I'd done to get him away from them, he went back. All the murders and the uprising, and the attempts on my life meant *nothing* to him. Just because I wouldn't be with him, he went back. Like this was some sort of morbid punishment.

I heard Calvin's laughter again and my composure snapped. "Is that *Calvin*?" I demanded.

"What do you care?" Derek said just as acidly.

"I care because they might have killed Heather. And he tried to kill me! Not to mention the fact that Melissa just tried to *eat* me."

Derek ignored that. "What do you want, Faith? I'm busy."

"Do you even *care* that Heather is missing?"

"Not particularly. She was a pain."

I let out a gasp, unable to believe what I was hearing. This wasn't Derek. This was a monster.

"You know what?" I said. "Lucas was right all along. You *are* a leech!"

I hung up before he could contest.

I curled my hands over my face, crying out with loss and frustration. I hated Derek for going back to the vampires and I *hated* this fear. I wasn't this weak person.

I sniffed loudly and straightened. I couldn't live my life like this. I couldn't do anything about the uprising, but I could certainly help my friend. I had to at least *try*.

But I needed some help to do it.

I needed—damn it, I needed Lucas.

At the thought of asking him for help, the scars I'd built around the wound in my heart twanged with an almost unimaginable pain. Suddenly, his voice was in my head, too loud to ignore as I usually did. *I won't be too proud to accept your help.* It only made me grit my teeth harder against the idea. It wasn't just pride keeping me from approaching Lucas again after all this time. It was fear. Seeing Lucas would probably send me right back to that pathetic ball of tears I used to be. But he'd be able to help me. And I had no other options.

I drew in a big breath, snatched up my phone and marched up to Lucas's room, making it all the way to his door before doubt halted me.

What if he opened the door and I found him with someone else? What if he'd moved on? What if he didn't care that Heather was gone? And that I was scared out of my mind that I would be next? What if he told me to go away?

What if he wasn't even *there*?

I shook my head, shoving the doubt away, and pounded my fist on the door before I could stop myself. *Okay, it's over. I did it. I knocked. Now I just have to wait until he—*

Lucas opened the door immediately. His eyes met mine and blazed silver, but he blinked and they were brown once more. It happened so quickly I wasn't sure if I'd actually seen it.

We stood there staring at each other for what felt like an eternity. Now that I was there, looking at him after all these many weeks of longing to see his face, I didn't know what to say. Words seemed so inadequate. Kissing would be much more appropriate or maybe crying hysterically.

The seconds continued to pass as though we were stuck in a time warp.

My skin caught fire beneath his gaze, and the flames rippled deep down into my bones. My only thought was him. *Lucas, Lucas, Lucas.* Over and over like a train fallen off its tracks, wild and aimless, heading toward disaster.

Then there was a sound. A sound I'd dreamt of, soft and grating like the low end of a guitar. Rough to the ear, but somehow perfect. Somehow better than any other sound in the world.

"Is something wrong?" Lucas asked.

It took a moment for the shock to wear off. For me to realize that I had to answer.

"Yeah," I whispered.

"Tell me."

Then I stopped being amazed that I was actually talking to him and really took him in. His expression was blank. No scowl. No smirk. Nothing. Not even a vibe to go off of. Just . . . indifference.

Somehow that crushed me more than anything else up to that point.

He didn't care that I was there. He didn't care that something was wrong. He just wanted me to go away. To leave him alone. I almost did it, but then I thought of Heather. This wasn't just about me. She needed my help, too.

"Heather's missing," I said. "The people that were killed last night—I was supposed to be with them. I think . . . I think the vampires are coming for me."

Something flickered across his features, but he hid it too quickly for me to read.

"Okay," he said. "I'll take care of it."

I felt my eyebrows drop into a frown.

"Take care of it. . . . ," I repeated.

"I'll get a pack member to guard you. I can ask Katie if you want her. Or Julian."

I looked away, gasping with the pain of those words. It was like being consumed by fire from the inside out. I wouldn't have been surprised if my fingers started turning black and cracking off. My mind was screaming, *Tell him you want* him. *Tell him!*

But my mouth didn't listen.

"That will be fine," I said, emotionless. "Thank you."

Lucas just nodded, his expression growing softer the longer he looked at me until finally, I saw the yearning I felt reflected in him. "You're hurt," he said softly, touching his fingers lightly to the place where I'd hit my head.

I should have told him about Melissa, but I couldn't stand being around him a second longer. Besides, he had to smell her on me, and he obviously didn't care enough about it to "take care" of it himself. I had to get out of there, start healing myself all over again.

I swallowed hard and took a step back, turning slowly so I wouldn't go nuts and start running away from him the way I'd done every day for the past two months. I blinked and he was gone. There was only the long hallway that led to the stairs, and surrounding the edges of my vision, scalding yellow flames. I took two steps away from him. Smoke clouded my lungs, making my eyes tear up. It was so hard to breathe. I could think only of collapsing like the building he'd painted those many months ago.

My life was on fire now, all right, but I was trapped inside one of the windowpanes, unable to escape while the fire licked my skin into oblivion.

You can do this. Just walk away. Walk away and let him go.

The thought was enough to make tears spill down my cheeks and threaten to bring me to my knees.

Then Lucas's voice came from behind me, low and hoarse as though parched.

"Faith."

For a moment, I wasn't sure I'd I heard it. Was I hallucinating? Was I that desperate?

I stopped walking and I heard it again, softer this time, and pleading with me . . . begging me to stay.

I spun around and ran to him, unable to stay away a second longer. He gathered me in his strong arms and held me, murmuring my name over and over as he pulled me so close I thought I would sink into him completely. I cried freely as I ran my hands down his back, his sides, over his shoulders, his neck . . . everywhere. Was this a dream? Could this really be happening? I held his face between my hands, halfway believing I *was* asleep and at any moment, I would awake to find my hands empty. Unable to even conceive of the thought, I rose up onto my tiptoes and smoothed my cheek against his, reveling in the mix of stubble and soft skin for as long as I could. If this was all I had—this one blissful dream—I wasn't going to waste it.

He turned his head, murmuring something I couldn't understand, and our lips touched.

Immediately, the flames died. My body calmed for the briefest of moments, soothing everything, down to my soul. And then it erupted again, but with a different kind of heat. It was an all-consuming fire and it rippled through my veins like crackling fireworks, making me absolutely crazy. I started to pull back, panting, but Lucas only clutched me closer with a warning growl as if daring me to try it again.

As if I ever would.

He kissed me hard, snatching me around the waist as he pulled me into his room and slammed my back against the door. His hands were everywhere, searching me up and down as I had, as if unable to believe I was real. His mouth was crushing on top of mine, and I loved it. I crushed him right back and yanked his T-shirt over his head so I could dig my nails into the perfect, caramel skin on his back. I smiled at his hiss of pain. He reciprocated with a sharp nibble on my lower lip and then a smile of his own when I gasped into his mouth.

Everything was Lucas. Everything was hot, burning me, melting away all thoughts of caution or control. Everything was about wanting him, needing him. All of him.

"Lucas," I said through his lips.

He just moaned, shaking his head against my interruption.

"Don't stop," I breathed. "Please, don't stop."

He paused, panting. His sweet breath inoculated me, taking me to a new level of abandon as his eyes searched mine. I saw doubt pass through them, concern. And then they began to smolder; they strayed to my lips and scorched them. I lurched forward to kiss him as I wrapped my legs around his waist. He didn't say a word. He hefted me up and lowered me to the floor, not even thinking to bother with the bed. My jeans came off, then his. He tugged my shirt off and then undid my bra as I fumbled around with his boxers.

He chuckled in my ear and paused to pull them down himself. Any other time, his amusement might have bugged me, but I couldn't have cared less.

All I cared about was his lips on mine, his body moving over me, and his voice saying my name, telling me he loved me. All that mattered was Lucas and me, loving each other for as long as we could.

• • •

Much later, we lay together on the floor, staring up at the ceiling and grinning like a couple of idiots.

Lucas turned his head to mine and said, "Wow. . . ."

I laughed. "That's an understatement if I ever heard one."

He snuggled closer, burying his face into my hair and inhaling deeply. "I didn't hurt you, did I?" he whispered in my ear.

I shook my head. "You were surprisingly gentle . . . after the first time."

Lucas groaned, half laughing as though embarrassed. "It's been a while," he admitted.

"But you didn't change," I said, awed.

"Because of you. You kept me in control." He nuzzled his nose into my throat and made my body tremble with aftershocks.

"I wasn't sure I could do it," I admitted. "Since I was so, you know . . . distracted."

Lucas laughed softly as he rested his head on my chest. "It was perfect."

I smiled and said, "I know." I hesitated before saying what I wanted to say next, not wanting to bring it up and ruin the moment. But it was bursting out of me. "I've missed you," I whispered finally. Lucas pressed his lips against my skin, his brows drooping into a frown. "I felt dead without you," I said. "Like a shell . . . like I was burning." I felt a sob try and choke off my words, but I repressed it. I had to get this out. "I'm so sorry. I was so wrong. About Derek, about what he is. You were right to be jealous. I would have been."

Lucas rose onto his elbows and looked down at me. His eyes were sweet, warm, and seeping into my soul like they'd never left at all.

"I was a jerk," he said. "I was selfish. I wanted all of you. But I can see now that Derek has a place in your heart that I can't ever be a part of." I started to protest but he put his fingers on my lips. "It's okay. I know now that the part Derek has is only friendship and that you've been so crazy over him because you feel guilty. You probably don't want to hear this, but I think you gotta tell him that you're the one who made me bite him. You gotta ease your guilt and start living your life again."

I nodded as tears trailed across my cheeks. Lucas wiped them away with his thumbs.

"You're right," I said. "I never should have made you bite him in the first place. It was the biggest mistake of my life."

Lucas shushed me. "You made that choice out of love, out of compassion for your friend. Just because it didn't turn out exactly like you'd hoped, doesn't mean it was a mistake."

"Yes, it does," I sniffled. "I should have just left him to be a vampire. Then at least he'd have a place in the world."

"Faith, if you'd let Derek become a vampire, he'd be fully dead inside. No soul left, none of his personality. Now, because of you, he's still himself. Now, he can make a choice—something none of us ever get the chance to do—about whether he wants to be like the vampires or not."

I sniffled again as Lucas went on, stroking the tears away with his fingertips. "A bad thing happened to Derek. He got bitten by Vincent because he was trying to help the girl he loved." He placed a soft kiss on my cheek. "But what happens after that—the choice he makes now—that's got nothing to do with you. Just because you're plagued with a curse, doesn't mean you get a license to be a monster."

Deep down, I knew he was right. I wasn't sure if I could let Derek go, but I had to try. I couldn't keep trying to control everything. Because there was very little of life that *could* be controlled. Not my power, not my friends or the choices they made, and not my relationship with Lucas. I couldn't control the horrible things going on around me, and sometimes I couldn't even help stop them—but I could learn to deal with them like an adult instead of throwing a hissy fit and acting out. "He's hanging out with the vampires again," I said. "I don't know when he'll be back or even *if* he'll be back. I might not ever get the chance to talk to him. I totally failed. He's one of them now." I buried my face in his chest. "What are we going to do? The uprising is happening and now they have Derek."

"Hey," he said, shushing me. "Look, maybe it's not too late. He's upset, but maybe not irreparably. Do you want to go upstairs and see if he's there?"

I recoiled at the thought of leaving the floor, of leaving Lucas's arms when I'd waited so long to return to them.

I let my hand slide down Lucas's flat stomach, and I flashed him a mischievous smile.

"Maybe later," I said.

Lucas's eyes smoldered as he caught where I was going, but then his brows knitted together and he said, "I didn't mean it, you know."

I turned my head to the side, confused.

"What I said that night. About not wanting to be with you. You gotta know it was all a lie. I love you. Being with you is the best thing that's ever happened to me. The trigger thing is manageable, especially now that you're learning to control your power. And it's fading for whatever reason. Maybe one day it'll be gone. Even if it's not, I don't care. I just want you. For as long as I'm allowed. One lifetime or a thousand. I want you."

I wanted to believe him so badly, but something stopped me. *No relationship can last an eternity.* . . . I didn't need eternity, but I did need a future with Lucas. If he could leave me so easily once, he could do it again. And as much as I loved him, I had more self-respect than to let someone treat me like that.

"But what about what you said before?" I asked. "You told me that no relationship was strong enough to last eternity. And I know you're probably right, but—I love you. And I want you forever. And I know that it'll never happen because I don't want to be a werewolf. But I at least want you for *my* future. The fact that you could just leave me again any time you want . . . I can't handle that,

Lucas. I won't let you do that to me again."

Lucas grabbed my arms. "Forget everything I said before I fell in love with you. I don't even know who that person is, cuz that sure as hell isn't me anymore. Sure, before you, I believed love couldn't last. But now there's nothing else on earth I want more than being able to love you forever."

He pulled me to him, enveloping me in warmth. "I'm sorry we can't have it," he whispered. "I'm sorrier than you'll ever know." He ran his fingers through my hair. "That night in Gould . . . well, I was eavesdropping a little bit and I heard what Yvette said about picturing my life after you died. I'm not saying I want to be away from you for a month, but I did picture it. And a life without you—it's not a life at all. It's just existence."

"I can't do that to you," I said, pulling back. "I'll . . ."

"What?" he took my cheek with the smallest smile. "Let me change you? I don't want that for you. I'll sacrifice my eternity for yours." He rubbed his thumb across my cheek. "Because I love you."

"I'm so sorry," I said, choking.

"I'll be fine," he said dismissively as he took up my hands. "You and me will go live alone in a beautiful house in the woods where nobody will bother us. Maybe have some kids, you can do your photography, I can . . . well, I can do whatever I want." He smiled and swept his palm across my cheek.

"Kids?" I croaked.

"Maybe one day. I've always wanted a couple. And that way I'll have a piece of you to love after you're gone."

I felt a twist of sadness at that, but smiled for him.

"After we deal with the vampires," Lucas said. "Our life will be perfect. Because we'll have each other. And if anybody tries to tell us otherwise, I'll set 'em straight. You forget, babe, I'm a werewolf. Nobody messes with me and mine."

I puffed a joyless laugh. "Oh right. And when I'm eighty, I'll try not to be jealous of your next, young sexy girlfriend."

Lucas's vibe was all exasperation. "There won't be any girls after you, my match. You're it for me."

Lucas wrapped me in his arms again and touched his lips to mine with such fragility it made me cry. Or maybe it was because of everything he'd said. I no longer doubted the depths of Lucas's love for me. It was bittersweet, though, because our love had to end someday—not because he would ever leave me again. No, I knew he'd stay with me for good this time. But death, inevitably, would be the end of our love. I kissed Lucas harder, overwhelmed by the odd surge of grief and love swirling through me.

He rolled over with me, and we were quickly lost in each other again. We slipped below the surface of life to a place where it was just Lucas and I, our bodies melded together, swirled into each other, riding that moment of ecstasy together.

When we would resurface, I could never know.

GOOD-BYE

I watched Lucas fall asleep. My eyes begged me to do the same, but my mind was still buzzing. I needed to talk to Derek. I'd told Lucas that I would try to convince him to leave the vampires again, but I knew there was only one way he'd consider that: if he had me. And I couldn't bear to lose Lucas again no matter what the cost. Which meant I had to say good-bye to Derek.

I sat up, dragging Lucas's leaden arms off of me and got dressed. I grabbed my phone and placed the silver necklace I kept in my sweater pocket around my neck. Stepping over Lucas's legs, I went outside to the bottom floor of the building where I was pretty sure he wouldn't hear me if he woke up.

I took a long, steadying breath and called Derek.

He answered on the first ring.

"It's me," I said. "I have to talk to you. Meet me on the football field if you still want to say good-bye." I hung up before he could answer, too scared that he would blow me off.

I forced myself to go outside. It was unlikely that Melissa would try to get me again tonight with dawn approaching, and as for the wolf . . . I wasn't entirely sure that it meant me harm anymore.

I walked along the winding campus sidewalks, shivering in the night air. I took my time getting to the field, planning out everything I wanted to say.

When I reached the stadium, I saw that one of the gates had been left ajar. I crept through the gate and walked the long dimly lit hall to the field. The stadium glowed beneath the moonlight. Almost out of habit, I looked up at the pale white moon, noting its fullness. It was getting close again.

A lonely black figure stood in the center of the field. His hands were shoved into the pockets of his charcoal blazer; his head was lowered, almost like he was afraid to look up.

I stopped before Derek, and he finally met my gaze. Neither of us said a word for a long while, we only looked at each other.

"You were with him," he said finally. "I can smell him on you."

I struggled to keep my voice level. "We're together again."

His nostrils flared, and he looked away, curling his lip. Finally, he looked around again. "Guess I saw that coming." His vibe was a tangle of defeat and misery, but something else danced at the edges—urgency. "I knew I was taking a chance by hanging out with the vampires again, but I never thought you'd go back to him after he left you like that."

"He didn't leave me," I said firmly. "I left him. I chose you, remember? I chose to help you, and you took advantage of me. Lucas was right. You're relentless. And it would be sweet, except that you've crossed the line."

Derek's face crumpled into a frown.

"Derek, you know I don't love you romantically anymore. You've always known it. You have to learn to accept it now." I took a deep breath, bracing myself to hurt him. Again. "I choose Lucas. I *have* to be with him; he's my blood. He's my life."

Derek began shaking his head. "If you only knew," he murmured. "If you only knew what I'd done for you. To keep you safe."

I drew back. "What are you talking about?"

"It's so ironic. All he's ever done is put you in danger, and all I've ever done is try to rescue you from it, and you choose him. It's just . . . so ironic."

"That's not true," I argued. "You bit me. You took me on that trip—"

"The trip you *asked* to go on!"

I shook myself, throwing away my fury in a heavy sigh. "Whatever. That's not the point."

Derek stepped closer, expression pleading now. "I never wanted to say good-bye, Faith. That was never why I asked Katie to talk to you. I needed to tell you something, and I knew you wouldn't meet me if I just asked you."

Realization of what he was attempting to do slammed into me. Even now—even after betraying my trust and returning to the monsters who'd killed Heather and countless others—he had the audacity to try and turn this around on me. I smiled bitterly. "You tried to trick me out here so that you could apologize, right? To try and make me the bad guy again, so you can go on feeling like the victim because I won't forgive you for going back to them."

"What? No, I needed to—"

"Stop it, Derek. Stop trying to manipulate me. God, Lucas was so right! I am so incredibly blinded by guilt. Here I was thinking you were just trying to be my friend—*really* trying—when as soon as Lucas was out of the picture, there you were, moving in on me when I was ill-equipped to defend myself."

"Faith, just listen. I wanted to talk to you so that I could warn you. That guy on Gould who attacked you was right. The vampires are coming for you."

"I know that! You don't think I know that? That I couldn't figure it out after what they did to Heather? After what *you* did! I'm sure you helped them, after the way you talked to me on the phone."

"Faith, they can hear through the phone, I had to say those th—"

"No. No more lies. No more wheedling your way around my heart. I'm done. I came here to say good-bye to you, and that's what I'm doing. I'm saying good-bye."

Derek's face fell, and he stepped back from me.

"What are you talking about?" he asked.

I just stared at him, making my face convey the word I couldn't bear to say again. *Good-bye.*

"But . . . no," he whispered. "You're all I have." He reached for me, draping his hands over my arms.

I wriggled away, but it was like his hands took away a piece of me when they parted from my skin. Something inside me wrenched. "Derek, I can't be here for you anymore. I know I said I always would be, but I can't anymore. Not if you can't get over me."

"Yes, you can, you can." He reached for me again and I withdrew. "I won't try anymore, I won't—"

"Derek, I'm the reason you're like this!" I exploded, unable to hold the truth in any longer. "I made Lucas bite you back in December."

Silence for a beat.

"*Made* him?" Derek finally asked. "How could you—?"

"That's not important," I cut him off. "The point is that I forced Lucas to bite you after Vincent did. I made you this way."

Derek faltered, gaping. "But . . . Lucas said he lost control." Then he blinked, and it was as though he was seeing me for the first time. "You? You *made* him?"

Tears bit at my cheeks. "Yes. I'm the one you should be blaming for this. Not the werewolves. Not Lucas. He was crazed at the time, and he didn't even know what he was doing. It was me. I did this to you. And I'm so sorry."

I started to reach for him, but he recoiled, his face a wild mess of emotions I couldn't begin to read or understand. When, at last, he turned to look at me, he was furious. "So, this is all *your* fault. I mean, when you think about it, if I hadn't followed you to the barn . . . if you hadn't started dating Lucas." His eyes flared. "If you had just listened to me and let yourself love me instead of him! None of this would have happened!"

An erratic, volatile energy began to flow in Derek's vibe, but there was nothing I could do to stop it.

"And now you've chosen him again!" he raged. "After everything you've done, after all the pain I've had to suffer because of you—you can't even *try* being with me."

"I did try," I choked. "I—I tried as hard as I could but I—"

"Shut up! Just shut up, Faith. God, you know, I came out here to *warn* you. I can't believe what an idiot I am!" He let out a loud half-roar, half-howling sound that jarred my bones. He slammed his fists into the turf, making humongous holes in the dirt. I almost screamed, but it happened too quickly.

"You know what? You're right," he said, straightening slowly. "You're right about one thing. You and me. Never gonna happen. This is good-bye, Faith. You think you're the one who's done? You don't even know the meaning of the word. I. Am. *Done*."

With that, he sped off in a blur of gray, and was gone.

Forever, this time.

MURDER

Lucas and I spent Sunday morning in bed, unable to get enough of each other. I didn't have a problem with this. In fact, those were the happiest hours of my life.

Things took a deadly turn for the worse when we left the room that afternoon.

As Lucas and I walked across the courtyard to my building, it was immediately apparent that something was up. There was an intense collective vibe of anxiety and fear rippling through the air, making me antsy. Students milled about in the courtyard, talking in hushed tones, as if exchanging information.

And that wasn't the worst part. There were about five news vans in the driveway outside my building; police cars, paramedics, people in suits with plastic name tags bustled by. Some girl from my building was being interviewed by a reporter. She was crying.

"What's going on?" I asked slowly.

He shrugged, glancing around the courtyard. "We should—"

Then I heard my name being shouted from a small group of people right outside my building. It was Ashley and Courtney and some other people from my floor. I walked over, somewhat embarrassed at my attire. I'd put on Lucas's leather jacket because my bra had been ruined by his . . . enthusiasm, and I felt weird without one.

"Hey," I said. "What's going on?" I eyed the yellow CAUTION tape blocking off our doorway. This was definitely bad.

"Oh, God!" Ashley gushed. "You didn't hear?"

"No," I said.

"She was probably too busy bed hopping," Courtney jibed.

Ashley giggled, and I flushed dark red.

Lucas slung his arm over my shoulder looking totally at ease, even smug. Courtney glared at me viciously. At first, I was slightly confused by the intensity of her hate. She was so insignificant to me that I wondered how she could despise me so much.

And then I remembered.

I was dating her ex-boyfriend.

I had to smother a chuckle. *Ohhhh, the irony. The beautiful, beautiful irony.*

I smiled and turned to Ashley, completely ignoring Courtney.

"Yeah, I was busy last night," I said, hugging Lucas closer. "Tell me what happened."

Ashley, who'd experienced my post-break-up depression first-hand, looked from me to Lucas several times and then gave me an I'm-so-happy-for-you smile.

Then she lowered the boom.

"You won't believe it," she hissed. "You know Kira Wilcox? From the room next to ours?"

"Uh-huh," I said warily.

"She was *killed* last night! In her room!"

My mouth dropped to the floor. I felt Lucas stiffen next to me.

"No," I gasped.

"Yes!" Ashley practically sang. "They think it was *him*. The serial killer!"

"But, how did he get in?"

"Kira *let* him in," Ashley said. "They have it all on the security camera. It's the first look they've got at the guy."

My mind was reeling. If someone had let a vampire into my building, there was no way I could ever go in there again after dark.

If he had been in my building, could he get into my room, too? Did it work like that? Or what if it had been a blood bitch that killed Kira? If it had been a vampire, the body would be exsanguinated, but if it was a blood bitch it would be killed in a different way. Stabbed. Choked. Beaten, or whatever. If it was a blood bitch, then the daylight hours were no longer safe. I needed to know which it had been, but figuring that out was something of a problem.

"Did they see what he looked like?" Lucas asked calmly.

"It's all on the news," Ashley said, sounding slightly annoyed. "But they're not letting anyone in the building until the investigation is done with, so it's not like we can watch it on TV. We're gonna be stuck out here all freaking day."

I couldn't hide my disgust at her selfishness.

"A girl died here last night," I said sharply. "Do you know how easily it could have been you?"

Ashley fell silent and Lucas massaged my shoulders gently, murmuring soothingly in my ear. As nice as that was, sweet nothings and a back massage weren't going to solve this problem.

"Here, look," Courtney said thrusting her phone at us. "I have Wi-Fi. You can see the news report."

I took her glitter-encrusted phone and held it between Lucas and me. The newscast was several hours old, but it showed a clip from the security camera. I saw Kira standing just inside the doorway, her long blond hair tied into a braid and a smile on her face. I watched in silent horror as she held the door open for her murderer. From the angle of the camera, it was close to impossible to see who it was, though my instincts said it was a woman. Something in the willowy grace of her walk tipped me off. My immediate thought was that it was Melissa, since she had been here last night. But then again, all vampires were graceful and some were small. It easily could have been a man. The clothing, too, was wrong—dark pants and a sweatshirt covering most of the features. Melissa had been wearing a miniskirt and Manolos.

There was something else I noticed. As Kira let the murderer in, someone else slipped past them—a girl. She seemed oddly familiar, but she was facing away from the camera too, so it was hard to tell.

"Who's that coming in with them?" I asked, handing back the phone.

"Dunno," Ashley said. "The police asked the whole building— well, except you, I guess—and nobody identified her."

She'd seemed really familiar, but maybe it was just someone from our building. Or someone I'd seen around campus. It annoyed me that I couldn't place her, since whoever it was might have details on the killer.

"We gotta go," Lucas said, pulling on my hand.

Courtney sniffed a mocking laugh. "You can't go anywhere. The campus is on lockdown. There are police guarding all of the exits."

"Did I ask you for permission?" Lucas sneered and towed me away into a secluded spot next to his building.

"So, what do you think?" I asked, hugging my arms around myself. "Was it a vampire?"

"Hard to tell. If it was, he was acting human for the cameras. Or trying to fool the girl, I don't know."

I took notice of his use of pronouns. "It looked like a woman to me."

"Does it matter?"

"It could have been Melissa. She knows where I live. She ah . . ." I hadn't told him this yet. "She kind of attacked me. Last night."

"*What?*" Lucas half yelled.

I glanced around, embarrassed. "Don't have a heart attack. Listen—" And I told him about Melissa's appearance last night. How she had orders to take me back to the lair, but got distracted when I started bleeding. I even told him about the heather-gray wolf, and that it seemed to be following me. I looked up at his irate expression when I finished and mumbled, "I'm sorry I didn't tell you."

Lucas rubbed his temples, muttering profanities to himself. "This is . . . a lot, Faith. How could you not tell me about this werewolf thing?"

I shrugged. "At first I thought it was nothing. And then when I decided it was actually following me, I don't know. Every time I tried to tell you, something else was in the way or more important."

"There's nothing more important to me than you," Lucas hissed fiercely. "You should have told me."

"I know." I looked tentatively up at him. "Do you know any wolves that are that color?"

"Gray? Tons of them."

"So you couldn't identify him?"

"Sure I could," Lucas said. "If I saw him. Or smelled him, maybe. But you telling me it was a gray wolf is like me telling you I saw a human with brown hair. It could be anyone."

"Well, it's not important now anyway. We need to focus on the vampires."

Lucas glowered away from me, shaking his head. His vibe was still livid, but he was trying to calm it for my sake.

"Can you smell her?" I asked. "The one who was here?"

"No, there's too many bodies obscuring the scent. I wonder how the Kira girl died. Did the report say?"

"It just said that she was murdered. I guess they're keeping that part to themselves until they know more."

"People will assume it's the same guy who's been exsanguinating girls," Lucas observed. "But if the body's not drained, then it might not have been a vampire."

"That's what I was thinking, but who is it, then? A blood bitch?"

"Maybe. Someone sent to get you. It was sheer dumb luck you chose last night to come to me. If you'd gone back to your room after the attack, instead of coming to mine. . . . God, they could have had you." Lucas's eyes burned into mine with a fervency that took me aback. I hugged myself closer. "Sorry," Lucas said. "I didn't mean to scare you. I'm just trying to examine all the angles." He took my arms and dragged them away from my body. "Look, I'm gonna go call Rolf and tell him about this. Go up to my room and change. I kept your clothes where you left them."

I blinked. "What? Why didn't you tell me that before?" I asked like this was the most important thing happening.

"I don't know," he said. "I didn't want you to think I was creepy for keeping your bras and stuff lying around."

I smiled, rolling my eyes at him.

"Okay," I said. "Then what do we do?"

"We gotta get off of this campus before dark. It's not safe here anymore, even if it was just a blood bitch who killed Kira. It's only a matter of time before they come for you again."

I shivered.

"The thing I don't get though," he said slowly, "is if they want you so they can blackmail Derek into helping them, then why are they still trying to get you? He already joined up with them, right?"

I nodded stiffly.

"So what do they want you for?"

I shrugged. "Turn me for the army? That's what Silas and Vincent said when they attacked me."

Lucas nodded, but made a face that led me to believe he doubted me.

"Where will we go?" I managed croakily.

"Gould," he said. "That's the only place I know you'll be safe. Now go upstairs and get changed. We have a long drive, and I wanna get there before dark."

"It'll be close," I said, looking at my watch.

"I can make it."

"How are we even going to get off campus? It's on lockdown, remember?"

"Let me worry about that." He thrust his keys into my hand. "Meet me at the driveway in fifteen minutes. Try not to talk to anyone."

"Why not?"

"That girl who came in with them . . . you never know. She might be a blood bitch, and if so, she's probably hanging around."

I nodded shakily and started to turn when he caught my arm.

"Hey," he said, voice tender and low now. "I love you. I promise you'll be safe, all right? I won't let them find you."

"Why does every vampire in Colorado seem to have it out for me?" I said, only half joking.

"Because you're so damn sweet." He kissed me briefly and slapped my butt as I walked away. I gave him a playful glare.

I changed clothes and tried to call Heather again, even though it was pointless. She didn't answer, but I stuck my phone in my back pocket just in case a miracle occurred.

At the door, I gave the reddish room one last look, praying like hell that I'd live long enough to see it again.

ACCIDENT

It was dusk and we still had an hour to go until we made it to Gould. Lucas had talked to one of the cops on the scene, who just happened to be a member of the pack, and we got through the barricade without an issue.

The problem now was time.

We were running low on daylight. Fast. And that meant nobody was safe anymore.

I didn't realize how tightly I was squeezing the sides of the seat until Lucas's hand drifted over mine.

"Calm down," he said gently. "We've got plenty of time. Gould's just an hour away."

I flipped my hand over and squeezed Lucas's instead, suddenly filled with an uncomfortable blend of happiness and dread. I grimaced, facing the window. It would have been nice to think that our time apart had solved all of our issues, but now I could see that it hadn't. Not even a little bit. And our problems were largely my fault, given the secrets I'd been keeping from him. I loathed the idea of ruining the moment, but if I was going to die—and it looked like I might with the way things were going lately—then I wanted to at least die knowing that I was open and honest with the boy I loved. I still had secrets, things I hadn't wanted to tell him for fear that he would leave me. Now, there was no excuse. Lucas was with me for good, and I owed it to him—and to myself—to be honest from now on.

But, damn, this was going to suck.

"I have a confession to make," I said loudly.

"Stop it," Lucas chided. "Don't act like you're gonna die."

"I might. And I have to get this off of my chest. I don't want to die a slut."

"Okay. . . ."

I drew in a deep breath and said, "I kissed Derek. While we were dating."

The loudest silence in the history of the world filled Lucas's car. "I know," he said.

"You *know?*" I gasped, turning to him. "How on earth could you know that? Did Derek tell you?"

"No. That night, when he bit you, I smelled him on you stronger than ever . . . all over you. I could taste him on your tongue."

I winced. "I did it to try and distract him; I didn't *want* to kiss him, I swear."

Lucas moved his thumb over my knuckles. "I know, baby. I'm not mad."

Why did those words feel like knives in my lungs? "I'm sorry," I whispered hoarsely.

"Stop, saying that. It's done with. I don't wanna talk about it anymore, okay?" He shot me a small smile as he drove. "That's all done with."

I shook my head, still hating myself. "That night," I said. "When you stopped Derek from biting me, how did you even know to come? Did you hear us?"

"Kind of. I heard you in my head. It wasn't so much your voice, as it was an instinctual thing. Like I could feel you asking for help. So I went upstairs and then I heard you yelling at him, smelled the blood. . . . It wasn't rocket science."

"Well, thank you," I said. "I don't know how you knew—it doesn't make sense—but I'm glad you did."

For a long time, I stared at the dense, green forest rolling by on the edges of the highway. The setting sun colored the leaves in varying, auburn tones. Dew sparkled on the window, marbleizing the view, while my breath made mist over the glass. It was dream-like, whizzing through life in silence. Lucas by my side, finally. "Knockin' on Heaven's Door" played over the radio, which I thought was morbidly fitting.

I forced myself to ruin the mood, yet again.

"I have another confession," I said.

Lucas groaned.

I ignored him and went on. "It's not a big deal. Well, no. It is." I fixed my gaze on the window again and said, "I went on that ski trip with Derek to find out why the vampires are building an army."

I heard Lucas let out a puff of air. "You're not nearly as smooth as you think you are, babe."

I frowned over at him.

"I knew that," he said. He laughed at my shocked expression. "You're a really bad liar. Maybe the worst in history."

"You would know," I grumbled.

"How else do you explain me following you there?"

"I just figured you didn't trust me with Derek."

Lucas nodded, raising his eyebrows. "Well, yeah. There was that, too."

"So if you knew I was lying the whole time, why'd you even let me go?"

"I didn't want to be an overprotective asshole who doesn't let his girlfriend out of his sight. But at the same time I knew the vampires would be there, and I wasn't about to leave you alone with them. And I knew you were up to something insane, as usual.

So I followed you."

"But how?"

"The vampires aren't the only ones with private jets. I just left from a different airport so you wouldn't see me hanging around."

I glowered at the dashboard, angry that my awesome plan had never been all that awesome, and then said, "Well, don't you want to know what I found out?"

He glanced at me sharply. "I figured you didn't find out anything."

"Why?" Did he really think I was that impotent? It hadn't been a *total* wash, after all.

"Because you didn't tell me anything," he said.

"Well, I didn't really get the chance to, did I?"

Lucas ran his hand through his hair, making it stick up in funny directions. "You gonna tell me?" he grunted.

"I found out the name of their leader. Arabella. I think she's the leader, anyway."

"The monarch," he corrected. "Anything else?"

"Calvin and Silas talked a lot about the Ancestors. Do you know about them?"

"Bits and pieces. They're pretty clandestine."

"Well, from what I got, there are like, two groups of vampires. Ones who worship the Ancestors and ones who think they're a bunch of crazies. Calvin was with the latter, and Silas got mad that he was committing treason by making fun of them, or whatever. Anyway, Calvin and Silas said that the Ancestors are planning something—something big, I gather—and that Arabella is helping them. Calvin said she needed stuff. Literally, he said *stuff*. And that it would somehow help them with the younglings leaving dead bodies all over the place. But I don't know what stuff they were talking about or what the plan is. I'm guessing it's like we thought—the uprising against the werewolves."

"Makes sense," Lucas murmured. "Damn it, I wish I knew what they wanted, though."

"Well, we know they want Derek, but that doesn't explain what the *stuff* they were talking about is."

"If it was Derek they wanted, they coulda had him ten times over by now." He shook his head with a dark glower. "No, I think they're up to something else. Derek is just a weapon—he can't help them with hiding the dead bodies. They've got something up their sleeves, and I'll be damned if I know what."

"I'm sorry," I said. "I should have tried harder to get more out of them."

Lucas gave me a flat look. "You know that's not what I meant. It's just frustrating. Vampires don't usually do things like this— scheming against us and killing so obviously. They're usually real quiet about it, stick to skulking around in the night and hiding from us. Their sudden boldness is really unnerving the werewolf community, even outside the pack."

"Really," I gasped. "So Rolf finally alerted everyone?"

He snorted. "Hardly. But rumors are flying, and he's been getting a lot of heat from the other pack masters, especially the more powerful ones in Canada and Germany—not to mention my old buds in Russia." Something in his tone said he had one of his macabre stories to accompany that statement, but now wasn't the time to ask about it. "They've all been exchanging info. Seems that this type of organized killing has been happening in other places. Small towns—remote areas where stuff gets overlooked. But when you piece it together, it's clearly the vampire broods. And now with what you're telling me about the Ancestors, it only reaffirms our theories. They're organizing worldwide. Gathering numbers for the revolution."

I suppressed a shiver. "So what do we do?"

"*You* don't do anything. You keep yourself outta the way."

I made a face, but remained quiet. He was right anyway—I was just going to cause trouble if I interfered.

"This little vendetta the vampires seem to have with you will disappear once we eliminate the Denver brood," he continued. "And then . . . well, depending on what Derek does with school, I might have to return to pack duty."

"If he drops out and turns vampire, you mean?"

"Yep. I'm only assigned to him while he's at school. If he drops out, I'll have to go back to Gould."

I frowned. "But . . . all this time, you haven't been watching him."

Lucas remained silent, his vibe going haywire beneath his calm exterior. Jealousy. Hurt. Heartache.

It hit me in an instant.

He knows.

He knew about Derek and my fling. He'd been keeping watch over Derek—and me—this whole time and I never knew. My throat suddenly seemed like it was stuffed with cotton.

"I'm . . . so . . ." I wanted to say sorry, wanted to erase that night with Derek.

"Don't," Lucas rumbled. "We were broken up. You had every right to . . . to do what you did. It's none of my business."

My heart was shattering. I hated this—that he knew.

"Lucas, I—"

"No." He didn't look over, but his voice was pleading. "It's over."

We collapsed into uneasy silence. After a while, it was Lucas who broke it.

"I might have to leave Colorado if Derek quits school," he murmured.

"What do you mean?" I asked, jolted. "Why? Where are you going?"

"To the other packs that are having this vampire problem. We have to get this uprising thing taken care of before they get too far."

"You mean the packs in Canada or Germany?"

"Yeah."

"And you expect me to stay behind, I take it?" I kept my tone light, but he must have heard the clip at the end. Lucas didn't say anything, so I took that as a *yes*. "If you're going someplace I'm coming with you."

"Like hell you are," he growled deeply. "You're staying here. In school. Where it's safe. End of story."

I gave him a meaningful stare. One that said, *we're not done talking about this*, but decided to move on. It wasn't happening now, and there were too many more pressing matters to discuss.

"So do you think what I found out from Calvin and Silas will help you guys find the lair?" I asked.

"Not to dampen your glory, but probably not."

I deflated into the seat. "Well, do you know who Arabella is? Maybe if someone knows the name then they can remember around where they saw her . . . or something."

Lucas smiled down at me endearingly.

"I've never heard of her," Lucas said. "But I bet Rolf has if she's been here any length of time. We'll talk to him about it when we get to the house."

I gazed out of the windshield again, watching the sun set.

"How long will that be?" I asked.

"About forty minutes."

"We won't make it before dark."

He didn't respond.

• • •

W e drove into the night and up through the mountains, snaking along the desolate, dark roads that led to the werewolf mansion. It was about half an hour past sunset, and we were minutes from our destination when I heard a loud rumbling from behind us. I turned around in my seat and saw two bluish headlights approaching us as breakneck speed.

I assumed they were drunk drivers, since nobody in their right mind would be going that fast at night where there were no streetlamps.

"Lucas," I said. "There are idiots coming up behind us."

His eyes flickered into the rearview mirror and then shifted silver. He cursed savagely and slammed on the gas. My heart careened into my throat as I became pasted to the seat.

"What is it?" I gasped, clutching the ceiling handle in a vice.

"Vampires." He cursed again, punching the dashboard so hard it dented the plastic. "I thought this might happen. Shit!"

My mind reeled, trying to make sense as we rocketed around a corner.

"How do you know it's them?" I asked, wincing as Lucas shifted gears and charged faster.

"I saw someone tailing us for a while when we left campus, but they disappeared. They must have stopped somewhere and let the vampires pick up the chase at nightfall. Damn it, I knew this was going to happen." He continued to blabber profanities and murderous grumblings. "We're almost to the house," he muttered. "Almost there . . ."

I watched the speedometer climb to ninety, a hundred . . . higher.

I spun in my seat, but all I could see were the blinding white lights of the car behind us. They were already on top of us, so close I could have reached out and touched the hood.

"Sit back!" Lucas yelled as the car sped ever faster.

Another car drove up beside us, a little black one with tinted windows. The passenger's window rolled down, and Melissa's perfect face appeared. I saw another vampire driving.

"Oh, God," I whispered. Melissa had survived the fight. Terror ravaged my brain. "Oh, God . . . Lucas. Go faster!"

"I am!" He hit it harder, and we blasted forward. The vampires were right with us.

Melissa laughed and made obscene gestures at us. Then she licked her long, pointy teeth and made an uh-oh face. She held the top of the car like she was bracing herself.

"Lucas!" I screamed. I tensed, readying myself.

Lucas's arm shot out in front of my body, and he shouted something I couldn't understand.

Then the vampires rammed their car into ours.

BROOD

First there was the jar of the impact. It slammed us sideways, and we flew into the air. I heard myself screaming. Glass stung my face.

Then we hit again. The ceiling caved in; the windshield cracked. Lucas's arm went limp. We rolled, over and over, and finally stopped when we were upside down. I hung there, still rolling around on the inside.

My ears buzzed, and my vision faded to black, off and on. I blinked and managed to turn my head. Lucas was hanging beside me. Unconscious. There was a large gash in the side of his skull, pouring blood onto the roof. Beneath it all, I saw the dull white of bone.

Heat hit me next. Intense heat, licking my face and my feet. The front of the car was on fire.

That's when I really woke up. My breath felt like waves of nausea, torturing my insides, and I couldn't stop coughing from the smoke. Three forms materialized in front of the hood, flames licking their shadowy forms like demons from the underworld.

I began shaking Lucas, yelling for him to wake up, but I couldn't hear my own voice.

And he wasn't waking up.

I tried to unbuckle myself, but my hands were shaking so badly I couldn't work the buckle. I started crying, which only made things worse. Then the side of the car ripped off, and I turned to see Melissa standing there, smug as ever. She tore the seatbelt from my chest and watched me fall in a heap on the roof of the car.

I wriggled around and watched the same thing happen to Lucas, only he wasn't moving.

I fought to get to him, but two iron hands took hold of me and yanked me away. I yelled and kicked, ignoring a tremendous pain in my right side. I was pretty sure something was broken in there.

Melissa threw me to the ground and cursed. Her eyes were coal-black with the crave. She was going crazy for the blood covering my body. Frustration welled in her vibe like a tsunami. She whirled around, stamping her foot.

"Stop, damn it," she snarled. She wedged her hands into her head.

One of the other vampires shouted at her from across the car. "Get a grip, Melissa!"

"I am!" She shrieked and her eyes faded. She rounded on me. "Come on, tramp, this time I'm not letting your blood get the better of me. I'll bet it tastes like garbage anyway."

I tried to squirm away, but Melissa dragged me by my underarms to the street. There were no cars to see us, no werewolves to help us, but I screamed for help anyway.

The other vampires tossed Lucas's body, lashed in silver chains, into the back of the other car and then approached me holding a rope and a leather bag.

"Am I going to have to use these, sweetheart?" one asked me.

"Screw off!" I yelled and tried to kick him in the groin.

He dodged me easily, clucking his teeth. He snatched up both of my legs in one hand and lashed them together without effort. Shrieking, I writhed as he tied my arms behind my back, and the other vampire shoved the bag over my head.

I continued to scream as they tossed me into the back with Lucas.

"Shut *up!*" Melissa hissed.

I ignored her, yelling louder just to piss her off.

She must have hit me then, because there was a blinding pain above my left temple and then . . . nothing . . .

• • •

I was thrown onto something cold and hard; I assumed it was the floor. I felt my arms and legs become free. The bag was jerked off of my head and then I could see.

Only I wished they had kept the bag on.

I was inside the vampire lair. I had to be.

The room was hexagonal in shape. It wasn't particularly big, but it was dark. The only lights came from candelabras burning against the black walls. Wax dripped from the votives, pattering on the floor like the sound of trickling blood. I could hear talking, low whispers and murmurs, words too fast to understand.

I rose to my feet, quivering. Vaguely, the pain in my side twanged, but I was too terrified to worry about it. Something smelled charred in the air, like something was cooking . . . *flesh.* Bile climbed up my throat, and I just barely swallowed it down.

Vampires huddled along the walls in cliques; Melissa was off to the right side with my abductors, and I spotted Calvin standing alone in front of what seemed to be the centerpiece of the room.

It was a chair. Not a big throne thing with jewels and gold and filigree. No. It was just a small iron chair.

It was empty for now.

I tried to get Calvin's attention, wanting him to see the hatred I held for him, but he wasn't looking at me. He seemed strangely subdued. His signature cocky smirk was gone and his indigo eyes were cast to the floor.

I think it was this fact that scared me more than anything.

I turned away from him to glance behind me and found Lucas was there—chained in silver. He was unconscious, bleeding out onto the cement floor. His blood seeped toward me in a river of red gore; he should have healed by now, but the silver chains were impeding his regenerative powers. I started toward him, wanting to staunch the blood flow, but the room hissed, and I stopped. Every dead-cold eye in the room was on me, daring me to try and move again.

I restrained myself, glancing around, instead, to try and see a way out. I got the feeling we were underground, which made sense if we were in their lair. Was that water rushing behind the walls? I looked up and saw a small wooden door on the ceiling above Lucas's head. *What in God's name is that used for?*

Quickly, I counted the vampires: ten. More than enough to kill me, but I couldn't dwell on that. Two guarded Lucas's broken body. Three stood on one side of the room, four on the other. Calvin stood alone at the front.

Then two more vampires entered. All eyes focused on the chair at the front of the room as an invisible door creaked open. A lethally beautiful woman entered, followed by a man in a long black cloak. The collar was popped, and he kept his head bent low, shading his face. But I knew that man. I knew that man with every inch of my body.

It was Derek.

Hatred exploded in my chest—complete and total loathing. I

felt my lips wrinkle into a snarl as I watched him glide into the room and stand opposite of Calvin like a pair of undead sentries. He refused to look at me.

Then the woman lowered herself into the chair. Her face was flawlessly beautiful, and she had slanted features, as though her entire face had been pulled up at the edges. She wore a long, flowing gown, black and sparkling in the low light of the room. The top was corseted, and there was a spidery necklace over her décolletage. Her big gray eyes fell on me, amused and slightly expectant—like she was waiting for me to do a flip or something.

All of the vampires had gone silent. The only sound remaining was the pattering of the wax and that gentle buzzing in the background.

Then a groan came from behind me and I turned. Lucas was stirring. *Thank God he's alive!*

"Do you know who I am, human?"

I spun back around and realized that the dangerous chick was talking to me.

I decided to take a wild guess and go with, "Arabella."

The woman's pencil-thin eyebrows twitched up and she nodded slowly. "You have been well informed," she said with a voice as clear and crisp as a glass of champagne. "Do you know where you are?"

Lucas moaned deeply and I heard the silver chains jingling.

I swallowed as my stomach wriggled uncomfortably. *Please, be okay, baby.*

"I'm in a vampire lair," I said.

"And do you know why you have been brought to my lair?"

Not wanting to give them any ideas about turning me, I went with my second-best guess. "Because someone told you I know what you're planning." I made sure to stare Derek down as I said this, but it was like he couldn't even hear me.

Arabella's eyes twinkled. "Tell me what I'm planning, human."

Lucas's hoarse voice came from behind me. "Don't . . . say anything."

I turned and saw that he was kneeling on the floor. The chains cut into his skin, scorching him, but he was awake, at least.

"Tell me," Arabella cooed pleasantly, "or your doggie dies."

"I know that you're planning an uprising against the werewolves," I ground out. "That's why all those girls have been dying. Because you can't keep your younglings in check."

To my surprise, Arabella's crimson lips turned upward in a vague smile.

"Is that what they're saying over there in the kennel? An uprising?" Her smile widened, and she stood and walked slowly around the room as though floating. Her dress seemed to be made of shadows; it snaked and coiled along the floor in a long ghostly train. My nerves skyrocketed as she stopped in front of Lucas.

She put her silken hand on top of his head and petted him like a dog. Lucas jerked his head away, disgust on his face. But Arabella tugged the chains, forcing Lucas to be still as she stroked his hair.

"Such vanity," she purred. "Such ego the mongrels have." She clucked her teeth, petting Lucas all the while. I wanted to jump over there and stab her with something long and wooden. "This is not about you," Arabella said to him. "I admit that you are partly correct. We *have* been increasing our numbers quite exponentially, which has caused our dear humans to pay a sad price. But a war against the dogs is not our goal. We would *never* want to eliminate you. Not at all." She bent low to Lucas's ear and whispered, "You know, I have always taken a fancy to a hint of wolf blood. Some say it is bitter, but I find it exhilarating."

Lucas's face tightened as she lowered her head to his neck.

I started forward. "No!" I yelled, lunging. Calvin was on me before my feet left the floor. He restrained me while I writhed around, watching in horror as Arabella sunk her nasty fangs into Lucas's skin.

He didn't scream, hardly even flinched as Arabella took a long pull out of his throat. She straightened and shivered violently. Blood continued to gush in red rivers down Lucas's chest, but none of the other vampires looked even remotely interested.

"Lovely," Arabella said, licking her lips. She patted Lucas's head. "You have old blood, dog. Very strong. It's a shame to see you go. But it must be done. I cannot have you gallivanting around, spoiling our plans."

She spun to face me, and I found her pupils had widened completely making her look like a walking corpse.

"Bitch," I ground between my teeth.

Arabella smiled coldly, licking her lips again. "Let her go, Cal, honey. She poses no threat to us."

Calvin released me roughly and returned to his spot without a word as Arabella resumed her seat. She sighed and regarded me. "I suppose you wish to know what we are planning, but I'm afraid you will have to wait until after you are turned to find out."

Fear shocked through my body. *Turned? Here? Now?* Was this seriously the reason I'd been brought here? So that they could turn one insignificant girl? What was the big deal about me?

Arabella seemed pleased by my astonishment. "Atonement must be made for the crimes you and your dog have committed against our kind. Vincent Stone and Silas Zircon were two of my oldest and most skilled subjects. Their lives must be repaid." She turned to Lucas. "Vincent's life was accounted for when you infected our dear Derek. But that leaves Silas to be recompensed. I think Faith shall do nicely. I do enjoy the pretty ones. They always come out looking so lovely."

My body went numb as Lucas began shouting curses and struggling behind me. I refused to turn around, unable to watch him in pain, but I heard the chains jerk and he yelped, falling ominously silent.

This couldn't be how our story ended, with me a vampire and Lucas murdered in front of my eyes. But there was nothing I could do to stop it. It was so *frustrating.*

And Arabella's whole spiel about repayment just seemed, well . . . dumb. Who was she kidding? She didn't want me for repayment. She wanted me for her army. She had to be lying about the war, trying to throw us off. And I was going to get her to admit it. I at least wanted that much if I was going to be turned against my will. I wanted the truth.

"I don't buy it," I said.

Arabella quirked her head.

"This can't be the first time someone's killed a vampire in your brood, right?"

Arabella swelled with indignation.

"You guys don't go hunting down humans for repayment every time it happens," I said. "So why are you doing this? Why me?"

For a moment Arabella appeared stunned, and after testing her vibe, I felt her panic. She hadn't expected me to confront her. But she kept her expression level.

"Vincent at least told me the truth," I said. "At least he admitted that it was for the army. So why are you making up this whole compensation crap?"

The vampires hissed at my disrespectful tone.

"Just be honest," I spat. "It's so I can help you win the war against the werewolves."

"There is no war!" Arabella shouted. "War with the dogs, as much as it displeases me to say it, would mean the elimination of our race. We are not, and will never be, as strong as the wolf packs."

A few of the vampires muttered dubiously.

"We do not work together," Arabella continued, glaring around at her brood. "We cannot unite in the way the packs do. And so we will never beat them. The Ancestors know it, and so does every one of you, regardless of whether you choose to acknowledge it."

Everyone quieted.

"So what then?" I demanded. "Why are you building an army?"

Arabella's lips pursed. "You'll have to wait until you have been turned."

I let out a frustrated noise. "Why do you want *me* so badly? So my boyfriend killed a couple vampires. Big deal. I'm sure it's not the first time it's happened, so why go through so much trouble for me? You killed a car full of people, got a girl to let you into my dorm room, sent Melissa and then *two* carfuls of vampires! I'm not that special!"

"But you *are* special," she purred. "Derek here, tells me of your unique gift. You read emotions, do you not?"

I refused to answer, glowering at Derek instead, who continued to study the floor. *Traitor*, was all I could think.

"Tell me," Arabella commanded.

I clamped my jaw shut. How could Derek tell them? Even the other vampires kept my secret, but Derek? *Derek* was the one who sold me out?

"Tell me," Arabella growled, "or I will make your doggie suffer terribly on his way to hell."

"I do," I spat. "I can read emotions. But I won't keep my power if you turn me." I didn't know if this was true, but I was grasping at straws.

"Is that what you think?" She snickered softly behind her hand. "Tell me, how did you come to this ludicrous conclusion?"

"I—I don't . . ." I didn't want to tell her about Yvette.

"You must never have met Kevin, have you?" She waved a hand empirically and one of the vampires standing next to Melissa came forward. He looked to be in his late twenties, tall and ruggedly handsome with flyaway curly hair and wide brown eyes. He bowed slightly before Arabella as he came to stand beside me.

Arabella gestured to the man. "Faith, meet Kevin. Kevin, this is Faith. She is like you."

I gaped up at Kevin, and he glanced briefly at me, contempt written on every inch of his flawless face.

He had no vibe.

It was true, then. He had the sense. This was *the* Kevin. The man Yvette had spoken of. He hadn't been killed, after all, but turned.

"His power remains intact," Arabella said victoriously.

That was cool and all, but if that was true then why hadn't they used him to get to me? He could have controlled the entire pack and made them give me up. I turned to face him. "Really? What can you do?"

"I can read emotions." His voice was smooth and deep as dark chocolate, but saturated with distain.

"That's all? You can't . . . do anything . . . else?" I didn't want to give anything away, but it ended up making me sound dense. A couple vampires snickered at me.

"No," Kevin said. "Nothing."

"Oh, well . . . cool." Was he lying? Yvette had said he could control the werewolves, too. So did that part of the power die with his body? Or had he simply lied to the vampires to keep them from using him? It would seem that it was the former because if he was on the vampires' team now he'd *want* to help them. Right?

"So you, see?" Arabella sang. "You have nothing to fear, Faith Reynolds. Your power will remain, and you will become a valuable asset to our army. Kevin here is quite useful when dealing with liars and thieves. We value him greatly." She waved her hand, and Kevin melted back into the shadows with the rest of the brood.

So this was all because of my power? I didn't want to believe it, but the timeline fit perfectly.

I'd scorned Derek after we kissed, and he returned to the vampires. He must have gotten wind that I was going out with that Harrison guy, grown jealous and angry, and then told the vampires everything. Made them want to turn me even more than they already did. Melissa had come for me the following night. And then when I hurt Derek again on the football field, Kira Wilcox had ended up dead the same night. Derek had access to my building. He could have let the killer in. He could have *been* the killer.

I stared at him, willing him to look up at me so I could shout something at him, but he was so, so still. How could he do this to me? Had I really hurt him so badly that he wanted me dead?

And then it dawned on me.

No, he didn't want me dead. He wanted me turned. So that I could be with him and not Lucas. The gravity of his betrayal all but took my breath away. Who was this person I used to call my best friend?

Vaguely, I realized Arabella was still speaking—not to me, but to one of the vampires. Melissa.

"I called her," Melissa was saying. "No answer. I dunno. Maybe she changed and left her phone someplace."

"Well, we cannot wait all night for her."

"I don't know what you want me to do," Melissa said, throwing her hands up. "She didn't answer. I called fifty times!"

Arabella's lip curled. "You know, we bend over backward for this tramp and then she doesn't even have the decency to show up." Her nails clacked on the iron armrest of the chair. "I suppose we should just continue without her. It's taken weeks to get them here, and after tonight it will be impossible to do so again. She'll just have to understand."

Another vampire spoke up. "But what if she doesn't give us the stuff?"

"She will. We're completing our end. And she'll complete hers. Besides, even if she doesn't, our Derek is back for good now." She gave him a fond look. "And he'll be more than happy to oblige us of anything we ask, won't you Derek?"

Derek nodded.

Arabella smiled winningly and straightened in her chair, clapping her hands together. "Well, then, who would like to do the honors? I know our dear Derek would enjoy it, but as we know, that is impossible for him."

"I should like to do it," Calvin said. "I have been waiting to taste her for quite some time now."

Arabella evaluated me for a long minute. Then she said, "So it shall be that Calvin Carnelian turns Faith Reynolds on this night. You have my permission, Cal. Go forth and add to our brood."

"Like hell!" Lucas roared. The chains rattled again as he struggled against them, but I couldn't look.

Calvin's pupils began to dilate as he stepped slowly toward me. Involuntarily, I backed up a few steps, and then stopped, knowing that running would be futile. Calvin came to a stop before me, and then my legs gave way. I slumped to my knees. Some of the vampires around me hissed and cackled. Lucas roared, fighting his chains.

I just stared up at Calvin. My fate had finally caught up with me. I was about to be turned.

Calvin knelt beside me and took up my wrist, sneering lustfully as he brought it to his mouth to inhale deeply the aroma of my skin. I turned away to face Derek instead.

His bright blue eyes were on me now, focused completely. They were so blue, almost purple. I turned away, unable to look at him. He couldn't be the last thing I saw as a human. I wanted to see Lucas, to remember what it felt like to love him and hold him close for those last few seconds of my life.

I craned my neck around as Calvin's teeth pressed against my wrist. Lucas screamed and fought against the chains. His eyes were shining like tiny stars, and his body shook violently with the will to change.

I loved him so much.

Acute pain in my wrist made me gasp and blink furiously. Then a draining feeling in my arm accompanied by a rush of vertigo. Numbly, I looked around. Calvin was drinking deeply from me like some wild animal, crazed with hunger.

It was only a matter of seconds now, before the venom seeped into me . . . before I was paralyzed.

31

TURNING

B ut it didn't paralyze me. I felt just as wide awake and mobile as I always had. I glanced around, confused as hell and feeling slightly faint. Calvin was taking a lot.

Why wasn't I passed out? Why wasn't I paralyzed?

I looked into Calvin's eyes and saw something . . . odd. They weren't Calvin's eyes. They were lighter, and there was no crave in them anymore. No blackness.

I looked up at Derek, standing against the wall; to those intense too-blue eyes. Tortured eyes . . . *trapped* eyes. His face was tight as though he was straining against some unseen bonds; veins popped out of his forehead.

I looked back at Calvin, sucking greedily, and *Derek's* eyes looked back at me. Light blue and sweet as a bowl of sugar. It was impossible, but . . .

"Derek?" I breathed at Calvin.

He winked.

Suddenly, Lucas changed. There was a massive roar and the boy drinking my blood—Calvin or Derek, I had no clue which—was pulverized to the floor. The room erupted into a frenzy of fangs. The vampires charged Lucas—all except Arabella, who remained, stunned, at her throne.

I was pushed away by someone and thrown against the back wall, insignificant as ever.

Then a lot of things happened at once. The boy who had bitten me changed into a slender white wolf. At the exact same moment, the person I'd thought was Derek standing by the wall screamed horribly and fell to the floor. When he stood up, he was Calvin.

Holy hell.

Calvin lunged into the fight, which was now Derek and Lucas—both wolves—against ten vampires.

Arabella leaped out of her seat, screaming, "What in the hell is going on here!"

I found myself wondering the same thing.

The vampires descended on my werewolves, stabbing with silver knives and biting viciously. The werewolves' shriek-like howls filled the room, reverberating until it made my ears ring. But they fought back, ignoring the sting of the blades. They tore vampires from their backs, slamming them to the floor, and ripping skulls apart with their bare teeth. Lucas flung one against the wall, sending the knife she was holding flying at me. I ducked and took up the blade with numb fingers, not knowing what good it'd do me.

A vampire chick lunged at Derek and sliced his muzzle with her nails. She raised her arm to strike again, but Derek dodged and ripped her chest open. She let out a ragged screech, fell to the floor, and then Derek yanked her head off, killing her. Now, Calvin was there. He had no weapon, but it didn't look like he needed one. He leaped over Derek and landed on his back, sinking his fangs into Derek's side. Derek yowled and writhed around, trying to get at him.

I clutched my knife harder, thinking that I should help—but Lucas, having thrown off two more vampires—darted to Derek's aid. Already, I could see his body shaking slightly. He didn't have much time.

I watched the fighting continue, so incredibly confused and scared. And bleeding out. I was worried the loss of blood was going to be a problem so I used the knife to cut the bottom of my shirt off and tied my wrist with shaking fingers.

Arabella screamed like a two-year-old pitching a fit as her vampires got picked off one by one. They weren't very skilled and, as Arabella had said, they didn't work together at all. They just darted in one by one and let Lucas or Derek gut them.

There were only six left when Calvin was killed. Lucas had managed to dislodge him from Derek's back and throw him to the floor, but Calvin sprang back up immediately and reared back to punch him. Before he could swing, Derek jumped in and snapped his head right off. I heard a high-pitched scream erupt from somewhere in the room, but was unable to tell who it came from.

I didn't spend time worrying about it, because just then, I noticed how violent Lucas's tremors had become.

Another vampire attacked him, and just as Lucas was about to dodge—he changed.

Derek intercepted the attack, leaving Lucas to fall to the ground in his human form, panting. But at an earsplitting scream from Arabella, the vampires all froze and Derek's foe retreated.

Derek crouched low to the floor, growling warningly at the room. Lucas, seeing me alone by the wall, swiped me up from the floor in an ultrafast movement that left me seriously disoriented. I was now standing in between wolf-Derek and Lucas in the center of the room.

Everything was silent—nobody moved.

Arabella stood by her toppled-over chair, fists clenched at her sides, blinking rapidly. She wasn't looking at us, but down at Calvin. Decapitated Calvin.

Dead Calvin.

Slowly, she raised her gaze to Lucas and, to my astonishment, I saw she was crying.

"He—was—my—first," she choked. "My first—creation. My mate." Her expression turned stormy. "You will PAY!"

She flew at us.

The room exploded again as the five remaining vampires attacked. I screamed and crouched down to the floor, head pressed hard on my knees by Lucas's weight. He was surrounding me, his arms a shield against the attack. His head was next to mine, and I heard his voice in my ear, crying out in pain. The sound rattled my heart. His body jerked as someone tried to pull him off of me. He made gurgling sounds, and I was willing to bet he was choking on his own blood, but he held tight to me, shielding me.

I heard Derek fighting, racing around the room. Squelching sounds reached my ears. Two more sounds of death.

Three left.

Something grabbed my ankle and yanked me out of Lucas's grasp. I screamed when I saw Melissa had me. I struggled, twisting my knee, and then Lucas vaulted for her and sprayed me with blood as his fist went through her chest.

I was so stunned, I couldn't even move. Lucas cracked her spine in his fist, pried her head off, then turned and grabbed my arm. As he tugged me across the room, I saw Derek fighting Arabella and a dude vampire—Kevin. Derek's coat was hardly white anymore—just a collage of pink, dark red, and filth.

I didn't want to leave him, but I didn't have much of a choice, either.

Lucas raced to the door on the ceiling and scooped me up. He jumped high, breaking the door with his back and running with me in his arms. We were in a wide, dark alley that smelled of grease and chemicals. I looked around Lucas's shoulder as he ran and saw that a vampire dude was coming after us.

"Lucas!" I yelled, pointing.

He cursed and stopped, slamming me against the wall as his body shook. He changed.

The vampire jumped, and Lucas met him in the air, crushing his body to the ground. I watched, huddled in the corner as Lucas fought off the vampire. Watching him, I suddenly realized how deluded I'd been to think I could handle the vampires alone. I was definitely more than happy to let Lucas and Derek save me.

It didn't take long for Lucas to finish off the vampire. Once Lucas had pinned him to the ground, he knocked the knife away with his muzzle and started ripping.

I turned away as Lucas tore up the vampire's throat, spilling muscles out onto the grimy street like bloody spaghetti.

Lucas's body trembled and he changed back. His face was covered in gore, and he wiped it with his arm as he came to me, panting.

"You're not paralyzed," he said, kneeling in front of me. He held my face.

"N-no," I said, shaking. "It was Derek. They s-switched bodies somehow, I don't know."

Lucas nodded, though I could tell he was confused about what had just happened as well. Screams and sounds of fighting continued to sound from the lair down the alley.

Lucas glanced in that direction and said, "I have to help him.

Stay here. I'll be right back for you."

I nodded jerkily and watched Lucas zip down the street.

In the silent, lonely moments that followed, I began to relax in tiny increments. After a minute or two, I began to breathe more normally, and after throwing up behind a trash can, I felt considerably better. I leaned against the wall, panting as the sounds of battle slowly drifted away.

Then a high-pitched screech—and then another and another. *Oh, God.* . . . There were more vampires down there. More had come to help Arabella.

I had to do something—help my boys. But what could I do? My power was useless against the vampires. I could only control the pack.

The pack!

I rose to my feet and tugged my cell phone from my pocket. It took me three tries to get the right number in, but when I did, Julian's voice came through the phone.

"This is Julian," he said.

"It's Faith," I said. "We need you. We're in major trouble."

"Faith? Where are you? You were supposed to be here—"

"That doesn't matter now," I said angrily. "Where are you?"

"At the house," he said. "Where are you?"

I faltered. "I—I don't exactly know. We're at the vampire lair." There was more yelling and bodies thudding together. I heard Lucas's voice above the others. He was human again, and for once, I wished for a full moon. "We need help! You have to come help us!"

"I don't even know where you are. How can I do anything?"

I held the phone away from me, staring at the screen. "Wait—

I think I have a GPS thingy." I started fiddling around, trying to figure it out, when something whizzed in front of me. I shrieked, dropping the phone. Julian's muffled voice sounded through the receiver, asking if I was still there. Then a dial tone.

He'd hung up.

I looked up to see what had distracted me from finally being the savior, and my jaw hit the floor.

It was Heather.

I stared for a moment, out-of-my-mind-relieved to see her. And then it penetrated my brain that Heather didn't look like herself. She stood in front of me, dressed like a sexpot, with gloved hands on her hips. Her normal, gentle vibe was snarled with otherness, and her face was pale as the moon.

She had been turned.

"Miss me?" she said. She smiled and long, pointed teeth glittered at me.

"Heather," I murmured. "Oh, God . . . I'm so sorry."

"Sorry for what? For being a jerk to me practically every moment since you met me? Whatevs. You know what they say. Karma's a bitch."

I swallowed hard. "But, we made up. I tried to warn you about the drugs and now . . . just look at you."

"You're so stupid. Like I gave a crap about anything you said. I *wanted* this, you idiot. What did you think, I didn't know what I was taking? Why do you think I never mentioned it to you—they forbade me because the vampires like to kill bloodies for fun. When they found us, it was sheer luck they kept me alive long enough for me to convince them to turn me."

"Turn you? Why would you want that?"

She bent and leered in my face. "So I can eat that fucker Pete once and for all—suck the life out of him the way he did to me."

I couldn't breathe, couldn't even stand properly, I was so horrified. My poor Heather . . . how could I have let this happen to her? "Please," I begged. "I'm sorry for everything, but you have to help me. They're going to kill Lucas and Derek."

"Don't worry. You'll live through it," she said. "I did when Pete dumped me." Then she feigned an epiphany and put her finger to her glossy red lips. "Oh wait. I *didn't* live, did I?" She made a mock sad face. "Well, after I'm through here he'll be a goner, too. And so will you." She grabbed me and ran down the alley with me over her shoulder like I was a pile of logs.

She jumped down the hole that led back to the lair, and her shoulder knocked the air out of me on her landing. The room was oddly quiet. Heather put me on my feet and pinned me to her body as she walked me to the center of the room, where Arabella stood, seething.

Her face was ripped open with slash marks, but there was no blood, meaning she hadn't eaten in a while. I saw the shining pink wounds healing already, returning to perfection. More vampires filled the room now, at least twenty of them, and I saw Kevin still among them, battered but alive . . . ish. Lucas was being restrained with silver again, but this time there was much more of it, and he was completely immobilized. Knives stuck into his limbs and pointed at his throat, threatening to slice his flesh open.

Derek was still in wolf form. Six or so vampires held him down, but that didn't look necessary. He was unconscious.

Heather released me when we reached the front of the room and drifted into the crowd, leaving me—her so-called friend—to face the wrath of the vampire monarch.

I shook involuntarily. I couldn't bear to look at her and stared at Lucas's tortured face instead. He looked right back, defeat in his gaze, and in that moment, I knew we weren't getting out of this alive.

I turned to Arabella and she immediately slapped me so hard I felt the skin on my cheekbone split. Lucas snarled ferociously, but I righted myself, not wanting him to do anything stupid.

"You have cost me my best subjects," Arabella cried. "Not to mention my mate! Your debt to me has been increased tenfold. You will never live long enough to repay it. You will be punished. I will not kill your dog. I will let him live. I will make you hurt him. I will make you lash him with silver and watch the life drain from his mongrel eyes. *I* will be your sire so I can force you to do anything I like. You have eons of pain in your dismal future, Faith Reynolds."

She bent and I felt her teeth hit my skin. In the corner of my eye, I saw Derek stirring, shaking his head as if waking up from a nap. I almost smiled at him. He'd saved me, after all . . . or at least, tried to. His white wolf-eyes widened as he watched Arabella's mouth slide toward my collarbone.

He struggled like crazy, but there was no way he could free himself.

Then, without even a word of warning, Arabella's teeth sunk below the surface of my skin, dipping into my blood like deadly quills into ink. It hit me in a blast of heat, followed immediately by coldness. Frost spread from her fangs throughout my body and all the way down to my soul. My vision swam as she pulled.

I hit the floor, ears ringing oddly, unable to move. I could only stare straight at the ceiling as my body froze. I was so cold . . . so incredibly cold. But I could hear. I could hear perfectly, maybe even better than normal.

Lucas roared so loud it made my ears ring, and Derek struggled against the vampires, causing them to shout and strike him. The other vampires hissed and cackled, some jeering. Then a sound like water trickling, and Arabella's face appeared in front of me. Her wrist was bleeding my blood tainted with venom. The venom that would kill me. Inside, I fought. Inside, I screamed.

But outside, I just laid there.

Paralyzed.

She began to tilt her wrist toward me. I felt warmth on my chest, my cheeks, sliding ever closer to my mouth. I wanted to shut it, but I couldn't. This was it. There was no escaping death now.

Then Arabella jerked her hand away and looked up, as if listening. At first I couldn't hear what she heard, and then it was there. The ground began to shake, and the thunderous sound of footfalls hit my ears.

A single howl bit through the night.

The werewolves.

Arabella vaulted to her feet and began screeching out orders. The vampires mobilized. I watched them blur by me and heard them whizzing through the air and into the alley.

And then the howling started.

The glorious howling of the pack, like heralding trumpets calling out victory. Except that there would be no victory for me. I was dying. No matter what happened now, I would die.

• • •

The sounds of battle began to fade until all I heard was sobbing and moaning. The crying came from behind me and then someone was talking. Two or three people—all male. I wished they would move so I could see them.

Then Lucas's face was above me, his human face. His perfect human face—all mangled up with scratches and blood, but still him. Derek's face was next to his, human now, too. My boys . . . my saviors. I prayed they'd get along after I was gone. That they wouldn't kill each other like idiots.

More talking, angry fighting and crying. Lucas's crying. His eyes dragged with tears that cleared clean paths in this filthy skin. He held me in his arms and I suddenly felt a million times better, even though he was so sad. He clutched me to him possessively, as though guarding me. Suddenly, he was yelling.

"You don't know what that will do to her!" he shouted.

"She'll die, Lucas," Derek argued. "Katie told me it would work."

"Katie doesn't know what she's talking about!"

"We have to at least try. She's dying!"

"He's right," I heard a third voice say. Was that Rolf? "There is nothing else to do for her. We don't have much time. If it fails, she would have died anyway."

Lucas held me closer.

"I'm sorry," he choked. "I'm so sorry, baby. Please, please forgive me."

I wanted to tell him not to be sorry. That this wasn't his fault. I wanted to say good-bye to him, and thank him for the happiness he'd brought to my life. I wanted to tell him it was okay to move on after I was dead . . . but all I could do was look at him.

He kissed my frozen lips, and I felt his tears drip onto my cheeks. Then his grip on my body loosened. He tilted my head back. Derek's bleeding wrist appeared. It was punctured, like he had bitten himself. Why would he do that?

I felt something warm and gritty fill my mouth and slide down my throat—something metallic.

"Enough," Lucas said. His face appeared in front of me again, so perfect, and so twisted with worry. I wanted to tell him that I wasn't in any pain. It would all be over soon.

"Her eyes are closing. . . ."

Everything was starting to go dark around the edges . . . fuzzy. I heard more yelling. It sounded like Derek this time. I frowned. I didn't like yelling. Yelling at Lucas . . . no . . . his face was staring to fade. The world was beginning to ebb. I felt almost good. Like I was about to fall asleep.

Well, if this was what it felt like to die, it wasn't so bad. It was pleasant, even. I could see Lucas; hear the grating of his voice someplace in the back of my mind . . . maybe even smell him, too. Or was that my mom's macaroni and cheese . . . ?

THE OTHER SIDE

I heard voices. Two voices, both soft, yet starkly different. Two boys . . . they sounded muffled, like they were in a different room, or maybe a different life.

"It's been four days," one said. "I don't think it worked. I think we need to try something else."

"There's nothing to try," another said. He had a low, crumbly voice that sounded dead with defeat.

"You could bite her," the other said. "Then she might be like me."

"She's already got enough magic in her blood. Any more would just make things worse."

They fell silent for a long moment.

"You really love her, don't you?" said the one with the mellow voice. It was sweet like low wind chimes.

"Of course, I love her," the crumbly voice said. "I love her more than my own life. I'd gladly have given it, if it could have prevented this."

Again there was silence.

"I love her, too," the mellow voice said. "I've loved her since the moment I saw her. I've been with her through everything. I can't lose her."

"You don't have to. You could keep her, if you just knew how to love her without wanting her."

"It's not like I can help it," the mellow voice snapped. "She's . . . she's perfect."

"Yeah," the crumbly voice said. "I know." He sounded almost resentful about this. "She might be different when she wakes up. She might be a lee—a vampire."

"Would that be so bad?"

No answer for a moment and then, "Yes. She'd be dead."

"You wouldn't love her if she was dead." He said it as a fact, not a question. "I would love her no matter what she was."

"That's because *you're* dead," the other shot. "And I never said I wouldn't love her."

Silence.

"You never said you would, either."

More silence filled the caverns of my mind and I drifted off, thinking that was the strangest dream I'd ever had.

• • •

I smelled Lucas. He smelled of woods and musk and something too delicious to put into words. I inhaled deeply and let my eyes flutter open. I saw a white plastered ceiling and a fan oscillating slowly. Light poured into the room, red light like I was in a darkroom.

Then I felt something warm slide over my stomach. My head fell to the side as the bed shifted and saw Lucas sleeping next to me. I smiled and then stopped because it hurt.

"Ow," I croaked.

Lucas's eyes popped open and he leaned over me, his gaze urgent and terrified . . . apologetic, even. What could he possibly have to be sorry for? He saved my life.

He and Derek saved my life.

"Hey," I rasped. My voice sounded like it'd been rubbed with sandpaper for a week.

Lucas suddenly collapsed on top of me, grabbing me up in his arms and hugging me so tightly it hurt. He kept saying he was sorry over and over, kissing my neck.

For some reason I was limp. It took tremendous effort to even breathe. Lucas finally set me down, and I smiled up at him. Again, smiling was painful so I stopped.

"Why does everything hurt?" I asked.

Lucas had tears in his eyes. He petted my hair away from my forehead. "I'm so sorry, baby," he said. "Are you okay? Can you move everything? I'm so sorry."

"Stop—being—sorry," I gasped. "I can't . . . breathe."

Lucas's face tightened. "What? What's wrong?"

"I can't move," I said. "It hurts to breathe. What's wrong . . . with me?"

Suddenly Lucas sat up.

"*Rolf!*" he shouted.

He vaulted out of the bed and my body shook with the bedsprings, sending agony racing through my bones. I blacked out.

• • •

I saw darkness. Only darkness. It was navy blue, like a winter night. I blinked and rubbed my eyes. Then I let out a cry of relief. I was rubbing my eyes. . . . I could move!

I sat up, but I must have done it too quickly because my vision spun and I had to lie back down. I looked out the window. It was nighttime.

"Lucas?" I called out.

Nothing.

"Derek?" I asked more softly.

Instantly the door banged open and Derek was there. He bolted to my side.

"You're awake!" he said. "Can you move? How's your breathing? Does anything hurt?"

I smiled and waved my hands around to show him I could move.

"I think I'm okay," I said. "What . . . what happened?"

Derek took up my hand, kissing it a million times, apologizing between each kiss.

Why was everyone apologizing so damn much? They had nothing to—

Suddenly, a terrible thought hit me. What if they *hadn't* saved my life? What if I was a vampire?

"Derek," I said. "Am I dead?

He pressed his lips together. "I don't know," he said finally.

Ice water drenched my veins. I was dead. I gasped for breath, over and over. My head spun. I was dead.

"I'm getting Lucas," he said. He dashed out of the room and reappeared five seconds later with Lucas by his side. All thoughts stopped when I saw him, all concern or remnants of pain. In that moment, it didn't matter if I was dead or not. Lucas was there. He was hugging me, within a breath.

I hugged him back, smiling even though the force of his arms was hurting a little.

"You're moving," he said hoarsely. "You can move?"

I nodded, crying. He wiped the tears from my cheeks and kissed them. He put his forehead against mine, and I felt the warmth sink into my skin. It felt warmer than normal.

"I love you, Faith," he whispered. "You can never know how much."

I smiled. "I think I have an idea."

Derek cleared his throat pointedly. Lucas pulled back and sat down on the bed, motioning for Derek to come closer. He sat in the armchair next to my bed, still looking worried.

Then I remembered that I might be dead.

I gulped and looked over at Lucas. "I don't feel dead," I whispered. "But I remember her biting me. I remember Derek's wrist bleeding." Derek nodded, confirming it.

Lucas took up my hand. "You're not dead, baby. It's only been six days, not even close to the full moon."

"But she bit me," I protested. "I remember being paralyzed."

"You were," Lucas said. "But then Derek fed you some of his blood."

I looked at Derek, who nodded again. "Remember when I told you I gave Katie some of my blood to test?" he asked.

I wrinkled my eyes up, trying to remember.

"Well, she did," Derek continued without me. "I asked her to do it. I wanted to know what it would do to a human if they drank it. Turns out, it heals. It's like antivampire blood."

I gaped. "Why didn't you tell me this?"

"Because I was trying to keep it secret from the vampires. I thought if they knew what I could do, they'd want to use me like you always said they were. I didn't want you knowing about it. It could have put you in danger."

"So you healed me?" I asked, amazed.

"Yeah," Derek said and shrugged. But his expression was anything but nonchalant. I'd never seen so much love pouring out of one being before—not even Lucas.

"Thank you," I said, thinking that those silly little words were nothing compared to the gratitude I felt.

"Don't," he murmured, looking away. "You almost died because of me."

"I'm *alive* because of you, Derek."

"You don't get it." He looked up at me urgently in his eyes. "After we . . . ended things, I went back to the vampires and I found out that they *were* looking for you after all. I knew they were planning to turn you for some reason and I didn't do a thing. I—I even told them about your power." He must have seen the hurt on my face because he tried to defend himself. "I was mad at you for what happened between us. For still loving him after how bad he hurt you." I cast a glance at Lucas and saw him hang his head. Derek continued, "I was so mad. But I swear, I never thought they'd go through all that trouble to find you—just to turn you. Once I told them about your power, though, you became their main focus. I'd never forgive myself if I let them turn you. This life—it's not one I'd wish on my worst enemy, let alone you.

"But I was being proud. I didn't want to go crawling back to you. Again. So I tried to just call you, tried to protect you without you knowing it. But you wouldn't talk to me, and it was only a matter of time before they got to you. So I realized I had to have a plan. That time on the football field? I wasn't just trying to warn you, I was trying to tell you what I had planned, what I could do . . . but then you kind of surprised me with that whole I'm-the-reason-you're-like-this thing, and I got distracted. By the time I got over it, it was too late. Melissa got into your dorm and killed that Kira girl and I knew you were done for."

"I still don't get it, though," I said. "What was your plan?"

Derek smiled ruefully. "I was going to bring you to the lair myself and pretend to turn you. It sort of worked at first, but Lucas changed and things went a little nuts."

"How was I supposed to know what you were doing?" Lucas grumbled.

"It wasn't your fault," Derek said. "I should have told you guys what I had planned. It's just that after the pack was all 'we don't need help from a mutant traitor,' I was reluctant to ask for your help." He shrugged and Lucas nodded understandingly.

"I still don't get it," I said, irritated that I was so slow. "How could you *pretend* to bite me? They know you don't have venom."

Derek contemplated me, and leaned in. "I can change forms," he said intently.

I blinked. "*Duh.* How does that explain anything?"

Derek frowned and waved me away. "No, you don't get it. I can change into *anything.*"

Silence echoed through my brain.

"It's not just wolves. I can shift into anything I want, so long as it's got a heartbeat."

"But vampires don't have heartbeats," I protested.

"Yeah, well, I can't be sure of course, but I think the reason I can shift into them is because I'm part vampire. Like my brain works the same way as theirs or something."

"I guess that makes sense." I lay back on the pillows, reeling. "Wow. . . ."

"Faith?" Lucas put his hand on my forehead. It was so hot, like a blanket of sticky magma. "Are you okay?" He turned to Derek. "Maybe we should wait to tell her everything else. She needs to rest."

I sat up suddenly. "No, tell me. I can handle it." I didn't know how true that was, but the curiosity was killing me. "Okay, so the plan was to knock Calvin out and switch forms with him, and then pretend to kidnap/turn me, right?"

"Yeah," Derek said.

"But, wouldn't the vampires figure out that you weren't Calvin? I mean, can't they smell that stuff? And the eyes were different, too. How'd you keep them from noticing?"

A smile spread across Derek's pale lips. "That's the other thing I never told you guys. I can use hypnotics. And not just on humans, but on vampires and werewolves, too."

This was just getting weirder and weirder, but I went with it to speed his explanation along. "So, you hypnotized the vampires into believing you were Calvin?"

"No, I hypnotized them into thinking Calvin was me. The problem wasn't getting them to believe I was Calvin. They don't pay much attention to each other, but I definitely think they'd notice two Calvins running around. So I made them see Calvin as me, and I shifted into Calvin's form."

"Why not just hypnotize them into believing you were Calvin, and save yourself the trouble of changing into him?"

He puffed a laugh. "I'm not that strong, Faith." He grinned at my scowl. "It takes a lot of concentration to hypnotize that many people, and the more things I need to hide, the harder it is. I had to practice for weeks on humans to get this good. And I needed to hypnotize Calvin, too, so he would do whatever I wanted. He was like a puppet. It was freaking great." He leaned back in his chair, smirking. "The only bad part was that . . . well, I have to drink human blood in order to use hypnotics. A lot of it. And I didn't have enough donated stuff left, so I had to use a few pets. I could have used just one, I guess, but I didn't want to accidentally kill anyone, so I used three."

I wrinkled my nose at that, but didn't say anything. It had been necessary. I certainly wasn't going to admonish him for it. I felt sorry for whatever pets had been forced to give blood, but if they'd had the same experience I'd had with Derek's fangs, they couldn't have been too broken up about it.

"So," I said. "Once you'd bitten me in front of everyone, you'd what? Hypnotize them into thinking I'd been turned?"

Derek nodded. "Yeah, which is another reason why I wanted to shape-shift into Calvin instead of using more hypnotics."

"Yeah," I said. "Does it weaken you like it does for the vampires?"

He made a face. "In a way. It makes me vulnerable to silver. I felt it last night, when I was fighting. I kept getting hurt worse than usual, and the wounds wouldn't heal quickly. Some still haven't closed completely." I noticed his arms were still wrapped in bandages even after six days. "But it was worth it," he said. "It was a perfect plan. The hypnotics and the shape-shifting. And if you got hurt, I'd have your blood in me to heal you. I—I gotta admit I was a little scared about that part. I wasn't sure it would work. I mean, Katie said it would, but it was scary as hell waiting for you to wake up." He made a pained face, and I put my hand on his arm. "And, I think the blood might have had some side effects."

"What?" I gasped. "Why do you say that?"

Derek looked to Lucas for help.

Lucas took up my hand, rubbing the top of it softly. "Feel how hot I am?"

I nodded.

"That's because you're a little colder than normal. It's nothing to be upset about, but you're temperature has been in the seventies for a few days now. And . . . ah, you look a little different."

"Bad? Am I all pale and icky?"

Derek sulked.

"Sorry," I said quickly. "But am I?"

Lucas kissed my cheeks. "Just a little. Nothing a trip to San Diego won't cure."

"Can I even *go* in the sun?"

"Sure you can," he said. "You're fine. Totally and completely fine. The vampire venom will burn itself out as Derek's venom cleanses it. And, ah—there's another benefit. According to Katie, you're immune to further infection from vampires."

"What?" I sputtered. "How—I don't understand."

"Neither do we," Derek said. "Katie's the chemist here, not us. She says that something about the integration of my blood with yours . . . I dunno, it like, reproduces or something so that when your body makes new blood cells, my blood sticks to them and keeps you safe forever. It's a permanent cure."

So Derek was a part of me. Forever. I didn't need his blood inside me to know that much, but the fact that there'd always be a little of him in me . . . it was enough to get me choked up.

Derek's lips turned up at the edges, in what had to be the most heartbreaking smile I'd ever seen. I wiped the tears out of my eyes and sighed, trying to gather myself.

"What happened after I passed out?" I asked thickly. "I thought I heard the pack. Did I imagine that?"

"No," Lucas said, and somehow, I didn't see any of the old jealously or anger in his expression, even after what Derek had said. He just seemed grateful. "It was a miracle," he continued, "but somehow the pack made it in time. Turns out the vampire lair was in an old water treatment plant about an hour outside of Gould. It was sheer luck that the pack was running near there, looking for the lair, actually. They should have been in Denver, but after the attack on CSU, they figured it might be somewhere close by. And we have you to thank. Julian said you called him."

"Yeah," I said. "He got the GPS thingy?"

Lucas nodded. "Smart thinking."

I blushed, which felt really warm on my cheeks. This was going to take some getting used to.

"So the pack came," I prompted. "And they killed the brood?"

"Most of them," Lucas said. "Arabella is dead, but a few of the lesser vampires got away in the scuffle. If we'd had the whole pack there, they would have been annihilated." He sighed wistfully.

I glanced nervously at Derek, wondering if he was upset that his vampire buddies had been killed by the pack.

"Are you okay?" I asked him. "About everything?"

Derek met my gaze, steady and resolute. "Yes. I'm glad those guys are gone. I was such an idiot. I didn't realize they were the bad guys. I didn't realize they really *were* using me."

"Using you?" I asked. A glimmer of hope shone in my chest. Had Lucas and I been right all along? "To get to me?"

"No, actually. Ah . . . it turns out all my lying and sneaking around, trying to keep my abilities a secret was useless. The vampires found out what my blood can do. I don't know how they figured it out, but they did. That's why they were so nice to me. You were right, Faith. They were just using me."

Somehow the triumphant I-told-you-so speech I'd had planned for this moment, just didn't fit. It felt mean now, when Derek looked so dejected.

I just shrugged and gave him what I hoped was a comforting smile.

"So, when I went back to them, after you and Lucas made up," Derek continued, "Arabella told me everything. I think she wanted to make sure I stuck with her this time. I don't know. Anyway, she told me that the reason they'd been building their numbers, wasn't so that they could rise up against the werewolves like you thought. It was so that they could finally come out of hiding. They wanted to take their places as the 'superior race.' Take over, basically. But they knew the werewolves would eventually find out what they were doing and try to stop them. Most of the brood thought they'd win for sure, but Arabella knew better. She convinced the Ancestors that they'd never beat the werewolves with the numbers they had, and the Ancestors agreed to test their plan first. So they started in small towns like Fort Collins, where a string of unexplained murders wouldn't cause too much of a stir worldwide."

I remembered Lucas telling me in the car about how this sort of thing was happening all over the world, and I looked over at him to see that he was nodding gravely. It all added up.

"But they ran into problems," Derek went on. "They underestimated the humans. When the national news started covering the murders they had to stop. Then, after I woke up and they met me, figured out what my blood did, they realized I could be the key to their uprising. They wanted to use my blood as an antidote to their venom—that way the younglings wouldn't kill their victims and leave them all over the place, which would keep their plan a secret from the wolves long enough for them to gain the upper hand."

Derek shifted in his chair, watching me as though I might break at any moment. "You okay?" he asked.

"I'm fine. Just processing. Continue."

"Okay, so Arabella told me all of that stuff, told me how special I was, and whatever. So I asked her why she didn't just create another viran? Another one of my kind. But apparently, it doesn't work the same way every time. It depends on how much blood you drink—where the werewolf bites you, if it happens on the full moon, or not. It all changes the chemistry of the infection. They agreed that trying to create more creatures like me would only complicate things given how powerful I am." A shadow crossed Derek's features and he said. "Some wanted to try, though. Start capturing humans and doing experiments. They were gonna kill the failed attempts so there weren't a bunch of superpowerful hybrids running around. The only reason they didn't was because I told them I don't know what kills me. Silver is nothing and a stake, I can heal from. I have a feeling decapitation might be the only way." He rubbed his neck absently. "But I'm not about to try it. Just in case."

Derek shook his head, leaning back in his seat with his hands tucked under his armpits. "If they can figure out how to kill me—or the other hybrids—they might start experimenting. For now, though, I'm the only one who can help the vampires take over. All they need is enough of my blood to fill a vial, and then they can start reproducing it in a lab or whatever. Katie said she doesn't know how to do it, but there is a way. And if they get my blood, they'll sure as hell figure it out."

He looked away now, anger and fear written all over his face; his vibe, too, was a mishmash of emotions, changing so quickly I couldn't pin them.

"They're dead now," I said, trying to comfort him. "You don't have to worry about them anymore."

Derek sniffed with bitter laughter. "Faith, the plan went all the way up to the Ancestors. Fort Collins was just a test run. The same thing is happening in other towns all over the world. Once the Ancestors find out that Arabella's brood failed to recruit me, they'll come for me and take my blood by force. And there's no place on earth I can hide. Not from five of the strongest, oldest vampires in the world."

"We'll think of something," I said, though even I could hear how frail my voice sounded. "We have to."

Lucas wrapped me in his arms, murmuring sweet things that almost made me feel better. He was so hot, scorching me, and I loved it. It was the best, warmest most amazing feeling in the world, and I was so glad I was alive to feel it.

That I still loved him.

I heard Derek's chair scuff against the carpet as he stood. "I'll, ah . . . give you guys a minute."

But, I pulled away from Lucas. "No," I said, glancing between the two of them anxiously. "Actually, I want to talk to you. Alone. Ah . . . if that's okay." I looked tentatively at Lucas and he nodded, giving my hand a brief squeeze as he walked away. Derek's face was stained red from Lucas's room, and he watched me worriedly from beside the bed. "Sit," I said.

He obeyed and leaned in, his forearms resting on his knees. "You're not going to yell at me are you? Because I know how stupid I've been—about everything and I—"

"Stop," I said, holding up a hand. "It's not about that. We all made mistakes. If we'd all just been honest with each other, I think a lot of what happened could have been prevented. But we're okay—for now." I sat up a little straighter, trying to gather myself. "What I have to say to you isn't about what happened. It's an apology."

Derek frowned slightly, but waited quietly for me to go on.

"I'm sorry," I started. "I'm sorry for how I've treated you since, well, since we came to CSU."

"No you didn't do anything, I—"

I put my hand up. "Just listen." I drew in a deep breath. "I've been jerking you around ever since that kiss on the La Poudre. I wasn't doing it on purpose, obviously, I was just confused. I *was* in love with you once. And you were right before when you said I was scared to love you again. I thought that if I fell in love with anyone they'd just betray me. It was all I knew. But then everything changed when I met Lucas. He fixed what you couldn't. And when we broke up I was crushed. Again. And I know you weren't doing it to hurt me, but I wasn't ready for another relationship. I wasn't over Lucas. And I think you knew that."

He nodded, lowering his face to the floor.

"But I was wrong to tell you we could only be friends," I said. "We'll never *just* be friends. We need a word stronger than friendship because you're so much more than a friend to me, Derek. You're a part of me. And not just literally. You stood by me throughout everything, even all of this . . . craziness." I cracked a small smile and then grew serious again, wanting him to grasp the finality of my words. "But we'll never be involved romantically. Not while I love Lucas. I'm sorry if this is confusing, or wrong or hurtful. I'm just trying to be honest."

Derek shook his head, meeting my eyes again and then looking away to stare at the bed behind me. "No, it's . . . I guess I already knew. You and Lucas—there's just something *right* about it. I don't exactly know what it is, but I know we'll never have that. I can't love you enough for the both of us." He shrugged sadly and looked at his hands.

"That doesn't mean we can't be a part of each others' lives," I said. "I really meant what I said on the phone before. I was wrong to cut you out of my life. I'm sorry for that, too."

He shrugged again, but I could sense that he was taking this hard—that his heart was breaking. I wanted to fix it, wanted to make him understand. "Derek, there's a reason we can never be together. And it's more than just loving Lucas inexplicably. There's an actual tangible reason."

"What is it?" He sounded like he didn't really care, but was playing along for my sake.

"We're matched," I said. "Lucas and I. It's ah . . . part of my power."

At that, Derek began paying attention. "The vibe thing?"

"Yeah. Listen . . ." And I told Derek everything. I told him about Yvette and Kevin, the others like myself, told him all that I could do and that Lucas and I had a sort of divine connection, stronger than with any other werewolf. It was what had drawn me to him in the first place and him to me, and part of why I loved him so completely. And it was why Derek could never fill that place in my heart, no matter how much he or I wanted to.

When I finished, Derek seemed more than a little dumbstruck. He sat silently for a long, tense moment, absorbing and sorting everything out while I leaned against the pillows. This conversation had taken a lot out of me, and I was beginning to feel the effects. My body yearned for sleep, but my mind spun around like a loose wheel. I tried to calm it, focusing on how happy I was to be alive rather than on the coming danger.

"I guess I should go now," Derek said.

"What?"

"You should sleep," he said. I tried to catch his eye, but he kept them hooded by his lashes, refusing to look at me.

"You don't want to talk about what I said?"

"There's nothing to say, really. It just—it sucks, all right, Faith? What do you want me to say? I'm happy that there's an extra special reason why we'll never be together? Just let me . . . let me deal with this. I—" He stood and turned away toward the window, locking his hands behind his head. I heard him murmur a curse. He lowered his hands, but didn't turn around, and his voice was flat when he spoke. "I'm not mad. I just need some time."

"Okay," I said meekly.

He looked in my direction—not at me, but toward me—and said, "I'll check in later." He started toward the door.

When he reached it, I called out, "Derek?"

He stopped with his hand on the doorknob, half turning to face me. "Yeah?"

"Thank you. I'd be lost without you. Thank you."

I saw his throat move as he swallowed. He looked on the verge of saying something for a long while, but then he nodded with a jerk and left.

As the door shut, I collapsed back onto the pillows again. I was burnt out, but still unable to relax. I missed Lucas. I wished I had the energy to get up and find him, but I was too weak to lift my arms, let alone stand. I opened myself up, trying to find his vibe among the lazy hum in the back of my head that was the rest of the pack members in the house. *Lucas?* I called, mostly to myself as I tried to locate his vibe. *Are you there?*

Nothing.

Discouraged and spent, I took his pillow from the bed and hugged it to myself instead, trying not to picture the way Derek's face had looked while I told him everything.

Then the door popped open and Lucas was there.

"You called?" he asked, with a wry grin.

I sat up. "You heard that?"

He came to the bed and sat in Derek's chair. "Yeah. It was like the night Derek bit you and I felt you in trouble. I just kind of knew you wanted me around. So I came."

I smiled drowsily. "Well, that's not exactly a hard thing to intuit. I always want you around."

He leaned forward, taking up my hands and pressing them to his scalding hot lips. "I'm not used to you being so cold," he murmured over my skin, his breath searing me.

"Me either. It'll go away right?"

He nodded. "Give Derek's venom time to work."

"So I guess his venom doesn't cure werewolf," I mused. "That night when he bit you . . . it didn't cure you."

Lucas shook his head. "Nope. Still me. Katie's doing some more tests, but it looks like it only cures vampirism."

"We have to think of something," I said. "We have to figure out how to keep the vampires away from Derek. And how to stop them from this world domination thing. But mostly Derek. If they don't have him, they'll never take over before the werewolves stop them."

"I know," Lucas said. "And we already have a plan."

"We?"

"Me and Derek. It's crazy as hell and we'll probably die in the process, but we gotta give it a shot. The alternative is unacceptable. The vampires taking over? That's a world of darkness on the horizon. . . . That's a world I'm not keen on seeing anytime soon."

My pulse accelerated at the thought, and I actually *felt* the warmth as my blood surged faster through my veins. "So what are we going to do?"

He cupped my face. "You're going to go back to sleep and get better. Let me and Derek worry about the vampires."

I began to protest, but he shook his head, laying me down against my pillows and kissing my forehead in this irritatingly chaste way.

"This is highly unfair," I mumbled. "I'm damaged. You should indulge me."

His lips curved upward. "You need to rest. I promise I'll tell you everything once we get the plan in order. For now, just sleep."

"Will you sleep with me?"

The look in Lucas's dark eyes said *yes*, but he shook his head. "Derek and I gotta do some planning."

"What's with all the, *Derek and I* talk? What are you two friends now?"

He shoved his hands into his pockets. "I don't think I'll ever be friends with the guy who's in love with my girlfriend, but he's okay. For a leech."

I felt a smug smile tug at my mouth. "I knew you'd warm up to him eventually."

He ignored me with a dry look. "Sleep," he directed, passing his hand over my cheek lightly. "You only have two weeks to recover."

I yawned hugely. "Why? What's happening in two weeks?"

Lucas's smile widened considerably.

"The wedding."

AT PEACE

The ceremony took place at dusk on the night before the full moon. The pack congregated in the backyard, which had been transformed from a barren expanse of grass to something resembling a snow globe.

Everything was white. The decorations were a swirl of crystal and icy satin and even the guests had been instructed to wear only white or black. It was beautiful and ethereal—just like the bride.

Melanie had never looked more stunning standing calmly next to Julian at the front of the room. Rolf, who married them, stood between them. He was the only thing that looked out of place in the room. While most of the men looked sleek and handsome in their tuxes, Rolf looked almost comical. It was like someone had stuffed a bear into a tux two sizes too small.

But all eyes were on the couple promising to spend their lives together. Of course, only the pack members and I knew the gravity of that particular promise. Melanie's family, who sat on the opposite side of the pews, was unaware of Julian's condition. I wondered if they'd be told when Melanie was infected.

It was happening tonight.

Suddenly, music started up and everyone began clapping. Lucas blew a loud whistle between his teeth and stood with the crowd. I looked up to see Julian sweep Melanie's veil away and kiss her gently on the lips. I smiled, watching as he bent her backward in his arms to give us a show.

Then they pulled back, both of them beaming, and ran down the aisle, and out of the ivory tent. There wasn't a bridal party— Melanie had wanted to keep things simple—so the wedding guests followed the bride and groom into the reception area.

It took place in another massive tent where music played, hors d'oeuvres were served on trays by straight-faced waiters, and people milled around talking and trying to find where they were supposed to sit.

For a few hours, Lucas and I sat at our table, laughing and talking, eating roasted chicken—Lucas had two plates—and dancing the Macarena with Katie and Derek, who both did extremely silly versions involving a lot of exaggerated pelvic thrusts and blushing on Katie's part.

Lucas wasn't thrilled to watch Derek's hands all over Katie, but I didn't mind. I was just happy to see Derek smiling again. He'd been in a funk ever since our talk, and things still weren't the same between us. But it seemed like he was cheering up. At least, Katie cheered him up.

At eleven, Melanie tossed the bouquet—which I did *not* catch— and then pretended to get into a limo with Julian to go on their honeymoon. Really, they were going up into the mansion to change clothes and prepare for the infection ceremony coming up.

As the music began to slow and Melanie's family started trickling away, grabbing the floral centerpieces and hiking out to their cars, Lucas turned to me and whispered deeply in my ear. "Come with me?"

I nodded, grabbing my clutch, and let him tow me out the back of the tent where the woods lay. Amber light from the tent spilled out over us; music swelled and sank in my ears as we rounded the tent and went up to the house to sit on the back porch. Lucas pulled me down into one of the chaise lounges and sat in the one next to me, his knees touching mine. He looked absolutely unreal in a tux with his hair styled and his face clean-shaven. The moonlight shadowed his features, and a nervous smile quirked his lips. *Is he nervous?*

I gave him a questioning look, placing my clutch on the seat beside me.

"I want to give you something," Lucas said.

"You do?" I said, immediately interested. He'd never given me a gift before, except for on my birthday and Valentine's Day, but those were obligatory. Impromptu gifting was so much more romantic. I smiled coyly. "What is it?"

"Don't get all excited," he warned.

"Too late."

"It's not a big deal—well, no. It is a big deal, but probably not for you."

I reached out and grabbed his hands. "What are you talking about?"

The vulnerability in Lucas's voice filled me with adoration. It was so unlike him—so *human*.

"It's something I've always wanted to do, but it never felt right, until now. It's a tradition. From . . . my time."

"You mean when man invented fire?"

He answered that with a withering look and said, "It's a gesture. Men would give something to their betrothed—"

My eyebrows flew up at that word, but Lucas quickly covered.

"Not that we're betrothed," he said. "I don't even believe in marriage, so—"

"What?" I choked, as another wave of shock rang through my body.

"Aw, don't go all female on me. It's not a big deal."

I made a face, crossing my arms over my chest. It was kind of a big deal.

"Listen," he said firmly. "I don't need to participate in some man-made institution to prove how much I love you. Wearing a tux and signing some dumb document that the government files away into a database doesn't prove love. Actions do." He took a deep breath, pulling my arms from around my chest and taking my hands again. "That's why I'm gonna make a gesture. Like I said, it's a tradition from when I was human. People don't really do it anymore, but I never got to and I . . . well, I've always wanted to." The smile on his face was almost bashful—something I'd never seen in Lucas before. This was obviously a big moment for him and I felt certain it would be for me as well.

"Okay," I said cautiously. "What's the gesture?"

Lucas reached into the pocket of his jacket and pulled out a square of thick argyle cloth. The pattern was faded almost beyond recognition and the edges were frayed, but it was unbelievably soft as he pressed it into my hand. "I know it probably seems silly to you—or weird. Or both. But back in my day, there were clans—like families. And each family had a specific pattern of cloth they wore, called a tartan. When two people wanted to get married, they exchanged a patch of their tartan with each other. It's a symbol of unity—of love." He squeezed my hands over the cloth. "I can't imagine ever finding anyone in this time or any other who's as perfect for me as you are. You're a part of me. In ways I don't even understand. You are truly my match. And for as long as I have you, I promise to be faithful. To love only you. And once you're gone from this world, you'll remain in my heart. Forever."

He brought my hands up to his, and kissed each one with a tenderness that made me want to cry. Then he released them and shrugged, seeming a little embarrassed. "I know it looks like just a dumb piece of fabric to you, but—"

"No," I said, clutching the square to my chest. "No, I love it. Is it actually from your family's . . . ?"

"Tartan," he supplied. "And yeah, it is. I kept what I had left of it in a high-security bank vault in Washington. There are some other things in there . . . things that hold particular value to me. I had this sent here." He nodded at the square in my hands. "For you."

I smiled at him, realizing that I was tearing up. They spilled over my cheeks, and I wiped them away daintily, lest I smudge my makeup. "Thank you. I wish I had something to give you back."

"Nah," he said waving me off as he stood. "It's dumb anyway."

I rose to my feet, too, catching his arm when he tried to turn away. "It's perfect. Much better than some silly wedding."

He searched me for signs of dishonesty, but I'd been truthful. I didn't need a wedding gown or a ring or any of that ridiculousness. I needed Lucas. And that was exactly what he'd given me. I rose up onto my tiptoes and kissed him. "I never thought I'd be able to trust anyone like I trust you," I said softly. "I'm sorry I don't have anything material to give you, but I do have this: I have one life. A blink for someone like you, but it's everything to me. And I give it to you. Fully." I wrapped my arms around his neck, cuddling into his chest. "I think it was always yours."

We were silent for a moment, arms wrapped closely around each other.

"Well, I'm wearing a white dress and you're in a tux," I said, jokingly. "And we just promised our lives to each other. So does this make us married?"

"Not legally, we're not. But we are where it matters." He brought my hand to his chest, and I felt the steady beat of his heart. "Right here," he whispered, gathering me in his arms again.

He rested his head down on the top of mine, sighing. I let my walls come down completely, and felt his emotions enclose me in an effervescent beam of golden sunlight. They seemed to fuse with mine and form something new—something I'd never felt before. It was almost a connection, but different—less tangible. I clung to it, letting it sink down into my soul, illuminating everything it touched and become a part of me. My heart raced, my hands tingled, and he looked down at me.

"Do you feel that?" he asked.

I could only nod because my power had suddenly revved up without my control. It blasted through my body and into Lucas. I felt him jump.

"What're you . . ."

"Hold on," I said, calm despite what was happening. "Let me try something."

Suddenly, it was as if I was Lucas. I could feel everything he felt, hear everything he was thinking—*what is she doing, this feels weird. . . . I can feel the change coming, she'd better hurry. . . .*

Sure enough, I felt it, too. Some sort of dark, tangled thing deep down in the recesses of his mind began sprinting to the forefront. But I wouldn't have this moment ruined with his curse—not if I could stop it. I shoved the darkness back, replacing it with the golden beam inside me. The beast shoved back, and I could hear Lucas's confused thoughts, but I ignored him. *Stupid trigger. Go away!* I released another powerful beam, and the darkness inside him began to retreat. Lucas stopped resisting. *Holy hell . . . how did she . . .*

I continued coaxing the beast away until there was absolutely nothing left. Nothing but Lucas and me—the way it was always supposed to be. Lucas's emotions leveled out, and I sent him only warmth and love. There was no trace of the curse left inside him— no danger. Just Lucas. Human and perfect.

"That feels amazing," he murmured. "It's like I'm . . ."

"I know," I whispered.

He looked down at me, his eyes the deepest, warmest brown I'd ever seen them. Human eyes. "How did you . . . ?"

I grinned, touching his cheek. "No clue."

"Don't stop."

He kissed me. Instantly, the change began to surge again, but I quelled it, taking my time feeling his lips moving over mine.

Finally, the beast began gaining ground, and my strength failed—the curse came rushing back in an unstoppable wave of fury, and I only just managed to pull out of his head in time. I leaned back, gasping, but Lucas was smiling.

"It's okay," he said, rubbing my back absently. "I'm just me again. Guess it couldn't last forever."

"What did it feel like? To kiss me like that?"

He closed his eyes and pressed his lips together as he remembered. I heard him let out a small contented sigh. "Peace," he whispered at last. He looked down at me, brushing his hand through my hair, and coming to rest at the nape of my neck. "Complete peace."

• • •

I returned to the reception not long after that. Lucas had gotten a call from Julian asking to see him—apparently he was having a minianxiety attack at the thought of what Melanie would be enduring in a few hours time. So Lucas went up to the mansion and I sat at my table alone, watching Derek and Katie dance to Michael Bublé as though they were doing an old-fashioned waltz—a very *bad* waltz. At the end of the song, Derek and Katie returned and collapsed at the table.

"That was . . . interesting," I said. "Really smooth."

Katie giggled. "You're such a dork," she said to Derek.

He looked as if she'd just told him he'd won the Super Bowl.

Katie was about to say something else when one of the runts—a girl in her late teens with pretty blue eyes and a drop-dead sexy dress—came up to Derek. "Will you dance with me?" she asked shyly, an odd contrast to her appearance, since anyone wearing that dress couldn't be as bashful as she was acting.

But Derek didn't seem to notice anything but that dress and the body it (barely) clothed. He jumped up and swept her onto the dance floor, where he did a much more sophisticated version of his dancing with Katie.

I studied Katie as she watched Derek dance with the girl. Outwardly, she seemed fine with it, but the jilted, dejected feel in her vibe indicated that she was obviously upset, and I realized at once what was going on. Katie had a thing for Derek.

It should have made me jealous the way it had when he'd dated Courtney, but it only had the opposite effect. I thought it was great. Katie was awesome. Though, at the moment, I felt bad that she was being forced to watch Derek's hand creep lower and lower down the girl's back, and their bodies cling together in the slow dance.

"Come on," I said to Katie.

"Huh?" She jerked out of her trance and looked at me.

"I'm hot in here. Let's go outside."

"Oh . . . okay." She rose to her feet and shuffled slowly past the dance floor as if hoping Derek would notice she was leaving.

We went to the back porch of the mansion where Lucas and I had sat, and I leaned against the railing, watching the human guests continue to slowly make their way across the yard. Soon they would all be gone, and Melanie would be infected. Changed forever. I sighed. How much easier my life would be if I wanted it, too.

I sighed, looking down at my white-sequined dress and watched the moonlight play games with the sparkles. "Were you scared? When it happened to you?"

"Oh, hell yes," Katie said, shooting me one of her toothy smiles. "Who wouldn't be? It's the unknown. There's nothing more terrifying than that."

"And was it worth it?"

"Yes."

"You think I'm weak for not wanting it too, don't you?"

"No. I think you're smart not to get sucked in by the romance of it. Being with Lucas forever would be great, but not if you're stuck being something you never wanted. Yeah, I love being a werewolf, but it's hard. Really hard. The triggers, worrying about hurting innocent people—losing your mind. If you're not ready for all that, if you're not *absolutely sure* that's what you want, you'll spend eternity regretting it."

I fingered my purse where the tartan Lucas had given me was

stowed away, and wondered suddenly if he'd bury me with it.

I shivered. Too depressing.

"I know you like Derek," I said, switching subjects abruptly.

Katie whirled to face me. "I—I don't . . . it's nothing, I just—"

"Chill. I'm not upset."

Katie didn't look so sure.

"No, really," I said. "Derek and I are strictly friends now. And I just want him to be happy. If you make him happy—and I think you do, because I haven't seen him smile like he does with you in months—then I'm okay with it."

Katie flushed, but then she looked down at the railing between her hands. "He doesn't like me back, though. I know he doesn't."

"Give him some time," I encouraged. "What he and I went through . . . it was sort of traumatic. But he'll get past it eventually. And who knows? If you're still interested, maybe it'll work out." I bumped her shoulder with mine. "Believe me, I'd rather you had him than Slut-dress in there."

Katie giggled, but then shook her head.

"It's stupid anyway," she said. "He's leaving and everything, so it's not like it'll work out."

"What do you mean he's leaving?"

Katie suddenly straightened, pressing her lips firmly together.

"Katie!" I exclaimed. "Tell me."

She shook her head. "Lucas made me promise. I can't believe I told. Oh, my gosh, he's going to murder me."

"Katie!" I grabbed her arm, trying to pull her back, but she darted away.

"I can't, Faith. You have to go ask Lucas. I'm sorry." She turned and practically ran into the house, slamming the door behind her.

I had to find out what was going on. Now. I turned and walked briskly back into the tent, where Derek sat at our table with Slut-dress, whispering playfully in her ear. I marched up to them.

"You," I said, pointing at him. "Come with me. Now."

"I'm busy, Faith."

"No!" I all but screamed. "I mean it. It's vital."

He stood with a wistful glance at Slut-dress and followed me out of the tent, where it seemed the last of Melanie's family had finally left and the pack was now preparing for the ceremony. I pulled Derek out of the way of the bustling werewolves and sequestered us in the shadows alongside the silken tent.

"Why did Katie just tell me you were leaving?" I hissed.

Derek studied his shoes. "I'm not really sure I should—"

"Derek," I warned in a low voice. "I will *literally* stab you with the end of my stiletto if you don't tell me what's going on *right now*."

"God," Derek said, looking abashed. "Dramatic much?"

I glared at him.

"All right," he said, making motions with his hands for me to calm down. "But don't tell Scooby I told you. He'll have a major freak out."

"Whatever. I'm not scared of him. And stop calling him names."

Derek let out a satisfied smile and said, "It's part of his master plan to keep me away from the vampires. We have to turn invisible. We have to leave the country and hide out for like . . . a long time. Lucas says he knows some werewolves who live in the wild up in Québec or something. He says we have to go where it's cold, and the werewolves there will help us stay under the radar. We're leaving—" He winced for a moment with a pitied expression. "We're leaving tomorrow night, Faith."

Something dull and painful yanked at my chest as Derek's words hit me. "We?" I managed. "As in you and Lucas?"

Derek nodded, looking away as he realized the news that Lucas would be leaving as well meant more to me than the news that *he* was going. I felt guilty, of course, but I couldn't help my reaction. Part of me had always known that Derek would have to hide out for a while in order to keep away from the vampires. But it had just never occurred to me that he would go so far. Or that he would take Lucas with him.

"Why didn't you tell me?" I asked. "Why did I have to find out like this?"

Derek put his hands up defensively. "Hey, don't get mad at me. I was told he'd handle telling you. If it were up to me, I'd have told you right away, but he seemed to think waiting would be . . . safer."

"Safer?" I spat. "What does that even mean?"

But before Derek could answer, a shadow appeared at his side—Lucas. His face was grave and shaded in suspicion.

"What's going on?" he asked.

I whirled on him. "Derek was just telling me how you plan on going to *Québec* tomorrow without even telling me."

Derek looked utterly betrayed, and I realized too late that I wasn't supposed to tell Lucas that I'd found out from him.

Oh well.

Lucas shot a murderous look at Derek, who made an annoyed noise in the back of his throat. "She was going to find out anyway," he said. "Why'd you take so long to tell her? And why'd you tell

Katie? She can't keep anything a secret."

"Because Katie's playing a role," Lucas said. "And a few others. We'll discuss it later." He turned to me, apologetic now. "I didn't want you to find out like this."

"How did you want me to find out?" I asked, voice like a hiss. "In the morning when I woke up and found you missing? What, were you going to leave a note on my pillow? *Gone to Québec with Derek, be back never?*"

"I didn't want to give you time to—" He broke off and made a face.

"What!" I shrieked, beside myself with fury. After everything we'd gone through, people were *still* keeping secrets?

"I didn't want to give you time to plan anything, all right? To somehow sneak along with us. It seemed like something you'd do. Se we're leaving tomorrow night on the full moon so you can't . . . so you can't follow us."

I was silent for a moment, equal parts furious and flattered that he'd known I'd find a way to go with him, given time. But none of this mattered anyway, because one thing had become completely clear. They were not planning on taking me with them on this trip.

And that was not an option. If they were going, I was going with them. I hated—straight-up *hated*—the thought of leaving CSU, because despite everything that had happened, I really loved it here and wanted to finish school. But there were some things that were more important—family being one of them. Derek and Lucas were my family, and I wasn't going to abandon them.

"I'm coming," I said. "Don't argue, Lucas. I mean it. I'm not going to just sit behind going to class while you two run off and risk your lives. I refuse." I turned to Derek. "Am I right?"

Derek looked to be in extreme pain and dread emanated from his every pore. "No," he said, flinching as if the word hurt his tongue. "You can't come, Faith. It's too dangerous."

I let my gaze flicker between Lucas and Derek several times. Both were apologetic, yet resolute. They actually *agreed* on this. And the most infuriating part about it was that they were right.

It was this realization—perhaps more than any other—that pushed me past my breaking point.

"Fine!" I screamed, making both of them cringe. "Leave. I don't give a shit. Stay in Québec or Russia or China or wherever for as long as you want. Take up my whole lifetime hiding in the forest like cowards. When you finally come back, I won't be here! I'll be dead and you'll have wasted—everything. You'll be . . ." Tears shattered my vision and cut off my voice. "I hate—the both . . . of you. Hate. . . ."

I felt Lucas's arms around me and I struggled to get away, but he was too strong and he wouldn't let go. I cried into his chest, half hitting him as he shushed me.

When at last I calmed, he released me slightly, still holding me close.

"I'm sorry," he said. "But you're human. And your life is too fragile. I can't devote myself to keeping Derek away from the vampires if I'm constantly worrying about you. I'll arrange for you to have protection—I already have a few pack members who volunteered. It'll be a long time. And it'll be hard. But this is the price we have to pay to keep Derek's venom out of the wrong hands." He bent and held my face trying to get me to look at him, but I refused, staring at the makeup-smudged lapel of his tux instead. "This is bigger than just me and you, Faith," he said, a little more firmly now. "If the vampires get Derek's venom you know what'll happen. They'll finally have what they need to take over everything. I can't let that happen."

It was selfish and immature, but in that moment, I didn't care about humanity. I didn't care about vampires or venom or anything. The only thing in the world that mattered was that Lucas was leaving. And he might never come back.

"Faith, look at me," he said.

"No," I whispered. "I can't look at you." I jerked away from him again, and this time he let me. Vaguely, I noticed that Derek had left, probably when Lucas started holding me.

"How long will you be gone?" I demanded, already knowing what the answer would be.

"I don't know."

"Estimate."

"Ten years? Fifteen? As long as it takes to stop them."

The words *ten* and *fifteen* were like bullets through my chest. "And you expect me to wait around, wasting my life away? Without you? What was all that bullshit about spending my lifetime together? Loving me forever?"

Lucas looked down at his shoes, wordless.

"Why'd you say all that to me?" I asked. "Why'd you give me this—" I reached into my clutch and yanked out the tartan. "To remember you by? I don't want some stupid piece of fabric to hold while I miss you for fifteen years! I want *you*. I want to go *with* you. I'll brave any danger I have to, just please don't do this." I was begging now and it was pathetic, but there was no other choice. I had to make him see that while leaving me for fifteen years seemed like nothing to him—it was a big chunk of my life. It was my best years gone. When he came back—if he came back—I'd be old. I'd be a different person. I didn't even know if I'd still love him. How could I love someone who left me like this? After he'd promised—*promised*—he would never leave me again?

"I don't want this either," Lucas said, eerily calm, as though he had rehearsed these lines earlier. "But you'll be safer here. I've almost lost you too many times. I don't think I'll make it if you really died. So I know this is hard, but it's the only way I can see that you'll be safe."

I flung the tartan at him, hitting him in the chest with it. "You can keep your ridiculous tartan. And you can keep the lifetime you promised me. And you can *keep* the love you gave me! Because I don't want any of it if I don't have you!"

My last sight was Lucas's face—a pale, stricken expression I'd never seen on him before—and then I swung around and ran. My heels made holes in the grass, tripping me up as I weaved in and out of the crowds and into the only place I could think to go where nobody would find me: the woods.

I thrust myself into the forest, stopping only to kick my shoes off, and ran hard. I dodged trees and low-hanging branches as I pushed myself harder, ignoring the sting of the underbrush cutting into my feet. This was dangerous, but I was glad for it. Lucas was so scared of me getting hurt that all I wanted to do was hurt myself— put myself in the danger he feared so much. Just to spite him.

So I ran farther, not even caring as my dress tore and snagged in the brush. When a tree branch scraped swiftly against my cheek, I finally stopped, clutching my face. Warmth gushed between my fingers.

"Damn it," I gasped to myself. I stood there panting for a minute, reveling in the endorphin rush, and then started walking to ease the painful throb of my heart. I wasn't paying attention to where I was going. I just focused on the movement itself.

Get away from Lucas.

Get away from Derek.

Get away from myself.

I shook my head, trying to erase the memories of what I'd said to Lucas—his face when I'd thrown the tartan back at him. Part of me wanted to turn around and take it back, to tell him I'd wait an eternity for him. But another part was happy I'd shown him how I really felt. He wanted me to be honest, right? Well, that was more honest than I'd ever been with him.

Still, it was probably time to turn around and go back to the party. The initiation would be starting soon and no matter how mad I was at Lucas and Derek, I didn't want to miss it.

I stepped past an ancient spruce and came to a halt. I'd entered a small clearing around a felled evergreen with cracking bark the color of dust. Deadened grass surrounded it, gray and anemic-brown. And crouching right behind, its coat so close to the color of the grass that, at first, my eyes slid right over it, was the heather-gray wolf.

34

BETRAYAL

I saw its eyes before I felt its vibe—two glowing pinpricks of acid green hovering behind the felled tree. I should have been scared, but I wasn't. I think a part of me knew it would be here—that it had survived the fight with Melissa and was waiting to catch me alone. My body was totally numb, my heart beating too fast to feel.

The wolf rose onto its feet, slowly stepping around the log and advancing on me. Vainly, I tried to ignite the connection, knowing all the while what would happen. The wall. The same wall that resided in Derek's head, that had kept me out that night in the courtyard when the wolf had tried to corner me. The same resistance I felt when Lucas and I had practiced blocking.

In a rush, I realized that this werewolf knew how to block me. This werewolf *knew* what I was.

It dawned on me, then, that this was the end—this was the moment it would finally kill me.

I was sort of mad about it. I'd survived countless supernatural attacks, a car crash, a vampire-werewolf battle, and the monarch vampire's bite, and now I was going to be mauled to death by some random psychopath werewolf? It just didn't seem fair.

I backed up against the spruce, supporting myself with the solid bark of the tree, and said, "What do you want?"

The wolf's ears flagged at my voice, and it stopped its slow advance, body tensed.

"Why are you following me around?" I demanded. "Change. At least tell me why."

The wolf's iron muzzle wrinkled over its snout as it snarled. A fresh hit of adrenaline swept through me, making my hands shake.

"Just tell me why," I said, less brazen now.

A deep growl was all the answer I got. It lowered itself, shuffling its shoulders as it poised itself to lunge.

I pressed myself harder against the spruce, cringing. Why did I come out here? Why wasn't I spending my last night with Lucas in his arms instead of acting like a spoiled brat out in the woods? Alone.

Damn it, I didn't want this to happen. I wanted to live. Frantically, I tried to ignite the connection again, but the wall shoved me back out. The wolf jerked forward, barking as if saying, *stop that!*

"Then tell me why!" I screamed, beating my fist against the tree.

That's when it pounced. I heard myself scream, felt my body curl into itself as I covered my head in my hands and crumpled to the ground. Claws dug into my ankle, yanking me into the air and whipping me around like a chew toy. A bone in my leg *cracked* when I hit the ground. I cried out, digging my fingernails into the earth, trying futilely to escape.

The wolf released me and I began to drag myself away using my arms, but then I felt the weight of its paws on my back, felt its claws tear open my flesh. I screamed again, overcome with agony. All I could think was *don't bite me, please, don't bite me.* . . . Claws on my arm this time, digging in and breaking my bones. It flung me across the clearing, and I landed hard on the ground, my body flush with the fallen log.

Sight faded in and out—I might have lost consciousness if it weren't for the pain. I couldn't move, couldn't breathe for a moment. And then I used my good arm to push myself into a sitting position against the log, still trying stupidly to get away. It was hopeless, of course, but I couldn't stop myself from fighting as long as I was able.

The wolf stood before me, hate and vindication emanating from its vibe like poison.

"Screw you," I croaked, wincing as my broken shin twanged. The bone was jutting out of my flesh. Nausea surged and I looked away, forcing myself to focus on the wolf instead. "Whoever you are—Lucas is going to . . . murder you . . . for this." Panting, I clasped my hand over my arm to try and staunch the blood flow.

Then I could swear I saw a leer cross the wolf's features.

It lunged at me, but instead of attacking, it shifted in midair and came to stand before me as a girl—a naked girl with auburn hair and emerald green eyes that pierced me right down to my soul. She wore her customary smirk.

"Danni?" I gasped. "I—I don't understand."

"What's not to get? I'm a werewolf. You're a bitch. And I'm going to kill you." She smiled snidely and walked around to the other side of the log. I didn't turn to watch her because it hurt too much, but when she reentered my field of vision she was clothed. She must have stashed a wardrobe change for this—meaning she'd planned it. I wondered if she would have come and gotten me if I hadn't been dumb enough to enter the woods tonight.

"Kill me?" I grunted through the stabbing pains. "Why? I thought we were friends."

"Ha!" Danni barked a laugh. "Seriously? You really believed everything? I'm better at this than I thought. I should join the CIA. Honestly, I can't believe you didn't guess immediately. I just assumed you didn't know about me." She came closer, leaning her hip on the log and looking down at me. I focused on the trees, praying someone would come out of them and save me from this.

"Doesn't my name mean anything to you?" she asked.

"Danni? No. Why?"

"Not Danni, idiot. *Danielle*."

Somewhere in the fuzzy mess of torment burning in my brain, the name shot off an alarm bell. *Danielle. Danielle the werewolf. . . . Lucas and Danielle.*

I felt my mouth part on its own. "You're his ex-girlfriend," I said. His crazy ex-girlfriend. The stalker. God, why didn't I put this together? Why didn't *Lucas*? "But he said you'd left," I protested.

"No way. I couldn't go when there was still a chance he might change his mind."

"You're insane," I said. "He doesn't love you anymore."

Danni grabbed a handful of my hair, yanking my face up to hers. I gasped, stars blooming in my vision. "He doesn't love *you*, bitch. You're a disgusting, weak human. If he feels anything for you it's just his protective nature—werewolf instincts. He was always a sucker for the pretty chicks. Saving the damsels, falling for them, and then realizing they're nothing but tools, and ditching them. You're no different."

She released my hair with a jerk and I ignored the fact that she was right about Lucas leaving (even if it was for my safety), saying instead, "What about you, then? You're a werewolf and he left you. What's your excuse?"

"He *had* to leave," Danni said dismissively. "He was being followed by some crazy vampire. Now that's over with. And this hiccup with you will be taken care of momentarily. Then we can finally be together again."

God, she's really, really crazy.

"So, killing me is going to make him realize he loves you?" I asked incredulously. "Yeah, that'll work."

"Well, obviously, this is plan B."

"What was plan A? Throw sand in his eye and slice his tires?"

"Shut up," Danni snarled. "I'm not a moron. I know he'll never want me if I kill you. Which is why I tried to get the leeches to do it."

I blinked. "What? No. They wanted me as repayment for killing their friends. And because of my power. They told me so."

"No, babe," Danni said, crouching down beside me. "They wanted you because I made a deal with them. I told them I'd get them Derek's blood if they turned you for me."

I struggled to understand amidst the agony ripping through my body. I was also losing blood fast and feeling seriously faint. If Danni didn't hurry up and kill me, I'd already be dead. That'd really piss her off.

"But you don't have Derek's blood," I protested.

Danni grinned darkly. "Yes, I do. I stole it from the CSU lab where that idiot werewolf girl with the yellow eyes left it."

In my head, I heard Derek tell me that the vial had gone missing—that Katie had to take another sample. Danni had stolen the original. I remembered Derek's weird conversation with Katie as he told her to throw something away; he must have been talking about the other sample. To keep it secret.

"So why didn't you give it to them?" I asked. "They did what you told them to do. They took me and Lucas, and Arabella bit me."

"Yet, here you are. Still human." Danni's green eyes glittered.

"So you still have the blood?" Was there a chance Lucas could get it back from her? Even if I died here—and it looked like I was going to—he still might be able to stop the uprising. But if Danni gave the sample to the vampires or if one of them stole it from her, it was all over.

"Of course I still have it," Danni said. "You think I'm dumb enough to give it away for a half-ass job? I was supposed to be there to watch it happen. Melissa didn't call me like she was supposed to. She was ticked because I messed her up so bad that night outside your dorm room. Little bitch."

Now that strange exchange in the vampire lair made sense. Arabella had been talking to Melissa about their part of the bargain, waiting for someone to show up. They'd been waiting for Danni. "Lucas would have seen you, though," I protested.

Danni rolled her eyes. "I wouldn't just stand there in the open, obviously. I'd watch where nobody could see me. It would have been epic."

But something still didn't make sense. If Danni had been the heather-gray wolf the whole time, why had she saved me? "That night outside my room . . . you saved me from Melissa. Why didn't you just let her take me?"

Danni made an annoyed noise in her throat. "I was going to. Why do you think I didn't kidnap you when we were alone at that barn? Why do you think I drove so slowly to keep you out past dark? Melissa was *supposed* to catch you and take you to the lair that night. Then I was going to go fetch Lucas, and bring him, as well. But then you had to go and bleed and screw everything up. She was going to drain you. And that wasn't the plan."

I let out a bitter puff of laughter, which hurt me more than I thought it would. "So what *is* the plan, Danni? Because I'm a little confused. Do you want to turn me? Kill me? What? How is any of this going to make Lucas realize he loves you?" I said this last part with heavy sarcasm, since I knew Lucas *didn't* love her, but Danni didn't catch it.

"I wanted Lucas to watch you be turned," she hissed. "That was the original idea. To make his lover into the thing he hates more than anything on earth. To watch him be forced to hunt you down and kill you. And I'd be there to comfort him all the while." She smiled wistfully and then sighed. "But that's not going to happen. Derek messed it all up with his obnoxious venom."

"Too bad," I said flatly.

"It's all right," Danni said, rising to her feet. "Because I would have hated missing the drama. You won't be turned, but you'll be out of the picture and that's the goal. Lucas won't be here to watch you die, either, but it's better that way. I have to pretty much eat you to hide your body from him and I don't think he'd be able to get over me eating his girlfriend, do you?"

I just stared at the ground, feeling angry, frustrated tears stinging the back of my throat. I held them in, not wanting her to see me cry.

"So go ahead," I ground out. "What are you waiting for?"

"I'm gathering my strength," Danni said, walking lazily around the clearing as if enjoying a sunny day.

I snorted a laugh, but stopped quickly because it was agony. "Right, like you need to gather strength to kill me. I'm nothing to you."

"True," Danni said. "Physically, you're hardly a threat. But you're not entirely human are you, Faith? You're something else." She watched me from off to my right. "Aren't you curious about why you can't read my emotions? About how I know how to block you?"

"Yes," I admitted reluctantly.

"The vampires captured a dude like you once," she said. "I forget his name—Kenny or something—"

Kevin, I thought immediately.

"They made him divulge everything about his power," Danni continued. "The sense, the connection, everything. But most importantly, he showed them how to keep their emotions—what scant ones they have left anyway—a secret. When I went to them and asked them to turn you, they agreed. But only on the condition that *I* do all the dirty work and get you to their lair. They told me you had a power and that you'd be able to tell I was a werewolf the moment you saw me. Obviously, this made getting you to their lair a lot more difficult."

"Why?" I grunted. "You could have just blocked me out and yanked me away."

"Well, first off, you're really well protected. There was hardly a moment when you were alone, even in class. You didn't know it but your little *boyfriend* is an overprotective freak. He had pack members guarding you pretty much twenty-four/seven. But on the odd occasion that I did catch you off guard, I ran into trouble with the whole blocking thing. I can't do it for too long because it takes a hell of a lot of concentration to pull off. So using force wasn't really going to work.

"So I thought that if I managed to befriend you, get you to trust me, then I could lure you into the lair more easily. But in order to do that, you had to think I was human. So I worked at it for a while with Kurt or whatever, and eventually managed to make my energy chill out. At least enough so that you wouldn't immediately realize I was a werewolf.

"But making you trust me was a serious chore. I went the wrong route and tried making friends with that chick you like, Heather. I sold her vampire blood, hoping you'd want some, too. But you freaked out about it and then I had a lot of backtracking to do. It was slow-going. And dull. Humans are *so* depressing when they're high. So when I finally caught you alone here in these woods a couple months ago, I tried to just ambush you as a wolf and drag you off, hoping you'd be too shocked to use your power. But you used your connection or whatever, and I hadn't figured out how to block you out when I was changed yet. When I met you again in the courtyard at CSU, I managed to block your controlling powers, but wasn't quick enough.

"By then the vampires were getting impatient. They wanted Derek's blood and apparently, he wasn't giving it up to them. I told them if they wanted to speed things up they could get off their asses and *help me*. So they sent Melissa. She lost her cool. I had to step in. You know the rest. They got you and Lucas two nights later, and Melissa didn't call me because she's a slut." She threw me a breezy smile. "Luckily, it all worked out. You and Lucas had a fight and you went all drama queen and ran into the forest, saving me the trouble of going out to get you. Kind of a bummer, actually. I had a dress picked out and everything. And killer shoes."

I shook my head, amazed at the hilarity of it all. It was so *not* funny, but the fact that it was happening—the fact that *this* was how I was going to die—well, it just brought a smile to my face. Or maybe I was giddy from the loss of blood. Part of me wished I'd die while Danni prattled on—just to annoy her.

"Well, now it makes sense," I said. "You made your vibe normal. Ish. And blocked me when I tried to stop you from attacking. You had the vampires track me down and try to turn me in exchange for Derek's blood. And now, since that plan went up in smoke, you're just going to kill me here. And eat me, apparently." I swallowed, tasting blood in my mouth. "Just so you know, I've been told I taste amazing. I hope you like peaches."

Danni's vibe, now unmasked to me, was a mash of fury and indignation at my flippant tone. She wanted me to suffer—to feel the pain she felt at losing Lucas. She wanted me to cry. To beg. To scream.

But I wouldn't do any of those things.

Instead, I closed my eyes and smiled. "He said he'd love me forever," I murmured.

A low snarl came from where Danni stood. "Shut up."

I pictured Lucas's shy grin as he handed me his family's tartan, and felt my smile widen. The pain began to ebb. "He said he'd love me even after I died."

"He won't. He lied."

"No. Lucas doesn't lie. He's my match." I could feel his arms around me now, hear the steady beat of his heart as my ear pressed against it in an embrace. I'd miss him. . . .

I'll miss you, Lucas. I'm sorry for what I said. . . . I hope you find happiness. Oh, and I hope you kill this bitch. What were you thinking, dating her? She's a jerk. . . .

"He loves *me*," Danni barked. Vaguely, I heard her come closer, felt her jerk me by my shoulders. "Stop it. Open your damn eyes."

I wish I could see your face one last time. I wish you were with me now. I need you.

Danni slapped me across the face, and my eyes flew open, the pain returning at once, but I kept my expression blank.

"That was rude," I said evenly.

"I hope you enjoyed your little daydream," Danni spat in my face. Her beautiful features had turned into a grotesque mask, and her eyes were alight with the change. "Because that's the last moment of happiness you'll ever have. I'm going to rip you apart. You're going to beg me for death."

But I just smiled at her and said in my sweetest, most mocking voice, "Please kill me, Danni. I beg you."

She changed.

The force of it knocked me backward, and her claws ripped into my flesh again. My legs shredded, bones cracking. I screamed hoarsely, laying face down on the grass, unable to move. I dipped in and out of consciousness. I was so weak—there was nothing to do but wait. Wait for the blow. The bite. The end.

"Faith!" a voice in the distance. The sound of feet pounding the earth. "Faith, where are you?"

It was . . . no. Impossible. How could he . . . and then it made sense. He heard me! He'd seen me go into the woods, and must have tracked me down when he heard my call. *Hurry!* I screamed.

Lucas burst into the clearing at breakneck speed, skidding to a stop when he saw the scene in front of him. Me, laying bloodied on the ground and Danni standing feet away, poised to strike.

Lucas's eyes were on Danni, silver and wide. "You," he whispered. "I'll kill you."

Danni growled viciously, and I felt a little surge of victory. I was still going to die, but at least Danni wouldn't get Lucas—at least he knew what she was.

"Faith, can you move?" Lucas asked.

"No," I rasped. "I think . . . my legs—broken . . ."

"It's okay," Lucas said. "It's all going to be okay."

Danni's low, throaty snarls filled the clearing again, followed by Lucas's. "You touch her again, and I'll rip your head off."

She just barked, stalking closer to me.

"I don't have time to deal with you," Lucas spat at her, also closing in on me. "Just leave and I'll let you live."

Another dangerous bark.

"I mean it," Lucas warned. I saw his long legs in my field of vision. "Go." He bent toward me, his hand coming so close to mine I could feel the warmth on my broken skin. I heard his voice in my ear. "It's okay, baby. I'm here."

Danni's vibe exploded with rage. I heard the deep, ripping sound of her snarl and felt the pounding of her paws on the ground as she rushed us. She pounced, and Lucas caught her around the throat, batting her backward. I heard a tree crack as Danni collided with it and saw Lucas run after her, changing in midstride. They clashed, biting and clawing each other. I couldn't tell how long the fight lasted—nor could I tell what was happening. As the darkness closed in on me, I heard Lucas's agonized yowl, heard his human voice scream, *No!*

Sharp pain in my stomach—burning pain. My eyes flew open.

I gasped.

She bit me.

Danni bit me.

Heat spread from the wound like a chemical fire. I writhed around into a ball to see Danni above me, green eyes greedy and eager as she lunged for another bite. Then a blur of black fur. Lucas's lupine body colliding into hers. The squelch of body parts separating.

My blood boiled beneath skin that felt like it was melting off of my bones. It was inescapable, irreversible, and all-consuming. Even my hearing was blocked out by the too-fast beat of my heart. Fear, anger—total hatred of everyone and everything—consumed my every sense, rocking my brain into insanity.

With what little vision I retained, I saw Danni fall to the dirt beside me. Dead. Then Lucas's body shaking, transforming back to human.

I heard the distant sound of screaming—my screams. Something welled in my gut—something terrible and powerful that rippled through my muscles and clawed at the inside of my skin, demanding to be released. Lucas's face appeared, his arms locking me tight in a prison of comfort I didn't want. I tried to struggle away; I couldn't lie still, couldn't see anything anymore—it was all red. Inside, my organs were exploding, brain turning inside out with terror.

He released me, letting me shake—letting me tremor.

The *something* in my gut swelled again, this time with a greater intensity, squeezing itself into all of my muscles, my bones, my mind. Then my body began to lose its shape—my bones popped out of their sockets, my muscles tore in two and reformed into new, impossible shapes. Nothing was left untouched; my skin prickled in a million different places, fingernails burned and elongated, teeth grew, sharpened, my spine curved and lengthened.

In a blast of white, my vision returned—my body stopped shaking, stopped burning, stopped hurting. But it wasn't my body anymore. It was a new body—a new world.

I was changed.

ACKNOWLEDGMENTS

When you do something like write a book, you don't do it alone. So to all of those people who helped me along the way, here's what I have to say to you:

First, I've got to thank my amazing agent, Tamar Rydzinski, for her unfailing support and awesome advice. It was you who said yes, and I'll never forget that.

While we're talking about amazing women, I have to mention my editor, Lisa Cheng. You always bring a smile to my face during those moments when I want to give up (usually this is right in the middle of a massive editing session, where I can see more red marks than black ones). The occasional "LOL!" in the margins is what helps me keep going. Thank you for your continued support. This book wouldn't be what it is without you!

To my amazing parents and sister, I give you ALL the thanks in the world. You deserve much more than my measly "thank you" for putting up with me throughout the writing of another book, but words are all I have. I hope you know how much you all mean to me. I especially want to thank my mom, because you slogged through that first draft like a champ and gave me so much love and support, even though we both knew it was garbage! Thanks for loving my garbage, Mom!

Husband of mine, thank you for listening to me as I plotted aloud, and rambled on about scenes you hadn't even read yet. Having someone to bounce ideas off of has been invaluable. You rock!

Children, once again I thank you for giving up your mommy for days at a time so that I could write this book. I hope that one day you'll read what I wrote and be proud of me. I love you both like crazy.

Everyone at Running Press, you're all amazing, and I can't thank you enough for all the hard work you did to make Blood Crave the best book it could be.

Lastly, I want to say thank you to YOU. If you've made it this far, gentle reader, you should know that you're awesome. And you completely rock for choosing to read my books. I'm insanely happy that you picked them up, and I sincerely hope that you continue to do so! I couldn't do this without you!